Also by Kathy Reichs

DEVIL BONES

BONES TO ASHES

BREAK NO BONES

CROSS BONES

MONDAY MOURNING

BARE BONES

GRAVE SECRETS

FATAL VOYAGE

DEADLY DÉCISIONS

DEATH DU JOUR

DÉJÀ DEAD

206 BONES

KATHY REICHS

POCKET BOOKS
NEW YORK LONDON TORONTO SYDNEY

Pocket Books
A Division of Simon & Schuster, Inc.
1230 Avenue of the Americas
New York, NY 10020

This book is a work of fiction. Names, characters, places, and incidents either are products of the author's imagination or are used fictitiously. Any resemblance to actual events or locales or persons, living or dead, is entirely coincidental.

This Pocket Books export edition February 2010

POCKET and colophon are registered trademarks of Simon & Schuster, Inc.

Designed by Erich Hobbing

Manufactured in the United States of America

1 3 5 7 9 10 8 6 4 2

Library of Congress Control Number: 2009014348

ISBN 978-1-4391-8261-1
ISBN 978-1-4391-6623-9 (ebook)

This book is dedicated to my colleagues in the forensic sciences who have demonstrated their professional commitment and aptitude by applying for and obtaining legitimate board certification.

The exam was a bear, but we did it!

Bravo!

American Board of Forensic Anthropology

American Board of Criminalistics

American Board of Forensic Document Examiners

American Board of Forensic Engineering and Technology

American Board of Forensic Entomology

American Board of Forensic Odontology

American Board of Forensic Psychology

American Board of Forensic Toxicology

American Board of Pathology

American Board of Psychiatry and Neurology

ACKNOWLEDGMENTS

My heartfelt thanks to Peter Bush, Laboratory of Forensic Odontology Research, School of Dental Medicine, SUNY at Buffalo, for his advice on scanning electron microscopy and energy dispersive X-ray spectroscopy, and to S. Kelly Sears, Facility for Electron Microscopy Research, McGill University.

My sincere gratitude to Michael Warns, who, as usual, researched many things. Who knew the Chicago burbs had so many quarries?

Michael Cook shared his knowledge of sewers. Renate Reichs aided me in mapping Chicago terrain. Jack Kenney offered tips on the Cook County Medical Examiner's office. William Rodriguez helped with forensic anthropology minutia. Michael Bisson enlightened me on CRM archaeology. Ronnie Harrison answered cop questions. And, of course, there was the nice lady who took my call at the Bibliothèque et Archives nationales du Québec.

I appreciate the continued support of Philip L. Dubois, Chancellor of the University of North Carolina at Charlotte.

I am grateful to my family for their patience and understanding, especially when I am cranky. Or gone. Credit to Paul Reichs for reading and commenting on the manuscript.

Particularly useful was the article by B. C. Smith, "A Preliminary Report: Proximal Facet Analysis and the Recovery of Trace Restorative Materials from Unrestored Teeth," *Journal of Forensic Sciences,* Vol. 35: 4, July 1990: 873–80.

Deepest thanks to my splendid agent, Jennifer Rudolph Walsh, and to my dazzling editors, Nan Graham and Susan Sandon. I also want to acknowledge all those who work so very hard on my behalf, especially: Susan Moldow, Katherine Monaghan, Paul Whitlatch, Emma Rose, Margaret Riley, Britton Schey, Tracy Fisher, Elizabeth Reed, and Michelle Feehan. And of course, I am indebted to the Canadian crew, especially to Kevin Hanson and Amy Cormier.

If there are errors in this book, I own them. If I have forgotten to thank someone, I apologize. You know the drill.

206 BONES

COLD.

Numb.

Confused.

I opened my eyes.

To dark. Black as arctic winter.

Am I dead?

Obeying some limbic command, I inhaled deeply.

Smells registered in my brain.

Mold. Musty earth. Something organic, hinting at the passage of time.

Was this hell? A tomb?

I listened.

Silence. Impenetrable.

But no. There were sounds. Air moving through my nostrils. Blood pounding in my ears.

Corpses don't breathe. Dead hearts don't beat.

Other sensations intruded. Hardness below me. Burning on the right side of my face.

I raised my head.

Bitter bile flooded my mouth.

I shifted my hips to relieve pressure on my twisted neck.

Pain exploded up my left leg.

A groan shattered the stillness.

Instinctively, my body went fetal. The pounding gained volume.

I lay curled, listening to the rhythm of my fear.

Then, recognition. The sound had come from my own throat.

I feel pain. I react. I am alive.

But where?

Spitting bile, I tried reaching out. Felt resistance. Realized my wrists were bound.

I flexed a knee toward my chest, testing. My feet rose as one. My wrists dropped.

I tried a second time, harder. Neurons again fired up my leg.

Stifling another cry, I struggled to force order onto my addled thinking.

I'd been bound, hands to feet, and abandoned. Where? When? By whom? Why?

A memory search for recent events came up empty. No. The void in recollection was longer than that.

I remembered picnicking with my daughter, Katy. But that was summer. The frigid temperature now suggested that it must be winter.

Sadness. A last farewell to Andrew Ryan. That was October. Had I seen him again?

A bright red sweater at Christmas. This Christmas? I had no idea.

Disoriented, I groped for any detail from the past few days. Nothing stayed in focus.

Vague impressions lacking rational form or sequence appeared and faded. A figure emerging from shadow. Man or woman? Anger. Shouting. About what? At whom?

Melting snow. Light winking off glass. The dark maw of a cracked door.

Dilated vessels pounded inside my skull. Hard as I tried, I could not evoke recollection from my semiconscious mind.

Had I been drugged? Suffered a blow to the head?

How bad was my leg? If I managed to free myself, could I walk? Crawl?

My hands were numb, my fingers useless. I tried tugging my wrists outward. Felt no give in my bindings.

Tears of frustration burned the backs of my lids.

No crying!

Clamping my jaw, I rolled to my back, raised my feet, and jerked my ankles apart. Flames roared up my left lower limb.

Then I knew nothing.

I awoke. Moments later? Hours? No way to tell. My mouth felt drier, my lips more parched. The pain in my leg had receded to a dull ache.

Though I gave my pupils time, they took in nothing. How could they adjust? The dense blackness offered not a sliver of light.

The same questions flooded back. Where? Why? Who?

Clearly, I'd been abducted. To be the victim in some sick game? To be removed as a threat?

The thought triggered my first clear memory. An autopsy photo. A corpse, charred and twisted, jaws agape in a final agonal scream.

Then a kaleidoscope sequence, image chasing image. Two morgues. Two autopsy rooms. Name plaques marking two labs. Temperance Brennan, Forensic Anthropologist. Temperance Brennan, Anthropologue Judiciaire.

Was I in Charlotte? Montreal? Far too cold for North Carolina. Even in winter. Was it winter? Was I in Quebec?

Had I been grabbed at home? On the street? In my car? Outside the Édifice Wilfrid-Derome? Inside the lab?

Was my captor a random predator and I a random victim? Had I been targeted because of who I am? Revenge sought by a former accused? By a conspiracy-theorist next of kin? What case had I last been working?

Dear God, could it really be so cold? So dark? So still?

Why that smell, so disturbingly familiar?

As before, I tried wriggling my hands. My feet. To no avail. I was hog-tied, unable even to sit.

"Help! I'm here! Someone! Help me!"

Over and over I called out until my throat grew raw.

"Anyone! Please!"

My pleas went unanswered.

Panic threatened to overwhelm me.

You will not die helpless!

Trembling from cold and fear, and frantic to see, I shifted to my back and started bucking my hips, stretching my hands upward as far as possible, oblivious to the agony in my leg. One thrust. Two. Three. My fingertips scraped hardness little more than a foot above my face.

I lunged again. Made contact. Sediment cascaded into my eyes and mouth.

Spitting and blinking, I rolled onto my right side and shoved backward with one arm and both feet. The rough ground abraded the skin on my elbow and heels. One ankle screamed in protest. I didn't care. I had to move. Had to get out.

I'd advanced a very short distance when I encountered a wall. Rectangular contours surrounded by mortar. Brick.

Heart hammering, I rolled to my other side and inched in the opposite direction. Again, I soon hit a wall.

Adrenaline flooded my body as terror piggybacked onto terror. My gut curdled. My lungs drew great heaving breaths.

My prison was no more than thirty inches high and six feet wide! Its length didn't matter. Already I felt the walls pressing in.

I lost control.

Scooching forward, I began yelling and beating the brick with my fists. Tears streamed down my cheeks. Over and over I called out, hoping to attract the attention of a passerby. A worker. A dog. Anyone.

When my knuckles grew raw I attacked with the heels of my hands.

When I could no longer flail with my arms, I rolled and lashed out with my feet.

Pain ripped from my ankle. Too much pain. My calls for help morphed into agonized moans.

Defeated, I fell back, panting, sweat cooling on my icy flesh.

A parade of faces marched through my mind. Katy. Ryan. My sister, Harry. My cat, Birdie. My ex-husband, Pete.

Would I never see them again?

Great heaving sobs racked my chest.

Perhaps I lost consciousness. Perhaps not. My next awareness was of sound.

A noise outside my body. Not of my making.

I froze.

Tick. Tick. Tick. Tick. Tick.

A cerebral crack opened.

Memory slipped through.

ANOTHER WRISTWATCH CHECK. ANOTHER SIGH. MORE SHIFTING feet.

Above us, a wall clock ticked steadily, indifferent to Ryan's restlessness. It was the old-fashioned analog kind, round, with a sweep second hand that jumped in one-second increments with sharp little clicks.

I surveyed my surroundings. Same plastic plant. Same bad print of a street scene in winter. Same half-empty mugs of tepid coffee. Phone. LCD projector. Screen. Laser pointer. Nothing new had magically appeared since I last looked.

Back to the clock. A logo identified the manufacturer as Enterprise. Or perhaps that was a name for this particular model.

Did people christen timepieces? Arnie Analog? Reggie Regulator?

OK. I was as edgy as Ryan. And very, very bored.

Tick. Tick. Tick. Tick. Tick.

Old Enterprise said it was ten twenty-two. Oh-six. Oh-seven. Oh-eight. We'd been waiting since nine o'clock.

Finger-drumming recommenced on the tabletop. Ryan had been performing off and on for thirty minutes. The staccato beat was getting on my nerves.

"He'll meet with us as soon as he can," I said.

"Our coming here was his idea."

"Yes."

"How do you lose a stiff in a morgue?"

"You heard Corcoran. They've got over two hundred bodies. The facility is overstretched."

While I have been described as impatient, Lieutenant-détective Andrew Ryan, Section des crimes contre la personne, Sûreté du Québec, takes the term to a whole new plane. I knew the routine. Soon he'd be pacing.

Ryan and I were in a conference room at the Office of the Cook County Medical Examiner, on Chicago's West Side. We'd flown from Montreal at the request of Christopher Corcoran, a staff pathologist with the CCME.

More than three years earlier, a fifty-nine-year-old woman named Rose Jurmain had taken a trip from Chicago to Quebec to view the fall foliage. On the fourth day of her visit she'd left her country inn for a walk and never returned. Her belongings remained behind in her room. No one saw or heard from her again.

Thirty months later remains were discovered in a forested area half a mile north of the inn. Decomposition was advanced and animal damage was extensive. I'd done the ID. Ryan had led the investigation. Now he and I were bringing Rose home.

Why the personal service? For me, friendship with Corcoran and an excuse to visit the old hometown. For Ryan? A free trip to the Windy City.

For Chris Corcoran and his boss? That would be one of my very first questions. Surely a CCME employee could have come to Montreal to collect the remains. Or a transport service. Until now the family had shown no interest in what was left of Rose Jurmain.

And why the request for our presence in Chicago nine months after resolution of the case? The Bureau du coroner had ruled Rose's death an accident. Why the special interest now?

Despite my curiosity, so far there'd been no time for questions. Ryan and I had arrived to find media vans lining Harrison Street and the facility in lockdown.

While parking us in the conference room, Corcoran had provided a quick explanation. The previous day, a funeral home had attempted to collect a body for cremation. Inexplicably, the corpse was nowhere to be found.

All hands were engaged in crisis control. The chief was spinning for the press. A frantic search was under way. And Ryan and I were cooling our heels.

"I suppose the family is going ballistic," Ryan said.

"Oooh, yeah. And the media is loving it. Lost bodies. Shocked loved ones. Embarrassed politico. It's the stuff of Pulitzers."

I'm a news junkie. At home I read, or at least skim, each day's paper from front to back. On the road, I tune in to CNN or a local station. Earlier, in my hotel room, I'd flipped between WFLD and WGN. Though aware of the story, I'd not anticipated the resulting chaos. Or the impact on us.

Sure enough, Ryan got up and began pacing the room. I checked my pal Enterprise. Inspector Irritable was right on schedule.

After logging roughly thirty yards, Ryan dropped back into his chair.

"Who was Cook?"

I was lost.

"Cook County?"

"No idea," I said.

"How big is it?"

"The county?"

"My aunt Dora's fanny."

"You have an aunt Dora?"

"Three."

I stored that bit of familial trivia for future query.

"Cook is the second most populous county in the U.S., the nineteenth largest government in the nation." I'd read those facts someplace.

"What's the largest?"

"Do I look like an almanac?"

"Atlas."

"Some almanacs contain census data." Defensive. After the trip from Montreal, I was no longer in the mood for teasing.

Though generally cheerful, Ryan is not a good traveler, even when the aviation gods are smiling. Yesterday they'd been grumpy as hell.

Instead of two hours, our flight from Pierre-Elliot Trudeau International to O'Hare had taken six. First a weather delay. Then a mechanical complication. Then the crew went illegal for dancing naked on the tarmac. Or some such. Annoyed and frustrated, Ryan had passed the time nitpicking everything I said. His idea of jolly good banter.

Several moments passed.

Tick. Tick. Tick. Tick. Tick.

Ryan was pushing to his feet when the door opened and Christopher Corcoran entered, dressed in lab coat, jeans, and sneakers. With his pale skin, green eyes, red hair, and freckles, Corcoran was a walking Irish cliché. And decidedly nervous.

"I'm really sorry for the delay. This missing body thing turned into an Italian opera."

"I hate it when corpses go walkabout." The old Ryan wit.

Corcoran gave a mirthless smile. "Especially when the decedent's under your care."

"It was your case?" I asked.

Corcoran nodded. As I looked at him, a million memories flooded my mind. A scrawny kid, all spindly limbs and wild carrot hair. Wrought-iron desks floor-bolted in long straight rows. Impromptu street games on hot summer nights. Interminable Masses on hard wooden pews.

As kids, Corcoran and I were back-fence neighbors in a South Side neighborhood called Beverly, and card-carrying members at St. Margaret's of Scotland. Keep in mind that Chicago Catholics map people by parishes, not geography. An oddity, but there you have it.

When I was eight, my father and baby brother died, and my family relocated to North Carolina. Corcoran stayed put. We lost touch, of course. I grew up, attended the University of Illinois, then graduate school at Northwestern. He studied at Michigan, undergrad through med school, then completed specialty training in pathology. It was forensics that brought us back into contact.

Reconnection occurred in '92 through a case involving a baby in a suitcase. By then Corcoran had married, returned to Chicago, and purchased a house on Longwood Drive. Though a little farther east and a lot upmarket, Corcoran had returned to the old spawning ground.

"Turns out it was here all along." Corcoran's voice brought me back. "The guy was so scrawny he got hidden behind an obese woman on an upper gurney shelf. The techs just missed him."

"Happy ending," Ryan said.

Corcoran snorted. "Tell that to Walczak."

It was said of Stanley Walczak that only his ego surpassed his ambition in raw tonnage. His cunning was fierce too. Upon the resignation of the previous ME nine months earlier, having forged a complex web of political connections, to the surprise of few, and the dismay of many, Walczak had called in his chits and been appointed Cook County Medical Examiner.

"Walczak is pissed?" I asked.

"The man detests bad publicity. And inefficiency." Corcoran sighed.

"We handle roughly twenty pickups a day here. Between yesterday and this morning the staff had to phone over sixty funeral homes to see if a delivery had been made to the wrong place. Four techs and three investigators had to be pulled off their normal duties to help check toe tags. It took three sweeps to finally locate the guy. Hell, we've got half a cooler set aside just for long-term unknowns."

"Mistakes happen." I tried to sound encouraging.

"Here, misplacing a body is not considered a career-enhancing move."

"You're a fantastic pathologist. Walczak's lucky to have you."

"In his view, I should have been on top of the situation sooner."

"You expect fallout?" Ryan asked.

"The family's probably lawyer-shopping as we speak. Nothing like a few bucks to assuage unbearable anguish, even when there is no injury. It's the American way."

Corcoran circled the table and we all sat.

"Walczak says he won't be long. He's closeted with the Jurmain family lawyer. You're gonna *love* him."

"Oh?"

"Perry Schechter's a Chicago legend. I once heard him interviewed. Explained his style as confrontational. Said being abrasive knocks people off their stride, causes them to reveal flaws."

"Character flaws? Testimonial flaws?"

"Beats me. All I know is the guy's a pit bull."

I looked at Ryan. He shrugged. Whatever.

"Before they arrive," I said. "Why are we here?"

Again, the mirthless smile. "Ever eat a Moo-Moo Bar or a Cluck-Cluck Pie?"

When Harry and I were kids, Mama had packed dozens of the little pastries into our lunches. Though uncertain of the relevance, I nodded recognition.

Ryan looked lost.

"Think Vachon," I translated into Québécois. "Jos. Louis. May West. Doigts de Dame."

"Snack cakes," he said.

"Thirteen varieties," Corcoran said. "Baked and sold by Smiling J Foods for two generations."

"Are they still available?" I couldn't remember seeing the little goodies in years.

Corcoran nodded. "Under new names."

"Quite a slap in the face to our barnyard friends."

Corcoran almost managed a genuine grin. "The J in Smiling J stood for Jurmain. The family sold out to a conglomerate in 1972. For twenty-one million dollars. Not that they needed the cash. They were bucks-up already."

I began to get the picture.

So did Ryan.

"Family fortune spells political clout," I said.

"Mucho."

"Thus the kid gloves."

"Thus."

"I don't get it. The case was closed over nine months ago. The Jurmain family got a full report but never responded. Though the coroner sent registered letters, until now no one has shown any interest in claiming the remains."

"I'll do my best to summarize a long but hardly original story."

Corcoran looked to the ceiling, as though organizing his thoughts. Then he began.

"The Jurmain family is blue-blood Chicago. Not ancient, but old enough money. Home in East Winnetka. Indian Hills Country Club. First-name basis with the governor, senators, congressmen. North Shore Country Day, then Ivy League schools for the kids. Get the picture?"

Ryan and I indicated understanding.

"Rose's father is the current patriarch, a sorry old bastard named Edward Allen. Not Ed. Not Al. Not E. A. Edward Allen. Rose was a black sheep, throughout her life refusing to follow any course Edward Allen deemed suitable. In 1968, instead of making her debut, she made the *Tribune* for assaulting a cop at the Democratic National Convention. Instead of enrolling at Smith or Vassar, she went off to Hollywood to become a star. Instead of marrying, she chose a lesbian lifestyle.

"When Rose turned thirty, Edward Allen pulled the plug. Deleted her from his will and forbade the family to have any contact."

"Until she saw the light," I guessed.

"Exactly. But that wasn't Rose's style. Thumbing her nose at Daddy, she chose to live on a small trust fund provided by Grandpa. Money Edward Allen was unable to touch."

"A real free spirit," I said.

"Yes. But things weren't all sunshine and poppies. According to her partner, Janice Spitz, at the time of her disappearance, Rose was depressed and suffering from chronic insomnia. She was also drinking a lot."

"That clicks with what we learned," Ryan said.

"Did Spitz think she was suicidal?" I asked.

"If so, she never said."

"So what gives?" I asked. "Why the sudden interest?"

"Two weeks ago, Edward Allen received an anonymous call at his home."

Corcoran was always a blusher, did so often and deeply when embarrassed or anxious. He did so now.

"Concerning Rose's death?" I asked.

Corcoran nodded, avoiding my eyes. I felt the first stirrings of uneasiness.

"What did this anonymous tipster say?"

"Walczak didn't share that information with me. All I know is I was tasked with overseeing a review of the case from this end."

"*Tabarnouche.*" Ryan slumped back in disgust.

I could think of nothing to say.

Tick. Tick. Tick. Tick. Tick.

Corcoran broke the silence.

"Edward Allen is now eighty-one years old and in failing health. Perhaps he feels like a schmuck for having driven Rose from his life. Perhaps he's still the same controlling sonovabitch he always was. Perhaps he's nuts. What I do know is that Jurmain called his lawyer. The lawyer called Walczak. And here we are."

"Jurmain thinks the case was mishandled?" I asked.

Corcoran nodded, gaze locked on the tabletop.

"Walczak shares that belief?"

"Yes."

"Mishandled by whom?" It came out sharper than I meant.

Corcoran's eyes came up and met mine. In them I saw genuine distress.

"Look, Tempe, this is not my doing."

I took a calming breath. Repeated my question.

"Mishandled by whom, Chris?"

"By you."

I GLANCED AT RYAN. HE JUST SHOOK HIS HEAD.

"You can't let on that I shared any of this." Corcoran looked more anxious than I'd ever seen him.

"Of course not." My tone was surprisingly calm. "I appreciate—"

The door opened. Corcoran and I sat back, casual as hell.

Two men entered, both wearing suits fitted by Armani himself, one blue, one gray.

I recognized Blue Suit as Stanley Walczak, peacock and legend in his own mind. Especially concerning his impact on women.

I had met Walczak at American Academy of Forensic Sciences meetings over the years, been favored by his attention on at least one occasion. For a full five minutes.

Why'd I bomb? Easy. I'm forty-plus. Though well past fifty, Walczak prefers ladies just out of training bras. Big ones.

Gray Suit, I assumed, was Perry Schechter. He had sparse black hair and a long craggy face that had taken at least six decades to form. His briefcase and demeanor screamed attorney.

As we rose, Walczak performed a quick but subtle assessment. Then he crossed to Ryan and shot out a hand.

"Stanley Walczak."

"Andrew Ryan."

The two shook. Corcoran jiggled keys in his lab coat pocket.

"Tempe." Yards of capped dentition came my way. Walczak followed. "Each time we meet you look younger and younger."

Digging deep, I managed to resist the famous Walczak charm.

"Nice to see you, Stan." I proffered a hand.

Walczak enveloped my fingers in a double-palm grip, held on way too long.

"I understand you and Dr. Corcoran are already acquainted."

Corcoran and I answered in the affirmative.

Walczak introduced Schechter.

There followed more pressing of palms.

"Gentlemen, Dr. Brennan." Again, a lot of teeth were displayed for my benefit. "Shall we proceed?"

Walczak strode to the head of the table and sat.

Ryan and I withdrew files, he from his briefcase, I from my computer bag. As Schechter settled beside Corcoran, I booted up my laptop.

"So," Walczak began. "I suppose you're both wondering why the passing of an eccentric old lady with severe alcohol and psychiatric problems necessitates such extraordinary inconvenience on your parts."

"Any death deserves proper attention." Even to myself, I sounded pedantic. But I meant it. I share Horton's worldview. A person's a person. No matter how eccentric. Or old. Rose Jurmain was not even sixty.

Walczak regarded me a moment. With his silver hair and salon tan, I had to admit, he was pretty. On the outside.

"Precisely why I've asked Dr. Corcoran to do oversight on this case," Walczak said.

Corcoran shifted in his chair, clearly uncomfortable.

"Dr. Brennan and I will be happy to answer all questions concerning my investigation, her examination of the remains, and the coroner's finding," Ryan said.

"Excellent. Then I'll turn this meeting over to Mr. Schechter and Dr. Corcoran. Please let me know if there's anything, anything at all, that you need."

With a meaningful look in Corcoran's direction, Walczak left the room.

"I'm pleased you speak English, detective."

A subtle tensing around the eyes suggested that Schechter's first words did not sit well with Ryan.

"*Mais oui, monsieur.*" Ryan's accent was over-the-top Parisian.

"Mr. Jurmain requests clarification on a number of points." Schechter's tone indicated that Ryan's humor was not appreciated.

"Clarification?" Ryan matched cool with cool.

"He is deeply troubled."

"You have copies of our reports?"

Schechter withdrew a yellow legal pad, a gold Cross pen, and a large white envelope from his briefcase. I recognized the envelope's logo, and the words *Laboratoire de sciences judiciaires et de médecine légale.*

"Dr. Brennan and I have prepared scene and autopsy photos to walk you through the investigation."

Clicking his pen to readiness, Schechter gave an imperious wave of one hand.

Ryan spoke to me in French. "Let's clarify this prick's head right out of his ass."

"*Certainement,*" I agreed.

Connecting my laptop to the projector, I opened PowerPoint, chose a file labeled *LSJML 44893,* and double-clicked an image. A wide-angle view of L'Auberge des Neiges filled the screen. Built of redwood, with carved and painted balconies and window boxes, the inn looked like something straight out of *The Sound of Music.*

Corcoran handed me the laser pointer.

Ryan began.

"Ms. Jurmain checked into L'Auberge des Neiges on twenty September, having reserved for two weeks. On twenty-three September she volunteered to other guests her intent to hike the following day."

"These other guests would be?" Schechter asked.

Ryan checked his notes.

"John William Manning of Montreal. Isabelle Picard of Laval. According to Manning and Picard, Ms. Jurmain appeared inebriated that evening, and had appeared to be so on several occasions spanning a period of three days."

Ryan slid several papers across the table, I assumed summaries of interviews with the auberge's staff and guests. Corcoran skimmed. Schechter took his time reading. Then, "These are written in French."

"My apologies." Ryan's tone was as far from apologetic as a tone can be.

Schechter made an indecipherable noise in his throat.

I switched to a wide shot of Rose's room. It featured a braided rug, lacquered pine furniture, and an overabundance of pink floral chintz. A suitcase sat open on a small settee, clothes oozing like magma from a sleepy volcano.

I moved to a picture of the bed stand, then to close-ups of the labels on five small vials. Oxycodone. Diazepam. Temazepam. Alprazolam. Doxylamine.

I aimed the laser pointer. As the small red dot jumped from vial to vial, Corcoran translated into generic names for Schechter.

"The painkiller OxyContin, the antianxiety drugs Valium and Xanax, and the sleep aids Restoril and Unisom."

Schechter drew air through his nostrils, exhaled slowly.

"When Rose got an idea into her head there was no reasoning with her. Always going off into the woods. Three years ago it was Quebec." He said *Quee-beck* with the disgust one might reserve for "Eye-rack" or "Dar-four." "Even though her"—he paused, seeking proper phrasing—"health was not good, she could not be dissuaded."

Ryan proceeded without comment.

"At fifteen twenty hours, on twenty-four September, Ms. Jurmain was seen walking alone along Chemin Pierre-Mirabeau, in the direction of Sainte-Marguerite. Though the temperature was near freezing, a motorist reported that she wore a lightweight jacket, no hat, no gloves."

As I projected a regional map, Ryan slid another paper to Schechter.

"Sunset that day was at approximately seventeen hundred hours. By nineteen hundred hours it was full dark. Overnight, temperatures fell to minus eight Celsius.

"On twenty-five September, it was noted that Ms. Jurmain had failed to return to the inn. A call was placed to an area code three-one-two number provided upon check-in. Subsequent investigation showed that line to be nonexistent.

"On twenty-six September, the SQ post covering Sainte-Marguerite was notified of Ms. Jurmain's disappearance. Woods bordering the road and surrounding the auberge were searched with tracker dogs. Unsuccessfully."

More paper.

"What is this SQ?" Schechter demanded.

"La Sûreté du Québec. The provincial police."

"Why not call the locals?"

Ryan launched into a primer on law enforcement Quebec-style, laying on a thick Maurice Chevalier where opportunity presented itself.

"In cities and larger towns there are local forces. On the Island of

Montreal, for example, policing is the responsibility of the Service de police de la Ville de Montréal, or SPVM, formerly known as the service de police de la communauté urbaine de Montréal, or CUM. Same force, new name.

"In rural areas, law enforcement is handled by La Sûreté du Québec, or SQ. In places without provincial police, meaning all provinces except Ontario and Quebec, it's the Royal Canadian Mounted Police, or RCMP, or, to Francophones, the Gendarmerie royale du Canada, or GRC. Occasionally, the Mounties are invited into an investigation in Quebec, but that's rare."

In other words, jurisdiction in La Belle Province can be as confusing as in any American state. FBI. State bureau of investigation. City. County. Highway patrol. Sheriff's department. Who you gonna call? Good luck. *Bonne chance.* Ryan didn't say that.

"L'Auberge des Neiges is located seventy-five kilometers north of the Island of Montreal, in the Laurentian Mountains. The nearest town is Sainte-Marguerite. Thus, Ms. Jurmain's case fell to the SQ. Shall I continue?"

Again Schechter flapped an arrogant hand. I wanted to reach across the table and smack the self-righteous little prick.

"Thirty months after Ms. Jurmain's disappearance, on twenty-one March, André Dubreuil and his son Bertrand stumbled on what they believed to be human remains. Their find was located twenty yards off a provincial road, approximately one half mile north of L'Auberge des Neiges. The SQ, the coroner, and the LSJML were notified. In that order."

As I projected a second map, Schechter jotted his first note of the morning. Then, "You are a homicide detective with this SQ?"

"Section des crimes contre la personne."

I translated. "Detective Ryan is with the equivalent of homicide, a section called Crimes Against Persons. He is assigned to special cases."

"And this case would be deemed special because . . . ?" Schechter elongated the last word of his unfinished statement.

"From the outset it was suspected that the remains in question were those of Ms. Jurmain. Since she was a non-Canadian national, an American, the case was assigned to Detective Ryan."

Schechter and Corcoran glanced at the police incident report Ryan slid to them. When their attention returned to the screen I moved through a new series of JPEGs.

The first provided a wide-angle view of a narrow two-lane blacktop, its gravel shoulder butting up to dense forest. The next six documented the route from the road to the body. On the ground, islands of snow overlaid dead vegetation, their perimeters darkened by meltwater runoff.

The eighth image showed yellow crime scene tape looping a stand of pines. In the ninth, people stood inside the tape. Ryan was there in a pea green parka and bright blue scarf. Two recovery techs wore navy jumpsuits stamped *Service de l'identité judiciaire, Division des scènes de crime.* So did I. Vapor billowed from every mouth.

Shot ten was a close-up of a small dark mound emerging from the snow. Embedded in the jumble of leaves, twigs, moss, and pine needles was a glossy brown object the size of a cabbage. A mass of matted gray hair lay to its right.

"The skull." I circled it using the laser pointer.

The next few shots focused on the partial skeleton, spread in a largely linear pattern from the skull. Mandible. Vertebrae. Ribs. Sternum. Pelvic halves. Sacrum. Right hand. Right leg. Everything was stained the same burnt umber.

One by one, I named the bones.

"Obviously human," Corcoran said.

"Animals had scattered bones over approximately twenty square meters," I said.

As I projected my site map, Ryan produced hard copies. "Dr. Brennan documented the position of each skeletal element."

When Corcoran and Schechter looked up, I resumed the presentation, moving outward from the central cluster through the dispersed remains.

"Each plastic cone marks the location of a bone or bone cluster." Advancing through the images, I again identified body parts. "Right femur, tibia, and patella. Right calcaneous. Right tarsals, metatarsals, and phalanges. Right radius. Right ulna and hand bones. Left lower central incisor. Right upper central incisor."

"Could we move this along?" Schechter said.

Ryan resumed.

"Given Ms. Jurmain's known history of alcoholism, the evidence of prescription drug abuse, eyewitness accounts, and the climatic conditions on the night of her absence from the inn, the coroner ruled manner of death as accidental and cause of death as hypothermia exacerbated by intoxication."

"You're saying Rose got drunk, wandered off, and froze to death." Schechter.

"Basically, yes. Shortly, Dr. Brennan will discuss skeletal identification and analysis of trauma."

"Not shortly. Now."

"Sir?"

"Enough of this ridiculous subterfuge."

Startled, I looked at Ryan. His face was a stone mask pointed at the lawyer across the table. Recognizing his expression, I jumped in.

"Detective Ryan has been providing background for the coroner's conclusion. But if your preference is to move on, we have no objection."

"I suggest we go directly to your report, Dr. Brennan."

"I suggest you specify what it is you want." Ryan's tone was a steel blade.

"Very well, Detective." Schechter's chin cocked up slightly. "My client does not believe his daughter died of exposure. He believes she was murdered."

Placing both forearms on the tabletop, Schechter laced his fingers, and leaned in.

"Further, he believes Dr. Brennan concealed that fact."

MY EYES JUMPED TO CORCORAN. HE CONTINUED STARING AT THE screen.

"Is that so?" Ryan's tone suggested trench warfare. "To what purpose?"

"That is what I intend to find out."

Schechter wiggled manicured fingers at the pointer.

I handed it to him.

"Project the close-up of the undisturbed remains."

Stomach knotted, I did as requested. As demanded.

The red dot appeared on the half-buried skeleton, drifted across the mandible, the clavicles, and the upper ribs. Coming to rest, it performed jerky pirouettes around the breastbone.

"That's the sternum," I said.

"I am aware of that."

The gut clench eased. Was that where Schechter was going? If so, he was a bigger dumbass than I thought. He must not have consulted an osteologist.

Closing the death scene file, I opened another containing photos taken at the LSJML. The first few depicted a body bag, zipped then unzipped, the latter displaying jumbled bones visible in the bag's interior.

The next series showed an autopsy table, dirt-encrusted skeleton atop the stainless steel. A few bones were connected by desiccated muscle or ligament. Most lay loose, in positions approximating those they'd occupied when the body was intact.

"Here you see the remains as they arrived at the morgue, prior to any manipulation. Shall I identify individual elements?"

Schechter gave another haughty wave. The old wheezer had quite a repertoire.

"Shall I explain my cleaning process?"

"Not germane."

"Dandy. Let's proceed to ID."

"My client does not question that the remains are those of his daughter."

"Groovy. Let's talk about trauma. Shall I clarify the terms antemortem, perimortem, and postmortem?"

"Succinctly."

"With skeletal remains, antemortem refers to trauma occurring prior to death, injuries sustained earlier in life and showing evidence of healing. Perimortem refers to trauma suffered at or close to the time of death. Postmortem refers to trauma inflicted after death, damage associated with decomposition, abuse of the body, animal scavenging, and such."

"How is this germane?" Clearly, Schechter liked the word.

"It is *germane* to your client's understanding of what happened to his daughter. And, perhaps more important, what did not."

Again the hand.

"I will not belabor the importance of distinguishing between perimortem and postmortem trauma. I would like to make clear, however, that, for the anthropologist, this distinction has more to do with bone quality than it does with time of death. It's a complex subject, so forgive me if I oversimplify.

"In fresh or living bone the moisture content is relatively high and the collagen, the component that gives bone its elasticity, is somewhat flexible. This permits a certain degree of bending under stress. With decomposition, moisture is lost and collagen degrades, so the bending capability diminishes. In other words, dry bone responds to loading like an inorganic, rather than an organic, material. It fails, or breaks, when subjected to smaller forces. Think of a green stick versus a dry stick. The former yields, the latter snaps under pressure."

Schechter made a note on his tablet but did not interrupt.

"Practically speaking, this means that fractures to dry bone are less clean and have more jagged edges. Fragments tend to be smaller. Breakaway spurs, relatively common in fresh bone, are rare. Concentric circular and radiating fractures, patterns produced by the transmission of energy through bone, are uncommon."

"Most impressive. We're all experts now."

Knowing his game book, I ignored Schechter's rudeness.

"Distinguishing an antemortem injury or defect is equally important in accurately determining manner of death. Since the first signs of healing are often difficult to detect, skeletal remains are examined on three levels, macroscopic, radiographic, and histologic."

"Let's skip the jargon." Schechter.

"Macroscopic means eyeballing. The first indication of antemortem repair is a narrow band of surface resorption immediately adjacent to the fracture site. This reflects inflammation at the point where the overlying membrane was torn away. Next, gradual erosion can be seen at the broken ends. These changes are evident anywhere from ten to fourteen days after injury.

"Radiographic means X-ray. Here healing appears as a blurring of the fractured edges, again roughly ten to fourteen days post-injury. The gap between the broken ends then widens as callus formation proceeds."

Schechter's eyes narrowed slightly.

"A callus is an unorganized network of woven bone that forms quickly at a fracture site. It functions like putty to hold the broken ends in place. As repair progresses, the callus is gradually replaced by true bone.

"Histologic means under the microscope. Here healing is first evidenced by spicules of woven bone within the callus. These spicules can be seen as early as five to seven days post-injury."

"Will we be getting to Rose sometime today?"

I opened a new PowerPoint file. Rose's skeleton was now in my lab, clean of soil and tissue. Each bone was aligned with anatomical precision, right down to the distal phalanges of the hands and feet.

"As Detective Ryan mentioned earlier, the remains suffered considerable postmortem damage due to animal scavenging."

I chose a shot of Rose's right thigh bone. Instead of a rounded knob on one end and condyles on the other, the femoral shaft terminated in long jagged spikes. I clicked to the tibia, then the fibula, demonstrating similar damage in the lower leg.

"Notice the cracking and longitudinal splintering. Those features, along with dispersal of elements away from the body, suggest large carnivore feeding."

Moving to a femoral close-up, I pointed the laser at one circular defect, then another.

"Those are canine tooth punctures. Based on size, I'd say the diners were *Ursus americanus.*"

"Black bears," Corcoran said.

"Bears eat carrion?" Schechter made no attempt to hide his revulsion.

"With relish," I said.

I proceeded to a tight shot of the lower jaw.

"But they weren't alone. Notice the lower edge." I ran the beam along the mandibular border. "See the parallel grooving?"

"Rodent gnawing," Corcoran said.

"Exactly. Once skeletonization was complete, the rats and mice moved in."

Corcoran was slowly wagging his head. "I've never understood the appeal once the flesh is gone."

"Dry bone is a rich source of dietary mineral and protein."

Schechter pulled on his nose with a thumb and index finger. "If your point is to shock me, Dr. Brennan, you fail."

"My point is to inform you."

"Let's cut to the chase." Schechter glared in my direction.

"Let's." I almost smiled. I was looking forward to deflating this arrogant gasbag.

"Bottom line." Leaning forward, I rested my forearms and interlaced my fingers as Schechter had done. "I observed significant damage to Rose Jurmain's skeleton, all of it postmortem in nature."

"What do you mean postmortem in nature?"

"I mean postmortem. As in, inflicted after death."

"By bears."

"And rodents."

"You observed no evidence of perimortem trauma?"

"Neither perimortem nor antemortem."

"What about the sternum."

"You heard me."

Schechter's mouth crawled into a reptilian smile. "Have you no image of the sternum, *Doctor*? Or are you reluctant to share it?"

Ryan moved forward in his chair. I laid a hand on his arm. He looked at me. I gave a barely perceptible shake of my head.

"C'est un ostie de crosseur." The guy's a flaming asshole. Roughly translated.

"He's going down," I replied in French.

I worked keys on my laptop. Rose's breastbone replaced her jaw on the screen. Beside it was an X-ray.

Snatching the pointer, Schechter danced the red dot around a small round defect two inches up from the bone's lower end. The dot then shot to the X-ray, where the defect appeared as a dark circle within the gray-white of the bone's spongy interior.

"You going to tell me bears did that?"

"No. I am not."

"How do you explain it?" Schechter demanded.

"How do *you* explain it?" I asked, almost sweetly.

"Clearly that's a gunshot wound."

"I see no evidence of that."

"Meaning?"

"No bullet fragments or metallic trace on the X-ray. No jagged edges. No shattered bits of bone. No radiating fractures or blowout fragments."

"You're saying the hole is antemortem trauma?"

"No. I am not." I knew it was childish to bait Schechter but couldn't help myself. The guy was so unpleasant I was looking forward to booting him under the bus.

"Explain."

"The hole did not result from trauma of any kind."

"Not trauma." For the first time Schechter's voice held a note of uncertainty.

"No."

"Elaborate."

"My explanation requires an understanding of sternal development."

Schechter did the hand thing. With a bit less flair than before.

I gathered my thoughts, then began.

"The sternum begins life as two vertical cartilaginous bars lying one beside the other. Eventually, the bars fuse along the midline. The cartilaginous sternum then ossifies, meaning it turns to bone. This ossification progresses from six centers, four of which form the body, or long thin part, of the sternum. If there's no objection I'll confine my comments to the sternal body, since that's where the hole is situated."

"Please." It was Schechter's first use of the word all morning.

I moved the laser sideways across Rose's sternum.

"Note the transverse ridges. Each marks the site of fusion of separate juvenile elements called sternebrae. Ossification begins in the first sternebra during the fifth to sixth fetal month, in the second and third during the seventh to eighth fetal month, and in the fourth during the first year after birth.

"That is, if things progress normally. But sometimes they don't. Occasionally a sternebra ossifies from more than one point of origin. In the lower sternebrae this variation usually involves two centers placed one beside the other."

I paused. To annoy? Maybe.

"Failed union of these side-by-side centers results in an anomaly known as a sternal foramen." I spoke slowly, a teacher addressing a dull student. "A variation resulting from incomplete fusion of a lower sternal segment as it ossifies from separate left and right centers."

Schechter scribbled, underlined, then spoke again.

"You're saying Rose had one of these things."

"Yes. It's stated on page three of my report, in the section headed 'unique identifiers.' "

As Schechter flipped pages I projected a new image. With a tight shot of Rose's foramen filling the screen, I listed characteristics.

"Single, circular defect, with a diameter of fourteen millimeters. Smooth, round edges, like a doughnut hole. Midline location, in the lower third of the sternal body. It's textbook."

"Could Rose have functioned normally with something like that?" Schechter's cheeks had gone blotchy.

"People do it all the time."

"Would she not have exhibited symptoms?"

"No."

"How common is this condition?"

"Sternal foramina occur in roughly seven to ten percent of the population."

No one spoke for what seemed a very long time.

Tick. Tick. Tick. Tick. Tick.

"You found nothing to suggest that Rose had been shot?"

"Nothing."

"No evidence of homicide?"

I shook my head. "No signs of strangulation, bludgeoning, stabbing, or slashing. No defense wounds on her finger, hand, or arm bones. Other than damage caused by bears, no signs of violence at all."

"Show me."

I took him through the skeleton, bone by bone.

Now and then, a mollified Schechter posed a question.

When my presentation finished we all sat mute.

Tick. Tick. Tick. Tick. Tick.

I could see Schechter's mind working, trying to classify new information. Perhaps tallying his billable hours for old Edward Allen.

"Tell me, Mr. Schechter. What prompted all this?" My gesture took in the screen, the reports, the four of us seated at the table.

"That's hardly—"

"Germane. Indulge me."

Schechter studied me, lips drawn into a thin hard line. I expected him to gather his pen and tablet and take his leave. To my surprise, he answered.

"Mr. Jurmain was informed that his daughter's death investigation had either been botched or deliberately falsified."

"By me."

"Yes."

"Informed by whom?"

Schechter hesitated, no doubt deciding how much to share, how much to hold back.

"The caller left no name."

Anger overrode any triumph I might have felt at besting the man.

"You launched this witch hunt based solely on an anonymous tip?"

"My client believed the call to be genuine."

"You could have counseled your client concerning proper protocol."

Again the long stare.

I stared back.

Tick. Tick. Tick. Tick. Tick.

Without comment, Schechter packed his belongings, snapped his briefcase, and walked to the door. Hand on the knob, he turned.

"You have an enemy, Dr. Brennan. I suggest it is in your interest to learn who placed that call."

With that, he was gone.

"RICHIE CUNNINGHAM WAS A BIG HELP IN THERE."

"Who?"

"You know. Richie and the Fonz? *Happy Days*?" Ryan pointed at his head. "Red hair?"

"You watch too much television."

"Improves my English." Again the hideous French accent.

"Chris gave us a heads-up on Jurmain's crackpot allegations." Though I defended Corcoran, I couldn't disagree with Ryan. My childhood pal hadn't exactly gone back-to-the-wall for me.

"Way to go, champ."

Ryan and I were traveling east on Harrison. I was at the wheel. He was riding shotgun. As at the airport and hotel, this arrangement had followed spirited debate. Ryan had claimed superior driving skills. I'd claimed knowledge of the city. A bit of a stretch, but my other argument had trumped his. My rental car, my choice.

"Chris has never been assertive," I said.

"A guppy is assertive compared to that guy. He should take lessons from Schechter."

"Right." I snorted. "Schechter's a peach."

"And you plucked him."

Ryan was grinning and doing that flicky thing he does with his brows.

Smiling, I raised my right palm. He high-fived it.

I drove a few moments, thinking a very unsmiley thought. Ryan voiced it.

"Schechter was right about you needing to identify the source."

"Yes," I said.

"Want me to talk to Jurmain?"

"Thanks, Ryan. I can do it."

"I keep going back to one question."

"Who's the scum-sucking bastard that made the call?"

"Well, yeah. But also, why? What's the motivation to jam you up? Have you pissed someone off lately? I mean, more than normal?"

I gave Ryan the Face.

"Eyes on the road. This stuff's slick."

Ryan was right. Sleet had been pelting the windshield as we'd made our way to the CCME early that morning. The stuff was now coming down even harder. Temperatures hovered around freezing, and the sun hadn't mustered the strength to penetrate the thick, cobalt clouds covering the sky. Semifrozen slush topped cars and mailboxes and lay along sidewalk borders and curbs. Harrison was coated with what looked like black ice.

"It has to be personal," Ryan went on. "Someone you've opposed in some context."

"That's my thinking. An insider, in all likelihood in Quebec. Who else would be privy to the fact that I'd worked Rose Jurmain?"

"Did the case draw attention?"

"I vaguely remember a line or two in *Le Journal* when the remains were found. Or maybe following the ID. But that was nine months ago. Jurmain got his call just two weeks back."

Anger began to blossom anew. I checked the dashboard clock. One forty. I changed the subject.

"What time is your flight?"

"Six thirty."

"Are you hungry?"

"Starving."

"Suggestions?"

"Your town. Your choice."

"Right answer."

"Where are we?" Ryan asked.

"Just west of downtown. In Chicago it's called the Loop."

"Why?"

"Something about the old el tracks forming a circle."

"El?"

"Elevated CTA tracks."

"CTA?"

"Come on, Ryan. You could figure that one out. Chicago Transit Authority. In this town, mass transit is part subway, part surface, part elevated. The whole enchilada is called the el, short for elevated."

"You're talking about commuter trains."

"Here it's never called the train, except by suburbanites or out-of-towners. To Chicagoans, the 'train' is Metra, which connects the Loop to the burbs."

"What does this multifaceted marvel loop?"

"Do you see me carrying a sign on a stick?"

"Meaning?"

"I'm not a tour guide."

"You said you knew this place like the back of your hand."

I had said that. What I *hadn't* said was that I'd moved from Chicago to Charlotte almost three decades earlier, and that my recall of detail might be hazy. But this one was a lollipop.

"The old el tracks run along Lake Street on the north, Wabash Avenue on the east, Van Buren Street on the south, and Wells Street on the west. Inside that loop is the city's original central business district. But I think the nickname might predate the el. I think it actually came from a streetcar loop that existed in the late 1880s."

"You're making this stuff up."

"You want a professional, take a Gray Line."

"Do you know where you're going?"

"Yes."

To our left, a Blue Line el clicked along ground-level tracks in the center of the Eisenhower Expressway. Around it, lanes of cars lurched and braked in truculent rivers attempting to flow east and west.

"That place looks a bit past its shelf life." Ryan indicated a Beaux Arts structure stretching for two blocks to our right.

"Cook County Hospital. I think it's now called Stroger. And I think there's a plan to tear it down. A lot of folks are opposed."

"Doesn't look that old on *ER*," Ryan said.

"Really. Too much TV."

"I turn it on for Charlie."

"Our cockatiel likes dramas?"

"Actually, he prefers sitcoms. Digs the laugh tracks."

Charlie was a Christmas surprise from Ryan. Part of the gift was that he kept the bird while I was away from Montreal. At first, I was skeptical. But the arrangement works and, despite his bawdy beak, the little avian has grown on me.

Ironic. Ryan dumped me, but my feathered pal stayed true.

"That part looks pretty good."

I glanced to my right. "We're beyond County now. That's Rush Presbyterian."

We were passing beneath a pedestrian bridge connecting the el to the Rush medical complex when *el turisto* struck again.

"Does that building get bigger from bottom to top?"

Without looking, I knew what Ryan was eyeing. "That's UIC. University of Illinois–Chicago. Used to be called Circle Campus."

"So what's the funky building?"

"University Hall. Houses faculty and administrative offices. Tapers out twice, so the top is some twenty feet wider than the bottom."

Ryan was craning forward to peer up through a wiper-cleared fan on the windshield.

"Brutalism," I said. "Ditto for the campus."

"That's harsh."

"The term was coined by an architect calling himself Le Corbusier—I forget his real name. Comes from the French *béton brut,* or 'raw concrete.' You should have picked up on that."

Ryan's face swiveled toward me. "What the hell kind of name is Brutalism? Why not call it Appallingism? Or Atrociousism? Or—"

"Complain to Le Corbusier."

"Obviously the guy was not into marketing."

"His invention, his choice."

"Describe the style."

I couldn't tell if Ryan was genuinely interested, just bored, or testing me. Whatever. I pulled from an article I'd read about a zillion years earlier.

"Brutalism involves the use of repetitive angular geometries and gobs of unadorned poured concrete. It was big from the fifties into the seventies, then lost favor."

"Gee. Why would that be?"

Ryan relaxed into his seat back. "Not bad, Brennan."

"How do you know I didn't make all that up?"

"Where are we going?"

"Greektown."

"Why?"

"Lamb and valet parking."

"Unbeatable combo."

I made a left onto Halsted, crossed over the highway, and, minutes later, pulled to the curb at Adams. When I got out of the car, wind whipped my scarf and drove sleet into my face. The ice felt like match heads burning my cheeks.

Accepting a valet ticket from a man in a parka and orange Bears hat pulled low to his brows, I slip-skidded to the restaurant. Ryan followed.

The Santorini's interior was exactly as promised by its name. Wooden tables with lattice-back chairs and crisp linen cloths, whitewashed walls, stone fireplace, copious fisherman paraphernalia.

Ryan and I hung our coats on a rack. Then a waiter with a Sonny Bono mustache and blue plaid shirt led us to an upper-terrace table. Only a few of the lunch crowd lingered, most wearing suits and retsina glows.

A second waiter brought menus. Same mustache, different shirt. I ordered a Diet Coke. Ryan asked for a Sam Adams.

"People rave about the seafood, but I like the lamb." Ignoring the menu, I brushed moisture from my hair.

"Not even a glance?"

"I know what I want."

Ryan studied the selections. "The Lamb youvetsi?"

I shook my head.

"Kampana?"

"Nope."

"You're being childish."

"Lamb artichokes."

"Not today, cupcake."

I checked. Damn. Ryan was right. Lamb artichokes were offered only on Tuesdays and Sundays.

"No problem." I leaned back, arms crossed on my chest. "Buttercup."

First the weather. I hate cold. Wet cold? Don't ask. Then meeting Schechter and learning of an anonymous enemy. Now no lamb artichokes. Or maybe it was proximity to Ryan. Or his use of the old endearment. My mood was heading into free fall.

Beside us, two men argued the pros and cons of hockey players whose names meant nothing to me. Outside, a siren grew loud, dimmed, faded. Glassware clanked somewhere off to my left.

When the waiter returned I ordered the exohiko lamb. Ryan requested the seafood combo and a second Sam Adams.

A very long time passed without conversation.

Ryan's mug was half empty when he finally said, "What are you thinking?"

"Don't men hate being asked that question?"

"Not me." Ryan beamed a little-boy smile.

I couldn't help but grin back. We'd been a team for so long, Ryan detecting, me working the vics. Though the breakup was difficult, I wanted this to continue. We'd been strictly colleagues once, could be again.

"I'm thinking we should eat and get you to the airport. With this weather, the trip to O'Hare could be a bitch."

"Very practical." Ryan nodded solemnly.

Minutes ticked by. Beside us, the men disagreed on the abilities of the Blackhawks' coach.

Our food arrived. Mine turned out to be chunks of lamb and cheese baked inside phyllo.

As I ate, unbidden memories elbowed for attention.

The beginning. My arrival at the Montreal lab, armed with a rule against office romance. Ryan's disregard for that rule. My eventual surrender.

The middle. Candlelight dinners in Vieux-Montréal. Walks on the mountain. Sofa suppers watching classic films on TV. Trips to the Laurentians. The Carolinas. Israel. Guatemala.

The end. Ryan's revelation of a newly discovered offspring, angry, addicted to heroin. Daddy's plan to reconnect with Mommy in an effort to save Daughter.

Our last meal, Ryan's words ripping a hole in my heart. I was out. Lily and Lutetia were in. *Adieu.* Sorry. Have a good life.

Then, months later, an admission of error, an apology, an invitation to reunite. Lily was in rehab, and he and Lutetia were living apart. Ryan wanted me. Wanted us.

Whoa, big fella! Do-overs ain't so simple.

Two months had passed since that conversation. I'd neither vetoed nor embraced détente with Ryan. Once burned, twice shy.

Trite, yes. But there's a reason some phrases grow into clichés.

"—ovabitch. They've shut down O'Hare." The words intruded on my reverie.

I glanced toward the next table. One of the sports critics was reading his BlackBerry.

"Did you just say the airport is closed?" I asked.

"Can you believe it?"

"Why?"

"A bomb threat, or a security breach, or some freakin' thing."

Ryan's mobile made an odd croaking noise.

"Text message. My flight's been canceled." He was already punching keys.

For the next thirty minutes Ryan spoke to airlines, then to a minimum of eight hotels. No flights. No rooms. Even the place we'd just left was fully booked.

"How'd everyone move so fast?" I asked.

"Apparently no one's checking out. And there are several huge conventions in town." Innocent choirboy look. "Guess you're stuck with me."

"You know I have plans."

"I suppose I could *try* for a rental car." Insincere.

Dear God. I couldn't take Ryan where I was going.

"Could be nasty, what with this weather, and me unfamiliar with the city," Ryan went on.

"Agencies provide maps. Or you can ask for something with GPS."

No go at Hertz or Avis.

I couldn't believe this was happening. Could the day get worse?

I thought of the evening ahead.

A lot worse, I realized.

"All right," I said as Ryan requested the number at Budget. "You can have my car. But you'll have to drive me to the burbs."

"Sounds workable. Surely motels that far out will have vacancy."

"Surely."

That's not how it went.

EVEN IN GONZO TRAFFIC, THE DRIVE FROM GREEKTOWN TO Elmhurst should take less than an hour. That afternoon it took two and a half.

By the time I reached St. Charles Road, the dashboard clock said six forty. Great. I'd given an ETA of four. Everyone would be there. If Ryan was spotted, my arrival would turn into a circus.

Sound melodramatic? Trust me. I know the crowd.

Ryan understood a little about my colorful in-laws. While driving, I'd given him the the current saga. I'd missed Thanksgiving, and would compound that felony at Christmas by taking Katy to Belize to scuba-dive instead of to Chicago to hang stockings by the fire. Thus, I was spending a couple of days with the Petersons tribe.

"Your former in-laws?"

"Mm."

Though we'd lived apart for years, my ex and I weren't technically exes. We'd never legally divorced. But that would soon change. Recently, fiftysomething Pete had slipped a diamond onto the finger of twenty-something Summer. Needless to say, Old Pete had also opted out of turkey this year.

"Your mother-in-law is making supper?"

"You just ate, Ryan."

"You rave about her cooking."

"She'll have a houseful."

"Aunt Klara and Uncle Juris?"

Over the years, I'd shared tales of Pete's alarmingly close and remarkably extended Latvian family. The annual beach trip, Easter egg–coloring contest, and Yuletide caroling to the Brookfield Zoo bears. The mandatory appearances at christenings, graduations, weddings, and funerals. The telephone network that makes the national disaster alarm system look like child's play. Apparently, Ryan remembered key player names.

Here's the story. Following World War II and the subsequent Soviet occupation of the Baltics, Pete's grandmother, her sons, and their wives decided it was best to seek greener pastures. According to family lore, the departure from Riga involved a dead-of-night dash and a harrowing voyage on a sketchy cargo ship.

Next came an extended heel-cooling period in "displaced persons" compounds, known as DP camps, up and down the German countryside. Undaunted by the long wait, the couples used their time to be fruitful and multiply. Madara and Vilis produced Janis, our very own "Pete," and his sister, Regina. Klara and Juris produced Emilija and Ludis.

After eight long years, a Latvian church in Chicago finally stepped up to the plate. In agreeing to sponsor the brave little band, the pastor and his flock guaranteed employment, housing, and a linguistically intelligible support network in the Windy City.

Upon their arrival, the family lived in an abandoned store. Not much, but it was home.

Working two jobs each, the brothers eventually managed to copurchase a wreck of a place in Elmhurst, a suburb close to the factories, the college, and the Latvian church. More important perhaps, Elmhurst's grand old trees reminded Omamma of her lost home far across the sea.

The house was a rambling frame affair with enough bedrooms to accommodate the whole ragtag clan. But that isn't family, American-style. In the U.S. we go to nuclear units, Ward, June, Wally, and the Beav.

A few more years and the brothers held separate mortgages. Pete and his parents and sister stayed in the big house with Omamma and a collie named Oskars. Pete's aunt, uncle, and cousins moved to a smaller property two short blocks away.

Homes, cars, TVs, and washers. College funds for the kids. Within a decade, the Petersons families were living the stars-and-stripes dream. Juris continued until retirement at the refrigerator factory. Vilis switched to teaching math full-time at Elmhurst College.

Almost a half century since the transatlantic odyssey, some things have changed. Old Omamma is dead now. So is Vilis. Pete's mother, now called Vecamamma, is ruling matriarch. Spouses have been added, and a new generation of cousins now shares the piragi. Though the ties that bind have multiplied through births and marriages, they're still forged of the same old-world steel.

"How's that feel?" Ryan asked. "Being with your ex's relatives?"

"Splendid."

"Not awkward?"

"Right now they think Pete's a dick and I'm Queen of Angels."

"That should work in your favor."

"Here's how my arrival is going to play out. I'll grab my bag and sprint. You'll drive away. Quickly. Got it?"

"Aren't we the drama queen?"

"Got it?"

Ryan gave a snappy two-finger salute.

As I turned north onto Cottage Hill, the car fishtailed wildly. I gently pumped the brakes until the rear wheels came back into line with the front.

I expected commentary from Ryan. Surprisingly, he offered none.

Ancient elms now lined both sides of the street. Beyond the trees, first-floor windows in large old homes cast rectangles of light onto slush-covered lawns. Ahead, at Church Street, two shadowy structures brooded like bunkers in the cold, wet night. Immaculate Conception High School and Hawthorn Elementary.

Right turn, then I proceeded a half block and slid to the curb in front of a white Victorian whose wraparound porch bulged into gazebos at each of its corners. The porch's ornately carved columns sat on a limestone outer wall that rose approximately four feet from the ground. The house's roof and right-wing and front-door porticos composed a trio of triangles facing the street.

Every edge now dripped electric white icicles. Ho. Ho. Ho.

I shifted into park and turned to Ryan.

"There's a Marriott on Route Eighty-three and a Holiday Inn on York Road." I pointed in the general direction of each. "If they're full, have the desk clerk call over to Oak Brook. It's hotel city out that way."

Hopping out, I opened the back door and snatched my purse and suitcase from the seat. Icy pellets blew horizontally into my face.

I met Ryan as he was circling the trunk.

"When you have a room and a flight, call me. Tomorrow we can figure out how to handle the car."

Ryan said something that was lost to the wind.

"And be careful." Shouted. "I declined the extra insurance."

With that I bolted for the house, one hand fighting my scarf, the other dragging my roll-aboard over slush that had frozen into choppy little waves.

Before my thumb hit the bell, the door opened and I was dragged inside. The air smelled of lemon polish, rye bread, and roasting meat.

"Who's driving that car?" Vecamamma asked after kissing my cheek. Never a buzzer or pecker, the old gal always planted a very firm wet one.

"A man I work with."

"A policeman?" One of my nieces was peering past us through the storm door. With her dark hair, green eyes, and ivory skin, Allie showed not a hint of her Baltic gene pool.

"Yes."

"Cool." Allie's younger sister, Bea, had wandered in wearing a very large sweater, very short skirt, black tights, and boots. On a six-foot blond the look was impressive.

"Is your policeman friend hungry?" Vecamamma was yanking my coat with enough force to rip pelts from wild game. "I'm making fresh ham. Men like fresh ham."

"He's eaten." I managed to slip free of both sleeves while retaining my arms.

"What's his name?" Bea was as forward as Allie was timid.

"Ryan."

"Is he cute?"

"We work together."

"Like, what? You never noticed?"

"Alise and Beatrise, finish setting the table." Vecamamma's command boomed from deep in the closet. "We'll be twelve."

Only a dozen. Not too bad.

Vecamamma emerged with hair doing a Kramer imitation. Death-gripping my arm, she ordered, "Leave the suitcase. Teodors will take it up to your room."

The house's main artery is a wide central hall. From it, in front, arched doorways open onto living and dining rooms, the latter used frequently, the former almost never. A central staircase rises from the hall on the left.

The kitchen is farther down on the right. Butler pantry. Opposite, two bedrooms and a bath.

Spanning the rear of the house is a wood-paneled room with green plaid carpet, a massive stone fireplace, and enough square footage to practice Hail Mary passes. Well, laterals, anyway. Chez Petersons' sports center, party pad, Speakers Corner, and family hearth.

Through the door I could see Ted, Ludis, and Juris watching a big-screen TV, each wearing a knit cap identical to the one on the Santorini valet. Ted had rotated the NFL logo to the back of his head. Old-school, Ludis and Juris had positioned theirs front and center.

"Tempe's here," Vecamamma warbled.

Ludis and Juris raised bottles of Special Export. Ted said, "Da bears!" All six eyes remained glued to the set.

Emilija's husband, Gordie, and Regina's husband, Terry, were conversing beside an overdecorated Christmas tree doing a Tower of Pisa imitation. Gordie is bald and paunchy and holds political views that make Limbaugh's look libertine. Terry is short and shaggy-haired and has voted Democratic all his life. At family gatherings each tries fervently and fruitlessly to persuade the other of the error of his thinking. When tempers flare, usually somewhere north of the third or fourth beer, Vecamamma and Aunt Klara signal disapproval by clucking.

I was following Vecamamma through the swinging kitchen door when realization struck.

Suitcase. Singular.

My hand flew to my shoulder. One lonely purse strap.

"Shit!"

Vecamamma cocked one wiry brow.

I was halfway down the hall when the doorbell bonged.

"I'll get it," I called out.

Bea was already there.

I heard the rattle of a chain guard, then hinges. A male voice. Giggling.

When I arrived, Ryan was in the foyer, my computer hanging from one sleet-drenched shoulder.

"Thought you might need this." He patted the case with his palm.

"Thanks." Stepping forward, I took the laptop. "Sorry to delay you."

"No trouble at all."

"Is it still coming down out there?" Bea asked.

"It's a real gullywasher."

Gullywasher?

"You should stay for dinner, give the storm a chance to let up," Bea said. "My grandmother always makes enough for an army."

"He has things to do." I squinted a warning at Ryan.

"Is this your policeman friend?" Vecamamma had steamed up behind me.

"I left something in the car. Detective Ryan was kind enough to bring it in. He's going now."

"Of course he's not. Look at him. He's soaked." To Ryan. "Officer, would you like to join us for dinner?"

"He's a detective, not—"

"I'm not exaggerating." Bea cut me off. "She makes tons."

"Something does smell mighty tasty."

Mighty tasty? Gullywasher? Great. Ryan was doing some warped Canadian version of the Waltons.

"I've made fresh ham and sauerkraut."

"I wouldn't want to be any trouble." Diffident smile.

"What trouble? Setting one extra plate on my table?"

"Tempe does go on about your cooking."

"Then that's settled." Vecamamma was showing a full yard of denture. "Bea, take the officer's jacket."

As THE OTHERS MIGRATED TOWARD THE FAMILY ROOM, I PULLED Ryan aside and gave him some ground rules.

"Don't drink Gordie's homemade wine. Don't talk politics with Ludis or Juris. Don't participate in competitive gaming of any kind. Don't discuss the job or details of what I do."

"Why?"

"Some of Pete's relatives share an alarming enthusiasm for the macabre."

Ryan knew what I meant.

We in the death business are often asked about our work, especially about cases flogged by the media. Ryan and I are both queried so regularly, our dinner invitations are often prefaced by hostess suggestions concerning appropriate table conversation. Never works. Though I don't volunteer, and sidestep when questioned, inevitably some guest persists in probing the blood-and-guts skinny.

It seems the world divides into two camps: those who can't get enough and those who prefer to hear nothing at all. Ryan and I called them Diggers and Dodgers.

"Diggers?" Ryan asked.

"Yes. Except for Vecamamma and Klara. Autopsy talk gives Vecamamma gas."

"Do they know about—" Ryan wagged a finger between his chest and mine. Us?

"No. But they have pack instincts." I continued my list of directives. "And don't even think of accepting an invitation to overnight."

"Holiday Inn all the way."

"And one other suggestion."

"I'm listening."

"Lose the John Boy routine."

Things went better than I would have expected. Ryan accepted and praised Gordie's rotgut bordeaux. He talked Big Moe and Bizzy Bone with Bea and Allie. He delighted Vecamamma, Emilija, and Connie by twisting the napkins into crook-necked swans.

No one asked about his marital status. No one queried our personal relationship. No one grilled him on current commerce in murder and mayhem.

Then, as we were gathering in the dining room, Cukura Kundze bustled in.

What to say about Mrs. Cukurs?

The Cukurs were pillars of the small church that welcomed the immigrant Petersons to the New World. More liberal than most ladies of her generation, over the years Laima Cukurs's exploits had inspired considerable gossip among her more proper Lutheran peers. The explicit sculptures. The colorful lingo. The hippie period mentioned only in whispers. The unfortunate tattoo.

Eighty-four, and widowed for a decade, Cukura Kundze had recently begun dating an octogenarian Hungarian named Mr. Tot. No one had gotten the gentleman's first name. Now, four months and many pot roasts and casseroles down the road, no one asked.

Or perhaps the more formal appellation just seemed more appropriate. Though Laima's first name had been known to the Petersons for half a century, Cukura Kundze had always remained Cukura Kundze.

Tonight, Cukura Kundze arrived Totless but bearing a torte.

"It's raspberry." Cukura Kundze handed the cake to Vecamamma. "Who's that?"

"A policeman friend of Tempe's."

"Good." Cukura Kundze wore glasses with clear plastic frames probably designed for combat soldiers. She nodded so emphatically the things hopped the hump on her nose. "Husbands cheat. Women have needs."

"Pete wasn't cheating." The cake smacked the table.

Cukura Kundze gave one of those harrumphs old ladies deliver so well.

"He and Tempe just decided it was time to skedaddle." Turning to me. "Right?"

Mercifully, Emilija emerged from the kitchen balancing bowls of kraut, limp broccoli, and sour cream cucumbers. Connie followed with tomato slices, potatoes, and gravy. Aunt Klara brought rye bread and some odd species of little gray sausage. Juris carried a platter of pork the size of Nebraska.

We all took our places. Plates filled quickly, then, just as quickly, began to empty. I made a preemptive conversational strike.

"Are the Bears having a good season?"

Ten minutes of sports analysis followed. When interest waned, I veered toward hockey.

"The Blackhawks—"

Cukura Kundze made an end run at Ryan.

"You carry a Taser?" Jabbing the nose piece of her glasses with a red lacquered finger. "People are getting their asses capped with Tasers."

"I've never used one."

"You have a real gun, right?" Ted's tone showed disdain for Cukura Kundze's question. "A Glock? A SIG? A Smith and Wesson?"

"Ever kill anyone?" Cukura Kundze was cranking up.

"Montreal has very little violent crime." Ryan nodded thanks as Gordie refilled his glass. I couldn't believe he was going for more. Pete once described Gordie's wine as a delicate Meritage hinting of goat piss and krill.

"But you must have sprayed some brains on a wall."

Dual clucking from Vecamamma and Klara.

"Will the Blackhawks make the playoffs this year?" I asked.

"Pass the potatoes?" Ludis said.

"I read about a biker war in Montreal." Cukura Kundze looked like a Hobbit between Allie and Bea. "You here to kick some Hells Angels butt? Or you working the streets, busting corner boys?"

"Ryan and I are here on administrative business," I said. "By the way, he's a Canadiens fan."

"Collaring pimps?"

"Nothing that exciting," Ryan laughed. "Tempe and I spent the day at the morgue."

"Potatoes?" Ludis repeated.

The spuds were passed, followed by the meat, et al. Then there was a lot of jockeying to find space for the bowls and platters.

Gordie poured Ryan more wine. Amazingly, he downed half the glass.

"Yep. Ryan is a Habs fan." Again I tried hockey. "Owns a Saku Koivu jersey."

"The Chicago morgue?" Cukura Kundze's eyes were wide behind the thick lenses.

"Our visit involved paperwork on a closed investigation."

"Like *Cold Case*," Bea said. "I love that show."

"You know people at the city morgue?" I recognized Cukura Kundze's tone. And look.

"I do." Wary.

"Do I ever ask favors, Tempe?"

The last request had been for an NYPD Crime Scene cap. Before that it was over-the-counter aspirin with codeine from Canada. I said nothing.

"Will you do something to make an old woman happy? Before I die?"

Vecamamma's snort fluttered the perm-crimped curls on her forehead.

"I really—"

"It's not for me, no, no. I wouldn't ask for myself. It's for poor Mr. Tot."

At an observatory high up on Haleakala, an intergalactic monitoring device beeped softly, alerted by a black hole of silence that suddenly popped into being in a midwestern suburb.

"Mr. Tot?" Total stillness. I could feel twenty-four eyes fixed on my face.

"His grandson is missing and the navy says the kid's gone AWOL. It's horseshit. Lassie would never have abandoned his duties."

"Lassie?" Klara's volume level told me she was not wearing her hearing aid. "Did she say Lassie?"

"Mr. Tot says the kid's gotta be dead."

"He might have amnesia," Allie said. "You know, be in some strange city and not know who he is. I saw that on TV."

"Lassie's a dog." Klara was loud enough to be heard in Topeka. "Like Oskars. Where is Oskars?"

The collie had died in 1984.

"Cukura Kundze," I said gently. "There's really nothing I can do."

"You could ask Richie Cunningham to check a few toe tags." Ryan's eyes had a jolly bad-bordeaux look.

"Wasn't Richie Cunningham that dork on *Happy Days*?" Ted said.

"Before that he played Opie," Connie said.

"Ron Howard," Susan said. "He's a filmmaker now."

"There's a guy at the morgue named Richie Cunningham?" Ludis.

"That's not his real name," I said, squint-staring at Ryan.

"Why'd he call him that?"

"Dr. Corcoran has red hair."

"And freckles." Ryan grinned a goofy grin.

Perfect. Detective Drinky Pants would not be driving tonight.

"Could this Richie friend look around, maybe see if the coroner's got Lassie on ice?"

You had to hand it to her. The old gal was persistent as herpes.

"Did Mr. Tot file a missing persons report?" I asked unenthusiastically.

"Right away. And went out looking himself. Course he didn't really know where to go. His bowling buddy, Mr. Azigian, went with him."

"What makes Mr. Tot think his grandson is dead?" I asked.

"They had tickets to see the Sox play the Cubs. At Wrigley Field. You think Lassie would pass that up?"

I had no idea what Lassie would do. What I *did* know was that every year a lot of folks simply walked out on their lives. I didn't share that knowledge.

"Can't hurt to give Corcoran a call," Ryan said.

A chorus of voices agreed.

"Fine." I forced a smile. "I'll phone tomorrow."

Over cake, Cukura Kundze revealed the following.

Almost four years earlier, during the week of his twenty-first birthday, Laszlo Tot left his barracks at the Great Lakes Naval Station, approximately thirty-five miles up the Lake Michigan shore from Chicago, on a weekend pass. Seaman Apprentice Tot failed to report for duty the next Monday or on any subsequent day. Following protocol, a military inquiry was launched and the civil authorities were notified.

Search efforts ensued, came up empty, and, in time, were discontinued. The navy reclassified Seaman Apprentice Tot as UA. Unauthorized absence.

Two months after the close of the investigation, a 1992 Ford Focus was found in the parking lot of the northeast suburban Northbrook mall. Records indicated the car was registered to one Laszlo Tot. The lead went nowhere.

When I headed upstairs, Ryan, Ludis, and Gordie were uncorking their fourth bottle. Debate was focused on gun control.

Sayonara.

• • •

Normally I have coffee for breakfast, maybe yogurt or a bagel. If feeling really jiggy, I might throw in cream cheese or jam.

Not Vecamamma's style.

After grapefruit, bacon, and pancakes with syrup and butter, I phoned the CCME. Corcoran picked up almost immediately.

He started out by apologizing for the previous day's debacle. I assured him there were no hard feelings. Then I provided a condensed version of Lassie Come Home.

Corcoran said he'd run a computer check for unknowns fitting Lazslo Tot's description. He promised to call back shortly.

I was disconnecting when Ryan entered the kitchen via the mudroom. His face was flushed and he was wearing Reeboks, gloves, a neck scarf, and sweats.

"*My kind of town, Chicago is*"—Ryan uncoiled and removed the muffler and finished with modified lyrics—"melting fast."

"You've been running?"

"Just five kilometers."

Given the tanker of wine consumed the previous evening, and I don't mean tankard, Ryan appeared to be in reasonably good shape.

Vecamamma turned from the stove, spatula held high.

"*Labrīt. Ka tev iet?*" Good morning. How are you?

"*Labi, Paldies. Et vous,* Vecamamma?"

"*Très bien, monsieur. Merci.*"

My eyeballs were rolling skyward when my mobile sounded.

Corcoran. I clicked on.

"The computer's down. Listen, why don't you stop by here? We'll visit. Then, when the system's back up, if there are remains that interest you, we'll pull them."

I'd planned to spend the day helping Vecamamma arrange snapshots in albums and bake Christmas cookies. But I knew my mother-in-law. She'd want me to help Cukura Kundze.

"Where's Walczak?" I asked.

"Milwaukee."

I glanced at Ryan, wondering if he'd need transport to O'Hare. Screw it. His best buddy Gordie could play chauffeur.

"I'll be there around ten."

CORCORAN AND I FOUND TWO POSSIBILITIES.

One was a heroin overdose victim, a white male with an estimated age of twenty to twenty-five. The naked body had been found sixteen months earlier on the city's South Side, near Forty-fifth and Stewart, between the Chicago & Western Indiana Railroad tracks and the edge of Fuller Park. No friend or family member had come forward. A records search had led nowhere. Ditto for dentals and prints. The man was still in the freezer.

The other was a skeleton. Descriptors had been entered as: white; male; eighteen to twenty-four years of age. The bones had been in storage for thirty-eight months.

We bombed on both fronts.

Though the information had yet to be entered into the system, Corcoran learned that Freezer Man had finally been IDed two days earlier. Turned out the body was that of a nineteen-year-old student from Ohio State, a schizophrenic who'd dropped out to hit the big city without calling home. What had happened on the mean streets was anyone's guess. Mom and Dad were awaiting delivery of the body.

By phoning Cukura Kundze, I learned that Lassie stood six-two and weighed roughly 190. Long bone measurements put Skeleton Man's height at five-six, tops.

I pulled the case to double-check the stature estimate. Right on.

"Not your boy," Corcoran said.

"No," I agreed.

We were standing beside a worktable in the CCME storage room. Corcoran was watching as I replaced Skeleton Man's bones in their box.

"Who does your anthropology?" I asked, snugging the lid into place.

"For years we used a guy out of Oklahoma. Now that he's retired, it's pretty haphazard. Sometimes a graduate student. Sometimes a resident doing a rotation here. Sometimes a staff pathologist."

"People who'll work for free," I guessed.

"Walczak claims there's no money in the budget."

"One day that approach will bite him in the ass."

"Hey, don't jump on me. I agree we should use only board-certified specialists. Would make my job easier."

"Who analyzed this fellow?" I laid a palm on Skeleton Man's box.

Corcoran checked the case file.

"AP. That would be Tony Papatados, a doctoral candidate at UIC. Excavates bones in Peru. Or maybe it's Bolivia. I don't remember."

"An archaeologist."

"Weren't you an archaeologist?"

"Yes. Don't get me wrong. Many bio-archaeologists and physical anthropologists are excellent researchers. Many know a lot of osteology, how to estimate age, sex, how to measure bones properly. But they're *not* trained in the full range of forensic issues. Most have little experience with modern populations."

Sudden thought. If Walczak had underqualified people working his anthropology cases, it was possible some remains had been improperly evaluated.

"Mind if I spend a little time in here?"

"Fine with me. Why?"

"Laszlo Tot was military. And reported missing. If he came here, even as a decomp, the ID would have been a snap with dentals and prints. But suppose his body wasn't found for a while. What if he was skeletonized and the bones were examined by someone with, shall we say, limited skills?"

"We could be overlooking him because the report is misleading."

"Or flat-ass wrong."

"I guess it's possible." Corcoran sounded dubious.

"Can you search your database for unidentified decomps and skeletons arriving during the past four years?"

Corcoran tapped the computer keyboard, peered at the monitor, tapped some more, then hit a single key.

"Hold on. There's a printer in my office."

He returned moments later with a list containing fourteen CCME numbers. He'd also pulled the police incident, morgue intake, and anthropology reports for each case.

Seven corpses had arrived badly decomposed. For those, the flesh had been stripped, then the skeletons cleaned by boiling. One individual had been burned, one mummified. For those, the remains had been left untouched. Five folks had rolled in as nothing but bone.

"They're all over there." Corcoran indicated the shelving to which I'd returned Skeleton Man in his absence. "But you're on your own. A battered toddler just showed up. I caught the autopsy."

"No problem."

Corcoran showed me where the necessary equipment was stored, and jotted a number should I have need of a tech. Then he was gone.

Starting with those who'd arrived as skeletons, I constructed a biological profile for each: age, sex, race, and height. When finished, I checked my findings against the case files.

At one fifteen Corcoran came to see if I wanted to break for lunch. Over a machine sandwich of very questionable-looking chicken salad, a six-pack of Oreos, and a Diet Coke, we discussed my intentions with regard to Jurmain. I told him I'd be phoning Edward Allen first thing in the morning, maybe even driving to Winnetka to pay a surprise call.

Corcoran apologized again. As before, I assured him he was not the target of my ire.

At one forty-five I returned to the storeroom.

By four I'd finished the skeletons. One Mongoloid female had been classified as Negroid. One elderly white male had a surgically pinned right "humerus" that was actually a femur from a very large dog.

No Lassie candidate.

Knowing I'd need X-rays, I skipped the mummified and burned individuals and moved on to the cleaned-up decomps. On the third set of bones I hit pay dirt.

During the first half of the twentieth century, Cook County was one of the leading producers of limestone and dolomite in the U.S. The bulk of the stone came from quarries situated in suburbs to the west and south of Chicago: Elmhurst, Riverside, La Grange, Bellwood, McCook, Hodgkins, Thornton. Most was shipped on the Illinois & Michigan Canal, later on the Sanitary and Ship Canal.

Though the golden age of quarrying has long since passed, the scarred landscapes remain. I'm not talking little dents in the ground. These pits are whoppers.

And great places to off-load bodies.

According to Police Officer Cyril Powers, on July 28, 2005, a decomposed corpse was spotted floating facedown just south of a bridge carrying the Tri-State Tollway over the Thornton Quarry. Powers contacted personnel at the Material Service Corporation, owners and operators of the quarry, then called for grappling hooks and a morgue van.

The remains were logged in as 287JUL05. A staff pathologist named Bandhura Jayamaran was assigned to the case. Jayamaran estimated PMI at two to three weeks.

Due to advanced putrefaction and severe cranial damage, including absence of most of the left side of the face and all of the lower jaw, only three teeth remained, the upper-right premolars and the first molar. None had a unique characteristic or dental restoration.

Fingerprinting was not an option. Concluding that little could be done with the body, Jayamaran ordered it cleaned and the bones stored pending anthropological analysis.

One month later, 287JUL05 was examined by someone identified only by the initials ML, who determined that the individual was a white male, approximately thirty-five years of age, with a height of five foot eight, plus or minus one inch. Age was based on the condition of the pubic symphyses, the small surfaces where the pelvic halves meet in front. Stature was calculated using the length of the femur.

ML noted trauma to the vertebrae, ribs, and skull, caused by the victim's fall into the quarry, and healed antemortem fractures of the right distal radius and ulna. ML ventured no opinion as to manner of death.

ML's descriptors were entered into a database at the Chicago PD missing persons unit, one week later into NCIC, the FBI's National Crime Information Center. Neither submission resulted in a positive ID.

287JUL05 went onto a shelf in the CCME storage room on September 4, 2005. He'd been there ever since.

OK, ML. Let's see how you did.

First, I arranged the cranial fragments into what resembled an exploded skull. Then I aligned the postcranial bones anatomically.

I began my assessment with gender, viewing first the skull, then the pelvis.

The right frontal bone bulged into a large, rounded ridge at the bottom of the forehead, above the orbit. The occipital had a prominent muscle attachment site dead center at the skull's back. The right mastoid, a hunk of bone projecting downward behind the ear opening, was impressive.

When articulated, the pelvis had a chunky pubic area, with an acute angle below the point where the two halves meet in front. Laterally, each side curved upward into a deep, narrow notch inferior to the hip blade.

OK. Agreed. 287JUL05 was male.

I made notes then turned to ancestry.

This was tougher, since little facial architecture remained, and the skull was too damaged to yield meaningful measurements. Nevertheless, I could see that the cranium had been moderate with regard to shape, not particularly long and narrow or short and globular. The cheekbones had been tight to the maxilla, the nasal bridge high, the nasal opening quite narrow.

Agreed again. 287JUL05 was white.

I made notes, then turned to age

On the left innominate, or hip bone, the pubic symphyseal face was badly eroded. Damage was less extensive on the right, and detail, though abraded, was observable. Taking the bone to a dissecting scope, I examined the surface under magnification.

And felt a tingle at the back of my neck.

Returning to the skeleton, I selected the fourth and fifth ribs and took them to the scope. At the sternal, or chest end, each rib terminated in a shallow indentation bordered by a smooth, wavy-rimmed wall.

Another tingle.

I made notes, then turned to stature.

After locating an osteometric board, I measured the right femur, tibia, and fibula. I was considering the estimates generated on my laptop with FORDISC 3.0 when Corcoran pushed through the door.

"Lord in heaven, girl. You're still here?"

"I may have found him."

"You're kidding."

I tipped my head at 287JUL05. "Someone with the initials ML examined this skeleton."

Corcoran looked thoughtful, then shook his head. "Don't recall an ML. I remember July of 2005, though. I was working a strange one, actually wrote it up for the *JFS.*"

"I think . . ."

"Listen to this. A sixty-eight-year-old female is last seen alive at a family picnic on the Fourth of July. No one hears from her for two weeks. The daughter finally checks, finds a corpse on the living room floor. Needless to say, by this time Mama's not looking too good.

"I do the autopsy, find nothing to suggest cause of death, so I sign her out as undetermined. Next thing I know, there's a cop telling me one of the grandkids has admitted to shooting the old lady. Apparently the little creep needed drug money and Grandma wasn't coughing up. I'm skeptical, because I've found no perforated organs, no nicked bones, no bullets or bullet fragments, no metallic trace on X-ray. Nothing."

"Uh. Huh." I didn't want to appear rude, but the case held no interest for me.

"But old Sherlock here goes back in. And guess what?"

I prepared my "I'm impressed" face.

"She must have been moving when the kid pulled the trigger. I find a bullet track shooting straight down the muscles paralleling the spine. Even though no vital organ was hit, the vic probably bled out." Corcoran beamed.

"You're a genius." I waited a respectful half second. "ML blew it."

"What? Oh."

I led Corcoran to the scope.

"Take a look at the pubic symphysis." I spoke as Corcoran adjusted focus. "That surface undergoes change throughout adulthood. Part of that change involves the formation of a rim circling the perimeter. See that gap on the upper edge?"

"On the belly side?"

"Yes."

"I see it."

"In young adults a hiatus like that is normal. The ventral, or belly, side of the rim is still forming. As adults age, the ends of the circle connect and the rim is complete. Then the rim begins to deteriorate. That's normal, too."

"First the rim forms, then it breaks down."

"Exactly. Those with little experience often confuse the two stages. Seeing that gap, ML misinterpreted formation as breakdown. He or she estimated age at thirty-five."

Corcoran looked up at me.

"This guy was closer to twenty when he died. But that's not the only problem."

Corcoran crossed his arms high on his chest.

"ML used an antiquated system for height determination, took measurements incorrectly, and relied on too few bones. He or she then chose inappropriate formulae for performing regression equations, and misinterpreted the statistical significance of the estimates those equations generated. Shall I walk you through the errors one by one?"

"No."

"ML put height at five-seven to five-nine. I put it somewhere between six feet and six-three."

"Bottom line?"

"Twenty-eight-seven-July-oh-five was a six-foot white male who died at roughly twenty years of age."

"Like Lassie."

"You've got it. Did the navy send antemortems so you'd have them in case you got an unknown fitting Tot's description?"

Corcoran hiked and dropped his shoulders, indicating he didn't know. "I can check. It's been less than five years. If we received Tot's records, they'd still be here."

There was a beat as we each thought about that.

"Any idea as to manner of death?" Corcoran asked.

"I saw nothing obvious."

"It doesn't make sense. Thornton is southwest of the city. Great Lakes is practically in Wisconsin. If this is your friend's grandson, he either went or was taken on a fairly long ride, and I think you told me his car was found north of the city."

Another beat passed. I pictured old Cukura Kundze, rheumy eyes eager behind the untrendy lenses. Deep down, I knew the victim in the box was Laszlo Tot.

Suddenly, I felt drained. I looked at my watch. Five fifty. I'd been at the morgue for almost eight hours. And *mañana* wouldn't be a cookie and album day, either.

"I can sort the trauma tomorrow," I said. "After I deal with Jurmain."

"That would be good."

Corcoran blushed.

I knew what was coming.

"Walczak won't pay you."

"No worries," I said. "This one's pro bono."

Snow was falling when I left the CCME, covering the dark muck frozen in the gutters along Harrison Street. Driving west on the Eisenhower, I let my thoughts wander.

Where had Laszlo Tot gone his last hours on earth? What had he done? Had he invited death by some act of stupidity? Of carelessness? Of greed? What was the day of the baseball game he missed? Friday night, Saturday, Sunday? Where had he intended to sleep?

Again, I saw old Cukura Kundze. If I could stop the pain barreling her way, I would. If I could magically morph 287JUL05 into someone else's sweetheart's dead grandson, I would do that, too.

I could do neither. Instead, I would search for answers. For justice. For Cukura Kundze. For Mr. Tot. For Lassie. Every person deserves to be accounted for. Old Horton, again.

Edward Allen Jurmain. What sleaze had filled the old man's ear with tales of my incompetence? My corruption? Why?

My grip tightened on the wheel.

How would I persuade Jurmain to share what he knew of his mysterious informant? Should I phone? Drive up to Winnetka? Could I manage to wangle my way into Jurmain's presence?

I thought about Pete and his melon-breasted, twenty-something fiancée, Summer. Were their wedding plans still on track? Did I give a rat's ass?

Katy. I knew my daughter wasn't enjoying her job at the Mecklenburg County Public Defenders Office. Had she quit? If so, to do what?

Ryan. I wondered if his flight had gone smoothly. If I missed him. I was heading home to Charlotte on Sunday. Would I want him to come for a visit? Would things ever be as they once were? Could they?

My head hurt. It had been a long day.

I pictured Vecamamma, busy at her ancient Tappan range. Today she was cooking lamb with carrots and cabbage. I wondered if she'd gone ahead and baked the cookies herself.

I smiled, happy someone was making me dinner. I didn't know who the other diners would be, or how numerous, but I was glad I wasn't returning to an empty house.

Yessiree. Family was just what I needed. Artery-clogging potatoes and gravy, bread and butter, rhubarb pie and ice cream. Throw-away conversation. Freedom from worries about Pete, Ryan, Katy, Jurmain. Distance from former husbands, old lovers, restless daughters, and back-stabbing tipsters.

Most importantly, distance from violent death.

ARRIVING AT THE HOUSE, I DID TWENTY MINUTES OF YOGA, THEN took a very hot bath.

While immersed in bubbles up to my chin, I pondered a plan for Cukura Kundze and Mr. Tot. I decided to call only after I'd finished with the bones and determined positively that 287JUL05 was Lassie. Hopefully, at that point I'd also be able to explain what had killed him.

I also considered my strategy for dealing with Jurmain. After some thought I settled on a home visit. I'd go directly from the CCME. Suppertime. I might take the old coot by surprise. What the hell? All he could do was have the butler throw me out.

The water was lukewarm when the doorbell started bonging.

Emerging from the tub, I pulled on jeans and a long red sweater. No blow-dryer. No makeup. Ain't family grand?

Between the stretching and the soaking, the knot in my stomach had eased and the headache had yielded.

Or maybe it was the aspirin. Whatever. I was feeling relaxed and rejuvenated. No corpses tonight. No accusations of professional misconduct. No double-edged teasing from Ryan.

Happily, this evening's gathering would be small. Perhaps that, too, was contributing to my newfound serenity.

Andrejs and Brigita were coming, though their parents would be absent for reasons of health. According to Vecamamma, Emilija's hemorrhoids had gained a quick fifteen pounds overnight. Gordie's ailment remained undisclosed.

Regina and Terry were committed to Thursday-night bingo at St. Ignatius. Ted was on duty at his night job. Bea had a paper due. Allie had a class. I'd not been looped in on other excuses.

Uncle Juris and Aunt Klara would, of course, be present. She was bringing pineapple Cool Whip Jell-O salad.

While tubbing, I'd also weighed the pros and cons of phoning Ryan. The cons won. Ryan was home now. My number was on his speed dial.

Muffled chimes continued, announcing the arrival of diners. I recognized voices by cadence and volume.

Following the fourth bong, Aunt Klara's alto bellowed up through the floorboards.

All present or accounted for. Time to socialize.

I was on the top step when, surprisingly, the bell sounded again. I heard the door open, then Gordie's voice.

"*Sveiki*, Vecamamma."

"*Vai tev iet labak?*" Was Vecamamma flustered? Gordie was about as bilingual as George Bush. Why query his health in Latvian?

"Couldn't miss your roast lamb," Gordie replied.

Vecamamma said something I didn't catch. Gordie answered. Laughter was followed by a second male voice.

"*Sveiki*, Vecamamma."

No.

"*Sveiki, monsieur.*"

"*Tabarnac*, something smells good."

"*Tabarnac, monsieur.*" Now Vecamamma sounded flirtatious.

Sighing theatrically, I trudged downstairs. Ryan and Gordie were coming up the hall, each wearing a mile-wide smile.

Gordie pistol-pointed two fingers at me. "Men are from earth. Women are from earth. Deal with it."

"George Carlin."

Ryan and Gordie smacked raised palms.

"Do vegetarians eat animal crackers?" Gordie.

"Carlin again," Ryan said. "Damn, I was bummed when he died." Pause. "If God didn't intend for us to eat animals, why did he make them out of meat?"

"Woody Allen?" Gordie guessed.

"John Cleese."

"Andy, my man. You know your comedy."

"You two spent the day playing Guess the Comic?" I was the only one not cracking up.

"Billy Goat!"

"Billy Goat!"

Tipsy high five.

"Lower, not upper!"

Palm smack.

When public road development began in Chicago in 1910, city planners came up with the idea of double- and triple-deck streets. Sound nuts? Not really. The arrangement was dictated by geography and traffic flow. This was the deal.

Many Loop streets crossed the river as bascule bridges, movable spans operated by complex counterweight systems. Bascule bridges accommodate boats nicely but require height clearance at their approaches to and over the river.

Railroad tracks were another complicating factor. Some ran along, others dead-ended at the water. Tracks also need clearance.

Thus, at points of closely spaced river crossings, a clearance zone was created. Many multilevel streets came into being as a result of falling within that zone. The idea was that local traffic would use the upper deck, while commercial vehicles and through traffic would travel below.

The longest and most famous multidecker is Wacker Drive, running along the south side of the main branch and the east side of the south branch of the Chicago River. Michigan Avenue is another.

The Billy Goat Tavern is located on Michigan's lower level. Apparently, Bud and Lou had experienced some confusion in navigating to their chosen watering hole. But they'd definitely found it.

"Did you know the Billy Goat inspired Belushi's 'Cheez-borger-Pepsi' sketch on *Saturday Night Live*?" Ryan asked me.

"Yes." Fake smile. "May I speak to you alone?"

"Sure."

"Please excuse us," I said to Gordie.

Without waiting for an answer, I turned and walked into the living room. Footsteps assured me that Ryan was following.

"What are you *doing* here?" Church-voice fortissimo.

"Gordie and I played racquetball. Then we had a few beers. The guy's a hoot, by the way."

"Why aren't you in Montreal?"

"Because I'm in Chicago."

"You know what I mean. I'm trying to spend quality time with Pete's family."

"They're great. Vecamamma's a—"

"I know. A hoot. You were supposed to go home today."

"The only flight I could get was at eight p.m. Vecamamma said I was welcome to stay for as long as I needed. Gordie offered racquetball, then a tour of the Loop. Ever been to Navy Pier?"

"Yes." My molars weren't clamped, but they were close.

Ryan shrugged. "Sounded good so I decided to hang for a while."

"A while?"

"I'll check with headquarters again tonight. See if anything's come up since I called in this morning. Otherwise, what the hell? I'm off duty until Monday."

"Your behavior is totally inappropriate."

"You're not the first woman to tell me that."

"Yo. Andy." Gordie was standing in the doorway. "Glass of wine?"

"A woman drove me to drink." Ryan opened the quote.

"I never had the courtesy to thank her." Gordie closed it.

"W. C. Fields," I said to an empty room.

Dinner went as you'd imagine.

When I retired at eleven, Gordie and Ryan were smoking cigars and doing stand-up. Vecamamma was flashing numbered signs to score their performances.

I descended at eight the next morning. Ryan was already in the kitchen, eating French toast as fast as my mother-in-law could slap it on his plate. Both he and she greeted me with *Bonjour.*

As we ate, I told Ryan about 287JUL05. In French. I wasn't yet ready to share what I suspected concerning Lassie Tot, and doubted Vecamamma's newly acquired linguistic skills would allow her to *comprendre.*

"You're convinced it's him?"

"Everything fits. Age, sex, race, height, time of disappearance. How many twentysomething white males standing six foot one vanish in any given year?"

I heard tsking from the vicinity of the range.

"Who did the original anthropology?"

"Corcoran didn't know."

"How'd the kid die?"

"I don't know. There are multiple fractures, but they may all be explained by the fall."

"How deep is the quarry?"

"I don't know."

"How'd he end up in it?"

"I don't know."

Tsk. From the stove.

I switched to English.

"This is delicious, Vecamamma."

"Pot roast tonight."

"Wouldn't miss it." I poured syrup on the refill she'd spatulaed onto my plate. "I'm really sorry about the photo albums." Too late for cookies. She'd made a zillion on her own.

"We'll do it another day. You help Cukura Kundze."

Reverting to French, Ryan delivered my first bad news of the day.

"Remember the old lady bludgeoned in her home a year and a half back?"

"In Pointe-Calumet?"

Ryan nodded. "Anne-Isabelle Villejoin. She was eighty-six. Lived with her eighty-three-year-old sister, Christelle. Christelle was never found."

Though I hadn't been involved, I remembered the case. All of Montreal was horrified by the brutality of the crime. And by the cold-blooded killing of such elderly victims. The search for Christelle had been exhaustive but fruitless.

"I got a call about an hour ago," Ryan continued. "Last night a guy named Florian Grellier was pulled doing one-forty on the TransCanada. A records check showed Monsieur Grellier had skipped the formality of actually purchasing the Volvo XC90 he was piloting.

"Grellier lawyered up with a courthouse crawler name of Damien Abadi. Abadi claimed his client had information on a missing old lady. After heated negotiation, in exchange for the crown prosecutor's absolute 'maybe,' Grellier decided it was in his best interest to share what he knew.

"Long story short, this morning they ran a nose around a field near Parc d'Oka."

Oh, no.

"The dog alerted?"

"Brayed like a goat in a grate."

"Cadaver dogs don't bark. They sit."

"OK. Fido parked his ass on the snow and signaled foul."

Please, no. I'd just left Montreal. I wanted to go to Charlotte. To see Katy and Birdie. To walk gloveless and bootless and need sunblock on my face.

"Did my name come up?"

"I was told Hubert would be contacting you."

Jean-Claude Hubert is Quebec's chief coroner and, currently, my main point of contact. If there was to be a disinterment, I knew Hubert would want me to direct it.

"What do you have going today?" Ryan switched topics.

"I plan to finish at the CCME. If the quarry skeleton is Lassie, I'll visit Cukura Kundze and Mr. Tot to break it to them personally. Then I'll drive up to Winnetka to see what I can charm out of Old Man Jurmain."

"Would you like company?"

"Oprah's tied up."

"I can be very charming." Ryan actually winked.

"Haven't you and your new best friend scheduled a field trip?" A creeping certainty that I wouldn't be going home to Charlotte was making me churlish.

"I fly out at six." Ryan also knew what Hubert would request. "Here's what I'm thinking. While you look at bones, I deal with changing your airline ticketing. Then, after visiting Cukura Kundze, we charm the jockeys off Jurmain, and head straight to O'Hare."

After breakfast I phoned the Bureau du coroner. We were both right.

Damn.

On the way to the car, I snatched the *Tribune* from the front steps.

My mood was so black, I allowed Ryan to drive. Wanting to avoid conversation, I unrolled the paper and glanced through the headlines.

And got my second wallop of bad news.

10

THE WHY-WOULD-ANY-RATIONAL-BEING-LIVE-HERE COLD RECEDED. The breath-fogged windows. The heater blasting arctic air at my feet.

Nothing existed but the print in front of my eyes.

"You're going to draw blood."

Ryan's voice snapped me back.

"Jurmain's dead." Unclamping my upper incisors from my lower lip.

"Edward Allen?"

"Front page, local section."

"What happened?"

"They found him yesterday at the bottom of his basement stairs." My voice sounded brittle. "The family doc is saying stroke."

"Autopsy?"

"There's none mentioned."

"Schechter did say Jurmain was not in good health."

"The old buzzard could have hung on another two days."

Ryan ignored that. "What else?"

"The story's mostly a tribute piece."

I read excerpts.

"Former president and CEO of Jurmain Foods, later Smiling J. Blah blah blah. Well-known personality in the snack food industry from the forties through the eighties. Blah blah blah. Died at his home in Winnetka at the age of eighty-one. Blah blah blah. Received some award for his service to SFA."

"SFA?"

"Snack Food Association. It's an international trade association representing over four hundred companies worldwide."

"The lowly Cheez Doodle has its own lobby?"

"According to the article, cheese snacks share representation with potato chips, tortilla chips, cereal snacks, pretzels, popcorn, snack crackers, meat snacks, pork rinds, snack nuts, party mix, corn snacks, pellet snacks, fruit snacks, snack bars, granola, snack cakes, and cookies."

"Who knew."

"The annual convention is called SNAXPO."

"Of course it is."

I read aloud. "Jurmain's association with the snack food industry began in 1946 after service with the Seventy-ninth Infantry Division in World War Two. Following—"

"That's probably more than I need to know."

"Damn, Ryan. How am I going to find the bastard who placed that call?"

"Maybe Schechter knows more than he let on."

"Maybe."

"How about this. I'll hunt lawyer while you examine Lassie. When you're done, we'll ambush Schechter instead of Jurmain."

"If the guy practices with a big firm, we'll never get past the receptionist. Those people are like samurai warriors guarding the king."

"Shogun."

"What?"

"They guarded the shogun. But you really mean the *hatamoto,* the higher-ranking warriors. Only the *hatamoto* served as the shogun's personal guard."

"Whatever." I wiggled my toes to generate warmth. "We'll never get to Schechter."

"You forget the old Ryan charm." Ryan winked at me.

"And when that fails?"

"I'll flash my badge."

"You have zero jurisdiction here."

"I'll flash it very fast."

We were in luck. The navy had hedged its bets, and the CCME still had Laszlo Tot's records on file.

Corcoran and I began by comparing Lassie's antemortem dental, chest, and right lower-arm films with postmortem X-rays made upon 287JUL05's arrival at the morgue. Despite the missing teeth, the skull damage, and the fractured ribs, we were able to establish positively that the man found in Thornton Quarry was, in fact, the missing seaman apprentice.

Maybe because intake was slow. Maybe because 287JUL05 now had a name. I didn't ask, just accepted my upgrade from the storage room to an autopsy suite at the back of the facility.

By ten I had Lassie laid out on stainless steel. Corcoran had disappeared to phone the Chicago PD missing persons unit and authorities at the Great Lakes Naval Base. Ryan had gone to ferret out Perry Schechter.

One by one I viewed skeletal parts under magnification. Arm, leg, hand, and foot bones. Ribs. Vertebrae. Pelvis. Clavicles. Scapulae. Sternum. Now and then I'd stretch, walk the room, compose in my head the sad news I'd deliver to Cukura Kundze and Mr. Tot.

Ryan and Corcoran returned together around noon. I was glad to see them. Though I was pretty certain by then how Lassie had died, I needed answers to several questions.

"Describe the Thornton Quarry," I said to Corcoran.

"It's big."

"How big?

"Really big."

I gave him the steely look. He blushed.

"Thornton's a mile and a half long and a half mile wide, one of the world's largest quarries. In addition to producing stone or gravel or something, it's used to prevent stormwater from overwhelming Chicago's sewage system."

"How so?" Ryan asked.

"There's a water control plan in the works called the Deep Tunnel Project. As part of it, the Thornton Quarry will serve as a reservoir to reduce the backflow of runoff and sewage from area rivers into Lake Michigan. I read somewhere that the Thornton reservoir already contributes a three-billion-gallon capacity, and is expected to contribute around eight billion when the system is completed."

"That's one monster holding tank," Ryan said.

"Tanks," Corcoran corrected. "There are at least five or six pits, or lobes, some abandoned, some active. The project is starting with two of them."

I tried to visualize the locale in my head. "We're talking just east of Halsted and just south of the Tri-State Tollway, right?"

Corcoran nodded. "A bridge carries I-294 and I-80 right over the quarry. At that point West 175th Street is called Brown Derby Road, named after a bar and dance hall built in the thirties. The joint actually has quite a history. In the early forties, a carousel and picnic grove were added, and political parties, companies, and schools held their annual picnics there. During the fifties the carousel was torn down and a new bar was built across the street. That was later—"

"Isn't the quarry secured?" Ryan interrupted the history lesson.

"I wondered about that, so I reread the responding officer's report. The complex is fenced and there's an observation building on-site. But Powers found that a gap had been cut in the fencing near the intersection of Brown Derby and Ridge Roads. By his estimate, the gap was large enough to allow entrance of a vehicle. Once inside the complex, Tot could have driven, or been driven, a few yards west along a dirt road right to the edge of the west pit. That's where the body was found."

"Assuming Lassie went into the water from up top, how far was the drop?"

"Maybe four hundred feet."

"That would do it," I said.

"Do what?"

"Look at this." I indicated a collection of loosely arranged cranial fragments.

The men stepped to the table. For Ryan's benefit, I kept it simple.

"These bones formed the base of Lassie's skull, the part that sat directly on top of his spinal column." With one gloved finger, I traced a crack that traversed several fragments in a curvilinear pattern. "This fracture extends anteriorally—"

I caught myself slipping into jargon.

"The fracture proceeds from back to front across the petrous portions of both temporal bones." I pointed to the two oblong bulges that encase the inner ears.

"The two ends of the fracture circle around to meet here, in the sella turcica." I moved my finger to a saddle-shaped prominence rising from the cranial floor, forward from the foramen magnum, the large hole through which the spinal cord enters the brain.

"It's a complete ring fracture. Ring fractures can be caused by jamming the head violently downward onto the spinal column—"

"As in a headlong fall," Ryan cut in.

"Yes. But ring fractures can also be caused by pulling the head sharply upward away from the spinal column."

"But now's when you tell us Lassie took a header." Ryan.

"Look closely at the fracture margins." I handed each man a fragment.

"The edges angle inward," Corcoran said.

"Exactly. The beveling is directed internally because the cranium was forced inferiorly against the spine. If the fracture had been caused by yanking the head upward, the beveling would be directed externally."

"Can a fall explain such massive maxillary and mandibular damage?" Corcoran asked.

"Sudden deceleration impact can tear the face right off the vault."

"So Lassie died as a result of a swan dive that forced his cranium down into his spine.

"No."

Both men did that male weight-shifting thing.

"I found rib fractures in addition to the cranial trauma. That's understandable. Lassie probably hit an outcrop or a ledge on his way down. What's odd is that his arm and leg bones are undamaged."

"The kid made no attempt to stop his fall." Ryan got it.

"A headlong plunge doesn't necessarily mean the victim is dead," Corcoran said. "Lassie could have dived. Or been unconscious."

"Good point." I selected two ribs and the right ulna. Crossing to the dissecting scope, I inserted one rib and adjusted focus.

"Check out this fracture."

Ryan deferred to Corcoran.

"The break has jagged edges." Corcoran spoke without raising his head. "Looks like a typical blunt force injury. As you said, he probably bounced off rock on his way down."

"Agreed," I said.

Corcoran yielded position at the scope. When Ryan had seen enough, I switched ribs, refocused, and stepped back. Corcoran moved back in.

"This break looks very straight. But that's definitive of nothing. I've seen straight-edged rib fractures that I knew were caused by blunt trauma."

"True enough. But did any look that clean? Kick up the magnification."

Corcoran did as I'd suggested, then repositioned the light source.

Several seconds passed. Then, "Are those what I think they are?"

"Striations. Now look at the fresh break on the ulna. Not the old healed fracture."

Corcoran swapped bones and squinted into the eyepiece.

"Cut marks?" Ryan mouthed over Corcoran's hunched back.

I nodded.

Fluorescent tubes hummed overhead. Muted footsteps clicked by in the hall.

Finally, Corcoran looked up.

"Chop to the ulna, stab to the rib. Ulna chop's probably defensive."

Corcoran referred to trauma caused when knifing victims throw up hands or arms to ward off attack.

"I found knife stab wounds on at least four ribs."

I held the other rib so Corcoran and Ryan could see the anterior, or chest, portion. A four-inch crack ran longitudinally along its surface.

Ryan whistled softly. "That's one hell of a weapon."

"Don't be fooled by appearances," I said. "Since fractures propagate with the grain of the bone, the length of a crack doesn't necessarily reflect the size of the blade that made it. But there is an indicator."

I pointed to a two-inch stretch within the longer defect. "Under magnification this portion appears very clean-edged. There's also a subtle squaring at one end. Together, those features suggest a two-inch-wide, single-edged blade."

Ryan started to speak. I held up a hand.

"When the rib cage is rearticulated, no cut extends between adjacent ribs. However, a cut on R-seven aligns perfectly with a square-edged defect on R-six. That pattern, also, suggests a single-edged blade."

"Striations mean serration," Corcoran said.

I nodded. "I'd venture the weapon has a single-edged, serrated, two-inch blade."

"Like a large steak knife," Ryan said.

"You think Lassie was dead when he went into the quarry," Corcoran said.

"In my opinion, the most likely scenario is that he was stabbed to death, then his body was dumped."

Murdered.

The word rolled in my head like thunder at the beach.

How to tell Cukura Kundze?

TICK. TICK. TICK. TICK. TICK.

I awoke disoriented. In my dream I was having sex. The sound was a fan spinning overhead. Too fast.

The man's face was a blur. Who was he? Was that why I was here?

But the sound wasn't whirling blades.

I was lying on my side, arms and legs flexed, palms pressed together under my cheek. The ticking was right at my ear.

I lifted my chin and felt something hard scrape my lobe.

A wristwatch?

But my Cyma was soundless. Whose watch was I wearing? Why?

I twisted my left wrist in front of my eyes. Hour and minute hands glowed faintly in the pitch black.

1:40? 8:05? A.m.? P.m.? I had no idea. No sense how long I'd been out.

Trembling, I tucked my hands between my thighs for warmth. My fingers were ice through the denim.

With the watch repositioned, I was again enveloped in complete and utter stillness.

As I lay seeing nothing, hearing nothing, the same questions arose. Where? How long? Who? Why?

I pictured myself as from a skycam, body curled, imprisoned in a very small space.

Google Earth.

Google Tomb.

Oh God.

The unseeable walls and ceiling seemed to shrink inward, to press down from above. My breathing grew ragged.

To block the claustrophobia, I focused inward.

Head: pounding.

Throat: parched.

Digits: numb.

Leg: throbbing.

Bladder: full.

Stomach: empty.

The awareness of hunger triggered thoughts of food. Seared ahi tuna, thick-sliced bacon, Thai soup with lemongrass and coconut milk.

I tried to inventory what I knew of my surroundings. My brain posted no list. Just more chow.

Mussels with garlic, tomatoes, peppers, and wine. Belgian fries dipped in thick mayonnaise. Ryan drinking a Bavik pilsner.

How long since he and I had shared that meal? Hours? Days? Was it the last time I'd eaten? Or had that supper been months ago? Years?

Was Ryan the lover in my dream? If not, was he real, or a construct of my subconscious?

My body was shaking, my teeth clacking in my mouth.

How was I dressed?

By wiggling against the ground I found the answer. Sneakers. Short-sleeved shirt. Jeans.

Sudden thought. If not in my purse, my BlackBerry would be in a pants pocket or clipped to my waistband. Had I checked for it? Of course I had. I wasn't an idiot.

But my thinking had been muddled. I'd been in pain. Yes? No? I couldn't remember.

Please!

By pressing my knees to the ground and angling my arms sideways, I was able to run the back of my left hand over my right front pocket. No BlackBerry.

Ignoring the pain in my leg, I reversed and checked the left. Nothing there either.

I went semi-supine, with legs up and knees flexed, and rocked from side to side. No bulge on my waistband or in either back pocket.

Tears of frustration sprang to my eyes.

No!

I rolled back onto my side. The ground felt frigid against my bare skin.

I had to do something to keep warm. To stay sane.

I needed a goal. A series of goals.

"First." I spoke aloud. "Free yourself."

My voice sounded leaden. Muffled by yards of brick and cement? Tons of earth? Acres of overlying forest or farmland?

Panic shot fresh tentacles into my chest.

"Second." Louder. "Find an exit."

"Third." Drill instructor bark. "Flee."

There. I had a three-part plan. A chart for organized action. Free. Find. Flee.

I began rubbing the backs of my hands fast up and down between the inseams of my jeans, mentally intoning the mantra.

Free. Find. Flee.

Free. Find. Flee.

Free. Find. Flee.

The frenzied movement ground the side of one elbow, but the friction kindled warmth in my fingers. Slowly, painfully, sensation crept back.

Nerves tingling, I scooched forward and ran my tethered hands over the wall, checking for a nail, a broken pipe, anything that might saw the ropes from my wrists.

Nada.

Methodically, I inched along, searching low, then rising as high as my bindings allowed. My prison was longer than I'd visualized. Small comfort.

Of less comfort was the fact that the masonry was frustratingly even.

I'd gone perhaps eight feet when my fingers picked out a malaligned brick protruding at a height of approximately eighteen inches. The brick's outer edge felt promisingly sharp.

I maneuvered into a hunched semi-sit and pushed down on the brick's upper surface. The mortar held firm.

"As you were, soldier!"

God Almighty. I was talking to stonework.

By flopping to my side and drawing my knees to my chest, I was able to create enough play in my bindings to get my wrists to the edge of the brick. I began rubbing feverishly.

Before long I lay back, arms screaming, head floating.

At this rate I'd exhaust myself while accomplishing little. New strategy. Two hundred rubs. Rest. Repeat.

And that's what I did, again mentally repeating the mantra.

Rub. Rest. Repeat.

Rub. Rest. Repeat.

Rub. Rest. Repeat.

During R&R, my neocortex would process data coming its way. The input was sparse. Cold. Dark. Newly raw flesh on my knuckles and hands. Faint yet oddly familiar smell.

Alone and terrified, I'd lie listening for the sound of a voice, a footstep, a turning key. I'd hear only my own labored heart and breath.

Exhausted, I'd drift into sleep.

Waking, I'd check the position of the glowing hands. Wonder. Had hours passed? Minutes? I had no concept of time.

I'd begin sawing again, arms stiff and shaky, every movement an agony.

Rub. Rest. Repeat.

Rub. Rest. Repeat.

Rub. Rest. Repeat.

Two hundred times. Four. Six. Ten thousand.

Following each cycle, I'd pull hard on my bindings, testing.

Finally, I felt, or sensed, a subtle yielding.

I yanked my wrists outward with as much force as my battered muscles could muster.

Again.

Again.

With the sixth heave I felt a hitch, then my left palm slipped relative to my right. Or had I imagined it?

"Break!" I screamed into the darkness.

I yanked and twisted, yanked and twisted.

"Break, you bastards!"

Tears streamed down my cheeks as my hands pistoned wildly.

"Break!" I tasted salt on my trembling lips.

"Break!" I wrenched my arms outward again and again.

At long last, some frayed strands yielded.

The ropes loosened. I managed to extract my left hand.

I fumbled free. Sat upright. Shook both hands. Blood rushed like fire into the deprived vessels.

I ran my fingers over my ankles, exploring the arrangement of the bindings. Finding the knots, I began clawing, desperate for freedom.

It was futile. My fingers were barely functioning and the knots were like rocks.

Again tears threatened.

Again, I banished them.

"Move!" my drill sergeant voice boomed.

Rolling to my stomach, I began inching through the darkness by dragging with my elbows and pushing with my legs. When that grew too painful, I rolled onto my bum and hitched forward with my feet and the palms of my hands.

I followed a zigzag pattern, determined to find a route to freedom. Or, that failing, an implement to free my feet.

My prison was long and narrow, perhaps a tunnel or passageway. As I proceeded through it, the musty odor grew stronger.

Now and then I'd stop for a time check. The glowing hands formed a horizontal bar. An L. *Overlapped to the right.*

Inevitably the periods of movement shortened. More and more often I dropped and went fetal. My elbows were bloody, my hands and feet numb from contact with the frozen ground. Despite my resolve, my efforts were waning.

Then, in a belly phase, my elbows pulled me forward and my shoulder brushed something. It wobbled. Settled back.

My hands reached out into the dark.

I heard a gravelly crunch.

My sensory-deprived brain computed the input.

Round. Hard. Roll trajectory two feet up and to the left.

Elbow-dragging my torso and legs, I groped the base of the wall. The smell was powerful now, a mix of mold and mildew and moth-eaten fabric, like clothes abandoned in an old attic trunk.

My bloody fingers finally grazed an edge. Pivoting to a hunch-sit, I teased the object up into my hands.

Gingerly, I hefted, weighing. I caressed the thing's outer surface. Explored its dimensions. Probed its contours.

With horror, I recognized what was sharing my darkness.

LIFTING MY FINGERS, I ALLOWED THE SKULL TO ROLL BACK TO ITS original position.

The searchdog's name was Étoile. Star. And she was one.

The grave had been under two feet of snow. Didn't matter. Étoile had nailed it.

Ryan had picked me up before dawn on Saturday. My window thermometer said minus six Celsius. Twenty-one Fahrenheit.

We talked little during the drive. Our flight from O'Hare had landed late, and it was midnight when I reached my condo in *centre-ville,* two before I got to sleep. Barely awake, I sipped the coffee Ryan provided and watched the city slide past my window.

My funk wasn't entirely fatigue-induced. I was still bummed by events in Chicago.

Ryan and I never got to see Schechter. Excuse was he was taking depositions in Rock Island. Consequently, I was still clueless about the viper who'd smeared my reputation with false accusations.

The conversation concerning Lassie had been as painful as anticipated. Throughout, Cukura Kundze wept as though she'd lost her own grandchild. The only upside was that Mr. Tot had insisted on informing his son and daughter-in-law personally concerning their son's fate.

In addition, I'd had another clash with my new neighbor, Sparky Monteil. Yeah, Sparky. Though built like a pear, the guy works hard at looking tough. Elvis hair. Badass tattoo on the side of his neck. My building superintendent, Winston, says the little twerp's at least fifty-five.

Sparky moved into my complex sometime last spring. His boxes weren't unpacked when the whining began. Seems Sparky hates cats. No, that doesn't do it justice. Sparky would have every feline on the planet rounded up, bagged, and tossed into the sea.

Granted, our home owners' association has a no-pets policy. But since Birdie and I are away so much in Charlotte, and since the little guy never sets paw outside the condo when in residence, I've been granted an exemption. Sparky is fighting to have that revoked.

Sparky exited the elevator as I was waiting in the lobby for Ryan. This morning's grievance concerned turds in the courtyard.

Sorry, pal. My cat's not with me this trip.

On top of all that, I was once again freezing.

The heater in Ryan's Jeep wasn't state of the art. The windows were frosted, and I could feel cold rising through my boots, up my legs, and into my pelvis. I suspected the only warmth I'd experience all day would be that leaching from the cup I clutched in gloved hands.

Our destination lay approximately fifty kilometers northwest of Montreal in Oka. When I hear the town name I think of three things: Mohawks, monks, and monastery cheese.

The last two are interrelated.

In 1815 a group of monks settled in Brittany and created a cheese called Port Salut. Six decades later their brainchild was the rage of Paris. Didn't matter. In 1880 the army of the French Third Republic seized the order's Abbaye de Bellefontaine, and the cheese-making Trappists were booted from the country.

At the invitation of Quebec Sulpicians, eight of the exiles set sail for Canada. From their vast holdings, the host brothers gave the immigrants land on the north shore of Lac des Deux-Montagnes. Naming the property La Trappe after Soligny-la-Trappe, the order's 1662 founding site, the new arrivals established L'Abbaye Notre-Dame du Lac.

At its peak, the monastery boasted upward of two hundred monks. By the early twenty-first century only twenty-eight remained, most over seventy years of age. Today, L'Abbaye is no longer a working monastery but serves as a nonprofit center for preservation of the site's heritage.

In making their transatlantic journey back in the day, the Trappist travelers brought with them their treasured *recette de fromage* and, once settled, the churning of cow's milk began anew. As in the homeland, the cheese was a box office hit.

As far as I know, the brothers still oversee the production of Oka Trappist Cheese, which, over the years, has evolved a new-world character uniquely its own.

The Mohawk thing is a bit more complicated.

In the summer of 1990, the "Oka Crisis" made international news. Essentially a land dispute between the town and the Mohawk community of Kanesatake, the confrontation lasted from mid-July until late September, and resulted in a commuters' nightmare, a public relations fiasco for the government, and the death of one Sûreté du Québec officer.

In a nutshell, here's what happened.

The town of Oka wanted to expand a golf course onto land containing a Mohawk burial ground and a sacred grove of pines. The natives screamed sacrilege. Their appeal was denied and construction of the back nine began. Incensed, tribal members barricaded access to the terrain in dispute.

No big deal. The cops clear the protesters, right? Wrong.

When the SQ restricted access to Oka and Kanesatake, First Nations groups began arriving from across Canada and the U.S. of A. In solidarity with Kanesatake, the Kahnawake Mohawks blockaded a bridge connecting the Island of Montreal with the south shore suburbs at the point where the bridge passed through their territory.

At the peak of the confrontation, the Mercier Bridge and Routes 132, 138, and 207 were all blocked. Traffic jams were vicious and tempers were fraying.

Enter the Canadian Armed Forces.

Ultimately, the Mohawks negotiated an end to their protest with the army commander responsible for monitoring the south shore of the St. Lawrence River west of Montreal. The lieutenant colonel's name was Gagnon.

Life has its ironies. The original cheese-bearing Trappists lived in a miller's cottage while awaiting completion of their monastery. The miller's name was Gagnon.

A fourth facet is Parc national d'Oka, one of a chain of Quebec wildlife reserves and tourist resorts. May through September, the park's twenty-four square kilometers host campers, picnickers, hikers, canoers, and kayakers. In winter, a few hardy souls still feel the need to bunk out in the cold, but the majority of visitors are snowshoers and cross-country skiers.

Wouldn't catch me. But I do like summer outings, biking the trails, sunning on the beach, bird-watching on the floating boardwalk into Grande-Baie marsh. No argument here. I'm a warm-weather wuss.

As Ryan headed north on the Laurentian Autoroute then west on Highway 640, I watched close-packed city buildings give way to equi-spaced and identical suburban houses, eventually to snow-covered countryside. Yellow smudged the horizon, then the sky oozed from black to gray.

Forty-five minutes after leaving my condo Ryan turned onto chemin Oka. By then the sun was a low-hanging white disk. Leafless trees cast long, fuzzy shadows across fields and blacktop.

In moments, we passed the main park entrance. Just inside the gate a small stone building announced Poste d'accueil Camping—Camping Welcome Center. A yellow diamond showed a turtle, lizard, frog, and snake in black silhouette.

Twenty meters beyond the park entrance, an SQ cruiser idled on the opposite shoulder, vapor pumping from its tailpipe.

Ryan made a U-turn and rolled to a stop. The cruiser's occupant set a Styrofoam cup on the dash, pulled on gloves, and hauled himself out. He wore an olive green jacket with black fur collar, dark olive muffler, and olive hat, earflaps tied in the up position. His name plaque read Halton.

Lowering the window, Ryan showed his badge. Halton glanced at it, then bent to inspect me.

I held up my LSJML card.

Halton flapped an arm toward the woods, then spoke in French. "Take the service road skirting the edge of the park. Party's at the river's edge."

"What river?" I asked.

"Rivière aux Serpents." Halton grinned. "Little bastards should be sleeping this time of year."

Ryan veered from the shoulder and we rolled forward, tires crunching on icy gravel. At our backs, across the highway, Le Calvaire d'Oka dominated the landscape. I'd once hiked the trail to its summit. A sort of woodland Way of the Cross, the path climbs five kilometers to a cluster of mid-eighteenth-century chapels. The view was kick-ass.

So was the poison ivy. I itched and oozed for weeks.

"Yield to reptiles?" Ryan's lame joke suggested anxiety.

"And amphibians," I said.

Ryan looked at me.

"The sign depicts herpetofauna. That includes amphibians." It was way too early for a biology lesson.

"What's the difference?"

"Amniotic egg."

"I prefer scrambled."

"Reptiles can reproduce out of water."

"Breakthrough moment. When did it happen?"

"Over three hundred million years ago."

"You'd think they'd be traffic savvy by now."

I chose not to answer.

We were traveling a narrow road piled on both sides with snowplow off-load. Trees rose around us like tall, naked sentinels.

The downward gradient increased as we moved toward the river. Soon I spotted the shore. Lining it was the usual cluster of vehicles: a second police cruiser, a black transport van, a blue crime scene recovery truck.

A uniformed SQ officer waved us to a stop. Her name tag read Naveau. Again, the warm welcome of law and order.

We identified ourselves. Naveau told Ryan to park at the back of a rustic wooden structure that was probably a warming hut for cross-country skiers.

Ryan did as directed, then we both tugged on hats and got out of the Jeep. The sun was higher now, casting smudgy-edged shadows from tree trunks and branches. The air was so cold it felt crystalline.

Good news. A plastic tent had been erected over what I assumed was the spot that had interested the cadaver dog, Étoile. Freshly shoveled snow lay mounded to one side.

I recognized the setup from an exhumation I'd done years earlier on an Innu reserve near the town of Sept-Îsles. On that occasion the temperature had peaked at minus 34 Celsius. I knew that inside the tent a portable heater was pumping air through corrugated piping, warming the interior and melting the ground.

Four men stood outside the tent. Two wore coveralls and jackets stamped with the same logo as the crime scene truck. *Service de l'identité judiciaire. Division des scènes de crime.*

One wore a black Kanuk parka not unlike my own sky blue one. In the thickly padded anorak, Joe Bonnet, my new lab tech, looked like a marshmallow on a stick. Mercifully, Joe's head was covered by a tuque. He thought the gel-spiked platinum hair looked punk. I thought it looked goofy, especially on a guy waving bye-bye to his thirties. But I never said so.

Joe was competent at his job but fragile. And needy. It wasn't enough to refrain from censure or criticism. With Joe, you had to constantly praise and reassure. I suck at warm fuzzies. Most people know and accept that about me. Joe wasn't getting it.

Needless to say, there had been blow-ups and pout-outs. His, not mine. Even under cease-fire, Joe and I were like stranger pets thrown together at Grandma's house. Always edgy, always sniffing the mood of the other.

Partly my fault. Two years, and I was still bummed by the loss of my longtime assistant, Denis. What's this retirement thing, anyway?

The fourth man wore an overcoat that barely buttoned across his ample midsection. Jean-Claude Hubert, chief coroner of the Province of Quebec.

Hubert waddled in our direction. His face was very flushed and very chapped.

"Detective Ryan. Dr. Brennan." Hubert's accent was upriver, perhaps Quebec City. "Thanks for coming out so early."

"What's the story?" I had the basics but wanted Hubert's version.

"Jailhouse canary's singing about a woman missing two years."

"Florian Grellier," Ryan said.

Hubert nodded. Three chins rippled above his muffler. "The victim was Christelle Villejoin. Grellier says she was murdered and buried out here."

"Murdered by whom?" Ryan asked.

"Claims he doesn't know."

"How'd Monsieur Grellier happen upon this information?"

"Says he met some guy in a bar. Swears he never got the guy's name, hasn't seen him since the night they banged shots together."

"When was that?" Ryan.

"Sometime last summer. Grellier's a bit hazy on that."

"You bring him out here?"

"No. He provided good landmarks, the road, the warming hut, the river. We ran a cadaver dog, she alerted." Hubert gestured an upturned mitten in the direction of the tent. "Handler says there's a ninety percent chance someone's gone south in the dirt over there."

"Pretty detailed mapping for a drunken recollection," I said.

"Yeah." Hubert puffed air through his lips. They badly needed ChapStick.

"What have you done so far?"

"Secured the area, shot photos, cleared snow, set up the tent. The heater's been going since yesterday, so the ground should be thawed."

"*Bon,*" I said. "Let's do it."

Hubert was right. The ground was sufficiently soft to dig. And another thing worked in our favor. Human nature. Either lazy or nervous, the perp had buried his vic only eighteen inches down.

By one, Bonnet and I had exposed the entire skeleton. Most of the bones we'd left in situ. Those found by sifting dirt through a screen we'd sealed into evidence bags.

I'd done an inventory, detailing everything but the phalanges. Those I merely counted.

One skull, including all twenty-one cranial bones and the six from the inner ear. One mandible. One hyoid. One sternum. Two clavicles. Two scapulae. Twenty-four ribs. Twenty-four vertebrae. One sacrum. One coccyx. Six arm bones. Six leg bones. Two innominates. Two patellae. Sixteen carpus. Ten metacarpus. Fourteen tarsus. Ten metatarsus. Fifty-six phalanges.

Two hundred and six bones. Damn, we were good.

Throughout the exhumation, Ryan and Hubert had come and gone. Turned out the heater recognized only two settings: Off and Tropic of Cancer. Though we'd opened a flap, the temperature in the tent rose to roughly 90 degrees Fahrenheit. Bonnet and I had peeled by layers, ended up working in T-shirts and jeans.

Now, as I made notes and Bonnet snapped photos, Ryan and Hubert stood peering into the pit. Their faces were flushed, their hairlines dampened by sweat.

The victim lay facedown, wearing bra and panties, with arms and legs twisted to the right. A fracture spidered the back of the skull.

"*Eh, misère.*" Hubert had uttered the expletive at least twenty times.

"Thoughts on body position?" Ryan asked me.

"Only preliminary."

Ryan nodded.

"I'm guessing she was hit from behind. Then she either fell or was pushed into the grave."

"Hit with what?" Taut.

"From the shape of the indentation, I'd say something flat with a raised central ridge."

"She?" Hubert had picked up on my gender reference.

"Yes."

"Because of the undies?"

"Because of cranial and pelvic features."

"The rest of her clothing rotted away?"

"I doubt it. Granted, the underwear is polyester, and synthetics outlast natural fibers like cotton or linen, but I'd have found zippers, buttons, snaps, something. I don't think she was wearing anything else."

"And no shoes or socks," Ryan pointed out.

"No," I agreed.

"Age?" Hubert asked.

Squatting, I lifted and rotated the skull.

Only eight yellowed teeth were present, their cusps worn flat. The remaining sockets were smoothed by bony infill.

The cranial sutures were fused. Both temporo-mandibular joints and occipital condyles were gnarled by arthritis.

"Old," I said, not trusting my voice to add more.

"Gotta be Villejoin. How many grannies go missing around here?"

I imagined the grisly scene. A terrified old woman, forced to strip and face death on the edge of her own grave.

Had she begged for her life? Realizing there would be no mercy, had she closed her eyes? Listened to the wind in the trees? To birdsong? Had she heard the sound of the weapon as it arced toward her head?

Suddenly, I had to get out of that tent.

13

BACK IN TOWN, RYAN AND I GRABBED LUNCH AT A LA BELLE Province. I had little appetite. The wet-wipes and disinfectant had gone only so far. I just wanted to shampoo and scrub the remaining dirt from under my nails. But Ryan was resolute. He often showed a bubbe streak, insisting I eat when I least wanted food.

Ryan ordered poutine, a Quebec delicacy that I've always found baffling. Take fries, top with cheese curds, cover with tasteless brown gravy. Yum.

I had pea soup and a salad.

We went directly from the restaurant to the Édifice Wilfrid-Derome in the Hochelaga-Maisonneuve district just east of *centre-ville.* The Laboratoire des sciences judiciaires et de médecine légale occupies the top two floors of the T-shaped structure, the Bureau du coroner is on eleven, the morgue is in the basement. The remaining footage belongs to the SQ.

Ryan took an unsecured elevator to four. I took a restricted one servicing only the LSJML, the coroner, and the morgue.

Any weekday the labs, offices, and corridors would have been swarming with white-coated scientists and technicians. That afternoon the place was quiet as a tomb. God bless Saturday.

Swiping my security pass for the fourth time since entering the building, I passed through glass doors separating the medico-legal wing from the rest of the twelfth floor, and proceeded down a hall with offices on the right and labs on the left. Microbiology. Histology. Pathology. Anthropology-Odontology.

During my absence in Chicago, window frames, bookshelves, cabinet doors, and refrigerators had been transformed. Each work area now reflected the sugarplum vision of its decorator. Plastic pine garlands. Lace doily snowflakes. Père Noël with his sack of goodies, reindeer, and sleigh.

My desk was heaped and my phone was flashing. Ignoring the hysterical red message light, I slipped my purse into a drawer and headed for the locker room.

Showered and dressed in surgical scrubs, I returned to the lab for case forms, calipers, and a clipboard. Then I took another elevator offering the same limited choices: LSJML, coroner, morgue.

In the basement, through another secure door, a long, narrow corridor shoots the length of the building. To the left are an X-ray room and four autopsy suites, three with single tables, one with a pair. To the right are drying racks, computer stations, and wheeled tubs and carts for transporting specimens to the various departments on high.

Through a small glass window in each door, I could see that here, too, nothing was happening. No police photographers, no autopsy techs, no pathologists. Some of the bulletin boards were decked out like the labs upstairs.

'Tis the season, I thought glumly, wishing I were home with Katy and Birdie.

I went directly to salle d'autopsie number four—my *salle,* specially ventilated for decomps, floaters, mummified corpses, and other aromatics.

As does each of the others, autopsy room four has double doors leading to parallel morgue bays divided into refrigerated compartments. Small white cards mark the presence of temporary residents.

But I didn't have to go there. The Oka victim lay on a gurney on the autopsy room side of the doors. Paperwork peeked from below the body bag.

A quick glance showed that the remains had been assigned LSJML and morgue numbers, and that Hubert had filled out a request for an anthropology consult.

I began by entering pertinent information into my anthropology case form. *Numéro de morgue:* 38107. *Numéro de LSJML:* 45736. *Coroner:* Jean-Claude Hubert. *Enquêteur:* Lieutenant-détective Andrew Ryan,

Section des crimes contre la personne, Sûreté du Québec. *Nom:* Inconnu. Unknown.

Last, I wrote the date and a brief summary of facts.

Tossing my clipboard onto the counter, I located a camera and checked to be sure the battery was charged. Next I pulled a plastic apron from one drawer, gloves and a mask from another, and put them on. Costumed and ready, I rolled the gurney to one side of the stainless steel table floor-bolted in the center of the room.

As a precaution, I took shots of the body bag closed, then unzipped with contents revealed. The bra and panties were visible, folded and tucked into one corner.

I checked undie labels, but the printing was faded beyond legibility. After measuring waist and chest circumferences and shooting a few more pics, I spread the garments on the counter.

Prelims finished, I began reassembling the skeleton. I'd completed an inventory at graveside, distinguishing lefts from rights, so the process went quickly until I got to the fingers and toes. Since individuation is so dreadfully tedious, those bones I'd merely counted and bagged.

A normal adult human has fifty-six phalanges. The thumbs and halluces, or big toes, have two rows each, proximal and distal. Every other digit has three rows, proximal, middle, and distal.

First, I separated hands from feet. Piece of cake for *les premiers.* Big toe phalanges are distinctly shaped and heftier than those in a thumb.

The reverse is true for pointer, middleman, ringman, and pinky. In those digits, finger phalanges are larger than toe phalanges. They are also flatter on their palm surfaces and more rounded on their backs, and their shafts are shorter and less laterally compressed.

Row position is all about joints. At its proximal end, a first-row phalange has a single facet, or concave oval surface for articulation with a metatarsal in the foot or a metacarpal in the hand. At its distal end are double knobs. A second-row phalange has double knobs at the distal end and double facets at the proximal end. A third-row phalange has a double facet at the near end, a tapered point at the far.

Setting the twenty-eight finger bones aside, I sorted toe phalanges by position. That done, I determined specific digits, two through five. Then I separated lefts from rights.

See what I mean by tedious?

By the time I finished with the feet my back was kinked and my face was itchy from the mask. I was doing overhead arm stretches when I thought I heard movement somewhere down the hall.

I checked the wall clock. 6:40.

I peered out the door in both directions.

Not a soul.

Back to the table.

Saturday-night loser. Scrooge neurons taunted from deep in my brain.

"Fa la la la la." My song rang cheerless in the empty room.

After another muscle stretch, I dived into the hand bones.

Proximal, middle, distal.

I was sorting digits when I heard the muted clink of metal on metal.

Again, I checked the hall.

Again, it was empty.

Printer recalibrating? Cooler kicking on?

The ghost of Christmas future coming to kick butt?

Achy and cranky, I turned back to the phalanges. I wanted to finish as quickly as possible. To go home, eat supper, maybe read a good book. Alexander McCall Smith. Or Nora Roberts. A story distant from this parallel universe of death.

Then I remembered. I didn't have a car because I'd ridden with Ryan. I'd have to take the metro.

Crap.

And it was probably a billion degrees below zero.

Crap. Crap.

As I worked, my mood grew blacker and blacker. I remembered there was no food at the condo. Dinner would be a frozen *tourtière.*

And I'd eat it alone. Birdie was in North Carolina. So was Katy. Since I wasn't supposed to be in Montreal, Ryan had Charlie at his place.

Where was Ryan? Probably out wining and dining with friends. Or maybe cocooned by a fire with his ex.

But Ryan swore he and Lutetia were history again. Were they?

Didn't matter. That ship had sailed.

Had it?

My eyes were burning and my back was seriously cramped. I had to force myself to concentrate.

Unbidden, lyrics came winging through my brain.

I'll have a blue Christmas without you. . . .

My eyes swept the room. Not a stocking or jolly Saint Nick in sight.

I was alone in a morgue ten days before Christmas.

I'd be alone at home.

Screw that. I vowed to call Ryan in the morning to ask for my bird. A cockatiel was better than no company at all. Maybe he and I could carol together.

"Four calling birds, three French hens . . ." I sang.

Screw tinsel and holly. What did Dickens say? Honor Christmas in your heart. Fine. I'd follow Old Charlie's advice.

Whoa.

Charlie. Charlie.

Until that moment, I hadn't noticed the coincidence.

Charlie, my cockatiel. Charlie, my old high school crush, now a lawyer in the Mecklenburg County Public Defender's office in Charlotte.

Charlie and I had barely started seeing each other when I left North Carolina for my late-November rotation in Montreal. And, to be honest, our first date had not gone well.

That's being charitable. I'd nose-dived from the wagon, binged on Merlot, then blown the guy off for a week.

I pictured Charlie Hunt, NBA tall, cinnamon skin, eyes the color of Christmas holly.

The vision did nothing to improve my mood.

Why was I stuck in this basement slogging through bones? What could I possibly accomplish tonight? I couldn't establish ID. Hubert hadn't bothered to provide Christelle Villejoin's antemortem records.

"Weenie's probably out swilling eggnog. Parked under mistletoe waiting for a mark."

I was now in full self-pity mode.

"Two turtle doves . . ."

Sighing, I snatched up another phalange.

Both joint surfaces were dense and polished, their edges lacy with bony overgrowth. Arthritis. Moving that finger would have hurt like hell.

My mind shot to the same tableau as in the woods. An old woman, trembling by a pit in her skivvies and bare feet.

The image morphed. I saw Gran's face the day she got lost at SouthPark Mall. The panic in her eyes. The relief upon seeing me.

Guilt drop-kicked self-pity into the night.

"So this is Christmas," I sang Lennon. ". . . and what have you done?"

I positioned the phalange.

I was selecting another when my mobile shattered the silence. I jumped, and the phalange flew from my hand.

My eyes flicked to the clock. Eight ten.

I checked caller ID.

Ryan.

Removing one glove, I snatched up the phone and clicked on.

"Brennan."

"Where are you?"

"Where are you?"

"I called your condo." Did Ryan sound annoyed?

"I'm not there."

There was a beat of silence. I listened but could hear no background noise.

"Are you still here?" Ryan asked.

"My answer would require knowledge of your present location." I retrieved the phalange and placed it on the table.

"You're in the morgue, right?"

"Technically, no. I'm in an autopsy room."

Rationally, I knew my discontent was not due to Ryan. But he was on the line, so he was taking the hit.

"It's Saturday night," Ryan said.

"Just eleven days left, Kmart shoppers."

Ryan ignored my sarcasm. "You've been here since three."

"And?"

"You working the Oka ID?"

"No, I'm knitting the old gal a sweater."

"You can be an Olympic pain in the ass, Brennan."

"Practice pays."

Pause.

"What's so urgent it can't wait a day?" Ryan asked.

"Once I finish the skeletal inventory, I can construct the biological profile and analyze the trauma. Then I can hike my hiney to a latitude where the mercury stands tall."

"Have you eaten?"

Ryan's question goosed my already significant irritation.

"Why this sudden interest in my diet?"

"Have you?"

"Yes," I lied.

"Would you like a ride home?"

I did.

"No, thanks."

"It's snowing."

"Joy to the friggin' world," I said.

"I'm upstairs."

"So I'm not the only loser lacking a life."

"What would it take to get you to ride with me?" Patient.

"Chloroform."

"Good one."

"Thanks."

There was a long silence before Ryan spoke again.

"I'm now primary on Villejoin, so I've been going through the file. I can fill you in."

I said nothing.

"Fatigue fosters sloppy thinking," he added.

Ryan's point was a good one. And I did want background on the Villejoin investigation.

I glanced at the disarticulated skeleton. Of the two hundred and six bones, only the hand phalanges remained unincorporated.

Tomorrow was Sunday. Barring a major disaster, the table would not be needed. The room was a secure area. I'd left remains overnight before.

And I was tired.

"I'll meet you in the lobby in ten," I said.

It was a decision I'd come to regret.

14

RYAN GOT HIS WAY BECAUSE I WAS TOO WEARY TO ARGUE. AND TOO hungry. That realization dawned as I was changing into the sweats I keep at the lab.

When asked my preference, I replied with the first foodstuff that popped to mind. Fish.

Ryan suggested Molivos. I agreed. It was a short walk to my condo from there.

Fifteen minutes after disconnecting we were slip-sliding along Avenue de Lorimier toward the Ville Marie Tunnel. The wipers were metronoming the windshield. Not a blizzard, but heavy enough snow.

While Ryan focused on driving, I checked e-mail on my BlackBerry.

Amazon wanted to sell me books. Abe's of Maine wanted to sell me appliances. Boston Proper wanted to sell me clothes. Delete. Delete. Delete.

The Humane Society wanted me to donate more money. Fair enough. Save.

A colleague wanted me to speak at a conference in Turkey. Save for polite refusal.

Katy reported that Pete and Summer had left for a week in the Turks and Caicos. She asked when I'd return to Charlotte. I replied that I'd definitely be there in time for our trip to Belize on the twenty-first.

I'd also received two offers of products guaranteed to please my genitalia, and three proposals to make millions through African banks.

As I slid the device into its holder, Ryan exited the tunnel onto Atwater. At rue Sainte-Catherine he turned right, then left onto Guy. The few pedestrians hurried with shoulders hunched, heads bowed. Sidewalks, sills, and steps were already blanketed, and car roofs and street signs wore fuzzy white caps.

Ryan parked in a stretch legal only on alternate Wednesdays from April through August between the hours of two fourteen and four twenty-seven a.m. For firemen and Freemasons. Or something like that.

Voilà, le parking, Montréal-style.

Ryan and I jaywalked across Guy, then hurried downhill. Inside the restaurant, a man with pockmarked skin and a wandering eye ushered us to a table for two.

"Two days, two tavernas." Ryan grinned. "Do I see a pattern?"

It was true. Same wooden furnishings. Same fishing nets. Same murals showing ruins or toga-clad deities. Here the tablecloths were blue-and-white checked.

"This place is fish," I said. "Chicago was lamb."

"I had the seafood combo."

"You failed to exercise good judgment."

"We should go to Greece."

"Uh-huh."

"Mykonos has some primo nude beaches." Exaggerated wink.

"In your dreams, Ryan."

"Oh, yeah."

Wandering Eye brought menus and inquired about beverages. Ryan asked for a Moosehead. I went with Perrier and lime. When the drinks came I ordered Mediterranean bass. Ryan chose snapper.

"Tell me about the Villejoin investigation," I said, wanting to avoid the perilous terrain of personal issues. Or shared nudity.

Ryan's smile morphed to a frown. He took a pull of beer and set down his mug.

"Anne-Isabelle was eighty-six. Christelle was eighty-three. Both were spinsters."

"Unmarried," I corrected.

"Right. They had lived with their parents in Pointe-Calumet. Serge Villejoin died in 'sixty-nine, Corine in 'seventy-seven. At that time the property went to the sisters."

I couldn't imagine an entire life played out in one house. Did I find such stability depressing or reassuring? I was too exhausted to gauge.

"Both worked as nurses' assistants. Anne-Isabelle retired in 'ninety-three, Christelle in 'ninety-six. After that the ladies pretty much stayed home, puttering in their garden, raising cats, crocheting gewgaws for church bazaars."

"What church?"

"Sainte-Marie du Lac in Pointe-Calumet."

Our fish arrived. We squeezed lemon, helped ourselves to beans and veggies, then ate in silence. Ryan broke it.

"A bazaar took place on May four, 2008. That was a Saturday. Normally the sisters would have walked the two blocks to the church, but they had a box of items for donation, so a neighbor offered to pick them up." Reaching back, Ryan pulled a small spiral notebook from his jacket and checked a name. "Yves Renaud. Forty-seven. A nurse at the Jewish General."

I waited while Ryan took several forkfuls of fish.

"According to Renaud's statement, he arrived at the Villejoin house around noon. He found it odd that two cats were wandering loose in the yard, since the animals were strictly indoor pets. He called out, got no answer, knocked, peeked through a window, yadda, yadda. Finally he tried the front door and found it unlocked."

"Were the women security conscious?"

"Renaud didn't know."

"Did they have an alarm system?"

"No. Renaud entered the foyer, called out again, heard nothing. He was about to leave when a third cat strolled by with blood on its nose. Suspicious, he looked around. The vic was on the kitchen floor with a pulverized face."

I noticed the subtle shift. Anne-Isabelle was now the vic. It was a distancing technique employed by cops. No names. I could tell the case disturbed Ryan greatly.

"Did you view the photos?" I asked gently.

Ryan nodded then wagged his head, as though movement could dislodge the horrific images.

"The room looked like a scene from a slasher movie."

"Recover a weapon?"

Ryan snorted his disgust. "The bastard beat her to death with her own cane."

"The perp brought nothing with him. That could suggest lack of premeditation."

"But a savage level of anger, which was triggered by something. Every bone in the woman's face was broken. So were the jaw, the right collarbone, most ribs, and both lower-right arm bones. But you probably know that. This was carnage beyond just killing."

We fell silent, thoughts pointed at the same ugly question. What monster could savage an eighty-year-old woman?

"I assume there was follow-up on Renaud?"

"LaManche did the post. Based on stomach contents and state of decomp, he put time of death at twenty-four to thirty hours. Renaud worked that Friday from seven until four. Coworkers and patients put him at the Jewish all day."

Ryan refocused on snapper. Through a window behind him, I watched flakes swirl light coning from a streetlamp on Guy.

When Ryan's fish was only bone, he laid down his utensils and leaned back. "The younger sister simply vanished."

"She didn't just vanish. Something was done to her. I remember the search. The publicity was massive."

"And fruitless. No one on the block had heard or seen a thing. Canvassing turned up zip. Ditto for phone checks. The vics had no credit cards and weren't computer savvy, so those avenues didn't exist. One neighbor thought he remembered Christelle talking about some distant cousins up in the Beauce. Those folks were never found. Local kids shoveled the snow, cut the grass, that sort of thing. The women's only known associates were either people in the immediate vicinity or members of the parish. Every last one alibied out."

"Wasn't there something about a bank card?"

"That was the only lead. On five May, around eighteen thirty hours, a withdrawal was made from Christelle's savings account at the Bank of Montreal."

"Made where?"

Ryan referred to the spiral. "An ATM at four-two-five-oh Ontario East."

"That's out east, near the Olympic stadium." Miles from Pointe-Calumet. "Did the sisters have a car?"

"No."

"Was the transaction caught on video?"

"No. The camera was down for three hours that night."

I thought a minute. "If LaManche is right about PMI, Anne-Isabelle was already dead by six p.m."

"Yes." Tight. "We missed the perp's photo due to a technical glitch."

"Did Anne-Isabelle have an account?"

"Both sisters used the same one."

Ryan drained the last of his beer. For a moment his thumb played over sweat fogging the outside of his mug. When his eyes met mine they were hard with resolve.

"I'm going to get this prick."

A fleck of foam hung on Ryan's lip. I fought an urge to wipe it away.

"I know you will," I said.

By eight a.m. there were sixty-seven centimeters blanketing the ground. Twenty-six inches. On any scale, that's a lot of snow.

Montreal is a champ at handling storms, but this time the city was brought to its knees. Between crowing about broken records, newscasters reported that only a handful of buses and metros were running. The airport was down. Church services were canceled. Businesses that normally operated on Sunday were closed.

Later it would become clear that most of the populace rose, looked out their windows, and crawled back into bed. God or the boss would understand.

I wasn't quite so complacent. I wanted to get to the lab to complete my analysis of the Oka bones.

After a breakfast of coffee, Grape-Nuts, and yogurt, I pulled on boots, donned my Kanuk, muffler, and mitts, and headed out, hoping to make it to the underground two blocks away.

No plow had ventured onto my street. No early riser had shoveled the walks. Why bother? The snow was thigh high and still coming down, the flakes tiny now, icy bullets that stung my face and bounced off my jacket.

On Sainte-Catherine, vehicles lining the curbs looked like lumpy white hedgerows. No buses. No cars. No pigeons. No people. Nothing moved. The hood was as deserted as Times Square in *Vanilla Sky.*

I arrived at the metro panting and perspiring inside my parka. A handwritten sign was taped to the grimy glass of the ticket booth.

Coupure de courant non programmée. Problème électrique. Unscheduled outage. Electrical problem. Below the words, the author had drawn a smiley face with a downturned mouth.

"Picture friggin' perfect." I was talking to myself again.

Fifteen minutes later, I was back at my building. As I turned into the corridor leading to my condo, I noticed a ziplock tucked behind the door knob.

Pulling off a mitt, I dislodged and checked the contents of the bag. Five small blobs, dry, crumbly, dark brown-black.

I unsealed the plastic and sniffed.

Excrement.

"Asshole!" The word echoed down the empty hall.

My neighbor Sparky had pulled this before. Once it was soiled litter, once a dead sparrow.

I definitely needed to vent.

After flushing the turds, I dialed my sister, Harry, in Houston.

I told her about Sparky's latest stunt.

She repeated my expletive, adding a modifier.

I told her about the snow.

"Doesn't ole blue eyes have a Jeep?"

"I can't crawl to Ryan every time I have a problem."

"Jeeps run in snow."

"So do Ski-Doos, but I'm not phoning Snowmobile Patrol."

"Is that a real thing?"

"Whatever. What are you doing?"

"Weeding my garden. It's so hot here the trees are bribing the dogs. Got to get at it early."

That made me feel worse. I said nothing.

"What else is new?" Harry asked.

I told her about Chicago, Cukura Kundze, and Ryan's sudden appearance at Vecamamma's house. Then I described the mysterious phone call to the late Edward Allen Jurmain.

"What kind of dipshit would pull something like that?"

"I intend to find out. It has to be somebody very nearby."

"That why your knickers are in a twist to work on a Sunday?"

Mentioning no names, I told her about the Villejoin sisters. She didn't interrupt. My sister can be impetuous, at times aggravating, but she's a crackerjack listener.

When I finished, Harry took a moment to respond.

"Gran was eighty-one when she died."
"She was."
"You working this thing with Ryan?"
"Yes."
"When you catch the bastard, do me a favor?"
I waited.
"Fry his balls."
I couldn't disagree with baby sister's suggestion.

MONDAY I AWOKE TO THE SOUND OF PLOWS BLASTING TRIPTYCH warnings to overnight parkers.

Wreep! Wreep! Wreep!

Déplacez votre voiture! Move your car! Move your ass!

Though the media were reporting that most main arteries were clear, through a side window I could see that my block still looked like a postcard from Finland. I knew the same scene was playing on side streets and alleys all over town. Shovels would be flying, and those who'd failed to relocate their vehicles would now do so only after heavy-duty lifting. Hospital ERs would be hopping.

Knowing traffic would be brutal and parking would involve angling ass-end into waist-high snowbanks, I opted for mass transit. Today my Nanook trek paid off. I rode standing shoulder to armpit with commuters smelling of wet wool and sweat.

At Édifice Wilfrid-Derome, small white mountains hid the fences surrounding the parking lots. Cars were wedged into every square millimeter of cleared pavement. Those blocking others had notes below their wipers. Courtesy? Or excuses to leave early?

Elevator talk was all about the storm. *La tempête de neige.*

Upstairs at the LSJML it was business as usual. Except in the medico-legal section. There, nothing had been usual since LaManche dropped his bomb one sparkling Friday in September.

Blocked coronary vessels. Bypass surgery in October. Medical leave until the new year.

In addition to myself and LaManche, the three other pathologists had been present that day. Michael Morin. Natalie Ayers. Emily Santangelo. So was Marc Bergeron, the lab's consulting odontologist. We'd all sat stunned.

Sure, the chief had suffered a pesky episode a few years back. But he'd recovered quickly. Once again arrived first each morning, turned the lights off at night. Triple bypasses were for frail, old men. LaManche was only fifty-eight.

I remember meeting LaManche's hound dog gaze. Dropping my eyes. Glancing out the window. This can't be real, I thought. The day is too beautiful. Irrational, but that's what I thought.

The following week, LaManche raised the issue of a temporary replacement. The decision was quick and unanimous. Ours was a congenial unit. There'd be no stand-in. Until the boss returned the pathologists would assign cases and make administrative decisions by consensus. The extra workload would be equally shared.

And that's how it was working, three months down the road.

Sort of.

After shedding my substantial outerwear, I snapped on a lab coat and headed to the staff lounge. At the exit from our wing, where the hall makes a turn, I passed a closed and locked door. Venetian blinds allowed a peek of an empty desk.

Beside the dark office, an erasable board announced daily staff whereabouts. *Congé de maladie* was scribbled in the box beside LaManche's name. Sick leave.

A lead weight settled in my heart.

The surgery went well. He'll be fine.

Still, the silent office and the Magic Marker entry gave me shivers.

LaManche had always been there for me, a voice of wisdom and reason. Of compassion and perspective earned by decades of working with the dead and with the bereaved left behind. That voice was now banished because of bum piping.

LaManche isn't old. Agitated, I swiped my card, missed, swiped again. The glass panels whooshed open. *It's not fair.*

Life's not fair. Gran's favorite retort zinged at me from the past.

Screw capricious fate. I couldn't imagine the LSJML without LaManche. Didn't want to.

Though the lounge was deserted, the puddled floor told me others had already been there. Dropping coins into an honor box, I poured coffee translucent as smoky quartz.

Back in the medico-legal wing, I hurried to the far end of the corridor. My watch said nine ten. Morning meeting usually kicks off at nine.

Our section's conference room is exactly what you'd envision in a government building. Algae green walls. Gray tile floor. Window blinds. Phone credenza. Gunmetal table and chairs. A blackboard/projection screen hangs at one end, a door opens to an audiovisual closet at the other.

Two pathologists sat with their backs to the windows. Sunlight warmed Ayers's chestnut hair and glinted off Morin's freckled brown dome. A third sat at the far end. Santangelo's slumping shoulders suggested fatigue.

Facing the old-timers was Marie-Andréa Briel, the new kid on the LSJML block. Briel had joined the staff the previous fall, during a period when I was away in Charlotte. Lab policy is that, for their first year, new pathologists do no homicide cases, so I hadn't really worked with Briel. Though I'd seen her in the halls, and we'd nodded across the table at staff meetings, we'd had virtually no personal interaction. I knew little about her from firsthand experience. What snippets I'd been given weren't golden.

One late afternoon, exhausted, LaManche had confided that an offer had been extended and accepted. In his opinion, the applicant wasn't the pick of the litter. But old Jean Pelletier had been gone for over a year and he and the others had been doing the work of five.

Though he'd yet to reveal it, the chief probably knew he was looking at surgery in the not too distant future. Another pathologist had to be hired.

Why such a prolonged search? The pay is low, and the LSJML requires fluency in French. You guessed it. The litter wasn't that big.

Ayers and Morin smiled when I entered. Santangelo flicked a wave.

"*Bonjour,* Tempe." Morin's French was that of the islands. "*Comment ça va?*"

"*Ça va bien.*" I'm doing fine.

"Couldn't stay away from our Montreal weather, eh?" Ayers knew my feelings on snow.

"No comment." I took a seat.

Briel glanced in my direction.

I nodded. Smiled.

Briel looked down at her notepad, vertical lines creasing the gap where heavy dark brows reached for each other over her nose.

I looked at Ayers. She shrugged. Who knows?

I tried again with my newest colleague. "I hope you're now feeling comfortable here."

Briel's face rose, frown lines in place. "*Oui.*"

"Not letting these old goats get on your nerves."

Ayers bleated softly.

"I can handle difficulties."

Marie-Andréa Briel was not blessed with beauty. Perhaps thirty-two, she had a substantial fundament, frizzy black hair, and skin the color of fluoridated teeth. That skin now went incandescent.

"I'm not implying that anyone is difficult. That's not what I meant. I'm very happy here. Thankful for the chance to learn."

Though grammatically flawless, Briel's French was oddly without accent or inflection. Definitely not Québécois or European. I made a mental note to ask about her origins.

Morin reached over and patted Briel's hand. "You're doing fine."

The frown lines relaxed. A micron.

"The old lady from Oka is downstairs?" Morin asked me.

"Yes. I started my analysis on Saturday, hope to finish today."

"Then outa here for a Dixie Christmas?" Ayers.

"That's the plan."

"Put elf hats on the hunting dogs?" Ayers loved to tease about my Southern roots.

"Yep. Then the cousins gather in my trailer to drink hooch and eat pork skins."

"*Bon.*" Morin distributed photocopied rosters of the day's cases. "Then let's not waste time."

I skimmed the daily morgue sheet. Eight autopsies. A typical Monday. Busy as hell.

Morin went over each case.

A Ski-Doo had slammed into a tree near Sainte-Agathe. A second snowmobile had then plowed into the first. Two dead. Alcohol intoxication was suspected.

An Argentine seaman had died in a home-rigged sauna in the Gay Village. The presumed host was in critical condition at the General. Alcohol and drug intoxication were suspected.

Two men and a woman had been discovered dead in their beds in Baie-Comeau. Carbon monoxide poisoning was suspected.

A man had been gunned down outside a convenience store in Longueuil.

A woman had been stabbed in her home in Lac-Beauport. The estranged husband was in custody.

Only the Longueuil shooting victim's identity was unknown. Prints were being run and a photo was being shopped to known gang members.

Nothing for the anthropologist. Hot damn. I'd be free to work on the Oka lady.

Though Briel offered, Morin assigned himself the stabbing victim. *Mo* went onto the roster beside that case.

Santangelo got the snowmobilers. *Sa.*

Ayers volunteered for the sailor and the gunshot death. Again Briel offered, but was refused. The shooting was clearly a homicide. The sautéed sailor was a foreign national. That meant potential diplomatic issues. *Ay.*

Briel's brow-pucker deepened as Morin wrote *Br* beside the chalet vics then tossed her a ziplock filled with vials of prescription drugs.

"Christelle Villejoin's antemortem records," he said, handing me an envelope whose size did not look encouraging.

"No X-rays?"

Morin shook his head.

"Dentals?"

"Apparently *les soeurs Villejoin* were not fond of medical professionals. Everything in the file looks pretty old."

Great.

Morin turned to budget matters. Additional cuts had been demanded by the ministry. Nothing new. Each year funding grew more spartan. The joke was that soon autopsies would be billed by the pound.

We were pushing from the table when Briel spoke up.

"I have taken on a student."

We all paused.

"A student?" Morin raised a questioning brow.

"I am beginning a new project and need a new research assistant."

"A project?" The brow floated higher.

"Montreal remains the last U.S. or Canadian city with a population over one million that does not fluoridate its water. Some communities in the West Island do fluoridate. Pointe-Claire, Dorval, Beaconsfield, Baie-d'Urfé, Kirkland, and parts of Dollard-des-Ormeaux and Sainte-Anne-de-Bellevue."

Ayers groaned softly. It was an old issue.

Briel ignored her.

"Though the Quebec government endorses and has offered to subsidize fluoridation in Montreal, the city refuses. I have read statistics stating that Montreal children have seventy-seven percent more cavities compared to children in areas of Quebec where fluoride is added to the water. The dichotomy on the Island of Montreal provides a natural laboratory. My assistant and I will be comparing the decay rates of unfluoridated city children to those of their fluoridated surburban counterparts."

"All costs will have to—"

"I have a grant."

"What happened to your old student?"

"I had to let her go."

"Who is the new student?" Santangelo asked.

"Solange Duclos. She is a fourth-year biology major at l'Université de Montréal. She will come for six hours each week beginning next Tuesday."

"Shouldn't this have been discussed prior to making a commitment?" Santangelo's voice had an edge. "There are security and safety issues."

Briel's cheeks flamed again, reminding me of Chris Corcoran. Which reminded me of Edward Allen Jurmain and his snake-belly informant. I would begin digging as soon as I finished with the Oka woman.

"—visibility for the lab. I plan to present my findings to the American Academy of Forensic Sciences. And to publish them in the *Journal of Forensic Sciences* and the *Journal of the Canadian Dental Association.*"

Ayers started to comment. Morin cut her off.

"You are new here. There is much to absorb."

Briel's shoulders hitched back. "I have completed a residency program in anatomic and clinical pathology. And several postdocs. I am not without experience."

"Our autopsy schedule is very demanding," Ayers said. "Look at today. You have two cases."

"I don't mind working late. Or on weekends. The research will be done on my own time."

Ayers shook her head. Santangelo wrote something on her roster.

"Access must be limited to our section alone," Morin said. "As with your previous student, Ms. Duclos must not enter the morgue or any other restricted area of the building. And she must, for security purposes, submit to a full background check."

"The background check has already been done."

"Have Ms. Duclos come to my office when she arrives on Tuesday." Morin looked around the table. "Other business?"

Nothing.

"Let's get cutting."

Downstairs, the Oka bones were as I'd left them.

The clock said ten past ten. Normally, I'd have begun with a full skeletal inventory. Since Hubert would be phoning soon, I decided to jump protocol and go straight to ID. Completion of the bone count could wait.

To avoid the influence of preconceived bias, I perform my analyses prior to viewing documentation. I see working in the dark as a sort of double-blind check.

Setting the antemortem records aside, I began to construct a biological profile.

By noon I'd determined that the skeleton was, in fact, that of a white female in excess of sixty-five years of age. Though I'd noted widespread osteoarthritis, advanced periostitis, and significant tooth loss, I'd found nothing sufficiently unique to positively establish ID.

I was sliding Christelle Villejoin's medical records from their envelope when I heard the anteroom door open. Seconds later, Briel appeared.

Though the frown lines were present, she made a lip gesture I chose to interpret as a grin.

"Taking a break?" I asked.

"Bones interest me. May I watch while you work?"

I matched her nonanswer with one of my own.

"I apologize for knowing so little about you. I'm away so much. You come to us from where?"

She misinterpreted my meaning. "My father was a diplomat. We moved a great deal."

OK. That explained the accent.

"Where was home before Montreal?"

"Montpellier, France."

"Ooh, climate shock." I laughed.

She did not. "My husband is from here."

"Still. In winter." I pantomimed weighing two objects, one in each hand. "South of France? Quebec? That's devotion above and beyond."

The perpetual frown never faltered.

"What does your husband do?"

"He is in private business."

Conversation was like pulling impacted molars. I remembered why I'd given up in the past. Nevertheless, I soldiered on.

"Do you live in the city?"

"We have a condo on Fullum."

"Handy. You can walk here."

"Yes. May I observe you?"

When working, there are things I avoid like a case of the drips. Cops trying to rush me. Prosecutors trying to sway me. Anyone trying to look over my shoulder.

I started to dodge her request. As I had previous ones.

"I'm sorry, but I've explained. I don't—"

"It's my lunch hour. My own time."

"I'm really humping to get this one done." I smiled modestly. "Besides, most of what I do is flat-out boring."

"I don't see it that way."

I was framing a firmer refusal when the door opened again. My second visitor was Ryan. His expression told me something was very wrong.

"What's up?" I asked.

Ryan chin-cocked the remains. "Is it Villejoin?"

"I haven't finished."

Ryan nodded to Briel, then spoke to me. "The situation could be nastier than we thought."

16

RYAN'S FINGERS RAKED HIS HAIR. TOUCHED HIS MOUTH. DRUMMED his belt.

"We may have a serial."

Beside me, Briel went very still.

"In Montreal?"

"No. In Saskatoon."

"Hardy friggin' har."

"I ran into your pal Claudel this morning."

Sergeant-détective Luc Claudel, SPVM. A city cop. Claudel and I were pals in the sense Hatfields and McCoys were buds.

"He's working an MP."

Ryan referred to a missing person case.

"Ten days ago a landlord named Mathieu Baudry dropped in on one of his tenants, Marilyn Keiser, a seventy-two-year-old widow living alone. Baudry was pissed about unpaid rent."

"Where's the apartment?"

"Édouard-Montpetit. The place looked abandoned. Unopened mail. Dead plants. Spoiled food in the refrigerator. The usual. Baudry asked around the building. None of the neighbors had seen or talked to Keiser in months. One suggested she might have gone south for the winter."

"Was that her pattern?"

"No. Keiser wasn't a snowbird. She drove, occasionally made short trips. Quebec City. Ottawa. Charlevoix. That was about it."

"Her car is also missing?"

Ryan nodded.

"Family?"

"Two kids, both married and living in Alberta. The only local relative is a stepson named Myron Pinsker. Baudry phoned Pinsker repeatedly. After a week of no contact and no returned calls he gave up and dialed nine-one-one.

"Claudel caught the case, did some digging, learned that since October Marilyn Keiser has missed medical appointments, book club meetings, a sit-down with her rabbi, and about a zillion other engagements. No apologies, no explanations."

"That's out of character?"

"Definitely. The stepson is a forty-four-year-old grounds worker at a West Island golf course. Beaconsfield, I think. Told Claudel he was unaware Keiser was missing."

"Maybe they aren't close."

"Maybe not. But someone cashed Keiser's last three old age insurance pension checks."

"Crap."

"Claudel learned that late yesterday. This morning he hauled Pinsker's ass to the bag."

"Detective Claudel thinks Madame Keiser is dead?"

Ryan and I glanced at Briel in surprise. She'd been so still, I think we'd both forgotten she was there.

"Doesn't look good," Ryan said.

"He suspects the stepson?"

"Pinsker better have a good explanation for those checks."

Ryan turned to me.

"Four elderly women in two years."

Three, yes. But four? I must have looked confused.

"Keiser. Anne-Isabelle Villejoin. This one." Ryan jabbed a thumb toward the bones behind me. "Jurmain."

"Rose Jurmain was hardly elderly," I said.

"But she looked old. Remember Janice Spitz's photos, the ones taken shortly before Jurmain's death?"

I nodded understanding. Maybe the drugs. Maybe the booze. Rose had looked decades beyond her fifty-nine years.

Again, Ryan gestured at the table. "Keiser's disappearance throws a whole new wrinkle into this ID."

I remembered Hubert's rhetorical question at graveside. How many grannies go missing around here?

Too many, I thought.

"I'll know within the hour if it's Christelle Villejoin," I said.

"Gotta roll. Claudel's interrogating Pinsker now."

With that, Ryan was gone.

A greedy relative? Or an anonymous predator targeting the weak?

I felt the usual riot of emotions. Anger. Outrage. Sorrow.

I needed a break.

Excusing myself to Briel, I stripped off my gloves and headed upstairs.

Thirty minutes later I was back in the basement. Coming down the corridor, I noticed Briel through the little window in the door to the large autopsy suite. She was speaking to Joe Bonnet while removing the brain from one of the Baie-Comeau corpses.

I paused briefly, wondering how the two new hires meshed. Joe was prickly, quick to take offense. Briel was as amiable as a statue in the park.

Briel said something. Joe listened, hair doing a latter-day Ric Flair in the fluorescent light.

Briel touched Joe's hand. He smiled. Actually laughed.

I continued on to Salle 4.

Taking the envelope that Morin had delivered to me from the Bureau du coroner, I spread the contents on the anteroom desk.

My pessimism was justified. There was little to spread.

Entries only went back to 1987. Nothing sinister there. Space in medical offices is limited, and paperwork is often destroyed when legally permissible.

For the past two decades, Christelle Villejoin had used a GP named Sylvain Rayner. Sparingly.

In 1989 she'd been diagnosed with shingles. In 1994 it was mild bronchitis.

The most recent entries dated to 1997.

On April 24 Christelle had complained of constipation. Rayner prescribed a laxative. On April 26 the problem was diarrhea.

Good job, Doc.

Christelle had no history of any bone-altering disease. No stents, pins, rods, or artificial joints had been placed in her body. She'd suffered no fractures. She'd undergone no surgeries of any kind.

No X-rays.

Nothing dental.

Christelle's chart was useless to me.

But there was a number for Rayner's office.

When I phoned, a robotic voice told me to take a hike. I'm paraphrasing.

On a hunch, I returned to the twelfth floor and tried Google on my laptop.

Sylvain Alexandre Rayner had earned his MD at McGill in 1952, retired from practice in 1998. A little more searching and I had a home number and directions to Rayner's residence in Côte Saint-Luc.

God bless the Internet.

My call went unanswered. I left a message and headed back downstairs.

I'd barely entered Salle 4 when the anteroom phone shrilled.

"Dr. Temperance Brennan, *s'il vous plaît*," a male voice said.

"May I ask who's calling?"

"Sylvain Rayner."

"The Sylvain Rayner who treated Christelle Villejoin?" I spoke loudly and slowly, a well-intentioned reaction based on a common and often false assumption. Rayner is elderly, therefore hard of hearing, perhaps dull-witted.

"*Oui.*"

"*Dr.* Sylvain Rayner?" I repeated the name, upping the volume and emphasizing the title.

"I can hear you, miss." The man had switched to English. "Yes. This is Sylvain Rayner. I'm returning your call."

Clearly, the good doctor had excellent ears. Or a dandy of a hearing aid. He'd even caught my Anglophone accent.

"Sorry, sir. Occasionally this phone distorts sound levels," I lied.

"How may I help you?"

"As I said in my message, my name is Temperance Brennan. I'm the forensic anthropologist with the coroner in Montreal. I have some questions concerning a former patient."

I expected the usual rebuff based on confidentiality. That's not what I got.

"You've found Christelle Villejoin," Rayner said.

"Perhaps." Careful. "Remains have come into the morgue. I've determined the bones are those of an elderly white female, but I've found nothing sufficiently unique to permit positive identification. The medical file I have is quite limited."

"I'm not surprised. The Villejoin sisters were blessed with remarkable genes. I saw both of them from the mid-seventies until my retirement in 'ninety-eight. They rarely had an ailment. Oh, a bellyache now and then. Common cold. Maybe a rash. Anne-Isabelle and Christelle may have been the two healthiest patients I treated in my entire forty-six years of practice. Never smoked, never drank. Took only drugstore vitamins, an aspirin now and then. No magic potions or lifestyle secrets. Just whoppin' good DNA."

"The coroner provided no dental records."

"The girls weren't so lucky there. Brushed and flossed like the devil, but still lost their teeth. Didn't matter how much I scolded. Both hated dentists. Got it from their mama, I think."

"I see." Discouraged, I slumped back in my chair.

"Fact is, they distrusted medicine in general. As far as I know, they gave up on doctors altogether when I retired. I referred their files to the young fellow who took over my practice, but he once told me he never laid eyes on either. Funny, them working all their lives at the hospital."

Is it? I thought. Maybe they'd seen too much.

"I remember the attack," Rayner said. "Poor Anne-Isabelle. I suppose the same demented animal also killed Christelle that day?"

"I'm sorry. I can't discuss an open investigation."

Rayner wasn't fooled.

"It's a harsh world we live in."

I couldn't disagree with that.

"Dr. Rayner, can you think of anything that might help me determine if this skeleton is Christelle's? Perhaps something you noticed while examining her? Something she told you? Something you spotted in older records that no longer exist?"

Down the hall I heard a door open, close. Footsteps. The pause continued so long I thought we'd been disconnected.

"Sir?"

"Actually, there was something."

Sitting upright, I said, "Tell me about it."

"Christelle had a ninety-degree flexion contracture in the proximal interphalangeal joint of her right little finger. When I asked about it she said her pinky had been crooked since birth."

"What about the other joints in that finger?" I grabbed pen and paper.

"They were fine. At first. Whenever I saw Christelle I checked her hand. Over the years compensatory deformity developed in the metacarpo-phalangeal and distal interphalangeal joints."

"Camptodactyly?" I guessed.

"I think so."

"Congenital?"

"Yes."

"Bilateral or just on the right?"

"Just the one hand was affected."

"Did you take X-rays?"

"I offered repeatedly. Christelle always refused. Said the thing never caused her any pain. The finger wasn't a complaint, and there was never any treatment, so I didn't chart it. Didn't seem important."

Suddenly, I was in a froth to get back to the bones.

"Thank you so much, doctor. You've been very helpful."

"Call if you need anything further."

Though an affected finger may look painfully distorted, camptodactyly is usually asymptomatic. And, like Christelle, many with the condition seek no medical attention.

Not particularly useful from an antemortem records perspective.

But two things *were* very useful.

Camptodactyly occurs in less than one percent of the population.

Camptodactyly leaves its mark on the joints.

After disconnecting, I shot upstairs, grabbed a Diet Coke, then practically danced back down to Salle 4.

Scooping the unsorted phalanges, I began to triage.

Row: Proximal. Middle. Distal.

Digit: Thumb. Two. Three. Four. Five.

Side: Left. Right.

Done.

I stared in disbelief.

17

IMPOSSIBLE.

Joe and I had recovered all fifty-six.

I checked every inch of the autopsy table. The entire skeleton. The gurney. The body bag. The floor. The counter. The sink. The plastic sheet I'd used to cover the remains.

I had no distal phalange from the right third finger and none of the three from the right fifth finger.

I checked again.

Nope.

Phalanges are small, often lost from corpses left out in the elements. Had the missing bones been carried from the grave by rodents? Wood rats are known to collect body parts in their nests. Had they been washed away by percolating ground water?

Or had I screwed up?

The skeleton had darkened to the same deep brown as the soil. Had I failed to spot the phalanges in the pit? Missed them in the screen? I'd dug an extra six inches below the skeleton. Had burrowing roots or insects dragged the little buggers deeper than that?

Was it something more sinister? Had Christelle's little finger been severed before she was placed in the earth? If so, what had happened to her middle finger tip?

And, more important, why? Did removal of the pinky imply a killer who knew his victim, a killer savvy to the forensic value of a finger deformity?

Sweet Jesus, this couldn't be happening. The camptodactyly was all I had. Hubert would be calling soon.

Wrong.

Hearing footsteps, I whirled.

Hubert's belly was rolling through the door. The rest of the coroner was right behind.

"Dr. Brennan." Cheek-popping grin. "What have you got for me?"

"Actually, I haven't quite finished."

Hubert retracted a cuff and checked his watch.

"I have no X-rays, dental records, or adequate medical history. With this other elderly lady gone missing—"

Hubert frowned. "What other elderly lady?"

I summarized Ryan's account of Marilyn Keiser.

"*Eh, misère.*"

"But I may have found something."

Hubert sighed through his nose. It whistled. "How long?"

"Soon."

"I'll be in my office."

When Hubert had gone, I made another sweep of the autopsy room. The phalanges were definitely not there.

I stood a moment, arms wrapping my waist.

Skeletal inventory sheet?

I checked.

At graveside, I'd indicated recovery of fifty-six phalanges. Beyond that, the information was useless. After identifying carpals, metacarpals, tarsals, and metatarsals, I'd merely tallied phalange totals, then bagged the hands and feet. Had I miscounted? Mistaken twigs for middles? Pebbles for distals?

Joe?

Thinking the tech might remember what we'd gotten, I hurried down the hall. The large autopsy suite was deserted. I called upstairs, got Joe's voice mail. Of course. Lunchtime.

Morgue photos?

It had been a Saturday. I'd worked alone. The bones had required no cleaning, so there'd been no risk of unintentional modification. Other than overview shots documenting condition upon arrival, I'd decided to delay photography until the skeleton was reassembled.

Scene photos?

Though a long shot, the right little finger might be visible in close-ups.

Climbing the back stairs to the main level, I exited to the lobby and took an unrestricted elevator to the second floor. A guy named Pellerin greeted me in the Service de l'identité judiciaire.

I requested the scene shots from the Oka recovery. Pellerin asked me to wait and disappeared into the back. After a short delay, he reappeared with a thick brown envelope. I thanked him and went back downstairs.

Sliding a spiral-bound album from the envelope, I started flipping through 5 by 7 color prints.

The opening sequence showed the usual terrain overviews, approach routes, and angles of a yellow-taped patch of earth. Only the tent was atypical.

I skipped quickly through those. My interest was in bones.

There were several photos of the skeleton lying in the pit, taken from a distance of at least six feet. Because the victim lay twisted to one side, the right hand and arm were difficult to see.

I tried a magnifying glass. It didn't help much.

I continued flipping through prints.

There were excellent close-ups of the skull, rib cage, pelvis, and all four limbs. In the grave. Beside the grave, lying on plastic.

Sixty-two pictures. Not a single tight shot of the hands or feet.

I sat back, dismayed.

Had I failed to recover key bones? I'm always painstakingly careful when working a scene. Some call me anal. But I had to admit to the possibility. It was hot in the tent. Cramped. Lighting was poor.

Then why the full count on the inventory sheet?

Had I lost the phalanges here at the lab? I'd been tired on Saturday. Awash in self-pity. Pinky phalanges are tiny little buggers. Had I rinsed them down a drain while cleaning my hands? Carried them off on a hem or cuff? Crushed them under a heel or gurney wheel?

Did it really matter? The bones were clearly not present. The question was, now what?

Hubert would be miffed if I'd left the phalanges in the grave. A return to Oka would involve additional expense and effort. The tent. The heater. The van. The personnel.

If I'd lost them after recovery, forget miffed. Hubert would be furious.

Bury the camptodactyly? After all, the crooked finger had been a long shot for an ID. The condition wasn't entered in Villejoin's chart. Simply tell Hubert my lead had not panned out? That *was* true. Sort of.

A zillion cells in my brain tossed a flag on the field.

Foul.

Ethics.

Crap.

Knowing it was futile, I tore the autopsy room apart, rifling drawers, emptying cabinets, running my fingers along baseboards and under counter ledges. Finding only detritus I don't want to describe, I gave up and walked every inch of the corridor, eyes to the tile.

No phalanges.

Hubert would want me to proceed with trauma analysis before reporting to him.

Delay of game.

Crap.

Moving slowly, I covered the bones. Removed my gloves. Washed my hands, carefully cleaning under the nails. Combed my hair. Recombed it into a ponytail.

Unable to stall any longer, I took the elevator up to ten.

The chief coroner was at his desk, jacketless now. His shirt was a coffee-stained pink that clashed badly with his red and green tie. Christmas trees with tiny banners screaming *Joyeux Noël!*

I tapped my knuckles on the door frame.

Hubert looked up. A cascade of chins disconnected.

"Ah, excellent."

A pudgy hand flapped me into the office.

Flashback. Perry Schechter. I made a note to inquire about Rose Jurmain. Kill two birds and all.

"*Bonnes nouvelles?*" Hubert asked.

"Actually, the news isn't so good."

Hubert slumped back, pushing the pink polyester to its tensile limit. The hand now flapped at a chair.

I sat.

Brushed lint from the knee of my scrubs.

Inhaled deeply.

"Are you familiar with camptodactyly?" I began.

"No." Coroners in Quebec are either doctors or lawyers. Hubert was among the latter.

I described the condition, then recapped my conversation with Sylvain Rayner.

"Sounds promising."

"Except for one thing."

Hubert waited.

"I don't have the right little finger phalanges."

"Why not?"

"Either they weren't collected or they've been misplaced."

"I don't understand."

I explained the tally I'd done on-site. And my fruitless search downstairs.

"Only those three are missing?"

"And the distal phalange from the right third digit."

"An error in recovery, documentation, or processing. An error that could compromise an identification. And you're uncertain which."

"Yes." I could feel my face flame.

"This is very disappointing."

I said nothing.

"This is a homicide."

"Yes."

"If the woman downstairs is Christelle Villejoin, this case will go very high profile. If a third old woman is dead, this Marilyn Keiser, that profile will go into the startosphere."

Feeling correction would not be appreciated, I held my tongue.

"Maybe these phantom phalanges were never there. Maybe the killer hacked off this woman's finger."

"Why would I record a total of fifty-six?"

"Carelessness?"

"I'll check the fifth right metacarpal for cut marks." I didn't believe I'd find any. I'd have noticed while sorting.

English speakers profane by reference to body functions and parts. Don't need to elaborate. French Canadians rely on liturgical reference. *Ostie:* host. *Câlice:* chalice. *Tabarnac* and *tabarnouche:* tabernacle.

"*Ostie.*" Hubert pooched air through his lips. "What about trauma?"

"I'm still working on that."

There was a beat of silence.

"Actually, there could be four," I said.

"Four what?" Hubert looked at me as though I'd been sniffing glue.

"Elderly women murdered in the Montreal area. *If* Marilyn Keiser has been murdered. And we don't know that, of course—"

"Who's the fourth?"

"Rose Jurmain."

"Who?"

"Last March a female skeleton was found near Sainte-Marguerite. Turned out to be a woman missing two and a half years."

Hubert shot forward. Rolls large enough to hide squirrels tumbled his torso.

"Of course." A finger jabbed the air. "Jurmain was a wealthy American. The father had connections. How could I forget? The old man was a pain in my shorts. You and Ryan just transported the bones to Chicago. But that woman wasn't so old."

"Fifty-nine." I explained Rose's prematurely aged appearance.

"*Tabarnac.*"

Hubert's face was now the color of his shirt. I decided to delay querying about my problem with Edward Allen.

"I could cut bone samples from the skeleton downstairs. Submit them for DNA testing." I knew it was dumb as soon I said it.

"Christelle Villejoin had one relative, a sister, now dead. You tell me she never had surgery, so we won't get lucky with hospital-stored gallstones or tissue samples. It's been two and a half years. The house has undoubtedly been cleaned of toothbrushes, combs, tissues, chewing gum. To what would we compare this DNA?"

"I thought there was family in the Beauce. Have attempts been made to locate those relatives?"

Hubert didn't bother to answer. Then I remembered. Ryan said that had been done. But done well? I made a note to ask him to double-check.

"Marilyn Keiser has offspring somewhere out west," I said. "We could at least establish that the skeleton is or is not hers."

"And if it's not we're still up shit creek."

"We could exhume Anne-Isabelle."

"Cremated." Hubert packed an encyclopedia of disdain into one little word.

"I'm happy to go back out to Oka."

Now the hand flapped at me.

The small office filled with tense silence.

What the hell? I was already on Hubert's list.

"This may not be the time, but I'd like to discuss an issue arising from the Jurmain case."

Hubert's stare was beyond stony and out the back door. Ignoring it, I began to explain my dilemma concerning Edward Allen's informant.

The phone chose precisely that moment to ring.

Hubert answered, listened, the scowl never leaving his face. Then, palming the mouthpiece, he spoke to me.

"I want your trauma report as quickly as possible."

A not so subtle kiss-off.

THE REST OF THAT DAY WAS DEVOTED TO THE OKA WOMAN.

Four hours with the bones revealed no further indignities to her person. No cut marks. No stab wounds. No bullet holes. No postcranial trauma of any kind.

The skull fracture, however, was a doozy.

When I surfaced at five, it had been dark for an hour. No new Demande d'expertise en anthropologie form lay on my desk. There were no urgent phone messages from cops or prosecutors. No update from Ryan.

Zipped, mufflered, booted, and gloved, I headed out.

The snow mounding curbs and sidewalks had already turned black. Along my route to the metro, aggravated drivers herniated themselves disinterring their cars. Exhaust fumes glowed red against a backdrop of traffic-stalled taillights. Salt crunching underfoot, I congratulated myself on my choice of mass transit.

Without Birdie or Charlie, my condo seemed dark and empty. For company, I popped in a Dorothée Berryman CD. Singing duets with Dorothée as she covered tunes by Mercer, Vaughan, and Fitzgerald, I whipped up a concoction of linguini, pine nuts, tomatoes, and feta. It wasn't bad.

After supper, I logged onto the Net.

Few things have improved my life more in recent years than the reinstatement of US Airway's incredibly fabulous direct nonstop service between La Belle Ville and the Queen City.

Good-bye, connection in Philadelphia! Hello, luggage in Charlotte!

Within minutes, I'd booked a seat on Thursday morning's flight. As I closed the laptop, my face wore a smile with the wingspan of a 747.

"Going home, going home, I'm a-going home."

Dorothée did not begrudge me my solo.

Tuesday I was up at seven, in the lab by eight.

The morning's autopsies included a worker crushed in a microbrewery and a bookkeeper who'd used timers and wrist leads to electrocute herself. Conscientious even in death, the lady had pinned a note to her sweater warning of potential hazard.

By ten, I'd drawn and photographed the Oka woman's cranial trauma and composed my report. Then I photocopied my diagram and printed superior, lateral, and interior views of the skull.

After downing a mug of very bad coffee, I hiked downstairs to the Bureau du coroner.

Hubert was in his office. The day's shirt was lavender, the tie still red and green. Candy canes and holly had replaced Monday's tree and banner motif.

"She was struck once from behind, once after she was down."

Hubert laid aside his pen.

Circling the desk, I placed the prints and diagram on his blotter. On each, I'd labeled the fractures alphabetically.

Using my finger, I traced a jagged break running from right to left across the back of the Oka skull.

"Letter *A* marks a radiating fracture caused by a blow to the right posterior parietal."

I indicated an indentation beside the sagittal suture at the top of the vault. A starburst of cracks spread from its center.

"Letter *B* marks a crush fracture."

"Caused by a blow to the crown."

"Yes."

A pudgy finger came down on an in-bending paralleling one side of the crush fracture. "*Bonjour.*"

"I'll come back to that. The letters *C* mark radiating and concentric fractures associated with *B*. Notice that every *C* terminates at *A*."

Hubert made a noise in his throat.

"Once formed, a crack will propagate until its energy is dissipated. In other words, when it hits an opening, it's done. So fracture *A* preexisted fracture *B*, and all its progeny, the *C*s."

Hubert got it. "The crown was hit after the parietal."

"Exactly. The first blow may have been lethal, but the killer was taking no chances. After she fell, he blasted her again to make certain she wasn't getting up."

"With what?"

I indicated the edge of the depression fracture that had caught Hubert's attention.

"The shape of the in-bending suggests a cylindrical object that widens into a flat surface with a raised central ridge."

Hubert studied the image. The phone rang. He ignored it.

Finally, "*Une pelle?*" A shovel?

"That's my take."

Selecting the interior view, I pointed to dark staining adjacent to both fracture sites.

"Hemorrhage." Taut. "Her heart was still pumping."

I nodded agreement.

Hubert did not raise his eyes to mine.

"A helpless old woman is forced to walk naked and barefoot through the woods. To watch her grave dug. Then she's bludgeoned with a shovel."

"Yes," I said.

"*Câlice.*"

Despite Hubert's pessimism, I returned to the lab, cut a bone plug from the Oka woman's femur, and delivered it to the DNA section. Then, with that case in limbo, I was free to focus on sniffing out Jurmain's informant.

Since I was currently not topping Hubert's hit parade, I decided to start with the case file. Perhaps somewhere in the minutiae of the investigation I'd find a clue to the identity of my accuser.

Dossiers are kept five years at the LSJML, then sent to a mountaintop in Mogadishu for permanent storage. Fortunately, Rose had disappeared only three years earlier.

After dropping my report in the secretarial office, I continued down the same side corridor to the library. Félicité Hernandez, a large woman with a penchant for Gypsy fashion and hair like Cher's after the bleach job, greeted me. We exchanged pleasantries, accompanied by much clacking. Félicité likes her accessories large and dangly.

I requested the master file for LSJML-44893, then took a seat. Five minutes passed. Ten. Though pleasant and thorough, Félicité is not speedy.

Finally, a corrugated binder hit the counter. Saying *merci,* I lugged the thing to my office.

For the next two hours I returned to Sainte-Marguerite, L'Auberge des Neiges, the yellow-taped mound in the pines. I reviewed the findings of pathology, toxicology, odontology, and fiber experts. Police incident reports. Witness statements. Information provided by family members.

I jotted names. Wondered with each. Did this person hint at professional dissatisfaction? At personal offense?

When finished I was as frustrated as when I'd begun. No answer had emerged. No theory as to motive had formed in my head.

Call the chief?

No way. I wouldn't interrupt LaManche's convalescence by drawing him back into the world of death.

I talked to Ayers, then Morin, then Santangelo.

Each laughed, said the allegation of wrongdoing on my part was ridiculous. Forget it, they counseled. The Jurmain case is closed. The old man is dead.

True.

Still.

I knew myself. Until I learned the identity of my accuser, the thing would keep eating at me. I'd never feel settled. Never be able to fully shut the door. And have no assurance that something similar wouldn't arise again.

Without mentioning specifics, I floated questions in the Service de l'identité judiciaire. In the morgue. In admin. In the secretarial office. No one had overheard or received complaints about me. No ruffled feathers. No bruised egos. No gripes.

Out of ideas and out of sorts, I went home.

The next morning, I flew to Charlotte.

* * *

On December 26, while Katy and I were diving off Ambergris Caye, Ryan sent a text message to my BlackBerry.

Break in Keiser. Call.

That evening, as Katy showered, I went out to the terrace and phoned. Ryan told me the following:

On Christmas Eve, a homeless man found a purse in a Dumpster behind a Pharmaprix drugstore on Boulevard Saint-Laurent. The contents included a comb, a hanky, and a nail file with the logo of a Hollywood, Florida, hotel.

Since the purse was found in Montreal, the SPVM caught the call. Hearing about it, and hoping for a Keiser connection, Claudel, the lead investigator on the case, went right to work. And scored.

At nine o'clock Christmas morning, Myron Pinsker identified the purse as belonging to his stepmother, Marilyn Keiser. Pinsker claimed to have given Keiser the file along with shampoos and lotions he'd bagged while vacationing at the Hotel Ocean Sunset in Florida the previous summer.

"Claudel says that after IDing the handbag Pinsker blanched and started shaking like he had the DTs. Claudel got him a glass of water, did the head-below-the-knees thing. As he's rebagging the evidence, Pinsker keels, the glass shatters, and blood flies everywhere."

"I assume Claudel did a deck dive, too."

"I see sun and sand have mellowed your take on humanity."

"Come on, Ryan. You know Claudel freaks at the sight of blood."

"I have to admit, Charbonneau's account was hilarious."

Michel Charbonneau is Luc Claudel's longtime partner.

"Picture this. Claudel's struggling not to toss his cookies, dialing for a medic, but his fingers are jumping all over the keys. Pinsker's on the floor with a shard up his ass. Or wherever. Claudel starts hollering for backup. Pinsker comes to, sees the purse, goes apeshit all over again, rocking and howling like a dingo."

"Genuine grief?"

"Precisely my question to Claudel."

"His answer?"

"'Do I look like a freakin' shrink?'"

I thought for a moment.

"How often is the Dumpster emptied?"

"Twice weekly. But the purse handle was hooked over an interior piece. There's no telling how long the thing was in there."

"The homeless man?"

"Harmless. Hoped his find would score him a six-pack."

"Latents?"

"Negative. The purse is fabric."

"So this big break is actually a nonstarter."

"So far."

"And the pension checks?"

"Cashed all at once at one location. No one remembers who brought them in. Signature's nothing like Keiser's. Name's illegible."

"The casher must have presented ID."

"Must have."

"What does Pinsker say?"

"Denies knowing anything about them."

Out on the bay, sails flashed tangerine in the last light of evening.

"What about my Oka samples?" I asked.

"Still cooling their heels in the DNA queue."

"Did you ask how long it would be?"

"They'll get back to me. When they stop laughing."

"Locate any relatives up in the Beauce?"

"Working on it."

No real news on Keiser, and nothing on Oka. So why the text message?

"When are you coming north?" Ryan's voice sounded lower, softer somehow.

"I usually get a call around January second."

With my free hand I twisted a bougainvillea vine.

"Remember the year we found Santa?"

Ryan referred to a bearded man who'd fallen down his chimney wearing long red underwear. His body was found three years later, on December 26, rigid as granite.

"Yeah." I smiled. "Good times."

"Charlie misses you."

"Give him a peck on the beak from me."

"He's practicing carols. Really nails the Chipmunk thing."

Though I laughed, a cold heaviness had curled in my chest.

"Please buy him a gift for me."
"Already got a cardigan with your name on the tag."
A soft breeze lifted my hair.
"Merry Christmas, Brennan."
"Merry Christmas, Ryan."

KATY AND I RETURNED TO CHARLOTTE ON DECEMBER 28, BRONZED and gorgeous. Or so we told ourselves. Pounds up and peeling was closer to the truth.

On the 29th, my daughter called for a late family Christmas. We met at Pete's house. My old house. It's easier now. Used to be a bitch.

Pete played chef. Standing rib roast for us. New York strip for Boyd, a very Ho Ho Ho kind of dog. Especially with a bellyful of steak.

Pete gave Katy a racing bike, the chow a rawhide bone, and me a gold David Yurman bracelet.

I was stunned, said it was way too much. Pete waved off my objections.

I wondered. Was my gift the reason for the surprising but delightful absence of the lovely and exceedingly busty young Summer?

Whatever. I kept the jewelry.

I spent New Year's Eve with Charlie Hunt. Dinner at the Palm, noisemakers, hats, slow dancing. After midnight we shook hands and went our separate ways.

Well, not exactly a handshake. But we each slept solo. Or at least I did.

Andrew Ryan: Tall, Nova Scotia Irish, sandy-going-gray hair, cornflower eyes.

Charlie Hunt: Very tall, exotically *mélangé,* black hair, jade eyes.

What was right with this picture?

What was *wrong* was serious history. And baggage roomy enough to swallow a Walmart.

Evenings, Ryan and I talked on the phone, but not as we had in the past. Our conversations stayed outside the guardrail, prudently distant from the dangerous ground of feelings and future.

We discussed LaManche. The chief had suffered a setback, an infection that would delay his return to work.

We hashed over the Keiser, Oka, and Villejoin investigations, everything we knew. Not much to hash.

Ryan had revisited those living on the Villejoin's block in Pointe-Calumet. Claudel had canvassed Keiser's building on Édouard-Montpetit. They'd learned which neighbors were neat, which drank, which were churchgoers, which were stoners.

Claudel had reinterviewed Keiser's stepson, Myron Pinsker, and again contacted her son and daughter in Alberta. Ryan had tracked down Yves Renaud, the nurse who'd discovered Anne-Isabelle Villejoin.

Everyone checked out. No one provided new facts.

Ryan had also reinterrogated Florian Grellier, the snitch who'd led them to the Oka grave, hoping to shake something loose. Grellier's story remained disappointingly consistent. He'd scored his info from an anonymous bar buddy. Beyond that, he knew jackshit.

On January 12, *Le Journal de Montréal* ran a short piece backgrounding Marilyn Keiser's disappearance and reminding readers about Christelle Villejoin. A flood of confessions and sightings followed. Stories ranged from "I killed them for their livers" to "I saw them in Key West with a tall black man." Apparently the guy was a snappy dresser.

A psychic swore Villejoin was still in Quebec, in a small, dark space. She'd seen no sign of Keiser.

Winter is my slow season up north. Waterways freeze and snow hides the land. Kids are in school. Campers and sportsmen stow their gear and grab their remotes.

Corpses miraculously found outdoors arrive solid as deer carcasses hung in a freezer. In those cases, the pathologist rules. Defrost. Y-incision.

Still, the wind-chill days generate plenty for the anthropologist. Folks die and putrefy in their beds. Folks crank up heaters or build fires that burn down the house. Folks off themselves in barns, bathtubs, and basements.

Perhaps Hubert still had a hard-on over the missing phalanges. Perhaps the tundra was atypically calm. Early January passed with no call from Montreal for my services.

While enjoying the sixty-degree sunshine in Charlotte, I examined three cases for the Mecklenburg County ME, worked on a research grant, cleaned closets, plastered and painted a cracked wall I'd been looking at for years.

In between professional and domestic chores, I spent time with my daughter. Unhappy with her job in the Public Defender's Office, Katy was considering a change, perhaps graduate or law school. I listened to her complaints and ponderings, murmured sympathy at appropriate points, rendered opinions when asked.

I also saw quite a bit of Charlie Hunt. He and I shared dinners, attended a few movies and a Bobcats game, played tennis twice. Though the kettle was racing toward a boil, I kept the lid on. A little neckin', as we say in the South, then home to bed with my cat.

Weeks passed.

The Oka woman remained *inconnue.* Unknown.

Marilyn Keiser remained *disparue.* Unfound.

On the 25th, as I was trimming Birdie's claws, my mobile rang.

Emily Santangelo.

Laying down the clippers, I hit speaker with one hand while pressing the cat to my chest with the other. Already peeved, Birdie began vigorous twist-and-push maneuvers.

"What's up?" I asked, tightening my arms.

Birdie meowed indignation.

"Am I catching you at a bad time?" Santangelo asked.

"Not at all."

Birdie started gnawing my knuckle.

"Stop that." Sharp.

"You all right?"

"Fine. Coroner got a stinker for me?"

"I'm not calling about a case."

Surprised, I thought for a moment.

"Have my DNA results come back?"

"No."

"Have Villejoin relatives been located up in the Beauce?"

"Not that I know of."

My blood turned to ice.

"LaManche?"

"No, no. The chief's fine. Well, relatively fine. He's responding to antibiotics, but will be out another six weeks."

Unconsciously, I relaxed my arms. Birdie wriggled free, launched himself, and shot from the room.

"Things just aren't the same without the old boy." Relief made me babble. "Did you ever glance over your shoulder and LaManche was just *there*? How does someone that big move so quietly?"

Santangelo ignored my blathering.

"Did Hubert contact you yesterday?"

"No." Brushing fur from my shirt. "Why?"

A click of hesitation in her throat.

"Emily?"

"This call is unofficial."

A tiny alarm pinged in my head.

"O-kaay."

"Come to Montreal, Tempe."

"You said no one needs me right now." I laughed. "Must be some flukey planetary alignment. Maybe Jupiter's getting it on with Venus and all of Quebec is awash in brotherly love. This has to be the longest stretch—"

"Fly up here."

Ping.

I clicked off speaker and placed the phone to my ear.

"Is Hubert still in a funk over those phalanges?"

A long, long silence rolled down from the north.

"Tell me," I prompted. "I can handle Hubert."

"He has them."

"What?" The fur-brushing hand froze on my chest.

"He has the phalanges."

"How?"

"Joe went back out to Oka. With Briel."

"How did *that* come about?"

"Briel offered to do it for the experience. Said she'd work Saturday to make up for any time missed." Santangelo's voice was flat, masking something under the words. "She argued that Joe would know what to do since he'd been present at the initial recovery. Hubert bought it. One of them spotted the phalanges while screening."

"When was this?"

"Friday."

"What the hell was a pathologist doing disinterring bones?"

"Apparently she took a course in forensic anthropology while on a postdoc in France."

I considered crushing or tossing the phone. Switched it to my left hand instead.

"Was Hubert planning to tell me?"

"He may not know. They finished late. I only found out because I was writing reports in my office when they got back to the lab."

A nonexpert crossing the line.

I took a deep, calming breath.

Exhaled.

"I'll be there Monday morning."

That night I saw Charlie again. Sushi. Sayonara.

Charlie knew I'd been burned by Ryan. And Pete. As on our previous nondates, he didn't press for more. I liked that.

So why the distance?

I didn't want to repeat last October's booty blunder. Or the embarrassing backseat high school romp.

But was that really it? I was free, so was Charlie. We weren't kids fighting hormones in Daddy's Buick. I thought of the statement that had so irritated Vecamamma. Women have needs.

Right on, Cukura Kundze.

So why the Puritan routine?

Was it Ryan?

Who knew?

What I did know was this. If I was keeping Ryan at arm's length, I was keeping Charlie somewhere on the edge of the Milky Way.

Monday morning. January 26. Back in Montreal and, thanks to Birdie, I was running late.

Still pissed over being ambushed by Dramamine, kitty carrier, and airplane the night before, the little drip fired through the open door when I turned to set the alarm. It took ten minutes of lobby searching and furniture moving to find him.

My neighbor Sparky Monteil happened in as I was scooping the escapee from behind the lobby sofa. Seeing the cat, he began ranting about filth and disease and the sucking of breath from babies.

Knowing I would miss the beginning of the Monday-morning meeting, and annoyed with Birdie, I failed to handle the situation with the finesse it required. Barbs were exchanged. Sparky swore he'd have me evicted, threatened that one day my pet might simply vanish.

Good thing Sparky's an Anglophone. Perhaps not. I can cuss like a sailor in my mother tongue.

At Wilfrid-Derome, I went straight to my office to shed my outerwear and grab pen and paper for the meeting.

Lisa is an autopsy tech with sun-tipped hair and a biblical rack. Cops attending autopsies always hope she will be the one handling their corpse.

As I unlocked my door, I noticed Lisa across the hall in the histo lab, deep in conversation with my assistant, Joe. Neither was smiling.

Spotting me through the window, both techs fell silent.

I waved.

Joe resumed logging organ samples.

Lisa gave a halfhearted flip of one hand.

Sexual tension?

Whatever.

Flinging my parka toward the desk, I dashed to the conference room.

Same green walls. Same table. Same roster of death due to malice, melancholy, folly, or fate.

Morin did the honors.

A dealer, held and punched by two rivals, dropped to the sidewalk and never got up. Probable homicide by rotation and hyperextension of the head.

A man noosed his neck to a tree and hit the gas in his pickup. Probable suicide by self-decapitation.

A meth addict slept naked on his balcony and froze to death. Probable accident by supreme stupidity.

As Morin talked, Briel made short quick strokes on her case list, frown lines going for a new personal best.

Santangelo alternated between drinking from and thumb-scraping the label off a bottle of spring water.

Ayers sat half turned from the table, focus fixed midpoint between the window and the blackboard.

Morin took the homicide, Santangelo the suicide. Ayers got the tweaker, Briel got a pass.

As paperwork was claimed, I studied my colleagues.

Stiff faces. Taut voices. No meeting of eyes.

First Lisa and Joe. Now this.

What the hell?

Sure, the Santas and elves were down, and February and March loomed long and dark. But I was sensing more than simple post-holiday letdown.

Anxiety over LaManche? Maybe. Budget cuts? Maybe.

Was I an issue? I was furious about the second Oka recovery. Were those around me picking up hostile vibes?

Morin turned in my direction.

"I suppose you've heard that additional remains were recovered at Oka."

Briel's eyes rolled up.

"Yes." Glacial.

"The coroner wants to know if an ID or exclusion is now possible."

"I'll talk to him." Nothing more. I'd decided to take my complaint directly to Hubert.

I couldn't help wondering why Joe had agreed to accompany Briel. He knew I'd be furious. Was redigging Oka his way of rebuking me?

When Morin queried new business, Santangelo cleared her throat.

"Actually, there is something."

We all settled back.

"I've taken a position with the Bureau du coroner." Santangelo's eyes flitted among Morin, Ayers, and me, resting only seconds before moving on. "I start February first."

Shocked, we just stared. Santangelo had been with the LSJML for fifteen years.

To my right, Briel paused, then recommenced doodling.

"I know this seems sudden." Santangelo palmed label scraps into a pile. "It's not. I've been thinking for a while that I need a change."

Santangelo's eyes flicked to me. I held them.

Why not mention this when you called me in Charlotte? Is this the reason for urging my return to Montreal? I asked neither question.

Santangelo looked away.

"Wow." Ayers slumped back.

"I know the timing sucks. You're still training new staff." Santangelo's tone was neutral. Evasive? "I'll help with the transition as best I can."

Ayers and Morin exchanged a quick glance. In it I could see a month of conversations.

"Are you sure?" Concern darkened Morin's already dark eyes. Perhaps weariness. Santangelo's departure meant another protracted hiring process.

"Yes." Santangelo dragged an outlier scrap to her pile.

"We'll miss you," I said.

"We'll still see each other." Santangelo tried to make it sound light. It didn't really work. "I'll be one flight down."

We all filed out. No jokes. No banter.

Coffee, then back to my office. After hanging my parka on the coat tree, I checked phone messages, then returned a few calls.

As I was disconnecting, my gaze fell on a letter that had worked its way out of the mound on my desk. The small white envelope was addressed to me at the LSJML, handwritten and marked personal. Curious, I picked it up and slit the seal.

A single sheet of paper had been scribbled with a one-line message.

Va-t'en chez toi maudite Américaine!!

Go home damn American!!

The writer had included no signature. Big surprise.

I checked the envelope. Local postmark. No return address.

"Thanks for the thought, chickenshit."

Sailing the note and its envelope back onto the heap, I crossed the hall to my lab.

And stopped dead.

BONES OCCUPIED EACH OF MY FOUR WORKSTATIONS. FLAKING AND warping suggested years of decay.

"What the f—" Under my breath.

"*Bonjour,* Doc."

I whirled.

Joe was washing his hands at the sink. "*Bienvenue.*"

Welcome back, my left buttock.

"What's this?" I flicked a hand at the two central tables.

"*Ossements.*" Smiling.

"Obviously they're bones." It came out sharper than I intended. Or not. "Who arranged them like this?"

The smile collapsed. "Dr. Briel."

"Under whose authority?"

Joe didn't move and didn't say anything. Behind him, water pounded from the spigot, bouncing tiny droplets onto the counter.

Striding to the closest set of remains, I rifled through papers secured to a clipboard.

My case form. My measurement list. My skeletal diagram. A request from Hubert for osteological analysis.

My brain lit up white-hot.

The door whipped from my hand so hard it slammed the counter. Ignoring the elevator, I flew downstairs.

Hubert was whaling up the corridor, mug in one hand, mail in the other. I closed in like a rat on a pork chop.

"What the hell is this?" Raising and waggling the clipboard.

Hubert's eyes flicked past me to check the hall at my back.

"Come into my office."

Damn straight.

Air whooshed from a cushion as Hubert planted his substantial derriere.

I remained standing.

"Have a seat."

I didn't move.

"Have a seat, Dr. Brennan." More forceful.

I sat, eyes lasering into Hubert's.

The chief coroner blew across his coffee, slurped, set down the mug. "Clearly you are upset."

"You sent Briel to Oka." Short and direct, not trusting my tongue.

"I didn't exactly send her."

"You authorized a pathologist to conduct a disinterment."

"You left half the burial behind."

"Hardly half."

"Dr. Briel offered."

"A freebie." Scornful. "On the house."

"Dr. Briel is an accomplished young woman."

"She may kick ass at the cha-cha-cha. But she's not an anthropologist."

"She has training and experience."

I shot forward in my chair. "Amateur hour!"

Hubert drummed the desk in annoyance.

"You said it yourself. This is homicide. If the case goes to court, you think Briel will qualify as an expert because she took some bullshit short course in anthropology?"

"It's only four bones."

"Four critical bones."

"Then you shouldn't have missed them."

"I'd have gotten them."

"You weren't here."

"I suggested a return to Oka before I left town. You declined my offer."

Hubert glared at me.

I glared back.

Seconds passed.

Hubert looked away first.

"You will analyze the phalanges, of course."

I said nothing.

"Is that it?" Message clear. Subject closed.

"That is definitely not it."

I yanked the Demande d'expertise form from Briel's clipboard and sailed it onto the desk.

Hubert glanced at it, up at me.

"And?"

"Replay the tape."

Deep sigh. So patient.

"Have you read the police incident report? Or did you storm down here totally unacquainted with the facts?"

"I read enough to know you asked a pathologist to do anthropology."

"*Câlice!* Not anthropology. Osteology. Simple sorting and counting. And again, I didn't *ask.* Dr. Briel offered."

"If she offered to shave your nuts would you let her do that?"

The chief coroner worked hard at looking prim. Didn't quite pull it off.

"There's no need for vulgarity."

True. But when that switch trips in my brain, civility boogies.

Hubert ran a hand down his face. Leaned back, flesh overflowing the armrests of the chair.

"Two weeks ago, SQ-Chicoutimi got a call about a man running bare-ass on a highway. Turns out it was some wingnut living near Lac Saint-Jean. Frontiersman type. Loner. Cops found him sitting in the snow outside his shack, gnawing on a rabbit. After bundling the guy off to psych, they tossed the property, found bones in an old storage locker.

"The coroner up there's a gynecologist name of Labrousse. The bones looked old, so Labrousse figured they'd washed up at the lakeshore, or eroded from an abandoned cemetery or Indian burial ground. Figured the happy hermit had collected and stashed them in his trunk.

"Bottom line, the remains came to us. Since you were away, Briel offered to take a look. I figured why not?"

"Here's why not." I tossed the whole clipboard not so gently onto the desk. "Briel went a whole *CSI* episode beyond"—I hooked quotation marks with my fingers—"taking a look."

As Hubert skimmed the pages, his brows rose, rippling his forehead.

"*Eh, misère.*"

"Age, sex, race, height. I'm surprised she didn't include Social Security numbers."

"I can see why you're upset."

"Insightful on your part."

"She means well. I'll speak to her."

"So will I."

Hubert picked up his pen and drummed it on the blotter, impatient for me to be gone.

I decided to power through. Why not?

"While I'm here, I'd like to discuss an issue arising from the Jurmain case."

Hubert aimed disinterested eyes at mine.

I reminded him of Rose Jurmain, L'Auberge des Neiges, the Chicago trip. Then I described the encounter with Perry Schechter, and related the tale of Edward Allen's tipster.

"I'm convinced the allegation came from this end, from someone with knowledge of my involvement in the case. Someone who was either too incompetent to know that no mistake was made or, worse, who wanted to embarrass me while knowing that no mistake was made."

"Ask the old man."

"He's dead."

First surprise, then irritation crossed Hubert's face.

"Are you accusing a member of my staff?"

"I'm accusing no one. Yet. But I will find the bastard who placed that call. I'm convinced it was someone working either at the LSJML or in the coroner's office."

Hubert thought about that.

"I'll pose some questions." Insincere.

"Thank you." More insincere.

I was at the door when Hubert spoke again.

"Dr. Briel is young and ambitious. I appreciate your understanding."

"I have a choice?"

By noon I knew the name of the old lady from Oka.

First I called Ryan. Then Hubert.

Each listened as I described the oddly deformed finger bones. Neither cared much about the camptodactyly. Both cared greatly about the ID.

Christelle Villejoin.

While I'd examined the phalanges, Joe had maintained a frosty distance. My assistant's fragile ego had obviously been bruised. Tough titties. Mine had also taken a hit. I knew I should have made a conciliatory gesture. Instead, I ignored the pouting.

But, as I'd worked, I'd been forced to make a not so proud admission to myself. I'd been as welcoming to Joe as I had been to Briel. Despite two years' proximity, I knew little about him.

Quick inventory. Joe was not yet forty. He lived alone, somewhere in the burbs, often biked to work. Disliked pickles. Drank Pepsi. Gelled and bleached his hair. Worried about being too thin.

Beyond those few inconsequential facts, I was blank on my tech's personal life. Was he divorced? Gay? Vegan? Sagittarian? I vowed to make more of an effort.

After reporting to Hubert, I went to apologize and appease. The histology, pathology, and anthropology labs were empty. Assuming Joe had gone downstairs for lunch, I did the same.

My assistant wasn't in the cafeteria.

But Ryan was.

Not in the mood for clever repartee, I dropped my eyes, hoping Ryan wouldn't spot me. Birdie's trick. If I can't see you, you can't see me. Stupid.

"Expecting George Clooney?" Ryan's form loomed above the table.

"Tiger Woods."

"What's the matter, buttercup?" Ryan deposited his tray and sat. "The other kids shunning you?"

I jabbed at my salad.

"Come on. Why the gloom-and-doom face?"

Christ. Where to start?

I told him about Santangelo's resignation.

"Can't blame a gal for moving on."

"No. But her leaving is . . ." What? ". . . symptomatic."

"Symptomatic?" Skeptical.

"Morale seems to have tanked in *médico-légale.*"

"Tanked?"

"What? Am I talking to a parrot?"

"Parrot?"

I rolled my eyes. Couldn't help it.

"Tell me, jelly bean."

"How's this for a morning? An asshole at my condo is trying to get me evicted because I own a cat. I have a new pen pal who thinks I'm the spawn of the devil. I had a bastard of an argument with Hubert. I ripped Joe a new anatomical part."

"Sparky-larky still on a rip?" We'd discussed my lunatic neighbor on more than one occasion.

I nodded.

"What's that guy do for a living?" Ryan downed a hunk of lasagna.

"I think Winston said he's with Montreal Public Works."

"Who's the pen pal?"

I shook my head, indicating I didn't want to pursue the subject.

"Think it could be greetings from the same creep who called Edward Allen Jurmain?"

I hadn't thought of that.

"I doubt it," I said.

Though few in number, I'd received hostile letters in the past. Typically, such mail was harmless venting by discontented next of kin or disgruntled convicted persons.

Full stop.

Might the letter have come from Sparky? I dismissed the thought. Anonymous intimidation wasn't really his style.

Poop in a package?

OK. Maybe.

"Why the blowup with lardass?" Ryan had moved on to the third on my list of complaints.

I described my trifecta in Hubert's office. The reexcavation at Oka. Briel's being allowed to examine the Lac Saint-Jean bones. Jurmain's nameless informant.

Ryan looked thoughtful. Or maybe he was trying to ID the brown goop oozing from the layers of his pasta.

"Lac Saint-Jean. Hm."

"Hm?"

"Maybe nothing. I'll do some checking, give you a call this afternoon."

"Any movement on Villejoin or Keiser?" I changed the subject.

"Not really. Claudel checked the airlines, VIA rail, local bus and taxi companies, Montreal travel agencies. If Keiser left town voluntarily, she either drove or went via hyperspace."

"Thumbed a ride on the Heart of Gold." I spoke without thinking.

"Blasted off with the Infinite Improbability Drive," he said.

Ryan and I were both fans of *The Hitchhiker's Guide to the Galaxy.* When a couple, we'd often sparred with our favorite quotes. Then it was fun. Now it just hurt.

Old habits die hard.

Ryan was smiling full on, eyes and all. Eyes like Bahamian waters. Eyes you could get lost in. Eyes I *had* gotten lost in.

But not again.

I looked away. "What else?"

"Claudel floated a nationwide APB on Keiser's vehicle. He checked local hospitals, and queried amnesia admissions across Canada. Or whatever term the psychobabblers use these days. Came up empty. Now he's looking at Keiser's neighbors, finding out how long each has lived in the building, previous addresses, that sort of thing."

"Keiser had an active social life."

Ryan chuckled. "Claudel told you?"

"Told me what?"

"The merry widow thought of herself as a child of the sixties. And a player."

"With men?"

Ryan nodded.

"She had boyfriends?"

"So she led the neighbors to believe." Ryan's smile could only be described as a smirk.

"Why is that funny? Because Keiser was elderly?"

Ryan formed a set of Vs with his fingers. Peace.

"Charbonneau's yet to locate a single old beau. He's working through the book club and knitting circle ladies. So far he's scored a lot of tea and cookies and one interesting tidbit. Keiser liked to spend time with nature."

"Meaning?"

"Sometimes she went off to the woods. To paint."

"Where?"

"She'd never say. She also frequented a place called Eastman Spa in the Eastern Townships."

It took me a moment to see the relevance.

"Retreats to the country. Sounds like Rose Jurmain."

Ryan nodded. "I'm running staff and guests, everyone connected with

L'Auberge des Neiges during the period Jurmain stayed there, cross-checking for overlap with Eastman. I'm also looking for any connection between Jurmain, Villejoin, and Keiser. So far, zilch."

Eastman Spa was upmarket, beyond my budget. "To afford Eastman, Keiser must have had something in her pockets."

"The estate isn't that big, maybe fifty thousand. There's a will. Pinsker gets five grand. The rest goes to the biological daughter and son. Claudel thinks both were genuinely shocked."

"At the paltry sum, or that they were primary heirs?"

"Both."

"Keiser and her offspring were estranged?"

"Yeah. Claudel's looking into why."

"Anyone profit from the Villejoins' deaths?"

Ryan shook his head. "The sisters owned the house and furnishings. They left a letter specifying that any proceeds of a sale go to the Humane Society."

Before heading upstairs, I bought a giant chocolate chip cookie.

Joe was at a microtome, slicing wax for specimen slides. I presented my bribe and did a mea culpa. Monsieur Moody seemed fractionally mollified.

I asked about his holiday. He said it was nice. Cooly. I asked if he had plans for the upcoming weekend. Exploration, he said. Really, I said. Of what? Stuff, he said, then refocused on his wax.

Okeydokey.

Conscience lightened, I turned to the Lac Saint-Jean case.

First, the evidence log that had been transported with the bones from Chicoutimi. No help there. The whole shebang had been bagged without reference to context. I assumed everything had been commingled inside the hermit's locker.

The gynecologist, Labrousse, was correct on one point. The remains were old. Bleaching, warping, and cortical flaking suggested long-term submersion in water.

The bones were also badly damaged. Many ended in jagged spikes abraded by years of wave action.

Though much was missing, it was clear I had four individuals, two adults and two kids. Briel had nailed that. But she'd misassigned a busload of elements. The adult female got several of the adult male's ribs and a juvenile radius. He got her right clavicle, left fibula, and sternum. Skull pieces had been jumbled all over the map.

The female looked white. Narrow nose, high nasal bridge.

From the broken facial segments, I could tell the male had remarkably wide cheekbones. Surprised, I checked maxillary fragments. All but one front tooth had been lost postmortem. I studied the lone incisor with a magnifying lense. Though abraded, the tongue surface retained a scooped-out appearance.

Interesting. Though far from definitive, flaring cheekbones and shoveled incisors were suggestive of Mongoloid ancestry.

For the kids I had too little to attempt racial assessment.

Briel came by around three, all lousy with enthusiasm. Expecting what? Praise? Thanks? Collegial discussion?

She got fiery disapproval.

Joe was cleaning beakers at the sink. He turned off the faucet. Over Briel's shoulder, I noticed his body go still. Listening.

Briel said little during my tirade. When I'd finished, she fled, jaw set, face scarlet as a tanager.

Joe turned and his eyes met mine. Flicked away. In that moment I saw censure. And something else. Disappointment? Disdain?

Again, I knew some gesture on my part was needed. Again, I let the moment pass.

I detest confrontation. Dislike change. Hubert. Joe. Santangelo. It had been an abysmal eight hours.

I was profiling the second Lac Saint-Jean kid when the lab door opened.

I looked up.

Until then, the day had been a love fest.

21

"KEISER HAD A HIDEY-HOLE." TYPICAL CLAUDEL. ARRIVING AT THE lab, he got straight to the facts. No *Bonjour.* No *Comment ça va?*

Surprised, I laid down the vertebra I was scoping with a hand lens.

"The building manager's a guy named Luigi Castiglioni, Lu to his close [illegible]. Yesterday, I'm doing follow-up with Lu, and the whole interview something's bugging me, like he's looking different than I remember. That, and the fact he's jumpy as hell. When I squeeze hard, the asshole lets slip he's just back from a six-month sojourn in the old country."

Quick calculation. July to January. That put Lu in Italy from the time Keiser disappeared through the time Claudel began to investigate.

I started to ask a question. Claudel held up a manicured hand.

"So I ask him. How's that work, you being overseas and here fixing toilets at the same time? Lu admits he's got a twin. Eddie. You believe that? Lu and Eddie. Sounds like some cheesy vaudeville routine."

I didn't interrupt.

"Conscientious citizen that he is, Lu doesn't want to get canned while he's on sabbatical, so he talks brother Eddie into acting as super in his absence. The scam flies. No one picks up on the swap. But the thing is, Lu's worked the building for twenty-two years. Probably schmoozing for tips. Whatever. He gets to know the tenants, learns what they're up to. Brother Eddie doesn't know jackshit."

I got the picture. Lu revealed something Eddie didn't know. New search. Bingo.

"Where was she?" I asked.

Claudel shook his head, as though amazed at the foibles of his fellow man.

"Turns out the old broad kept a getaway near Lac Memphrémagog."

I let the "old broad" reference pass. "She went there to paint."

Claudel dipped his chin. "Yeah. The place started life as her third husband's hunting shack."

"Third?"

"Got the lineup from the kids, Otto and Mona. They're a prize pair, by the way. Gotta revisit that."

"Oh?"

"Just a gut. Problem is, both were thousands of clicks from Montreal in Alberta when Mama dropped off the radar. There's no evidence of missing money. Still, I'm examining financials, looking for secret accounts, suspicious transfers or withdrawals, major debts, big purchases. Any flags over the past three months. Changes in routine, spending habits, income. It's a long shot, but we've got no short ones. I'm also checking the possibility of nasty habits—addiction, gambling, the usual. Doing the same for the stepson, Myron Pinsker."

"What about the three husbands?"

"Uri Keiser was numero uno. They married in 'fifty-eight, divorced in 'seventy-eight. He remarried in 'seventy-nine, moved to Brooklyn in 'eighty-two. Some bad blood there. Keiser's been in New York ever since. Pinsker was next. Married in 'eighty-four, taken out by an aneurysm in 'ninety-six."

"He'd be Myron Pinsker's father?"

"Yeah. Named Myron, too. Why would you keep saddling kids with a tag like Myron? That a Jewish thing?"

"I don't think so."

"Hubby three was Samuel Adamski. Keiser married him in 'ninety-eight. Interesting sidebar, the guy was fourteen years younger than his bride. She was sixty-one. He was forty-seven."

"Is Adamski still around?"

"Died in a boating accident in 2000. No tears there, at least not in Otto and Mona's world. Keiser's kids say the guy was a parasite and mean as a snake."

"When Adamski bought the farm, Keiser added electricity and plumbing to the hunting shack. Kept the whole deal secret. Property's still in Adamski's name, so it never popped on the radar."

"Her kids knew nothing about it? Her stepson?"

"Allegedly, no one did."

"Except Lu."

"Hard to believe, eh? Anyway, soon as Lu rolls on the shack, I haul ass to the country. Outside things look hunky-dory. Inside's a different story."

Claudel has a habit of rising up on his toes when he gets to the good part. He did that now. Descended.

"Interior's one room with a sleeping loft in back. Left-hand corner, by a wood stove, the carpet, one wall, and a sofa are burned to shit. Also one body."

I'd seen it before. A fire flames quickly, runs out of fuel, dies. One room can be toast, another undamaged.

"Where was the body?"

"Half on, half off the sofa."

"You sure it's Keiser?"

"Nah. My money's on Hillary Clinton."

I ignored the sarcasm. "You've told Keiser's kids?"

Claudel nodded. "Neither suggested they'd be booking airline reservations soon. Pinsker's on his way over here now." The thin lips went thinner. "Unless we got us one hell of a coincidence, it's Keiser."

I thought of Rose Jurmain. Anne-Isabelle and Christelle Villejoin.

"Any reason to suspect foul play?"

"Gee, how about Granny's pension checks turning up cashed? How about her purse being in a Dumpster a million miles from her crib? But there was no sign of forced entry, if that's what you mean. The place wasn't ransacked. No blood. The vic was fully clothed."

"Any obvious trauma? A gunshot wound? A blow to the head?"

"I am a detective. Not a pathologist."

Claudel's arrogance often goads me over the edge. Given the day's events, I was gripping the brink with my toes. But Claudel was right. My question was stupid.

That, too, made me cranky.

"Did you *detect* anything to suggest Keiser could have died elsewhere?"

"She was lying facedown. Contact with the floor preserved flesh on the chest and belly. Pooling looked right."

Claudel referred to the third of death's Triple Crown. Rigor mortis: stiffening in the muscles. Algor mortis: cooling of the tissues. Livor mortis: pooling on the "down" side.

Here's livor, short and quick. When the heart stops beating and chasing the blood around, gravity causes the heavier red cells to sink through the lighter serum and settle in the dependent parts of the corpse. The result is a purplish red discoloration known as lividity, or livor mortis, on the body's "down" side.

Like its colleagues, rigor and algor, livor works the clock, beginning twenty minutes to three hours after death and congealing in the capillaries in four to five. Maximum lividity usually occurs within six to twelve hours.

So. In addition to estimating postmortem interval, livor is useful in determining if a corpse has been moved.

Case in point. Had Keiser been lying prone while flying a purple bum, that pattern would have suggested she'd been moved after death. A darkened chest and belly were consistent with dying facedown.

"What about the car?"

"Parked in a lean-to in back."

I tried to picture the setup. Woods. Rustic cabin and shed.

"Is the property that isolated?"

"The nearest neighbors are a half mile away. Cottagers, gone since September. We're tracking them."

"Who's doing the post?"

"Ayers." Claudel tugged a very expensive cuff to check a very expensive watch. "Pinsker should be here by now. He's going to take a look at the clothes. What's left of them."

I got to my feet. "I'll ride down with you."

Petty, but I couldn't help myself. Claudel's phobia is the stuff of legend.

The man can calmly size up any crime scene. Blood-soaked sheets? No problem. Brain-spattered walls? Bring 'em on. Feces-smeared rugs? Groovy. To Claudel, crime scenes are telltale moments frozen in time. Violent moments, yes. But distant ones. And useful building blocks. In his thinking, each tableau is an exercise, a puzzle to be dissected and reassembled. Guts and gore talk, and one must listen intently.

But park a corpse on stainless steel and Claudel goes Jell-O in the knees. Yep. The guy can't handle cold flesh or morgues.

"Pinsker's identification of the body is a formality." Claudel tipped his head. The hawk nose shot a shadow across one cheek. "It's Keiser. I've got to get back on the street."

I watched Claudel's impeccably pressed buttocks disappear through the door.

An hour later it was Ryan.

"That the Lac Saint-Jean stuff?" Eyeing the bones spread before me.

I nodded.

"Looks old."

"It is."

"How old?"

"It's safe to say these folks didn't hang stockings this season."

"Forty years?"

I just looked at him.

"A Cessna 310 disappeared in 'sixty-seven en route from Chicoutimi to Quebec City. Gouvrard family. Parents, two kids. The last sighting was in the vicinity of Lac Saint-Jean, so thinking was the plane went down in the water. No wreckage was ever found."

Ryan handed me a paper. I glanced at it. Listed were the names and ages of four individuals.

Achille Gouvrard, 48
Vivienne Gouvrard, 42
Serge Gouvrard, 12
Valentin Gouvrard, 8

"Any chance there are antemorts after all these years?"

"File's on the way."

"You're good, Detective."

"Yeah, I guess I am."

"I owe you."

"I'll collect." Exaggerated brow flash.

Something stirred in my southern parts. I ignored it.

"Why did Lac Saint-Jean ring a bell for you?"

"Gouvrard's sister was married to a guy on the job, Quentin Jacquème. For years Jacquème floated a query on the anniversary of the crash. If anything turned up, he wanted to know about it."

"Got to admire such doggedness."

"Doggedness. Good word. The reminders stopped shortly after I came aboard, when Jacquème retired. Being former SQ, he was easy to locate."

"Thus the continued existence and quick access to a forty-year-old file."

"Thus."

"Sad about Keiser," I said.

"Yes," Ryan said. "But expected."

"Yes," I agreed.

When Ryan left I finished my analysis. Though each skeleton was fragmentary and most bones were weathered and damaged, there was sufficient data to determine that the family profile fit.

No one showed any obvious health or dental issues.

But what about Daddy's cheekbones and shoveled tooth? Probably normal variation.

Nevertheless, I'd have Ryan ask Jacquème about his brother-in-law's ancestry.

At four twenty I phoned Hubert to report Ryan's find.

"Nineteen sixty-seven." I heard leather strain as Hubert shifted in his chair. "So Dr. Briel's involvement becomes irrelevant. By the way, how did she do?"

"C minus."

Hubert made one of his indecipherable sounds.

"I can't sign off on IDs based on what I have," I said. "Antemorts are on the way, but I'm not optimistic. I've got very few teeth. None for the younger child."

"DNA?"

"Maybe mitochondrial, but that's iffy. Bone quality is very poor. What are the chances of locating maternal relatives?"

"*Tabarnac.* How many families could one lake hold?"

I remembered Hubert's words at Christelle Villejoin's grave. How many grannies go missing around here? I said nothing.

"Besides, the crash is ancient history."

"Ancient history can snap back in bad ways. *If* it's the Gouvrard family, legal issues might remain. Inheritance. Insurance. Liability."

"Madame Keiser is downstairs." Topic switch. Hubert's standard operating procedure when uncomfortable. "Ayers volunteered to do the autopsy first thing tomorrow."

I waited.

"Perhaps Keiser became disoriented and set herself on fire."

"There's no history of dementia."

"Shit happens."

I spent another two hours with the Lac Saint-Jean bones, listing details that might be useful once antemortem records arrived. I suspected Hubert was right. Mom, Dad, and two kids? What were the chances? Still.

Pelvic features told me the male and female were somewhere between the ages of thirty-five and fifty.

Gender determination is sketchy at best with preadolescent skeletons. I had only fragments of one, none of the other juvenile pelvis, so, in this case, the issue was a nonstarter.

The jaw and most of the head were missing from the older child, but arm and leg bone development suggested an age of ten to twelve years.

The younger child was represented by two vertebrae, three partial long bones, a calcaneous, and a handful of cranial fragments. Epiphyseal maturity in the proximal femur suggested an age of six to eight years. I also had three isolated molars, two deciduous and one adult. Wear facets suggested that all three molars had been fully erupted. Root closure suggested an age of six to eight years.

Why so little skull for the kids? Nothing sinister. The individual bones comprising young vaults are either separate or only partially fused. When the soft tissue sloughs, these bones often disconnect at the sutures, the squiggly lines along which they join hands.

All four individuals had cranial and thoracic fractures. The male had some lower-limb trauma. The smoothing of every broken edge made perimortem versus postmortem determination impossible.

La famille Gouvrard?

I reviewed my notes.

Adult genders: Consistent.

Adult and juvenile ages: Consistent.

Skeletal trauma: Consistent with an aviation accident. The male's lower leg injuries were as I'd expect for a person manning the controls.

Consistent.

Not enough. The male's cheekbones and shoveled incisor still troubled me.

I surveyed the empty lab. The silent printer. The winking message light on Joe's phone. The screen saver looping endlessly on his computer.

Usually Joe says *au revoir* when clocking out. Today he'd left without a word. Clearly, I'd need to lay in more cookies. But why the snit? Because I'd chewed out Briel? Try as I might, I could think of nothing major I'd done to deserve the current cold freeze.

Dejected, I let my eyes drift to the window. Twelve stories down, traffic flowed as streams of tiny red dots. Reflected in the glass was a slender woman, blurred features impossible to read. The tense shoulders suggested frustration.

Time to go.

After securing my calipers in a drawer and locking the lab door, I crossed to my office.

With the LSJML's new phone system, calls go directly to individual extensions. Unanswered ones roll straight to voice mail. Occasionally, contact to the main line is reported on paper.

I was zipping my parka when I noticed an old-fashioned pink slip amid the clutter on my desk.

I picked up and scanned the message.

Yes!

I snatched up the receiver.

CALLER HAS CONFIDENTIAL INFORMATION.

Perry Schechter's name was accompanied by a ten-digit sequence starting with 312.

Chicago.

Had Jurmain's lawyer discovered the identity of the bastard who set me up?

I dialed.

Four rings, then a way too smooth voice asked that I leave my name, number, and reason for phoning.

I did as directed, then slammed the receiver.

Could anything else go wrong today?

I checked the handwritten date and time. Schechter had contacted the lab at nine fifteen that morning.

The clock said six forty.

I decided to split and call again from home.

Sure. That'll work.

It didn't.

I tried once upon arrival, twice after sharing take-out pad thai with Birdie.

Vecamamma rang as I was collecting the dinner debris. She was considering cataract surgery, wanted my opinion. I told her to go for it.

I asked about Cukura Kundze. Vecamamma said that Laszlo's remains had been released by the coroner, and that his parents had organized a memorial service and interment. She'd attended, of course. Though sad, both Cukura Kundze and Mr. Tot appeared relieved that the boy was finally square with the Lord, at least from a funerary perspective. She described the coffin, the flowers, the music, the supper, Cukura Kundze's inappropriately magenta dress, and, of course, the minister's homily.

Familiar with policy concerning retention of samples in open homicide cases, I wondered how much of Lassie had actually gone into the ground. Didn't say it.

I asked about the investigation. Vecamamma knew nothing.

After disconnecting, I speculated for the hundredth time on what had happened to Lassie. Why had the kid been murdered? Where? By whom? I hoped his case wouldn't end up like thousands of others, in a forgotten box on the shelf of a police property room.

At eleven I went to bed.

The cat joined me sometime in the night.

I slept until eight the next morning. Driving to the lab, I had a session with myself. Hostility bad. Serenity good. Smell the roses. Better for health, longevity. Blah. Blah. Blah.

First thing, I called Schechter.

The same recorded voice smarmed the same directive. After dictating a second message, I recradled the receiver. Gently.

Staff meeting was the arctic affair it had been on Monday. No smiles. No jokes. No one wanting to be there.

Briel was absent. I learned she'd begun teaching a course at the med school in Laval.

As we dispersed, I pulled Ayers aside to ask why everyone seemed so down. Mumbling about fatigue and overwork, she hurried off to cut a Y in Marilyn Keiser's chest.

Back at my desk, I called the coroner's office. A new secretary picked up. I began my request. Stopped. Asked the woman's name. Adele.

I identified myself. Adele and I exchanged pleasantries. The new me.

"Has the Gouvrard file come in?"

"Un instant, s'il vous plaît."

I heard a clunk. Computer keys. A rush of air as the receiver was raised to an ear.

"*Oui.* Dr. Briel has it."

"What?" Sharp.

Silence.

I took a breath. "Sorry, Adele, but I'm confused. Why was the file sent to Dr. Briel?"

"According to the record she's handling the case."

"That is an error." So very polite. "Please replace Dr. Briel's name with mine."

Adele said nothing.

"If you have questions, please speak with Monsieur Hubert."

Two requests. Two "please's."

Adele hesitated, then, "Shall I collect the dossier and deliver it to you?"

"Thank you for offering. That's not necessary."

I was disconnecting when Joe stuck his head into my office.

"Anything for me?"

I started to ask for X-rays of the maybe-Gouvrard family. Remembered. Smiled.

Joe waited, face set in neutral.

Southern women are famous for knowing the right things to say. For conjuring words and phrases that put others at ease. It's a skill I admire but do not possess. That's being generous. When it comes to small talk, I suck.

At a loss for common conversational ground, I glommed onto a comment from yesterday's cookie enticement.

"Tell me something." A good Dixie girl opener. "You said you'll spend the weekend exploring. I find that intriguing." I didn't. My mind was on the Lac Saint-Jean bones. "Exploring what?"

Joe didn't turn away, but didn't exactly clamor for eye contact.

"It's just a hobby."

It wasn't really an answer.

"But the weather's so cold. What do you explore?"

Shoulder shrug. "Just stuff."

The dolt wasn't making this easy.

"Caves? Mines? Alternate dimensions?"

"Underground stuff. It's called drainsploring. It's no big deal. Do you want that girl poking around in the storage closet?"

The quick-change threw me.

"What girl?"

"Some chick's rummaging through your old cases."

So much for bonding.

"X-ray the Lac Saint-Jean vics."

Shooting to my feet, I crossed the hall to my lab.

The "chick's" back was to the door as she examined the contents of a box. Its label said LSJML-28723.

"Excuse me?"

When the girl whirled, two margarine braids whipped below a triangular bandana tied at the back of her head. Though easily six feet tall, she weighed about the same as your average middle-schooler.

"You startled me." Hand to chest.

I crossed my arms. Considered, but didn't tap a foot.

"And you would be?"

"Solange Duclos."

The name meant nothing. My face clearly said it.

"Dr. Briel's research assistant." Almost a whisper.

The Université de Montréal student. I'd completely forgotten.

"Who let you in here?"

"Dr. Briel gave me a key." She held it up.

I extended an upturned palm. Duclos dropped the key into it.

"Dr. Briel suggested I familiarize myself with dentition by going through old cases." Duclos's was the reddest lipstick I'd ever seen. Probably named Passionate Poppy or Chili Pepper Red.

I gestured Duclos out of the closet. Snatching up a spiral-bound reference, she scurried past me, book flat to her almost nonexistent breasts. After locking the door, I joined her.

Don't take it out on the kid.

"Did you check in with Dr. Morin?"

Duclos nodded, crimson lips twisted sideways.

"Other than *familiarizing*, did Dr. Briel leave further instruction for you?"

Duclos shook her head.

Great. Briel had a novice on the floor but wasn't even in the building.

Duclos held up a battered copy of Bass's *Human Osteology*.

"She gave me this. The chapter on dentition is really good. I know the teeth, of course, incisors, canines, molars, premolars, but I need to brush up on details." Not stammering, but close. "I'm shaky on mandibular versus maxillary, left versus right."

"Sit." I pointed at the only surface in the room not covered with bones. "There."

Duclos rolled a chair to the spot I'd indicated. As she folded into it I returned to the closet. Using a small round key on my personal chain, I unlocked a metal cabinet and withdrew a plastic tub.

Duclos watched my return with Frisbee eyes.

"Practice on these. Divide by categories, then sides, then uppers versus lowers."

The tub hit the counter with a crack.

After coffeeing up, I tried Schechter again.

Nope.

Next, I went to Briel's office. A gray envelope lay on her desk, return address SQ, Chicoutimi.

I humped back to my lab.

Psyched.

But not for long.

The Gouvrard records made the Villejoin file look rich in comparison. There wasn't a single X-ray. The medical and dental data were negligible. The typed reports were faded and smeared, probably the product of carbon copying. The handwritten notes were barely legible.

After three and a half hours of squinting and magnifying and translating from colloquial French, I had nothing more than when I'd started.

Achille, the father, had suffered from hypertension and eczema, conditions for which he'd taken medication. He'd stood five feet nine inches tall. Useless. I had no complete long bones. He'd broken three toes in an industrial accident at age thirty-seven. I had no foot bones.

An absence of dental records suggested Daddy wasn't into regular checkups.

Vivienne, the mother, had no medical condition that would have affected her skeleton. She'd had trouble with what would now be called acid reflux. She'd suffered from migraines. She'd lost a baby two months into a pregnancy three years prior to her elder son's birth. No height was recorded.

Mommy had undergone root canals in her first and second lower left molars. Both those teeth had been lost postmortem.

Serge, the elder brother, had fractured his right ulna at age six. That bone had not been recovered. He'd had measles at seven and chicken pox at nine. On his eleventh birthday, he'd suffered a mild concussion by falling from a tree.

Though the boy had visited a dentist and been treated for cavities, I had none of his teeth.

I looked at the clock. One ten.

Across the lab, Solange was still sorting and studying dentition. The neon lips made me think of the print they'd leave on a glass.

I tried Schechter again, left a third message.

Then I headed to lunch.

Natalie Ayers was in the cafeteria. She pointed to an empty chair opposite hers. I sat. Sensitive to the earlier brush-off, I avoided the subject of staff morale.

"Done with Keiser?"

Ayers nodded, teeth embedded in an egg salad sandwich.

"I assume it *was* Keiser."

"Yeah. Thanks to decomp and burning, her face and dentition were history. Fortunately, she wore a bridge. That survived. We got the antemorts. The thing was a match."

"What killed her?"

"Who knows? The internal organs were mush. X-rays showed no fractures, bullets, or foreign objects. I sent samples to tox, but I'm not optimistic."

"Did you find smoke in the lungs or trachea?"

Ayers waggled a hand. Maybe yes, maybe no. So it was unclear if Keiser was alive when the fire started.

"Was she a smoker?"

"According to Claudel, yes."

Ayers worked on the second half of her sandwich. I ate the remainder of my salad, then switched subjects.

"Briel's student is here but Briel's in Laval educating young minds."

Ayers snorted air through her nose. "No she's not. Our wunderkind is downstairs educating herself."

"Oh?"

"She came in as I was leaving, asked if she could look at Keiser. For the experience."

"She's something." I laughed.

"She is." No trace of a chuckle.

Ayers stirred her coffee. Tapped the rim of her cup. Laid down her spoon. "Sorry about earlier."

"No problem," I said.

"You're right, though. The atmosphere in our section has turned to shit."

"Because LaManche is gone?"

Ayers considered. "No. That's not it."

"Then why?"

"I don't want to tell tales. But I will say office tension is the reason Emily quit to work for the coroner."

"What do you mean?"

Ayers shook her head. "Ask Emily."

"She called me last week. Told me about Briel and Joe going back out to Oka, then urged me to get back up here fast. Never mentioned leaving the lab."

"Talk to her."

I vowed to do that as soon as possible.

Then events started crashing and the world seemed to veer off its orbit.

WHEN I RETURNED TO MY LAB, YOUNG SOLANGE DUCLOS WAS gone. Either Briel had corralled her, or the kid had left for the day. I didn't much care. I had tables full of bones and a coroner with a shortage of patience.

Naturally, it was an afternoon of interruptions.

I'd hardly stowed my purse when Claudel appeared. Anxious to resume my analysis of the Lac Saint-Jean vics, I asked few questions, just let him talk.

"*L'équipe du service d'incendie* has finished with Keiser's cabin."

Claudel referred to the arson boys, members of the chemistry section who determined cause and point of origin in suspicious fires.

"They picked up traces of accelerant on the carpet and sofa."

Arson.

"What was used?"

"They're working on it."

"Ayers couldn't tell if Keiser was breathing when the place went up," I said.

"This is not my first homicide. Dr. Ayers and I have discussed her findings."

Well, hot damn for you. I didn't say it.

I was settling with the Lac Saint-Jean vics when my cell phone buzzed in my lab coat pocket. I checked caller ID.

Perry Schechter. So badgering *can* pay off.

Unfortunately, the lawyer's "confidential information" was not the breakthrough for which I'd been hoping. While sorting Edward Allen's papers, Schechter had found a scribbled note containing a phone number beginning with a 514 area code. The accompanying message consisted of one word. *Rose.*

After disconnecting, I did a reverse look-up using whitepages.com. The number came back "unpublished or unlisted."

I called a contact at the SQ. He said he'd run the line and get back to me.

Ten minutes later he did. The number traced to a pay phone at the gare Centrale on rue de la Gauchetière Ouest.

Great. Montreal's downtown railroad station.

But Schechter's info wasn't totally useless. It told me two things.

Thing one: la gare Centrale accommodated both long-distance VIA rail routes and hookups to city and suburban metro lines. So my accuser could be a commuter, an out-of-towner, or a local desiring anonymity. Now I was getting somewhere.

Thing two: pay phones still exist. Who knew?

It was four fifteen when I finally got to refocus on the Lac Saint-Jean vics.

The lull didn't last.

I was opening the file of the younger son, Valentin, when male laughter razored into my concentration.

Ryan.

Joe.

Since the pathology, histology, and anthropology-odontology labs are all interconnected, I figured Ryan had entered at the far end and was cutting through toward my domain.

Rustling over the past hour had signaled that Joe was doing paperwork at his desk, directly in Ryan's path. I assumed the two were discussing carburetors or sports scores, or enjoying one of those frat-boy jokes that elicit the singularly annoying conspiratorial Y-chromosome guffaw.

The younger Lac Saint-Jean child, perhaps Valentin Gouvrard, was represented by two vertebrae, three partial long bones, a calcaneous, a handful of cranial fragments, and three isolated teeth. Ignoring the buddy-boy sniggers drifting in from next door, I arranged the sparse little collection.

Preservation was awful. A combination of soaking and wave action had removed most identifiable anatomical landmarks, and breakage had rendered accurate measurement impossible.

But the teeth allowed confirmation of my age estimate of six to eight. Here's why.

Unlike sharks or gators, humans are granted only two sets of choppers. Kids sport twenty. Grown-ups expand the assemblage to thirty-two by adding premolars and wisdom teeth.

Replacement goes thus. Around age six, the first permanent molars join the kiddy lineup. Around eleven or twelve the eight baby molars give way to eight adult premolars. During the teens and early twenties, two more adult molars join the back of each arch. No need to describe the incisor and canine action up front. We all know how that mess unfolds.

The younger child's first permanent and second baby molar had been recovered, both from the lower jaw on the right. Also the second baby molar from the upper right. I set the baby teeth aside.

I was examining the adult molar when a shadow fell on my hand. I glanced up.

Ryan looked uncharacteristically formal in a dark navy suit and crisp white shirt. His pale yellow tie had sprightly blue dots.

"Natty," I said.

"Thanks," he said. "Court day."

"Your testimony went well?"

"Wowed 'em."

"With your modesty." I returned the tooth to its vial. "Buttering up my assistant?"

"Not sure he's butterable."

"Meaning?"

"When I said you were thermally challenged he got all defensive, said I was being rude."

My left brow floated up.

"I was making a joke."

"Perhaps Joe is one of those people who believe that being rude is rude. Why the comment on my climatic capabilities, anyway?"

"Mr. Touchy was looking at pictures of a utility tunnel or something. I asked about it, just making conversation, couldn't have cared less. He described some nutball hobby. I said he must love the cold. He said that's what Dr. Brennan thought. I said—"

I raised a silencing hand.

Ryan took the hint. "Gouvrard antemorts gonna put this to bed?"

I shook my head. "So far the file's of limited use. Mama had migraines and bellyaches. Daddy had a rash. The older kid broke an arm, but I don't have those bones. Daddy smashed his foot but I don't have those bones."

"Find anything exclusionary?"

"No. The ages and adult genders play. Ditto the injury patterns. The bone quality is crap, but consistent with forty years underwater." I wiggled upturned fingers, indicating frustration. "There's just nothing unique, nothing to make me comfortable with a positive ID. Anything new on Villejoin?"

"Grellier's been leafing through mug shots the past couple days. Thinks he may have spotted his bar buddy. Punk name of Red O'Keefe. Aka Bud Keith. Aka Sam Caffrey. Aka Alex Carling. Creative guy. Usually these toads stick with the same initials. Makes it easier to keep the monogrammed tea towels."

"What's his story?"

"Four-time loser, all petty stuff."

"O'Keefe's in jail now?"

Ryan shook his head. "Been on the street since 1997. Served his full stretch, so he's not on anyone's call sheet. Former PO says his last known address was in Laval. While we're running him to ground I'll cross-check his rich list of monikers against names in the Jurmain and Villejoin files."

"Worth a shot," I said.

"Got nothing else."

"You talk to Claudel lately?"

"We keep missing each other."

I told him about the accelerant in Keiser's cabin. Likely arson.

Ryan opened his lips, as though to comment. Or share a thought. Instead, he checked his watch.

"Time to put the chairs on the tables and kill the lights."

"Meaning?"

"I'm outa here."

That night I picked up shrimp curry with veggies. Birdie downed the crustaceans but spit the carrots and peas on the rug after licking off the sauce.

I tried reading a novel but couldn't focus. I kept picturing Rose Jurmain alone in the woods. Anne-Isabelle Villejoin hemorrhaging on her kitchen floor. Christelle Villejoin trembling on the edge of her grave. Marilyn Keiser in flames on her couch.

I phoned Harry, but she was out. So was Katy.

Frustrated and antsy, I decided to assemble a chart. Perhaps a pattern would emerge once facts were placed on paper. Or converted to megabytes.

Opening a blank document on my laptop, I created three columns, then entered what was known about each woman.

Rose Jurmain

Fifty-nine, but looked older
American (Chicago)
Wealthy background, cut from father's will, estranged from family
Lesbian, lived with partner, Janice Spitz
Religion?
Suffered from depression
Prescription drug and alcohol abuse
Estate goes to?
Traveled to Quebec to view foliage, L'Auberge des Neiges
Body found on surface in woods near Sainte-Marguerite thirty months after disappearance, skeletonized, scavenged by bears
No perimortem skeletal or cranial trauma

Anne-Isabelle/Christelle Villejoin

Eighty-six, eighty-three
Pointe-Calumet, Quebec
Spinsters, lived together
Catholic, active in church
No alcohol or drug use
No car or travel
No extended family
Cats
Estate goes to Humane Society
Anne-Isabelle bludgeoned to death in home, overkill. Christelle disappeared on same date.
ATM card used on east side of city hours after attack

Tip from Florian Grellier following DUI arrest (info obtained from unknown bar patron; O'Keefe plus AKAs?) concerning Christelle
Christelle's body found in shallow grave near Oka eighteen months after disappearance, skeletonized
Cranial fractures indicate blows with a shovel (Anne-Isabelle beaten with cane)

Marilyn Keiser

Seventy-two
Widow, lived alone in apartment in Montreal, Boulevard Éduard-Montpetit
Married three times
Son and daughter, Otto and Mona, in Alberta, estranged
Stepson, Myron Pinsker in Montreal
Hippie. Active social life.
Jewish
Cabin near Memphrémagog. Existence known only to building super, Lu Castiglioni
Owned and drove auto, took local trips
Vehicle found at cabin
Fire. Accelerant indicates arson.
Found in cabin three months after disappearance, body decomposed and burned
Ayers autopsy. No obvious cause of death.

I stared at the lists, willing an idea to go off in my mind. Or on. Like an overhead bulb in a comic strip.

Didn't happen. Only questions emerged. I began jotting them down.

The Villejoins were Francophone. Rose Jurmain was American, undoubtedly Anglophone. Did Marilyn Keiser speak French or English? Or both?

Keiser's estate would go to her kids. The Villejoin sisters left everything to the Humane Society. Who stood to benefit from Rose Jurmain's death?

Keiser was Jewish. The Villejoins were Catholic. Rose Jurmain?

Keiser had two kids. The Villejoins and Jurmain had none. Did Rose's partner, Janice Spitz, have offspring?

An American lesbian with substance abuse problems. Two spinsters who rarely ventured from their home. A socially active grandmother married three times and estranged from her kids.

Did these women have anything in common besides violent death?

Keiser and Jurmain liked back-to-nature getaways. The Villejoins never left Pointe-Calumet.

Keiser and Jurmain had large families from whom they were disconnected. The Villejoins had only each other, maybe distant relatives in the Beauce.

The Villejoins were bludgeoned. Jurmain and Keiser had suffered no skeletal trauma.

Keiser was torched in her country chalet. Anne-Isabelle was left in her home. Christelle was buried in a shallow grave. Jurmain was dumped on the surface.

Were we looking for linkage that didn't exist?

I started anew, focusing on commonalities.

Every victim was female.

Every victim was old or appeared to be old.

Every victim died within the past three years.

Except for Anne-Isabelle, every victim was found in a remote wooded area.

Coincidence? I didn't believe it.

I was logging off when window glass exploded into the room.

Heart hammering, I dove for the floor.

I LAY BELLY TO THE CARPET, ARMS FLUNG OVER MY HEAD. I SENSED stinging on my left shoulder and cheek.

Traffic sounds drifted in from the street. A man singing. The hum of a transformer next to the building behind mine.

Inside the condo, nothing but quiet.

Cold air was rapidly chilling the room.

I opened my eyes. The upended lamp was out. Light from my computer screen sparked fragments of glass scattered around me.

Then, in the stillness, I heard a soft crunch.

A footstep?

My breath froze in my throat.

Pushing with my palms, I hopped up into a squat and twisted.

Birdie was staring at the window with round yellow eyes, one forepaw frozen like a setter on point.

"Birdie," I hissed. "Come here."

The cat kept staring.

"Bird." I reached out a hand. It was shaking.

Birdie took a tentative step toward the window, nose up and twitching, instincts roused by the unfamiliar scent of outdoors.

Keeping low, I duckwalked across the room, scooped and pressed the cat to my chest, then strained for further sounds. Did I sense another presence in the condo?

My ears picked up nothing but Birdie's breathing and my own racing heart.

As my vitals normalized, questions ricocheted in my head.

What the hell had just happened? An explosion in the restaurant across the alley? A collision in the street?

Had someone fired a missile? A cherry bomb? A bottle rocket?

Who?

Kids, drunk or stoned or simply careless?

Or had my window just taken a bullet? If so, had the shooting been accidental? A random drive-by?

Had the hit been intentional, the barrel aimed specifically at me?

Probably not, or the shooter had very poor aim.

To intimidate?

Sparky?

Was my neighbor escalating his campaign to oust me from the building?

Sudden recollection. *Go home damn American!!*

Was the letter from Sparky? Someone more dangerous? Should I have taken the message more seriously? Was the sender a genuine threat?

Why had I refused to discuss the issue with Ryan?

Simple. I'd traveled that road. I knew Ryan would kick into gear and tag me with round-the-clock guards. Or a listening device on my bedside lamp. Or an ankle bracelet that sounded an alarm if I raised my voice.

Had Ryan's tossed-off suggestion been right? Had the letter writer also placed the call to Edward Allen Jurmain?

Sparky?

Someone more malevolent?

Professional slander.

Hate mail.

Incoming projectiles.

Were the caller, the sender, and the window blaster one and the same?

I picked up the phone and dialed 911.

A unit showed up within minutes. The cops listened, dutifully checked the window, made a few notes. Then we all went outside.

Broken glass littered the lawn, but there wasn't a bullet casing or spent rocket in sight. We agreed on a probable point of origin, a cement ledge behind a pizza parlor across the alley. The spot is a popular hangout for kids and street people.

The cops were aware that I knew the drill, didn't try to fool me. Property damage, no personal injury. The skirmish would receive the same level of attention as a snatched pair of panties.

Unless I turned up dead in the immediate future. Then the incident would be investigated to Yonkers and back.

When the cops left I went to the basement for a piece of the plywood Winston keeps on hand. This has happened to me before, though with somewhat less flair.

I'd barely wedged a patch into place when Ryan called. The man's network makes the CIA look amateur. Nifty if you need info. Annoying when you're the gossip traded.

I assured Ryan I was fine.

"You think it's this dickhead neighbor of yours?"

"I don't know."

"Who else have you pissed off?"

I used silence as an answer.

"You there?"

"I'm here."

"Got any theories?"

"Kids with fireworks."

"Got any other theories?"

I reminded him of the letter, and granted that maybe, just maybe, he could be right concerning Edward Allen's informant. I'll give it to him; he didn't say I told you so.

"What do you intend to do?" he asked.

"Fix the window," I said.

"I could be there in ten minutes."

"I'm good."

There was a brief pause. Then, "I found something."

I suspected the segue was another shot at a foot in my door.

"I ran Red O'Keefe's name against the Villejoin and Jurmain files. Got nothing. Then I tried the aliases."

Ryan paused for effect. I waited.

"The Villejoins paid for everything by cash or money order, and recorded expenditures in a ledger. Unfortunately, they didn't bother with dates. But around the time of Anne-Isabelle's murder, a handyman removed a dead pine from the sisters' backyard. The entry appears as a one-hundred-fifty-dollar payment to one M. Keith."

"You're thinking it's Bud Keith." In French, *Monsieur* is abbreviated *M.* Monsieur Keith. Aka Red O'Keefe. "That could be huge."

"Could be."

That night I tossed and turned for a very long time. It wasn't just the window. Questions bombarded me from all cardinal points.

You know how you play games when you can't fall asleep? I envisioned four columns, similar to the three I'd created for Jurmain, the Villejoins, and Keiser. I even titled them. Mentally.

The Grudge. The Gouvrards. The Grannies. The Gloom.

Adrenaline-buzzed, my mind ping-ponged among them.

The Grudge: Though Ryan's comment had irked me, I had to admit his reaction was plausible. The letter. The accusation. Perhaps the assault on my window. Clearly, I'd pissed someone off.

Who? What was the gripe? How could I smoke the rodent from his hole?

The Gouvrards: The Lac Saint-Jean bones were in wretched condition. The antemortem records were useless, given what had been recovered. At least for the adults and the older child. There'd been so many interruptions I'd yet to read little Valentin's file.

Were the vics in my lab actually the Gouvrards? Would the degraded bone yield anything that could be sequenced? Could an appropriate relative be located? Without DNA, how would I resolve the issue?

The Grannies: In the past three years, four elderly women had rolled into the morgue, one fresh, two skeletal, one burned and decomposed. Though cause of death was unclear for Rose Jurmain and Marilyn Keiser, unquestionably Christelle and Anne-Isabelle Villejoin had been murdered.

Why such abuse of the old and frail? By whom? Red O'Keefe–Bud Keith? If so, what could I do to help nail his ass? Was O'Keefe–Keith responsible for more killings?

Did Myron Pinsker fit into the mix? Marilyn Keiser's daughter or son, Mona or Otto? How? If not a family member, who had cashed Keiser's pension checks?

If the deaths were linked, would it happen again? Was a predator out there even now, prepared to kill? What could I do to prevent that, to protect other old ladies?

I thought about murder in general. With each passing year the violence seemed to increase in frequency and decrease in rationality. People were shot for handing out pink slips, for taking too long to bag burgers, for driving too slowly or following too close.

My four grannies had all been murdered, I could feel it in my gut. For what? By whom? I wanted the situation to make sense, but it didn't.

The Gloom: Normally, I'd have sought counsel from my coworkers. But the mood at the lab was tense and unreceptive. LaManche was ill. Joe was sulking. Hubert was angry. Santangelo was leaving, and I didn't even know why. Ayers was acting cool and aloof. Briel's unrelenting pressuring was inexplicably grating.

On and on. Over and over. Faces. Names. Rose Jurmain. Anne-Isabelle and Christelle Villejoin. Marilyn Keiser. Myron Pinsker. Florian Grellier. Red O'Keefe–Bud Keith. Sparky Monteil. Achille, Vivienne, Serge, and Valentin Gouvrard.

The glowing orange digits said 1:15, then 2:18, 2:43, 3:06.

Then the alarm was chirping.

In a fog, I rolled over and palm-smacked the button.

The next sound I heard was a ringing phone.

Groggy, I reached out and dragged the handset to my ear. Clicked on.

"Mm."

"You OK?" Ryan.

"Dandy."

"Just checking."

"Jesus, Ryan." Sitting upright. "What time is it?"

"Ten fifteen."

I checked the clock.

"Shit!"

"You coming in? I've got some more—"

"Thirty minutes."

Flying across the room, I yanked undies from the bureau, then threw on yesterday's jeans and sweater. In the bathroom I had a thirty-second moment with the Sonicare, splashed water on my face, yanked my hair into a pony, and bolted.

I MISSED STAFF MEETING BY ALMOST TWO HOURS. ON THE ERASABLE board, the square by Morin's name said *Témoignage.* Testimony. I wondered if it was the same trial for which Ryan had been subpoenaed.

Sprinting down the hall, I happened to glance to my right. Natalie Ayers's door was ajar. She was at her desk.

My first reaction was surprise. Normally the pathologists were downstairs by that time of morning.

It took a moment for details to register.

Ayers was sitting with elbows on the desktop, shoulders hunched, head hanging between upraised hands. Discarded tissues littered the blotter.

Reversing, I gently pushed the door inward.

"Natalie?"

Ayers's head snapped up.

I looked into eyes that were red and swollen.

"Has something happened?"

Ayers shook her head, tried faking a smile. It was a lame attempt.

"What is it?" I prodded.

The teary eyes drifted over my shoulder out into the hall.

Without waiting for an answer, I closed the door, took a chair, and assumed a listening posture. Message: I'm here until you talk.

Ayers drew a shaky breath. Plucked a clean tissue. Leaned back.

"I screwed up on Keiser."

I wiggled my fingers. Give me more.

"The poor woman was shot." Ayers's mascara was everywhere, her face an ink drawing left under a tap.

"Go on."

"I checked the X-rays, looked for exit and entrance wounds, fragments, you know the routine. There wasn't a single indication of a gunshot wound. Nothing. Nada."

I nodded.

"She must have been rising up, or maybe doubling over to protect herself. The bullet was small caliber, entered at the shoulder, ran longitudinally down the right erector mass, and exited without nicking a bone or organ. I've never seen anything like it."

"You snagged the track by making cross-sectional cuts?"

"*I* didn't snag anything." Ayers swallowed. "Wonder girl found it."

"Briel?" I masked my surprise poorly.

Ayers nodded, causing tears to breach her lower lids. She jabbed the wadded tissue at her cheeks.

"When?"

"During her pajama-party autopsy session last night."

"You gave her permission to examine Keiser?"

Ayers nodded. "I figured hell, why not? She's an eager beaver, wants to learn."

"Did Briel report the discovery to you?"

Ayers snorted her contempt. "How would that advance her precious career?"

"She went straight to Hubert?"

"What do you think?"

I thought she probably had.

"And get this. Hubert's given her permission to speak to the press."

"When?"

"Tonight." She told me the name of the show. I'd heard of it, but never watched it. "Should make for great viewing. They'll probably sell the movie rights."

"How did the media learn Keiser had been found?"

Ayers shrugged both shoulders while blowing her nose hard.

"Why would Hubert allow Briel to go on air?"

Ayers flapped her tissue-free hand. "You've been away. You don't understand. The Keiser and Villejoin investigations have been going nowhere. The cops and the coroner have been taking heat. Finding Keiser makes everyone look like they're working hard."

"Sonovabitch," I said.

"Sonovabackstabbingupyoursbitch."

Back in my office, I sat motionless, tiny wings fluttering in my brainpan. My lower centers were trying to snag my attention. Why? What word or name had triggered the feeling?

Briel? Keiser? Hubert? Media? Gunshot wound?

Hard as I coaxed, the moth-notion refused to venture into the light of conscious thought.

I was still swinging mental nets when my desk phone shrilled.

Ryan skipped the preliminaries.

"Want to meet O'Keefe?"

I drew a blank.

"Earth to Brennan. Red O'Keefe? Florian Grellier's bar buddy?"

"You've got him?"

"The gentleman awaits as we speak."

Red O'Keefe. Aka Bud Keith. M. Keith?

"Does he admit to working for the Villejoin sisters?"

"Funny. I plan to discuss that very topic."

"How did you find him?"

"O'Keefe's former probation officer has one helluva network."

"What's his story?"

"Pumps gas part-time at a Petro-Canada station on Boulevard Décarie, lives in a flop around the corner. O'Keefe and I are about to have a chitchat. Care to observe?"

"When?"

"Now."

I glanced across the hall. Through the window, the Lac Saint-Jean bones lay as I'd left them.

"I'll be right down."

The SQ interrogation room could have been part of any cop shop on the planet. Blank walls, battered table and chairs. Today the small space smelled faintly of gasoline, the aroma introduced, I assumed, by the lone occupant's grease-stained parka.

Occasionally my presence is requested at the questioning of a suspect.

Today was one of those times. I assumed Ryan's motive was the usual. Afterward he'd want my take on the guy.

O'Keefe looked up when Ryan and I entered, hooded eyes hard and analytical, as though dissecting the world and everyone in it. His hair was stone gray, styled by someone probably calling herself a "creative director" and charging a bundle. The cut was an odd contrast to the blue-collar outfit.

Ryan introduced himself and held out a hand. O'Keefe's fingers remained firmly laced atop his wool tuque and mittens.

Ryan queried O'Keefe's preference of French or English.

The cold glare held.

We sat. Ryan placed a folder on the table. O'Keefe ignored it. Us.

Perhaps because of the surname, perhaps for my benefit, Ryan proceeded in English. "Thank you for coming in today, Mister O'Keefe. I'll try to take up as little of your time as possible."

O'Keefe's eyes slid to me, returned to Ryan.

"Dr. Brennan and I work together."

Vague. Let O'Keefe wonder.

"You are presently employed as a gas station attendant?"

O'Keefe remained impassive.

"I know this is tedious, but I need to verify facts for my report."

I'd seen Ryan conduct dozens of interviews, knew what he was doing. Start out easy, gain the suspect's confidence, causing him to reveal things he might otherwise hide, allowing him to contradict himself. Then move in for the kill.

Eyeballing this suspect, I wondered how successful the tactic would be. I knew from Ryan that O'Keefe had graced facilities in a number of provinces.

"It is O'Keefe, isn't it?" Ryan opened but did not glance at the file. "There seems to be some confusion on the name."

"Let's not dick-dance around. We both know I got a sheet." O'Keefe's speech was Anglophone, working-class, with an accent that sounded more Eastern Seaboard than Montreal.

"Let's not." Ryan's pleasant tone now had an edge. "Let's talk about Florian Grellier."

"Who the fuck is Florian Grellier?"

"Let's try this one. Bud Keith."

O'Keefe hitched his shoulders. "I got a stage name. So what? So did Judy Garland."

"You ever do yard work? Tree removal, that sort of thing?" Another of Ryan's ploys. Change tack. Switch to a probably touchy subject. Throw the interviewee off.

Not O'Keefe.

"Think she'd a got that star in Hollywood as Frances Gumm? Wait. I got a good title for the movie." O'Keefe arced a hand, as though spanning a marquis. *"A Star Ain't Born."*

No one laughed.

"Tree removal?" Ryan pressed.

"I've done a lot of things."

"Tell me about Pointe-Calumet."

"Hear it's nice in summer. Real green."

"Did you tell Florian Grellier you knew the location of a buried body?"

"What the fuck?"

Ryan waited. The silence worked.

"That what this dickhead Grellier told you?"

"Answer the question."

"How can I do that when I got no clue who this freak is?"

"I'll paint a picture. You're in a bar. Grellier's buying. You're eager to keep the shots coming."

"No cigar. I'm a beer man."

"Come on, Red. What was it? You got drunk, began running your mouth to impress your new pal? Or maybe you got creative to gain some street creds? The guy's buying, so you keep spinning."

"This Grellier. He finger me for this?"

"Picked your smiling face from a whole lot of others."

"Let me guess. His ass is looking to do time."

Ryan neither confirmed nor denied.

O'Keefe thought a moment. Then, "I was a cop, I'd be asking myself, a guy trades something like that? Why? What's to gain? I'd be thinking the shitbag's probably gaming the system."

Ryan didn't argue with O'Keefe's logic.

"Let's try another name. Christelle Villejoin."

"That some chick says I owe her money? Bad news, I got none."

"Christelle Villejoin was eighty-three. Someone cracked her skull and buried her in the woods."

I watched O'Keefe for signs of agitation. The guy's face remained a stone mask.

"Christelle's sister was eighty-six. She was beaten to death with a cane."

"You got some kind of hearing disorder? I already said. I never met your snitch. Know nothing about no stiff in the woods."

"How about we back the attitude down, Red. Or is it Bud?"

"Look, I ain't who I used to be. I've got gainful employment now."

"Spare me your Eagle Scout bullshit."

O'Keefe jabbed a thumb at the folder. "You got my sheet. I played some cons. Did snatch-and-drops. Credit cards. I ain't your guy."

"Where were you on May four, 2008?"

"Fuck would I know? Where were you?"

Ryan again used silence.

O'Keefe flipped his tuque, flipped it again. Smoothed it with one hand. Then, "This guy Grellier's a crackpot. You got nothing. Screw you."

"Screw me?" Quietly.

O'Keefe lunged forward, temples pulsing with tiny veins. "You reading me on this? I don't know no one named Grellier. Got nothing to do with dead old ladies. I don't know what the fuck you're talking about."

"I'm talking about murder, you dumb shit."

"You can wipe your ass with any more questions."

The two men glared at each other, noses inches apart. Tense silence crammed the tiny room. This time Ryan broke it.

"An officer will bring you pen and paper. You can write, can't you, Red? Don't sweat the spelling and punctuation."

O'Keefe slumped back and kicked out his feet. The hooded eyes again crawled to me.

"Your little friend don't say much, but she's smokin'."

Ryan scribbled in his spiral, tore off the sheet, and slapped it on the table.

"I'll need proof of your whereabouts on these dates." Pure ice. "Take your time. I know your social calendar probably stays packed."

Ryan got to his feet. I followed.

"And don't make travel plans."

A reptilian smile curled O'Keefe's lips. "That was good." Pointing at Ryan. "Got that Horatio Caine thing going. Get you some aviator shades, you're on your way."

Ryan and I walked to the door.

O'Keefe spoke again to our retreating backs.

"Smokin' doc, you come to the station I'll slip you a wax job."

"IMPRESSION?" RYAN ASKED.

"I need a shower."

"He said you were smokin'."

"The guy has good hair."

"Yeah. I noted that. Walmart clothes. Wall Street do."

It was past two, and the cafeteria was deserted. Ryan and I had just bought vending machine sandwiches. My ham salad looked like it might have been made during the Tet Offensive.

"Volatile personality."

"Agreed. The guy's coolness itself, then suddenly the temper slips its leash."

"Do you think he's dirty?"

Ryan set his briefcase on a table by the machine, pulled out and opened a file.

"O'Keefe was straight up on one thing. He's got no history of violence. There are some sealed juvies in here. I could get those if I need them. His first arrest was in 'sixty-eight. Purse snatching. Got probation." He flipped pages. "Busted in 'seventy-two for passing bad paper, more probation. Did his first slap in Bordeaux from 'seventy-five to 'seventy-eight. Credit card fraud." More pages. "Bump in the late eighties in Halifax, another in the early nineties in Edmonton. Credit cards both times. Last jolt was back here in Quebec, 'ninety-six to 'ninety-seven."

"Where's O'Keefe from?"

"Moncton. Real name's Samuel Caffrey."

"What does he do when he's not serving time?"

"Works various cons. Picks up jobs at day labor centers. Doing shift work for factories, working for local moving companies. Occasionally takes on part-time employment, like pumping gas."

"He ain't who he used to be." I mimicked O'Keefe.

"Imagine that."

We had the thought simultaneously.

"I'll check to see if anyone moved in or out of the Villejoin neighborhood around the time of the attack," Ryan said.

"Or had their house painted."

"Or roof repaired."

"M. Keith." As we crossed toward the elevators. "The name's not that common in Quebec."

"No it isn't. I plan to float O'Keefe's picture around Pointe-Calumet, see if any of the Villejoin neighbors remember him."

I told Ryan about my conversation with Ayers.

"Is Briel really that good?" First the phalanges, now the bullet track. He didn't say it.

"She blew it on sorting the Lac Saint-Jean vics."

"How's that going?"

"I plan to finish with the younger kid *tout de suite.*"

I was punching for an elevator when a question occurred to me.

"You said the Villejoins had a savings account, right?"

Ryan nodded.

"How did they pay the bills they recorded in their ledger?"

"I can find out. Why?"

"We know they didn't have credit cards or a checking account. They didn't use the Internet. Maybe they kept cash in the house."

"Go on."

"Say they hire a handyman, pay him. He sees the stash in the cookie jar, decides to return later and help himself. Maybe one of the sisters surprises him, things go south—"

I let the thought hang.

A ghost of a smile played Ryan's lips.

"Not bad, Brennan."

* * *

It was as if the gods were conspiring against me. Or at least one among them had a grievance.

Arriving upstairs, I found Duclos in my lab, idly thumbing through her osteology manual. Today the beyond-yellow hair was pulled into dual ponies, one sprouting from each side of her head. The lipstick was mauve.

I set down my half-eaten sandwich.

"Where is Dr. Briel?"

"Preparing for her interview." Perhaps in deference to her boss's upcoming appearance on CTV, Duclos was speaking English. "Is that cool, or what?"

"Two words, Ms. Duclos. Self starter."

Duclos's face went utterly blank.

"Is there nothing you could be doing?"

"Oh." Nervous giggle. "The teeth are in the cabinet. I couldn't get to them."

Valid point. Though no one gave a rat's petootie about Bergeron's dental collection, he insisted on keeping it under lock and key. Only Joe and I were privileged. Should one of Bergeron's students need entrée in his absence we'd each been granted access to the treasure. Woo-hoo!

I dug in my purse, then went to the closet to liberate the tub.

Duclos looked up at me, awaiting direction.

"Compare deciduous to permanent." Terse. Duclos was not my responsibility. Having to mentor her was making me cranky.

"Baby molars have bulbous crowns and slender, divergent roots." She spoke as though reading text.

"Yes." I dug an example from the tub and handed it to her.

Pointing the crown north and the roots south, she wiggled the molar through the air. "The itsy bitsy spider went up the waterspout." The nursery rhyme sounded strange in her accented English.

I finished the last of my sandwich, bunched the cellophane.

"The front teeth have scallopy biting edges, right?"

I shook my head, wondering what seasoning had been used in the ham salad.

"Not always." I tapped a finger on the Bass book.

"No sweat. I'll look it up."

I turned to the youngest Lac Saint-Jean kid.

More frustration. Joe had X-rayed the bones but had failed to take films of the teeth. After twenty minutes of searching, I found him in the break room downstairs, outside the morgue.

I was probably too abrupt. What the hell? It was late, and so far I'd gotten little accomplished.

Joe agreed to shoot apicals. Cooly.

Back to the twelfth floor.

Duclos and I worked side by side in silence. Now and then my stomach rumbled. Once she offered gum. I declined.

Some folks suffer headaches, others allergies, others gastric distress. I occasionally trip paths A and B. Never C. Thus, when hit with digestive symptoms, I'm totally flummoxed.

By late afternoon I needed something.

After trying Ayers, the secretaries, and the receptionist, I finally bummed an antacid from Morin. He insisted on describing the autopsy he'd just completed. It was three ten when I finally got back to the Lac Saint-Jean vics.

Joe had yet to collect the dentition for X-ray.

Feeling guilty about my brusqueness, I arranged the teeth on trays, separated by person. Twelve for the adult female, all in the lower jaw. Twenty-one for the adult male, some in mandibular, some in maxillary fragments. None for the older child. Three for the younger child, all isolated.

There. I'd gone the extra mile. Saved Joe ten minutes.

I was sliding the skeletal X-rays from their sleeve when my cell phone rang. Chicago area code. I clicked on.

"Tempe, it's Chris Corcoran."

"Hey." By now the sandwich was really kicking in. I tried to stifle a belch. It came out sounding like a guinea pig grunt.

"You OK?"

"Mm."

"You sound odd."

"I'm fine." Feeling a twinge, I pressed a hand to my belly.

"Good news. The cops think they've caught a break in the Tot case."

"Oh?" I felt bad about not having asked. I'd meant to for a week.

"An inmate at Stateville is looking to cut a deal for transfer to Pontiac." Corcoran referred to two of Illinois's maximum-security correctional facilities.

"What's so great about Pontiac?" Snappish.

"Ouch. You sure you're OK?"

"Sorry, I'm a little tired." I swallowed. "Go on."

"The guy says his cellmate's been bragging that he and a buddy rolled a kid and dumped his body in a quarry."

"When?"

Through the window I saw Briel power-stride up the corridor and into her office. Duclos shot from her seat and bolted out the door.

"The guy doesn't want to arouse suspicion by asking questions. So far he's just listening. But he's agreed to wear a wire."

"What's the cellmate in for?"

"Armed robbery."

My desk phone rang.

"Gotta go, Chris. Keep me in the loop."

I disconnected one line and picked up the other.

"Brennan."

"You nailed it. The kid who mowed the lawn and shoveled the walks for the Villejoin sisters says they always paid cash. Says the vics kept money in the pantry."

"A lot?" Feeling a sudden rush of heat, I pressed a hand to one cheek.

"He didn't know."

"How old is this kid?" I shifted the hand. My forehead felt clammy.

"Fifteen."

"That would make him what, twelve when the Villejoins were killed? Probably too young."

"And the kid's about the size of a meerkat. A small one. He wouldn't have had the strength."

"Or the wheels to get him to an ATM on the east side of Montreal or out to Oka," I agreed. "Any moving or painting crews in the neighborhood that week?"

"Dead end on that, but I'm checking with the day labor centers. The kid's father said they do get the occasional person hustling work door-to-door. I'm taking O'Keefe's picture to Pointe-Calumet now. Want to tag along?"

My stomach made a sound impossible to describe.

"You feeling OK?" I asked Ryan.

"Tip-top."

"What kind of sandwich did you buy from the machine?"

"Cheese."

"I'll pass. Let me know if you have any luck with the photo."

Palming another antacid into my mouth, I popped the first few X-rays onto the light box, unsure what I was hoping for. The Gouvrard antemorts suggested no condition or injury that would affect bone. At least not the bone that I had.

I was halfway through the films when my gut signaled again. Forget twinge. This was a card-carrying cramp.

My gaze drifted to the trays I'd organized for Joe.

I looked at the clock. Four thirty-five. Had he actually left without taking the films?

"Joe," I called around the corner.

What the hell?

"Joe!" I barked.

The top of my head flew off and my innards lurched.

I looked at the teeth. The bones. The useless X-rays.

These people had been dead for decades. They could wait another day.

Flicking off the light box, I locked up and headed out.

By the time I reached home the evil ham salad was goose-stepping across my gut, bellowing threats of a holocaust to come.

Entering the kitchen only to fill Birdie's dish, I stripped, yanked on a nightshirt, and fell into bed. Minutes later I was up and lunging for the bathroom.

The vomiting continued well past the emptying point. When it ended, my mouth tasted of bile and my intercostals and abdominals ached from the strain.

But I felt better.

Not for long.

The microbes ran me in twenty-minute loops. Hurl. Recover. Renauseate. Hurl.

By ten I was shaking and drained. Literally. My thermoregulators had long since thrown up their hands, leaving my body on its own to decide whether to shiver or sweat. At times it did both.

I was crawling under the covers after a session with the porcelain prince when my eyes wandered to my bedside clock. Eleven twenty-five. My pounding brain managed a cogent recollection.

Briel.

Clawing the remote into my palm, I clicked on the TV and found the right station.

The interview was a feature spot, one of those long pieces in which an unusual job or profession is highlighted. The interviewer was a tweed-jacketed guy who looked like he'd just finished high school. Maybe.

Tweed Jacket introduced Briel as though she were Our Lady of Forensics. He might even have said that. I was so ill by that time, looking back, I'm never sure.

Briel wore a white cotton blouse and black pants that showed far too much ankle. Her hair was pulled back and tied with a bow. The perpetual frown was firmly in place.

If the sandwich hadn't already laid me low, my colleague's grandstanding certainly would have. With Tweed Jacket lobbing softball questions, Briel spoke of her brief but illustrious career.

An exhumation in France. A case involving a mysterious poison. The elusive cause of death for Marilyn Keiser. Though Briel's face remained neutral, her tone was one of smug satisfaction.

To my horror, toward the wrap-up, discussion turned to Christelle Villejoin's missing phalanges.

"Do you know Dr. Temperance Brennan?" Tweed Jacket asked.

"She is my colleague."

"Her training is in anthropology, correct?"

"Yes. As is mine."

I shot to a sit.

"A short course! You took a bloody short course!"

"Isn't Dr. Brennan usually responsible for coroner-ordered exhumations?"

"Yes." Just the slightest hesitation. The winging down of brows. For effect? "Dr. Brennan led the initial recovery at Oka. The phalanges were missed."

Though I was chilled and shaking, my face burned.

Had I? Had I really missed them? I must have. But how?

My queasy brain scraped together an image of the tent. The pit. The earth-stained bones.

"—specialty training in forensic archaeology. What is needed in such situations is a team approach, the utilization of experts in excavation methodology, taphonomy and decomposition, and human soft and hard tissue anatomy and pathology."

"Do such teams exist in Quebec?"

"One. A private company called Body Find. Corps découvert. I am—"

My poisoned gut arced full cycle.

I stumbled to the bathroom on shaky legs.

When the retching stopped, I staggered back to bed.

Shivering uncontrollably, I killed the TV and light and pulled the covers to my chin.

THOUGH COLD-NUMBED AND ALMOST USELESS, MY HANDS EXPLORED the skull. From habit, my brain catalogued detail.

Large mastoids and brow ridges. Male. Edentulous.

"Who the bloody hell cares?" I screamed in frustration.

My cry sounded flat, deadened by brick and trapped silence.

I looked at my watch. The glowing hands now formed an acute angle pointing left. Two twenty? Four ten? Afternoon? Night?

I thought of my daughter. Wondered what Katy was doing at that moment. Harry. Ryan. Tried to imagine what was happening at the lab.

Surely I'd been missed by now. Surely a team was coming. Right, coming where?

"Help! Please!"

My throat felt raw. I coughed.

"Hello! Anyone!"

A bout of trembling gripped me. I hugged my body, felt my arm bones knock my ribs. My skin was cold and clammy to the touch.

Like a corpse at the morgue.

Panic flared anew.

I'm going to die. Alone in a dark tomb. No one will know where I went. Where the flesh is rotting from my bones.

I thought of the tweaker who'd frozen to death on his porch. How long could I survive before hypothermia killed me?

I hated my captor. Hated him for me. For Katy. For Harry. Hated him with a fury born of years spent with the battered dead. Hated him for the throat-slashed wives. The cigarette-burned babies. The bedsored grannies.

"Who are you?" I shrieked.

Forget him. Activity brings warmth. Warmth brings life. Use the anger. Move. Get out.

I took a deep breath.

Took another, shifting to my nose.

The musty smell was stronger here. Mold. Mildew. Creatures long dead.

Setting the skull on the floor, I rolled to my belly and began dragging myself forward, using the odor as a guide.

My raw elbows screamed. My injured leg spasmed.

Ignore the pain.

Arm-thrust. Pull.

Arm-thrust. Pull.

Soft echoes suggested a more enclosed space. A wall ahead?

Six thrusts, then my chest landed on bulk. Propping on my right elbow, I explored the object with my left hand. Gingerly. Careful not to move it.

Lumpy L, scaly with mold. Underside flat with a heel-shaped protuberance at one end.

A boot.

I reached left.

A second boot lay beside the first.

Heart hammering, I danced my fingers upward over mold-crusted fabric that crumbled at my touch. Running beneath the fabric were long tubular objects. I recognized their shape. Their meaning.

Leg bones.

Dear God, I was feeling up a corpse.

I pictured the body.

Swinging my legs right, I inched upward along the side of the torso, blindly probing in the darkness. My fingers picked out heavy round buttons.

I counted. Visualized. A jacket?

I applied pressure with my palm.

The jacket overlaid a series of rigid arcs. Lumps and knobs. A collapsed rib cage. Vertebrae.

I tried lifting the jacket's lower edge. My effort kicked up a tsunami of scent, rank and earthy and reeking of death.

I changed to breathing through my mouth.

Elbowing and kneeing in reverse, I cleared the boots and shifted left.

Beside the first, my trembling fingers encountered a second set of footwear. Trousers. Another jacket. A fleshless skull, spiderweb hair clinging to the crown.

Again, I hitched backward and dragged myself left.

A third corpse lay head to foot with the others. Or had, until the skull detached and sought new ground.

My hands recoiled in horror.

Mother of God! My prison was a crypt, more frigid and black than I could have imagined possible. Filled with complete and utter silence.

And decaying bodies.

Questions kaleidoscoped in my brain. Hysterical. Pointless.

How long? How many? Who?

Using my bound legs, I hitched myself aft of the third corpse and dragged myself left, hands fumbling in the dark.

Irrational, but I had to know.

Beyond the first three dead I found four more.

Brailleing for clues, I determined that everyone had been entombed wearing boots, belted pants, and jackets with heavy round buttons, probably metal. Four jackets were adorned with medals and insignia.

Dead soldiers?

It didn't matter. What did matter was the possibility that I'd soon join their ranks.

My breath began to catch, my chest to heave.

Reason weighed in.

No tears! Think!

A single word exploded in my brain.

Edges!

A desperate ghoul, I raided the dead and placed my booty in a pile. Medals. Buckles. Insignias. Three lower jaws with the front teeth in place.

Shifting to a hunch-sit, I spread my knees, leaned forward, and began sawing at my ankle bindings. One cord was all I needed.

One.

One.

How long did I gnaw away at those ropes? Long.

As with my wrists, it finally happened. A gentle yielding of pressure. A pop. My legs flew apart.

Electricity exploded from neuron to neuron.

I wanted to scream.

To shout for joy.

To kill the bastard who'd done this to me.

I wanted to escape.

Rounding my back, I massaged and flexed both ankles.

When blood flow returned, I eased onto all fours.

Not bad.

I flexed a knee, testing the injured leg.

Tender. Tolerable.

During my corpse crawl, I'd noted that the dead had been placed with their heads or feet to a wall. Apparently, I was at one end of the tomb.

Might a door be at the other?

Arms and legs rubber, I crawled toward the spot where I'd first regained consciousness, left hand periodically skimming the brick. One step. Five. Twelve.

Twenty steps. My outstretched palm smacked brick. Another wall was meeting the long wall at ninety degrees. I'd reached the other end of the tomb.

I began sidestepping right, hand groping for a door.

Sudden horrifying thought. If the bodies had been simply bricked in, there'd have been no need of a door. No one was ever entering again. Or leaving.

My tortured brain rode another illogical wave. Poe. "The Cask of Amontillado."

But Montresor was caught.

No. Fortunato died. Alone. Underground.

My movements became frenzied. Sitting on my haunches, I hand-swept the brick in wide jagged arcs.

Someone put you here. There had to be a way in.

There has to be a way out.

I almost gasped when my fingers brushed something set into the masonry. Flat. Smooth.

Wood!

I groped for a handle.

Zip.

A latch.

No go.

My frozen fingertips were sending little to my brain. I rubbed my hands together fast. Some feeling returned.

I began anew, more slowly. More carefully.

Eventually, my trembling fingers picked out an irregularity. Traced it.

My brain tallied the tactile, threw up a visual. A crack, outlining a door maybe two feet square.

Frantic, I began clawing at the gap with my nails. The narrow space was packed with a hard, crumbly substance.

Think, Brennan!

Fumbling back through the dark, I gathered my macabre assemblage. Then I scramble-crawled back to the door and began hacking and gouging.

Periodically, I'd roll to my back and hammer the wood with my feet. Or throw my weight from all fours, connecting with a shoulder or hip.

Sounds filled the stillness. The clink of my pirated tools. The tick of mortar falling on brick. The wheeze of air in and out of my mouth.

I was sweat-soaked and panting when the door finally popped free and dropped with a clunk.

I inched to the edge and peered out.

CLUNK.

I raised my lids.

The window shade was a muted gray rectangle outlined by strips of sluggish daylight. Again. *War of the Toxic Ham Salad: Day Three.*

Birdie was atop the bureau on the far side of the room. Below him, a framed photo of Katy lay angled to a baseboard.

Though better than yesterday, my body still felt like it had gone through a crusher.

I sat up. Groaned.

Bird looked an accusation in my direction.

Can cats do that?

Thursday was a blur. I could remember trying to change the sheets. To feed the cat. To shower. To eat crackers. My innards would have nothing to do with digestion. After each attempt at activity, I'd fall back into bed.

Fitful while sleeping, I'd kicked the covers to the floor. Reengaging them, I assessed. Though the fever and nausea were gone, my rib and abdominal muscles ached, and a low throbbing lingered behind my eyeballs. My nightshirt was soaked.

I looked at the clock. Ten twenty.

Bird had a point.

"You hungry, buddy?"

Prim nonresponse.

Peeling off the wet jammies, I donned sweats, then dragged to the kitchen to feed the cat.

Back to the bathroom. Already my energy level was tanking.

I studied my image in the mirror while brushing my teeth. Eyes rabbit pink. Face oatmeal. Hair pasted to my scalp and forehead in swirly wet clumps.

How would Harry describe my appearance? Rode hard and put away wet.

"Apt." My voice sounded croaky.

Lab today?

Maybe.

Shower?

Not yet.

Hair?

Later.

One system kicked in. Suddenly I was famished. Ten hours of vomiting will do that, I guess.

The refrigerator offered condiments, Diet Coke, moldy lettuce, and a trio of plastic containers whose contents would require a gas spec for ID.

I was contemplating a grocery run when I heard knocking at the front door.

Entrance to my building requires a key. Others must buzz. Only the caretaker or a resident should already be inside.

Sparky?

Merciful God. Not today.

I tiptoed down the hall and peeked through the peephole.

An impossibly blue eye stared back.

"I know you're in there." Muffled through the door.

"Go away."

"I have news. Open up."

Reluctantly, I did.

Ryan was bundled in hooded parka, muffler, and tuque pulled low to his brows. His nostrils were blanched, his cheeks flushed. He held a square white box in mittened hands.

"Klondike Pete called," I said. "They want the outfit back."

"It's twenty-two below." Shifting the bakery, Ryan palmed back his hood.

"You could not know I was here," I said.

"Shadow in the peephole. The cat moves low to the ground. I'm a detective. I read clues."

Ryan's eyes roved my body. My hair. A grin played his lips.

"Don't say it," I warned.

"Say what?" All innocence.

"I've been under the weather."

"Two-day blizzard?"

"You're a laugh riot, Ryan. You should take yourself on the road. Like, right now?"

Ryan proffered the box. "I brought breakfast."

I smelled pastry. Buttery eggs. Salty bacon.

"You'll do coffee?" Ryan had his faults, but he made great coffee.

"*Bien sûr.* I am the brewer of coffee and the fixer of glass."

"My hero." Stepping back. "Winston already replaced the window."

Ryan disappeared into the kitchen. I went to the bathroom to try to reason with my hair. Pointless. I finally yanked it into a knot on top of my head.

Lipstick and blush?

Screw it. I almost died of food poisoning.

Ryan had set two places at the dining room table. He sat at one, sipping coffee from my RCMP mug. The open box was one croissant down.

"Flu?" he asked when I reappeared.

"Deadly ham salad."

"But you emerge the victor."

"I do." I opened a croissant, considered, then removed the bacon, not up to another porcine encounter. "Let me guess. Someone in Pointe-Calumet recognized Red O'Keefe's picture?"

"No."

"OK. What's your news?"

"One Bud Keith was on the payroll of L'Auberge des Neiges at the time Rose Jurmain disappeared."

"Holy shit." Through a mouthful of egg and dough.

"The holiest."

"Doing what?"

"Kitchen worker."

"Bud Keith aka Red O'Keefe?"

"Our very own."

"Was Keith–O'Keefe questioned?"

"Yep. Cops ran him, saw he had a record, a string of aliases. But Keith cooperated, and, more importantly, served up an airtight alibi for the time period in question. He was bear hunting with friends near La Tuque. Six guys put him there the date Jurmain disappeared. Cops saw no reason to follow up."

"How long did Keith/O'Keefe work at the inn?"

"Split after a two-month stint. Gave no notice and left no forwarding address. Manager says he was a good worker, but moody."

"What does that mean?"

"He didn't like the guy."

"What does Claudel think?"

"He thinks it's worth follow-up."

"Is he making progress on Keiser?"

"He's got the vic's son, Otto, flying in from Alberta. Apparently Mona's divorced, has three little kids and nowhere to leave them. Claudel wants to run sonny around the apartment and the cabin at Memphrémagog, see if maybe something clicks. I'll probably join up for a look-see."

"You never know," I said.

"You never know."

A detail had been nagging at me since I'd heard about Keiser's visits to Eastman Spa.

"Something's been bothering me."

"You know I'm yours if you want me."

"I'll keep some bubbly on ice."

"I'm all over that."

"Marilyn Keiser made regular visits to Eastman. That's big bucks. Yet she had only modest assets. How did she pay for her pricey spa habit?"

Ryan got it right away.

"You're thinking home banking. She kept a cash stash, like the Villejoins."

"Could that be the link?"

"I'll pass the idea along to Claudel. Maybe he needs to go further back in Keiser's financials, look for large unexplained withdrawls. Also check with Eastman, see how she paid."

"How'd you guess I was here?" I reached for my second croissant.

"You weren't at the lab yesterday or today. Where else would you be?"

"I do have a life."

"Course you do."

To switch topics, I described Briel's television debut.

"What do you know about this Body Find outfit?" Ryan asked when I'd finished.

"Nothing," I said. "Yet."

"Want me to do some poking?"

"I can handle it."

"I'm sure you can."

I told Ryan about the call from Chris Corcoran. The inmate at Stateville.

"The Chicago cops think the guy's story is solid?"

"Apparently."

"I hope it pans out. For Cukura Kundze's sake."

"And Lassie's."

Ryan tipped a wrist to check the time.

"You heading in this afternoon?"

"Probably not." I surprised myself. Until that moment I'd been operating on the assumption that I'd go to the lab.

Ryan crossed to me, squatted, and placed a hand over mine. His face was so close I could feel his breath, smell the familiar Garnier shampoo.

"You deserve a couple of days off." Gentle squeeze. "I'm going to build you a fire. Light it when you want."

"Thanks." Barely audible.

When Ryan left I gathered the breakfast debris, called the lab to tell them I wouldn't be in until Monday, then took a long bubble bath. Lying in water as hot as I could bear, I pondered my decision to stay home. I never take an unscheduled break. Idleness makes me cranky.

Post-poisoning fatigue? Minus twenty-two temperature reading? Confidence that the Lac Saint-Jean vics would soon be IDed? Humiliation over Briel's public disclosure of my screwup in the Villejoin case?

Whatever.

The hot water and full belly acted like an opiate, drugging me into a state of total lethargy.

Avoiding my sweat-stained bed, I got a quilt, lit Ryan's fire, and stretched out on the couch. Birdie joined me.

I stroked his fur. He purred on my chest.

I closed my eyes, feeling drained of the ability to move. To read. To watch TV. To think.

* * *

I awoke to the sound of a ringing phone. Bird was gone. The windows were dark and the fire was nothing but embers.

Retrieving the handset, I clicked on.

"I didn't see you today or yesterday." Emily Santangelo.

"Food poisoning. I'll spare you the details."

"You OK now?"

"I'll live." My eyes drifted to the mantel clock. Four forty-five. "Beware vending machine sandwiches."

"You actually ate one?"

"Not the crusts."

Pause.

"Did you see Briel's interview Wednesday night?"

"A thing of beauty."

Longer pause.

"We need to talk."

My instincts sat up. Emily Santangelo was a reserved, almost reclusive woman, not one for office gossip or girlie exchanges.

"Sure," I said.

"You feel up to dinner, maybe something light? Chicken soup? I could bring it to you."

"I'll need to disinfect this place before anyone enters." I was thinking flamethrower. "How about meeting at Pho Nguyen on Saint-Mathieu?"

"Vietnamese?"

"They make great soup."

"That works. I can be there by six thirty."

"I won't look good."

"I won't call the press."

There was a subtle muffling of ambient noise, as though Santangelo had cupped the mouthpiece.

"Something's very wrong." Almost a whisper.

"Wrong?" I asked.

"See you soon."

The line went dead.

DÉCOR IS NOT A PRIORITY AT PHO NGUYEN. TWO STEPS DOWN from the sidewalk, the place has a white tile floor, white walls, and maybe a dozen Formica-topped tables. White.

But the soupe Tonkinoise kicks ass.

Santangelo was there when I arrived, seated in a back corner, perusing the menu. She smiled on seeing me. Waved.

"This cold will either cure or kill me." I pulled off my muffler and gloves and unzipped my parka. "Glad you called. I needed some fresh air."

"You walked?"

"It's not far." Pho Nguyen's other attraction is that it's only blocks from my condo.

Stuffing my accessories into a sleeve, I hung the jacket on the chair back. An Asian kid approached as soon as I sat. His cheekbones were high, his hair thick and black, with one platinum streak in front. A gold earring looped his right brow.

"I'll have a number six, medium."

"What's that?" Santangelo asked.

"Pho bo. Beef noodle soup."

"The same for me." Santangelo tucked the menu back into its holder.

The kid crossed to the front counter and bellowed our order into the kitchen.

"I'm not what you'd call an adventurous eater," Santangelo said.

"You'll like this."

The kid returned with small plates piled with basil, lime, and sprouts.

Santangelo shot me a quizzical look.

"I'll talk you through it," I said.

I brought Santangelo up to date on the Keiser and Villejoin investigations. On Ayers's distress over missing a bullet track. Fully engaged in transitioning to the coroner's office, she'd not kept current. When the soup arrived, we focused on adding hot sauce, soy sauce, and the fresh embellishments.

We'd been slurping and twirling for a while when Santangelo finally got to the subject on her mind.

"Do you know the real reason I'm leaving the lab?"

"No."

"The atmosphere has gone rancid. It's Briel." Santangelo practically spit the name. "She's poison."

Like Ryan, I used silence, allowing her to go on. She did. Big-time.

"The woman is ambitious to the point of ruthlessness. She's everywhere, has a finger in every pie. She's in the autopsy room at all hours of the night. Teaches a university course. Has a research grant. Plans to present papers at about a zillion scientific conferences. She's a callous, unfeeling, coldhearted climber."

"Don't hold back."

"It isn't funny, Tempe. Briel is determined to be a superstar and she doesn't care who she destroys on her march to glory. Did you know she fired her graduate student today? Had the girl in tears."

"Duclos?"

Santangelo nodded.

"Why?"

"Probably because the kid has warm blood in her veins."

"Why doesn't someone rein Briel in?"

"She has the other pathologists cowed and the chief coroner eating out of her hand."

Santangelo toyed with her soup using the little china spoon. Set it down. Picked up her chopsticks. Dropped them. Pushed her bowl toward the center of the table.

"You said you watched Briel's interview Wednesday night?"

"Yes."

"You heard her plug this Body Find outfit? Corps découvert? It's her husband's company."

"You're kidding." I couldn't keep the shock from my voice.

"I heard her talking about it with Joe Bonnet. She and her husband are going to be the next Mulder and Scully." Santangelo's voice was coated with disdain.

"Who's she married to?"

"Sebastien Raines. An archaeologist."

That surprised me. I thought I knew all the archaeologists in Montreal, at least by name.

"Is Raines on faculty with one of the universities?"

Santangelo shook her head. "He does cultural resource management."

Typically, CRM archaeologists work for governments and for businesses that must, by law, save archaeological resources threatened by development. Some do the archaeological portions of environmental impact studies. Some direct salvage digs.

Although many private sector archaeologists are very good surveyors and excavators, academics view them as a whole as second-rate. Why? They work on short contracts and rarely publish. Many are employed by companies that prefer nothing be found that would delay their projects. Rightly or wrongly, those at universities see opportunity for corruption in CRM work.

"Where did Raines train?"

"No clue."

"How does he figure into Briel's Mulder-and-Scully scenario?"

"Briel and Raines are starting this company, Body Find. Corps découvert. When everything is in place they plan to hawk it as one-stop shopping for law enforcement. Archaeology, anthropology, pathology, psychology, entomology, botany, geophysics, cadaver dogs, remote sensing. They'll find your body, ID it, determine PMI, cause of death. You'll only need a lab for complex testing like mass spectrometry or DNA sequencing. They'll even provide expertise in underground mine safety, mapping, ingress-egress methods. You name it, Body Find will be there for you! Better, quicker, cheaper!"

"Such companies already exist," I said. "NecroSearch International, for example. They do fantastic work. Although NecroSearch limits itself largely to victim location."

"There's one other big difference. NecroSearch is a nonprofit. Every team member is a volunteer. Body Find's objective will be to make bucks."

"Privatized forensics?"

Santangelo nodded. "And Briel is doing everything she can right now to raise her profile. When it's time to launch the business, she wants to trade on her status as the *Canadian Idol* of crime solving."

"Including anthropology," I said, seeing the implication.

"Yeah. Imagine that."

I stared at Santangelo. She stared back. Around us, china clinked and conversation hummed.

The waiter approached. Feeling tension, he left the check and quietly slipped away.

"Nail her, Tempe." Santangelo's tone was soft, but her words were edged with emotion.

"Why me?"

"Why not? You've never been afraid to take a good bite of charlatan."

Back home, the dragging fatigue again threatened to flatten me. Nevertheless, I did a Google search on Sebastien Raines. It turned up zilch.

Next I called Jean Tye, a colleague at the Université de Montréal. Tye knew little beyond the fact that Briel's husband had applied for a position at the U of M in 2007. Since Raines had done zero research, published nothing, and completed only a master's degree, he'd not been considered a serious candidate. He'd heard that Raines had also submitted an application to the Université du Québec à Montréal. UQAM had also declined to hire him.

Tye was aware that Raines was involved in contract archaeology. He remembered that Raines had done some fieldwork in France, and that his MA had been granted by an institution with which Tye was unfamiliar. His specialty was urban archaeology, digging up garbage dumps, abandoned cemeteries, and building ruins.

And one other thing. Sebastien Raines was active in a number of radical fringe separatist groups. According to Tye, Raines's desire for an independent French-speaking North American nation was so extremist that the guy offended most members of the Bloc Québécois.

Ryan called shortly after eight. He planned to meet Claudel and Otto Keiser at the Édouard-Montpetit apartment at ten the next morning.

Saturday. What the hell. I agreed to ride along.

By nine I was back in bed. New sheets. New nightie. Same old cat.

I was unconscious in minutes.

In sleep, I sifted. Organized. Played with patterns.

I saw Rose Jurmain's skeleton, gnawed and scattered in piney woods. As I watched, it rose, bones ghostly in the moonlight. Tendrils grew around its perimeter, rippling like seaweed under water. Written on each tendril was a name and identifier.

Edward Allen, the father. Perry Schechter, the attorney. Janice Spitz, the lover. Andre and Bertrand Dubreuil, the discoverers. Red O'Keefe–Bud Keith, the auberge kitchen worker. Chris Corcoran, the Chicago pathologist. ML, the Chicago anthropologist.

No. That's wrong. ML analyzed Laszlo Tot's bones.

The ML tendril went dark and drifted to the ground.

The scene morphed to Christelle Villejoin, buried in bra and panties in a shallow grave. Slowly, the old woman sat up. The undies looked zombie white against her earth-stained bones.

Christelle's tendrils were fewer in number than Rose's.

Anne-Isabelle, the sister. Yves Renaud, the discoverer of Anne-Isabelle. Sylvain Rayner, the retired physician. Florian Grellier, the tipster. Red O'Keefe–Bud Keith, Grellier's bar buddy. M. Keith, the handyman.

Bud Keith–Red O'Keefe. A Rose tendril gently overlapped with a Christelle tendril.

A figure appeared, face veiled, hand outstretched. In the palm lay four phalanges. A corner of the veil lifted, revealing features. Marie-Andréa Briel.

Briel's face darkened, then changed to that of Marilyn Keiser. Keiser's body was mottled black and purple. Though less luminous, her tendrils were the most numerous of all.

Uri Keiser, Myron Pinsker Sr., Sam Adamski, the husbands. Otto and Mona, the son and daughter. Myron Pinsker Jr., the stepson. Lu and Eddie Castiglioni, the janitors. Natalie Ayers, the pathologist.

The dream toggled to a new scene.

Ryan stood at a lectern, projector shooting a white beam of light into darkness behind him. Three students occupied chairs before him. Ryan fired question after question. The students answered.

If O'Keefe/Keith was guilty, why did he do it?

Money?

The Villejoins had little. Jurmain kept only a few dollars in her room at the auberge.

O'Keefe/Keith was small-time. Maybe a little was enough.

How did O'Keefe/Keith cross paths with Marilyn Keiser?

Might Myron Pinsker be the killer?

Rage? Jealousy? Fear of losing his inheritance?

Are there assets we don't know about?

Did Pinsker's life intersect those of the other vics?

Were Jurmain and Villejoin random, selected because of their age and gender?

What about the Villejoins' neighbor, Yves Renaud?

The janitor twins, Lu and Eddie Castiglioni?

Shotgun questions and answers, back and forth.

I kicked at the blankets.

Now Hubert was speaking from the lectern.

Cause of death was unknown for Jurmain. Villejoin was bludgeoned. Keiser was burned.

That's wrong.

Keiser was shot. Student three was now Chris Corcoran.

Ayers did the autopsy but missed it. Student two had become Marie-Andréa Briel.

Briel found the bullet track, Hubert said. Briel found the phalanges. All hail Briel.

A moth fluttered into the projector beam, wings frenzied in the stark illumination.

I saw its velvety antennae. The layers of silken hair covering its abdomen.

The moth flew directly toward me.

Its jaws opened.

30

RYAN WAS PROMPT. AS USUAL.

By nine fifty we were pulling to the curb in front of a U-shaped red-brick building in a neighborhood bordering the U of M campus. Crossing the front courtyard, I noted details.

Grounds litter free. Walks shoveled with square-edged precision. Bushes wrapped with burlap and tied.

Lu Castiglioni was at the door, looking like he'd rather be elsewhere. I suspected he'd just been grilled by Claudel.

As we followed Castiglioni inside, I continued my survey.

Twelve mailboxes, each with a button and speaker plate to announce arrivals. No camera. The security system relied on voice alone.

Claudel had assumed an Armani pose in the lobby. Leather gloves. Tan cashmere coat. Impatient frown. Beside him was a moose of a man bundled like a hunter just in from the Yukon.

Claudel introduced his companion as Otto Keiser. Ryan and I offered condolences to Otto on the loss of his mother.

Otto shook our hands, studied our faces.

Castiglioni led us to an elevator and pushed a lighted brass button. We rode to the third floor in silence.

Keiser's unit was at the far end of a newly carpeted hallway that smelled of fresh paint. We passed only one other door.

Castiglioni used a master key.

Abandoned homes develop a certain smell. Old food. Dirty laundry.

Dead plants. Stale air. The shades were drawn and the heat was lowered, but Keiser's apartment was wearing that perfume.

We entered directly into the living room. Down a hall shooting right I could see two bedrooms joined by a bath, all entered through doors on the left. Past the bedrooms, straight ahead, the hall ended at a dining room. Beyond that was a kitchen. Through a back-door window, I could see wooden stairs joining a porch.

Ryan and I went left, Claudel and Otto right. Castiglioni stayed in the corridor.

The living room had a bay of wraparound windows at one end. Strung beads covered the glass, annihilating what must have been the architect's intent.

The room was trimmed with crown moldings, chair rails, and baseboards painted a lime green that couldn't even have looked good in the can. The floors were wood, covered with rugs that were escapees from an LSD trip. Amateur landscapes and still lifes shared wall space with opera posters and low-quality prints. I recognized Picasso. Modigliani. Chagall. Pollock.

Figurines, vases, photos, snow domes, music boxes, and carved nudes crammed the mantel and shelves to either side of a fireplace whose brick had been painted the same unfortunate green as the trim. All paintings and bric-a-brac were evenly spaced in perfectly straight rows.

I glanced at the framed photos. Otto was recognizable in some older ones, as a toddler, then in scenes reflecting a typical childhood age progression. In many he was with a girl a few years younger, arm draped protectively around her shoulders. I assumed this was the sister, Mona.

The two also appeared repeatedly as teens. Yearbook portraits. Proms. Otto on the hood of an old Chevrolet. Graduation shots of Mona, high school and college.

Obviously Keiser loved her children. I wondered. Was she loved by them? By anyone? Saddened by the thought, I continued my survey.

The assemblage included one formal wedding picture showing a very young Keiser with a very thin man. Clothing and hairstyles suggested the fifties. Was the groom Uri?

A snapshot showed an older Keiser wearing a peasant dress and holding a small bouquet. Beside her was a short, dark man in a boutonnièred brown suit. The two stood outside the Hôtel de Ville, Montreal's old City Hall.

Ryan came up beside me.

"Think this is Pinsker Senior?" I asked.

"That scans. The guy's 'burns and lapels scream early eighties. Keiser and Pinsker tied the knot in 'eighty-four. Any Kodak moments of the Adamski nuptials?"

I shook my head. "What's your take on Otto's age?"

"Mid- to late thirties." Ryan did some mental calculation. "Uri and Marilyn were married a long time before they had kids. Interesting."

I waved an arm at the photo collection. "Another interesting observation. Beaucoup kiddie, teenage, and young adult shots. Nowhere does Otto or his sister look older than twenty-five."

"You're guessing an estrangement dating back ten years?" Ryan said.

"That, or every picture from the last decade was lost or destroyed."

"Seems unlikely. Keiser was a hoarder."

"A very neat hoarder. Check out the shelves. The stuff's arranged with the precision of a Presbyterian choir."

"Ten years." Ryan was thinking out loud.

"About the time Keiser married Adamski." I pointed out the obvious.

Two killer blue eyes swung my way. "Dr. Brennan. Perhaps you should apply for the detective's exam."

"Perhaps I should."

"I wouldn't feel threatened."

"Claudel might. Shall we join him?"

In the hall, I noted the security panel, a simple speaker with a buzzer button. Hardly state of the art.

I also noted a wall cabinet with a tiny gold key. I looked inside. Books.

Claudel and Otto were in the kitchen. While Ryan spoke to them, I slipped into the bedroom.

Another overdose of color. More paintings, knickknacks, curios, and photos. I checked the images but found no Adamski candidate.

A Chinese lacquered box was centered on the bureau. I lifted the lid. Jewelry sealed in individual plastic bags.

I opened the closet. Dresses, skirts, and slacks in eye-watering colors, all hanging from the rod at two-inch intervals.

Keiser's approach to storage was the polar opposite of mine. Shelved boxes were stacked by descending size. Clothing was separated by category, then color. Shoes were snugged into racks, again organized by shade and style.

Marilyn Keiser was one tidy lady.

The bathroom and guest bedroom showed similar attention to order and placement.

Obsessive-compulsive disorder? Making a mental note to inquire, I moved on to the kitchen.

Ryan was querying Otto on his mother's third husband. Otto's eyes were on his shoes.

"What did Adamski do?"

"Beats me."

"You never asked?"

"Yeah, I asked. You couldn't pin the guy down."

"Did he have his own income?"

"Who knows?"

I looked around. The kitchen was turquoise and tangerine, another victim of stuff overload. Baskets, ceramic pots, china plates, cookie molds, glass containers, silk flowers, framed cross-stitch masterpieces. You name the kitsch, Keiser hung it or placed it on a counter or shelf.

"You didn't like him, did you?" Ryan.

Otto looked up, face filled with disgust. "He was forty-seven. My mother was sixty-one. Would you?"

"That was it? The age difference?"

"The guy was smooth, always with an answer, you know? But underneath, there was this . . ." Otto spread his fingers, grasping for a descriptor. The palms were tough and calloused. ". . . hardness. I can't describe it. I'm a mechanic, good with engines, not words."

"Did Adamski take advantage of your mother financially?"

"Who knows?"

"Did she complain?"

"No."

"Were they happy?"

"Mona and I live out West." Shoulder shrug. "You go where the jobs are, you know? After marrying Adamski, Mom pretty much quit writing and phoning." Otto sighed deeply. "Look, my mother was flaky as piecrust. Thought of herself as bohemian. Do you know what she named us?"

Ryan and I waited.

"Othello and Desdemona. Can you imagine growing up with names like that? And a mother who wore tights and braids and sang opera to your friends? One time I brought a kid home, Mom's posing nude for some wack-job artist." Otto snorted mirthlessly. "As soon as I moved West I changed my name. Added a *t* and got the 'hell' out." Otto finger-hooked quotation marks. "Get it? Othello? Got the"—more hooked fingers—"hell out?"

I could only guess the number of times he'd told that joke.

"Mona did the same."

"Did you and your sister try contacting your mother?"

"When we called, she was always busy. I assumed she didn't need us anymore. She was happy and had a new life."

Claudel cleared his throat.

Ryan forged on. "What about Pinsker? You like him?"

"He was a nerd, but an OK guy."

I peeked inside a cabinet. The plates sat in evenly spaced stacks. The cups hung at identical angles on equidistant hooks.

"You know his son?"

"Not really. I was a kid when Mom married his father. Myron was already off on his own."

I closed the cabinet, opened another. Shipshape.

"He's in your mother's will."

"That's cool. Mom was married to Pinsker for twelve years. Besides"—Otto snorted again—"she didn't leave much."

"That strike you as odd?"

I noticed a subtle tensing of Otto's jaw. Quick, then gone. "What do you mean?" he asked.

"Are you surprised your mother had so few assets?"

Otto shrugged. He did it a lot. "Looks like she got by OK."

Impatient, Claudel shifted his feet.

"With so little money, how did your mother live as well as she did? This apartment. The spa trips."

Otto regarded Ryan as if he'd just dropped from the south end of a pig. "How the hell would I know? The last time I saw her was 2000."

"When Adamski died. Were you saddened by his death?"

"What kind of question is that?"

Ryan waited.

Another shrug. Otto was a real charismatic fellow. "Honestly? I hoped the prick would rot in hell."

"Your mother had income from her old-age pension." Ryan tried a fast cut.

"I suppose she did."

"Myron Junior helped her some. Ran errands, that sort of thing."

"So." Defensive. Guilt?

"Someone cashed three checks after she died."

"You suspect Myron?"

"Do you?"

"No. I . . ." Otto spread his feet. "You're trying to confuse me."

"Adamski drowned, didn't he?" Another quick veer.

"Yes." Wary.

"Where?"

"Someplace in La Mauricie. Near Trois Rivières, I think. Or Chambord."

Claudel had had enough.

"We've been over this, Detective Ryan."

"Repetition never hurts." Ryan's eyes stayed clamped on Otto's face.

"Mr. Keiser, you've noted nothing amiss in your mother's apartment?" Claudel asked.

"When are you guys going to listen to me? I haven't set foot in this place in years."

"You came to Montreal for Adamski's funeral?" Ryan ignored Claudel's interruption.

"There was no funeral."

"Why not?"

"How the hell would I know? Maybe the guy was an atheist."

"What was your purpose in coming?"

"To talk my mother into relocating to Alberta. I even offered to pack all her crap."

"No luck?"

Otto spread his arms to take in the apartment. "Does it look like she moved?"

"OK." Ryan nodded. "Let's go to Memphrémagog."

The cabin was about what I'd pictured, though constructed of logs, not boards. The roof was shingle. There was a metal exhaust pipe in back, I guessed from the woodstove, a crude porch in front.

The word *remote* doesn't adequately describe the location. The unpaved road off the blacktop seemed to go on for about ninety miles.

Ryan and I agreed: Keiser's getaway was not a place one would stumble upon. Either she was targeted and followed, or her killer knew of the cabin's existence.

The windows were intact. Ditto the door lock. Inside, we saw no signs of a struggle. No overturned chair or lamp. No broken vase. No cockeyed picture or painting.

Had Keiser let her killer in? Did she know him? Or had he overwhelmed her so quickly she'd had no chance to react?

The air was frigid and smelled of ash and kerosene. Other than localized fire damage and fingerprint powder from the crime scene techs, the cabin's interior looked jarringly normal.

Like the apartment, the place was jammed with paintings, and with what I suspected were local farmers' market crafts and collectibles. Old milk and soda bottles. Cowbells. Cheese vats. Antique tools.

While Otto and Claudel wandered, I checked the art. Keiser's initials signed every work.

In the unburned back corner I found her easel and supplies. The techs had been respectful while tossing the place. And foresighted. The upright brushes still formed perfect circles in their holders. The paint tubes still marched in parallel rows. The unused canvases still waited in graduated stacks.

Behind the easel was a small wooden sideboard covered by a handmade afghan. I lifted an edge.

The sideboard had one long drawer above, a pair of doors below that. The brass pulls and lock were tarnished and dented. The wood was overvarnished, gouged and splintered, as though once pried open by force. The piece looked old.

OK. I admit it. Occasionally I get snagged by an episode of *Antiques Roadshow.*

Vaguely curious, I used a pen to swing one door wide. The cabinet was empty.

I crossed to the bathroom.

And froze.

Psyched, I hurried to the loft and pulled aside a curtain forming a makeshift closet. A dozen garments hung from a rod suspended between twisted coat hangers.

"I've got something," I called out.

Six feet clomped up the stairs.

"SOMEONE STAYED HERE."

Six puzzled eyes stared at my face.

I spoke to Otto.

"Your mother kept her belongings precisely sorted and arranged. In her apartment closet, all garments hang exactly two inches apart, utilizing the whole length of the rod. On her bureau, on the mantel, on the bookshelves, every object is positioned equidistant from its neighbors, and every bit of surface is utilized."

Otto nodded slowly, brows pinched into a frown. "That sounds right. She'd get upset if we moved stuff."

"Your mother's paintings are studies in symmetry. Everything is balanced, even."

"Where are you going with this?" Claudel, too, was frowning.

I gestured at the closet.

The men took in the clothing shoved to one side.

Claudel started to speak. I cut him off.

"Follow me."

In the bathroom, Keiser's toiletries were bunched together on one half of a shelf flanking the sink. The other half was empty.

Claudel did one of those air poochy things he does with his lips.

"I suspect Mrs. Keiser was OCD. Her compulsion involved keeping objects spatially ordered. If so, she'd have been incapable of breaking that pattern."

"You're suggesting someone pushed Mom's stuff aside to make room for their own?"

"I am."

"SIJ and arson teams tossed this place." Claudel. "They probably moved things."

"I don't think so." I told them about the painting supplies. "But it's easy enough to check the scene photos."

Claudel's lips tightened.

"Supposedly, only one person knew about this cabin," Ryan said.

"Lu Castiglioni," I said.

"Who?" Otto asked.

"The super at your mother's building."

"What about Myron Pinsker?"

Good question, Otto.

My eyes drifted to the easel. The paints. The sideboard.

Sudden head-smack thought.

"Otto, when you were growing up did your mother keep cash at home?"

"A few bucks in her wallet. Maybe a grocery fund. No big deal."

"Did she ever talk about pulling her money out of the bank? Express concern about the safety of her deposits?"

"Mom was born in the thirties, had that Depression mentality. Banks scared the crap out of her."

"Did she ever act on those fears?"

"Yeah, actually she did. When she took a jolt in the market in 'eighty-seven, she sold all her stocks and put the cash into a savings account. After nine-eleven she threatened to withdraw every penny. It was one of the few times we'd talked in recent years. I didn't take her seriously. The markets were in chaos. Everyone was freaked. And, as I said, Mom was a flake."

"But did she do it?"

Otto shrugged. Who knows?

"Your mother wasn't one for locks, though, was she?"

Otto looked puzzled.

"At the apartment, she had a wall cabinet and a jewelry box, both with keys. She locked neither." I turned to Ryan. "Got a penlight?"

Ryan pulled a small flash from his pocket. Crossing to the sideboard, I squatted to inspect the doors. Close up, lit by the small beam, the gouging and splintering appeared fresh.

"This damage is new." I looked up. "I think Mrs. Keiser kept something locked in this compartment."

"The doors were jimmied." Ryan finished my thought.

"By this mysterious houseguest." Claudel's cynicism was starting to grate on my nerves.

I stood. "Who may have kept her prisoner until he got what he wanted."

Otto looked as though he'd been slapped.

"I'm sorry." I was. "I shouldn't have said that."

"How far back did you go with Keiser's financials?" Ryan asked Claudel.

Claudel was staring at the empty compartment. Ryan's question brought his face around to us. For an instant he looked as if he'd been caught off guard. Then he nodded and yanked his mobile from his belt.

"*Tabarnouche.* I'm getting no signal on this piece of crap. Charbonneau's working that angle. Once I'm on the road and back in range, I'll call and see what he's dug up. When I know, you'll know."

Ryan's mobile rang as we were entering Hurley's Irish Pub for lunch. He clicked on.

"Ryan."

As we took seats in the main room, in Mitzi's booth, I noticed that one small wrong had been righted. The name plate dedicating the corner to Bill Hurley's mother had been stolen one busy night. The little plaque was now back in place.

Really. How low can you go?

As Ryan listened, I mouthed the name Claudel. He nodded.

The waitress brought menus. I ordered lamb stew. Ryan gestured that he wanted the same.

The waitress collected the menus and left.

Ryan contributed a lot of "*oui*'s" and "*tabarnac*'s" to the phone conversation. Queried a location. A date. An amount. He was smiling when he disconnected.

"We got us a motive."

"Really?"

"Between the fall of 2001 and the spring of 2003 Marilyn Keiser withdrew approximately two hundred thousand dollars from her savings account at Scotiabank. There is no record of a deposit elsewhere."

"I knew it. She kept it in shoe boxes at the cabin."

"Not sure about the boxes, but, yes, your cabin theory skews right. And, by the way, Claudel is impressed."

"He is?"

Ryan was looking for the waitress, who had vanished.

"What did he say?"

"I'm impressed."

"Seriously."

"I've got to use the men's." Ryan slid from the booth. "Order me a beer."

"What kind?'

"The usual." He was gone.

The usual? I'd seen the man drink about every brand ever brewed.

Across the room, beer tap handles ran the length of the bar. Round ones, oval ones, wooden ones, green ones. I read the logos.

First the OCD. Then the locked sideboard.

Was it Wednesday and Thursday's purging? Had clearing my system enabled me to think better? Heightened awareness born of my battle with microbes? A third dot connected with an almost audible click.

Oh, baby, I was on a roll.

I was poking at the idea a second time when Ryan returned.

"This is nutso, Ryan. Wild barking mad."

"Where's my beer?"

I could barely sit still.

"Listen to me." I pointed two palms at Ryan. "Just hear me out before you scoff."

"I never scoff at you, buttercup."

"The floral endearment is scoffing."

Ryan made a give-it-to-me gesture with his hand.

The waitress arrived with our food. Ryan ordered a Sam Adams.

"That's it!" My palm smacked the table.

The waitress backed off.

"What are Red O'Keefe–Bud Keith's other aliases?"

"All of them?"

I nodded.

Ryan pulled his spiral from a jacket pocket, flipped pages. "Red O'Keefe. Bud Keith. Sam Caffrey. Alex Carling."

"He's using beer brands!"

Two kids at the next table slid glances our way.

I lowered my voice.

"He mixes and matches. Red—Red Stripe. Bud—Budweiser. O'Keefe—O'Keefe's. Keith and Alex—Alexander Keith's. Carling—Carling's Black Label."

"Sonovabitch."

"But listen." Again the stop sign hands. "Listen."

"I'm listening."

"Sam Adams."

Ryan raised his mug.

"Sam Adamski."

"Keiser's third husband?"

I nodded.

"He's dead."

"What if he's not?"

The mug halted en route to Ryan's mouth.

"According to Otto, Adamski's body was never recovered. What if he's alive?"

"What if he is?"

"Keiser and Adamski married in 'ninety-eight. What if she talked to him about sewing her money into the bedroom drapes? What if he looked her up this fall to check things out?"

"The drowning was staged?"

"Or the accident was real, but he survived. Maybe he saw his death as an opportunity to be exploited."

"Where's he been since 2000?"

"Maybe he changed his identity and hid out, left the country, got busted and did time under another name. Who knows? Adamski reemerges, needs bread, decides to look up his former wife."

"Why now?"

I ignored Ryan's question. I was spitting ideas as they came into my head.

"Or maybe the two kept in contact all along. Maybe they met at the cabin. Adamski knew about it. He built it, for God's sake."

"Why keep it secret that he's alive?"

"The kids hated him."

"They hated him throughout the marriage."

"OK. Maybe they weren't in contact. Maybe he shows up, holds her captive, smacks her around until she tells him about the money. Then he kills her."

"Take a breath."

I did.

"Otto said something this morning that got my wheels turning."

"What?" I asked.

"He remembered that Adamski drowned somewhere in La Mauricie."

"It was a boating accident. Do you suppose Adamski went down in the Saint-Maurice River?"

"I don't know. I'll find out. That's not important. You know what else is right there, not far from Trois Rivières?"

I shook my head.

"A little place called La Tuque."

It took me a nanosecond to make the connection.

"Bud Keith's alibi. He wasn't at L'Auberge des Neiges when Rose Jurmain was killed. He was off bear hunting at La Tuque."

Things were falling into place.

M. Keith, the Villejoins' tree removal man.

Bud Keith–Red O'Keefe, Grellier's bar braggart with knowledge of Christelle's hidden grave.

Bud Keith, the kitchen worker at Rose Jurmain's auberge.

Sam Adamski, Marilyn Keiser's third husband.

For the longest time Ryan and I just stared at each other.

Could Caffrey/Keith/O'Keefe/Carling/Adamski have killed all four women?

Why?

Means and motive didn't matter for now. We had the common link. The explanation of how the victims' lives touched.

Ryan reached for his mobile.

32

BY THE TIME RYAN DROPPED ME AT MY CONDO WE KNEW THAT Caffrey/Keith/O'Keefe/Carling/maybe Adamski was neither at home nor at work.

Ryan issued a BOL. Be On Lookout. I'd barely cleared the Jeep when he roared off, hands tight on the wheel.

He phoned that night around eight.

"He's slipped the grid."

"You'll get him."

"I *had* him." Ryan's voice was taut with frustration. "I *had* the sonovabitch."

"What did the neighbors tell you?"

"They're not the type to notice. Or to share insights with cops."

"What about the gas station?"

"No one's laid eyes on the guy since Wednesday."

The day Ryan interrogated him. I didn't say it.

"I faxed Keith/O'Keefe's mug shot over to Trois Rivières. They ran it out to the camp near La Tuque where Adamski was staying when he had his fatal boating accident in 2000. It's the same guy. *And* the same camp."

"No shit."

"They're the outfit that arranged Bud Keith's bear hunt during his sabbatical from kitchen duty at the auberge."

"Good work, Detective."

Ryan snorted in self-derision. "Except for the part where I let the bastard walk away without so much as a backward glance."

"He won't get far."

"He disappeared in 2000 and didn't resurface until two years ago. We have no friggin' idea where the prick was all that time."

Good point. I didn't say that, either.

"You confirmed that Adamski's body was never found?"

"Yeah." Ryan sounded exhausted. "Apparently he went out on the lake early one morning, alone. They found the boat belly-up, Adamski wasn't in it. They dragged the lake on and off for a week, found his wallet, hat, his fishing gear. No body."

"The locals didn't find that odd?"

"Apparently it's happened before. This lake's ninety feet deep in places."

Sudden flash of the Lac Saint-Jean vics abandoned in my lab. I felt my own stab of guilt. Quentin Jacquème had been waiting forty years for an answer concerning his brother-in-law Achille and the rest of the Gouvrard family.

Monday. First thing. No distractions.

"—gotta tell you. I'm beat."

I pictured Ryan doing that hair-rake thing with his hand. I imagined the clumps shooting in all directions.

I opened my lips.

Hesitated.

What the hell?

"Would you like to come over?"

"Thanks, Tempe. Really. But I promised Lily I'd pick her up early tomorrow. I can't screw up. I'd better call it a day."

"I understand." I didn't.

"You know where I'd rather be. It's just . . . Please. Ask me again?"

"Sure." My chest burned. I needed to get off the phone.

Birdie and I watched *Pretty Woman* on the old-movie channel, then crashed.

Sunday was a day to make Alexander Graham Bell proud. Or rich.

Harry called first, as I was reading the *Gazette.* She spent twenty minutes telling me about her latest romantic interest, then asked how I was.

I described my run-in with the ham salad.

Harry asked if I'd IDed the bastard who'd smeared my name with Edward Allen Jurmain. I told her I hadn't. She suggested modification of that party's genitalia, then asked how things were going with Ryan. To avoid the subject, I talked about the acid atmosphere at the lab, described Briel's television performance, and recounted my conversation with Santangelo.

Harry ordered me to take the day off, citing some cockamamie theory about germs and stress and karma and longevity. I agreed. Vaguely.

Harry pressed, made me promise. Eventually, I did. I knew my sister. Il Duce would call repeatedly to be sure I was home.

Katy phoned not long after Harry. She was dating a musician named Smooth. Smooth, thirty-two, was from Pittsburgh and played in a band called Polar Hard-on. Needless to say, my daughter's news caused a setback in my sister's karmic relaxation regimen.

But I did take things easy. Wrote reports. Plowed through e-mail. Read. Played with my cat.

Took Harry's calls, reassured her that I hadn't slipped house arrest.

All the while, I awaited news of Adamski's capture.

Chris Corcoran rang around four.

Planting a wire on the Stateville inmate had paid off. The cellmate, one Antoine "Pooter" Brown, had provided enough detail to hang himself for Laszlo Tot's murder. In exchange for consideration in sentencing, Pooter had admitted to being present at Lassie's killing, and had agreed to roll on his partner.

He and a genius calling himself Slappy spotted Laszlo in a video arcade. They followed him and tried to hijack his car. Laszlo fought back.

Slappy knifed Lassie. Pooter had watched, helpless to stop the attack. Uh-huh.

Following the stabbing, they'd emptied Laszlo's pockets and stuffed him into his own car trunk. They'd then driven aimlessly, debating their next move. Being from Thornton, Pooter thought of the quarry.

After dumping Laszlo's body, they'd ditched his car in a suburban mall and taken a commuter train back to the city. On Laszlo's dime.

When arrested, Slappy fingered Pooter as the blade man. Very original.

Ryan called at six. His mood wasn't exactly jubilant, but it was a million miles up from the night before.

"Break out the party hats."

"You got him?"

"We may have picked up his trail."

"Wowzer!"

"Did you really say that?"

"Where was he?"

"At approximately four p.m. Thursday a man fitting Adamski's description rented a Hyundai Accent from a Budget agency on Boulevard Décarie. You'll never guess the gentleman's name."

"Miller Moosehead."

"Good one. Alliterative. But no. Lucky Labatt."

"Lucky?"

"Lucky Lager."

"Never heard of it."

"Jack Nicholson drank it in *Five Easy Pieces.*"

"Renting a car requires a license, proof of insurance. Could Adamski come up with a new identity so fast?"

"Fake paper is one of his specialties. It wouldn't have taken him long. Hell, he probably kept extra documents in his underwear drawer. I've issued alerts here and nationwide with CPIC. I also notified the boys at the border. They'll nail him. You going to the lab tomorrow?"

"Oh, yeah. Hubert will be on me like green on Kermit."

"First wowzer, now a frog metaphor. You must have your strength back."

"Simile."

"What?"

"A simile uses words such as 'like' or 'as' to compare two ideas. A metaphor directly compares seemingly unrelated subjects."

"Yep. She's back."

"The Lac Saint-Jean bones have been sitting since Wednesday when I got sick."

"Aren't they the Gouvrards?"

"Probably."

"You have other possibilities?"

"No."

I heard a female voice in the background. There was a muffled sound, as though the phone had been covered or pressed to a chest. In seconds, Ryan was back.

"I've got to take Lily home."

"You two had a good day?"

"As good as they get."

"She's still angry?"

"As a bee in a bottle. Simile."

"Keep me up to speed on Adamski?"

"Roger that. Lady in the loop."

Monday, I fired from bed feeling like I could reforest the Amazon solo. Laszlo's killers were behind bars in Chicago. Adamski would soon be netted. I was cured. Life was good.

So was the weather. The sky was azure, the sun blinding. The temperature was expected to climb to a balmy 2 degrees Celsius.

Since the streets were clear, I decided to drive. That went well, my arrival did not. Due to the tonnage of snow taking up curb space, street parking around Wilfrid-Derome remained a nightmare.

After circling for twenty minutes, I forked over the cash and pulled into the lot. Big deal. It's only money.

I rode the day to twelve with cops and LSJML staff exchanging gossip and news of their weekend lives. Briel was in her office. Morin and Ayers had not yet arrived. Neither had Joe.

In my lab, the Lac Saint-Jean vics lay on the counter and tabletops. The Gouvrard file waited on my desk. In my office, the phone was doing some serious flashing.

I decided on a course of action. Phone messages first. Then little Valentin's antemorts. Then the younger child's bones.

No caller had left a plea or query requiring my immediate attention. Setting my scribbled list aside, I crossed to the lab and opened the Gouvrard file.

It took only minutes to spot an entry that sent my hopes soaring.

Tetracycline is a powerful antibiotic capable of killing a wide array of bacteria. Unfortunately, if taken during the period of dental formation, the drug becomes calcified in the enamel. The result is permanent overall gray or brown discoloration of the crown, or patterns of horizontal stripes of varying intensity.

In the 1950s, tetracycline was so commonly prescribed this type of staining was widespread. As recently as 1980, the drug was still given to kids and pregnant women.

Bad news for your smile. Good news for a forensic ID.

According to his record, Valentin Gouvrard contracted a streptococcal infection at age seven months. The baby took tetracycline for three weeks.

I flew to my bookcase, yanked down a reference manual, and checked a chart.

The deciduous second molars begin calcification between sixteen and twenty-four weeks in utero for the maxilla, between seventeen and twenty weeks in utero for the mandible. Crown completion occurs at around eleven months for the maxilla, ten months for the mandible.

Quick deductive reasoning.

Observation: Valentin Gouvrard took tetracycline when his baby second molars were forming.

Observation: Adult premolars replace baby second molars around age eleven or twelve. The child on my table died between ages six and eight, and, therefore, had his second baby molars at death.

Deduction: If the child on my table was Valentin, those molars would be discolored.

I checked my inventory. One adult first and two baby second molars had been recovered. Though I'd glanced only briefly at the baby teeth, once when doing inventory, once when laying them out for X-rays, I'd noted nothing but a possible dot of dullness in the enamel of the upper-second kid molar.

I was hurrying to check the remains when the phone rang.

"Dr. Brennan."

"Monsieur Hubert."

"I understand you've been unwell."

"I'm tip-top now."

"Good. Come down to my office."

"I've just found something which may be important in resolving the Lac Saint-Jean case. Perhaps—"

"Get down here, please." Sharp. "Now."

"Is something wrong?"

"Yeah." The coroner's tone could have crisped lettuce. "My whole fucking staff is inept."

HUBERT WAS IN HIS CHAIR, LOOKING LIKE DECADES OF WAY TOO much bakery.

"Have a seat, Dr. Brennan."

I sat, expecting a reprimand, clueless as to why.

"Let me ask you something." The coroner's expression was one of perplexed disappointment. "Do you enjoy working here?"

"What?"

"A simple question."

"Of course I do."

"Are you preoccupied with some personal crisis?"

"No." What the hell?

"Experiencing burnout?"

"No." What the bloody hell?

"This feud you're involved in. Could it—"

"I'm involved in no feud." Defensive.

"This situation in Chicago—" Hubert rotated a hand. It was so fat the knuckles showed no wrinkles.

"I can hardly *feud* with a nameless accuser."

"Something is impacting your work."

"Bullshit." Not clever, but it jumped from my lips.

"Must I lay it out?"

"Indulge me." The morning's buoyancy was gone, replaced by anger.

"Quentin Jacquème has called my office repeatedly since the discovery of the Lac Saint-Jean skeletons. Jacquème is retired SQ. His late wife was Achille Gouvrard's sister. Three weeks of calls, Dr. Brennan. And nothing to tell the man."

I focused on my breathing, trying to stay calm.

"On Friday, Dr. Briel asked permission to examine the remains. Since you were absent, I allowed her to do so."

"Well-done." I kept my eyes hard on Hubert's. "Now you have news for Jacquème. A nonexpert has been called in."

"*Au contraire.* I will tell him I am prepared to close the file."

Using one sausage finger, Hubert slid a paper my way.

The report was brief—ages, genders. The description of the younger child included a discussion of tetracycline staining in the baby molars.

Reading the final paragraphs, I translated to English in my head. To be sure.

> The tetracycline staining of the deciduous second right maxillary and mandibular molars is sufficiently unique, in combination with skeletal and dental development, to allow positive identification of the younger individual as Valentin Gouvrard, age eight.
>
> Given consistency in the demographic profile, including adult sexes and individual ages at death, the bone condition, and the pattern of perimortem trauma, it is my opinion that the bones recovered from the vicinity of Lac Saint-Jean on January 12 of this year are those of the Gouvrard family, vanished and presumed dead August 14, 1967.
>
> —Marie-Andréa Briel, M.D.

I looked up, stunned into silence.

"How could you have missed something so important, Dr. Brennan?"

I didn't trust myself with words.

"The staining is obvious. Briel saw it. When she showed me, I saw it. Tetracycline is discussed in the child's medical record."

Still, I said nothing.

"First the Oka phalanges. Now this." Hubert ran a hand over one jowl. "*Eh, misère.* I think you need a break."

"Are you placing me on leave?"

"I am placing you on notice." The leviathan belly rose, fell, as the coroner sighed deeply. "No more screwups."

"Are we finished?"

Hubert looked as though he wanted to say something else. Didn't.

I rose and headed for the door, anger radiating from me like heat from a teapot.

Downstairs, I went directly to the younger child. Uncapping the plastic vial, I slid the three small teeth onto the tabletop.

And stared in astonishment.

Both baby molars had dark brown bands wrapping their crowns.

Hubert was right. The defect was glaring, even with a cursory glance.

The upper-second molar also had a pinpoint of dullness on its proximal cusp. A restoration? Had I spotted that?

I checked my comments.

There was no mention of a filling. I made a note to check the dental X-rays.

Now the heat was in my chest.

How could I have missed the staining? A possible filling?

Was the coroner right? Was I distracted? Becoming careless?

Distracted by what? Ryan? My eagerness to escape on holiday with Katy? Obsession over finding Edward Allen's informant? Over putting Rose Jurmain to rest in my mind?

My cheeks still burned, now from shame.

I was still staring at the teeth when my mobile sounded. I almost ignored it. Instead, I slipped the phone from my belt.

"Do da dance! Sing da song!" Ryan. "Woohoo! We got our man."

"Adamski."

"No. Harry Houdini."

"That's great, Ryan." Flat.

"Try to curb your jubilation."

"I'm thrilled."

"Are you getting sick again?"

"I just went another round with Hubert." I rolled one of the molars around on my palm. "Where'd you nail Adamski? Or Lucky Labatt, or Keith, or whatever the dirtbag now calls himself."

"Genius was watching *Rockford* reruns at a cousin's flat in Moncton. Piece of work name of Denton Caffrey. Adamski's hometown, Adamski's real surname. Gee, who'd have thought to check Caffrey's place? The King of Beers is dumber than a bowl of noodles."

"Where is he now?"

"Claudel flew to Moncton this morning. We'll work Adamski as soon as his ass hits Montreal."

"Think you can crack him?"

"I have to." Ryan's vehemence was palpable even at a distance. "Adamski's dirty, I can feel it in my gut. But everything we've got so far is circumstantial. His marriage to Marilyn Keiser. His known alias, Keith, in the Villejoins' ledger. Florian Grellier fingering him for running his mouth about Christelle's body. His working at L'Auberge des Neiges when Jurmain turned up dead."

"Enough circumstantial evidence can make a case."

"Impressions. The statement of a convicted felon. Adamski's criminal record." Ryan snorted. "Juries want physical evidence. So far we've got zip."

"You'll get it."

"We're rechecking Keiser's cabin for latents, canvassing neighbors, stores in the vicinity to see if anyone remembers Adamski buying kerosene. Doing door-to-door in Pointe-Calumet, refloating his picture. Villejoin's cold a year and a half, Jurmain over three. It's tough."

"Then get a confession."

"That's the plan, ma'am. Claudel's going to schmooze Adamski on the plane. When we work him, he'll play good cop. I'll hit him with the two-by-four."

"Poor casting."

"Hey. The Emmy's as good as mine."

After clicking off, I sat staring at the baby tooth.

How had I overlooked the discoloration?

Returning all three teeth to the vial, I crossed to the window and gazed down.

I missed it.

Stupid. Stupid. Stupid.

I watched a barge slip silently upriver, not really computing what I was seeing.

Briel found it.

Molecules of an idea began coagulating. Lost. Lac Saint-Jean. Fleuve Saint-Laurent.

Twelve floors down, the water looked gray and forbidding. Deep. Unyielding.

The idea took shape.

Adamski's body was never found.

The Gouvrards were never found.

Did others lie forgotten in cold, wet graves?

Crossing to the computer, I called up Wikipedia.

I learned that Lac Saint-Jean is a crater impact lake in the Laurentian Highlands, two hundred kilometers north of the Saint Lawrence River, into which it drains via the Saguenay River. Lac Saint-Jean covers approximately a thousand square kilometers, and drops to sixty-three meters at its deepest point.

Quick calculation. Roughly four hundred square miles by two hundred feet deep. That's a whole lot of water.

I researched a number.

Dialed.

Worked my way through a dazzling hierarchy of voice mail choices.

When a nice lady finally answered, I made my inquiry. She asked me to hold.

I held.

In a while the nice lady came back on the line.

They had one source that might be of help.

Far from optimistic, I headed out.

Montreal has many libraries, both English and French. The Bibliothèque et Archives nationales du Québec, or the Grande Bibliothèque, is the newest, having opened in April of 2005. Located on Boulevard de Maisonneuve, near the Université du Québec à Montréal campus, the massive glass and steel structure houses Quebec's largest collection of recent, rare, and old editions, multimedia documents, reference materials, maps and prints. Auditorium. Exhibition hall. Café. Boutique. *Bien sûr!* It's all there *pour vous* at the BAnQ.

Following the nice telephone lady's instructions, I climbed to the first floor, walked to the north wing, and passed through doors marked *Collection nationale.* Bellying up to a counter, I asked for assistance.

Hands on bony hips, a not quite so nice lady listened to my request, frown deepening with my every word. When I'd finished, she told me I'd need to obtain a library membership. When I returned, card in hand, she indicated a set of microfilm readers and told me to wait.

Ten minutes later, she reappeared carrying a tray filled with small gray and yellow boxes. With an expression of gothic gloom, she asked if I knew how to spool.

I assured her I'd practically majored in spooling.

Telling me there was additional microfilm going back to 1897, she took her leave.

I checked labels. The dates ran from 1948 to 1964, the year the *Progrès du Saguenay* ended publication.

Deciding to start with the newspaper's most recent editions, I spooled up the first reel. The film scratched softly as I cranked backward through time: 1964. 1963. 1962.

The black-and-white images floated in and out of focus. At first I went slowly, checking every page. As my skill grew, I was able to zip through the irrelevant, focusing solely on news and obits.

After an hour I felt a twinge behind one eye. After two a kettle drum was banging fortissimo.

I looked at the tray. Only a billion little boxes to go.

Was my idea crazy?

Maybe. But I had to look. Had to satisfy myself I'd done everything possible.

Threading a new film leader, I began winding through the first half of 1958.

Just past midway, I found what I was after.

Recherche pour les Victimes Noyées Suspendue—
Search for Drowning Victims Suspended

As with Briel's report, I translated as I read.

> July 21, 1958. Following a week of intense effort, the search has ended for four victims still missing and presumed dead following a boating disaster on Lac Saint-Jean. A memorial marker will be erected in honor of three of the dead, Louise-Rosette, Melanie, and Claire Clemenceau, in the cemetery at Sainte-Monique during a brief ceremony Thursday at 1 p.m. The public is invited.

A boating accident. Missing bodies. Lac Saint-Jean.

Excitement jangled every nerve in my body.

A full marching band had now taken the field in my frontal lobe, so I'd fallen into a rhythm of fast-forwarding and periodically pausing to skim. Obviously the hit-and-run approach had been inadequate. I'd missed the initial coverage.

Like the phalanges. And the tetracycline staining.

I rubbed my eyes. Rolled my shoulders.

Drowning. That would mean spring or summer.

Rewinding to April, I began anew.

July 14. The incident was reported in heartrending detail.

Tragédie de Pique-nique—Picnic Tragedy

The headline topped an article taking up most of page 4 below the fold.

On July 13, 1958, a congregation from the small town of Sainte-Monique had held its annual picnic at Parc de la Pointe-Taillon. As was customary, activities had included pontoon rides out onto Lac Saint-Jean.

An afternoon thunderstorm had barreled in with such speed and ferocity, the boaters hadn't had a chance to react. The pontoon had capsized far from shore. Two men had survived. Four adults and five children had not. A man, a woman, and two little girls remained unaccounted for.

Heart hammering, I looked at the names and ages.

Richard Blackwater, 37
Louise-Rosette Clemenceau, 45
Melanie Clemenceau, 13
Claire Clemenceau, 7

I jotted the names and ages of those not recovered, and the date and location of the incident. Then, ignoring my throbbing head, I picked my way through the rest of 1958, reading every word, no matter the size of the print.

On the Tuesday following the incident, the first three victims had been buried, also in the Sainte-Monique cemetery.

Another article ran on July 16. The piece was brief, stating that the last two drowning victims had been laid to rest.

I pushed on.

After search efforts ended on July 21, there was no further mention of the tragedy. Or of the missing victims.

I sat back, staring at my notes.

It all fit. The PMI. The profile. The adult male's cheekbones and incisors. I was willing to bet the farm Blackwater was an aboriginal name.

Suddenly, "Sugar, Sugar" boomed from my purse. After an eon of fumbling, I found and disarmed my cell.

When I looked up, the not so nice library lady was closing in, face pinched into a murderous scowl. Mouthing "Sorry," I gathered my things. Unimpressed, the dragon waited, then bird-dogged me to the door.

Outside, darkness was settling over the city. Car windows were steamed, turning passengers and drivers into murky silhouettes. A damp wind skulked up de Maisonneuve, teasing trash and carrying with it the scent of oil and salt from the river.

Before pulling on my gloves, I checked my list of missed calls.

The number was Ryan's.

He answered right away. Adamski was at Wilfrid-Derome. He and Claudel would begin with him shortly.

Why SQ turf? Though Marilyn Keiser was reported missing in Montreal, and her case fell to the city cops, the possible link to the Villejoin sisters, perhaps Rose Jurmain, meant the Sûreté du Québec owned a piece of the action. At Ryan's suggestion, Claudel had agreed to conduct the interrogation at SQ rather than SPVM headquarters. Courtesy. Separate forces. Neither detective outranked the other. Besides, Adamski thought he was a person of interest because of Florian Grellier's link to Christelle Villejoin.

I wondered. Hadn't Adamski questioned why he was being hauled to Montreal by a city cop? If so, I was sure Ryan and Claudel had covered that detail.

I picked up the pace.

When I arrived on the fourth floor of Wilfrid-Derome, Ryan and Claudel were viewing Adamski on a monitor in an observation room. Both wore expressions of disgust.

Claudel swiveled when I entered, then looked a question at Ryan.

"Dr. Brennan has offered to share her impressions," Ryan said. We all knew I had no official reason to be present.

Claudel hitched one shoulder.

"How will you go at him?" I asked, noting several files in Ryan's hand.

"First we'll focus on the Villejoin murders. During the plane ride, Detective Claudel may have implied our reason for wanting Adamski was to shine a light on Florian Grellier."

"The guy who fingered Adamski for revealing the location of Christelle Villejoin's body."

"Yes, ma'am."

"You told Adamski you're investigating Florian Grellier?" That surprised me.

"Hey. It's not Detective Claudel's fault if the witness mistook his meaning. Anyway, we'll start with Grellier and Villejoin. Then Jurmain and Keiser will come at him like two tons of high-grade manure."

The good-cop-bad-cop boys left. I stayed by the monitor.

Adamski raised stony eyes when the detectives entered the interrogation room. As before, his hands remained clasped on the table.

When Ryan activated the sound system, the tinny sound of scraping chairs came through a speaker.

This time, Ryan skipped the niceties. "This interview will be recorded. For your protection and ours."

Adamski's face remained neutral. Though he was trying hard for tough, the guy looked nervous.

"Do you prefer this interview be conducted in French or English?"

Ryan waited a full five seconds.

"With no preference expressed, questioning will proceed in English. Ryan, Andrew, lieutenant-detective, Sûreté du Québec, and Claudel, Luc, sergeant-detective, Service de police de la Ville de Montréal, in interview with Red O'Keefe, aka Bud Keith, Alex Carling, Samuel Caffrey. Shall we add Lucky Labatt? Or shall we let that priceless gem go?"

"Look, I told you last time. I don't know nothing about no old lady got buried in the woods."

Ryan took Adamski over the same ground as last time, with questions framed to suggest the police had nothing new.

The performances were five-star all around. Adamski stonewalled. Ryan, feigning increasing frustration, grew more and more aggressive. Claudel interjected with the voice of reason.

After forty minutes, Ryan appeared to have reached his snapping point. Opening a file, he skipped a snapshot across the table. Though they were a bit fuzzy on the screen, I could see that the subjects were Christelle and Anne-Isabelle Villejoin, smiling before a Christmas tree, each arm-cradling a cat.

Adamski glanced at the photo, his expression never moving off cocky.

Ryan slapped down another. Christelle's skeleton lying in its grave.

"Jesus." Adamski jerked his eyes away.

Ryan shot from his chair, circled the table, and forced Adamski's head around with two hands.

"Look at her. Look at her, goddamn you!"

"Hey, hey, Lieutenant." Claudel placed a restraining hand on Ryan's shoulder.

Ryan released Adamski, spun the file, and snapped a third photo onto the table. Rose Jurmain, looking much older than her fifty-nine years.

"How about this one?" Adamski's lower lid twitched as he stared at the image.

"Or were you Bud Keith when you did her?"

"What the fuck?"

"Big career move? Stalk an old woman, kill her, pocket a few bucks. Better than credit card scamming. That stuff's for kids. But here's what I don't get." Ryan shoved his face into Adamski's, forcing him to arc backward over the chair. "What kind of dickless piece of shit does old women? Tell me. You sleep at night knowing you beat someone's grannie to death?"

"I didn't have nothing to do—"

"I'm going to nail you, you sick sonovabitch." Ryan's voice carried the menace of a sharpened blade.

Again, Claudel intervened. "Maybe we could all use a break."

Without a word, Ryan straightened, smacked the audio switch, and strode from the room.

Seconds later he joined me. I smiled. He responded in kind.

"Now what?"

"Now Claudel mentions Adamski's stint as Bud Keith at L'Auberge des Neiges. Maybe drops the name of the hunting camp in La Tuque, gets Adamski worried we're wise to the Sam Adamski alias, thus to Marilyn Keiser."

"Masterful."

"Oh, and Claudel just might reference the fact that Rose Jurmain was an American, drop a few phrases like *extradition* and *death penalty.* Hint that maybe it would go better for him to stand trial here."

"Jurmain died in Quebec," I said. "Her body was found here. The U.S. could never extradite her killer."

"We know that, but this dickhead may not."

On the screen we watched Claudel say something to Adamski, pat his arm, exit. Minutes later he returned with a Pepsi.

Ryan waited a half hour, then reentered the interview room carrying two cardboard boxes. Each had an evidence label, one SQ, the other FBI. Both were empty.

Placing his props on the floor in Adamski's sight line, Ryan activated the audio system and sat down.

"Lieutenant-detective Ryan rejoining interrogation." Ryan turned to Claudel. "Have you read the suspect his rights?"

"What the hell?" Adamski's head whipped to Claudel.

"It's a formality." Claudel, sounding uncharacteristically kind.

I studied Adamski as Claudel did the right-to-remain-silent bit. His left temple vein was pumping a gusher.

"Do you understand your rights, Mr. O'Keefe?" Ryan asked when Claudel had finished. "Or should we go with Adamski? Guess that one slipped the list."

Adamski almost winced at the name.

"Do you understand the statement Detective Claudel just read to you?"

Adamski only glared. Stunned at hearing the incriminating alias? Already spinning explanations?

"I'm free all night, Adamski. But someone wastes my time, I get real cranky."

"Who's this Adamski putz? Why you calling me that?"

"Your rights?"

"I ain't an idiot." With venom.

"Mr. Adamski has indicated that he understands his rights and obligations."

Ryan served up silence.

Though agitated, Adamski didn't fall into the trap.

"We're going to move on," Ryan said. "This interview now concerns the murder of one Keiser, Marilyn, and any and all related events and/or crimes."

Ryan asked Claudel to state the SPVM case number for the record. He did.

Ryan opened one of his files. "You were married to a woman named Marilyn Keiser from 1998 to 2000, is that correct?"

Adamski hesitated, weighing his options. "Things didn't work out. So what?"

"Marilyn Keiser was murdered three months ago."

"That's got nothing to do with me."

"Her body was found one week ago, in a cabin at Memphrémagog. She'd been doused with kerosene and set on fire."

"Maybe she pissed off Memphrie." Adamski snorted nervously. "You know? The monster from the lake?"

"You think this is funny?"

"I think this is a crock of shit."

"You built that cabin. Other than yourself and the victim, no one knew it existed." Ryan didn't mention Lu the janitor.

"Ain't that a coincidence."

"Mrs. Keiser kept money in that cabin. Having been married to her, you'd be aware of that practice."

"Marilyn was a wackjob. Everyone knew it."

"Your prints are all over that cabin." Ryan laid a hand on one of his empty cartons.

Adamski's eyes flicked to the box, away. "So? The place used to be—"

"You bought that kerosene. We're going to find the clerk who sold it to you."

"You're crazy." Now the bravado sounded forced.

"You killed your ex-wife, doused her, torched her, and walked away." Ryan was hammering hard.

"No—"

"You killed Marilyn Keiser. You killed Rose Jurmain. You killed Christelle and Anne-Isabelle Villejoin."

"No." Adamski's fingers were jammed together hard to stop the shaking. The maneuver wasn't working.

Ryan tossed down an autopsy photo of Keiser. Added a shot of Anne-Isabelle on her kitchen floor.

Again, Adamski looked away.

"Look at them. Anne-Isabelle Villejoin was eighty-six. Christelle was eighty-three. Your ex-wife was seventy-two."

Circling the table as before, Ryan yanked Adamski by the hair to force his eyes toward the pictures.

"Tell me this, you gutless sack of shit. Did it turn your stomach to murder these helpless old women? Did you smack them from behind to avoid seeing the terror in their eyes? Did they tremble? Did you? Like you're trembling now?"

"I don't know what you're talking about." Struggling to break free of Ryan's grasp.

Ryan shoved Adamski's face down until his nose was inches from the tabletop.

"We've got you at Jurmain's auberge. We've got you at Keiser's cabin. We've got you at the Villejoin house. We've got you running your mouth to Florian Grellier."

Adamski kicked out his feet and twisted from side to side. Ryan ignored his writhing.

"We're requesting surveillance photos from the ATM where you used the Villejoins' bank card. We're talking to everyone who ever set foot in Pointe-Calumet. We're talking to everyone who ever so much as walked past Jurmain's auberge.

"Know what's happening in Moncton right now? Cousin Denton's having a nice little chat with the cops. Think he'll rat you out on that big score you bragged about? Maybe roll on the money you stashed at his place?"

"Jesus Christ, back him off," Adamski croaked.

"For God's sake, Ryan." Claudel was on his feet. "Let the guy breathe."

Freeing Adamski, Ryan took an angry step back.

Adamski brought his head up and rubbed his scalp with a trembling hand.

Ryan nodded at Claudel ever so slightly.

Claudel resumed his seat and spoke in a calming voice.

"I'm not going to scam you, Sam. It looks bad. These ladies were old. Juries don't like that. They've got mamas, grannies, aunties. The physical evidence is piling up. Witnesses are going to come forward. Jurmain was an American." True but irrelevant. "If you come clean, maybe you can help yourself. Maybe we can help you."

"I never heard of no Rose Jurmain." Adamski's eyes were now clamped to the tabletop.

"We can talk about that."

Silence buzzed through the speaker. A minute. Two.

Above Adamski's sight line, the detectives exchanged anxious glances.

I held my breath. Like Claudel and Ryan, I knew Adamski's next utterance would signal thumbs up or down on the good–bad cop performance. I want a lawyer? I didn't mean to do it?

Slowly, Adamski lifted his head. When he spoke, it was to Claudel.

"I don't say shit while this lunatic's in my face."

35

IT WAS A NIGHT OF BAD COFFEE DOWNED WHILE SITTING ON BUTT-numbing chairs. Ryan and I watched Adamski/Keith/O'Keefe by monitor as Claudel spun his magic two doors down.

The story came out slowly, with Claudel doing empathetic, Adamski veering between boastful and whiny.

By two he'd owned Marilyn Keiser. By four he'd rolled on the Villejoins.

This was the creep's story.

Adamski's boating mishap was real. After capsizing, he managed to drag himself ashore. Lying soaked and exhausted, he'd had an epiphany. His current life sucked. Loathing lawyers and paperwork, he decided to turn the mishap to his advantage.

After seeding the lake with belongings, Adamski hitched a ride to Nova Scotia. In Halifax, he looked up a fellow businessman, invested in a new identity, and set out for greener pastures south of the border.

Life in America wasn't the dream Adamski had envisioned and, in 2006, he returned to Quebec. Using an old alias, Bud Keith, he got a kitchen job at the auberge near Sainte-Marguerite. During his tenure at the inn, an alcoholic old lady wandered off and vanished.

Eventually bored with scraping plates and scouring pans, Adamski headed for the bright lights of Montreal. Still living as Bud Keith, he met a waitress named Poppy from Saint-Eustache. Soon they were living together.

At first things were dandy. In due course, Poppy began nagging

Adamski to contribute to the cost of their cohabitation. Offering use of her Honda, she suggested door-to-dooring for handyman jobs.

Adamski spent the early part of May 4 in a bar, drinking beer and debating the merits of personal freedom versus a free roof and steady pussy. Pumped on Moosehead and self-pity, he then followed route 344 into Pointe-Calumet, and picked a house with a dead pine in the yard. Anne-Isabelle, his first mark, agreed to his tree-removal proposal, then paid from an oatmeal tin dug from her pantry.

Angry that the job had taken longer than anticipated, Adamski asked for more than the agreed-upon sum. Anne-Isabelle refused. An argument ensued, was concluded by Adamski grabbing the old woman's cane and clubbing her to death.

Hearing the commotion, Christelle came to investigate. Out of control with rage, Adamski demanded more cash. When Christelle produced a bank card, Adamski shoved her into Poppy's Honda, drove into the city, and forced her to make a withdrawal.

But time behind the wheel had a sobering effect. Afraid to hit other ATMs as he'd initially intended, and afraid to return to Pointe-Calumet, Adamski stopped to purchase a garden spade. He then killed and buried Christelle in Oka.

Adamski then ditched the Villejoins' bank card, scrubbed the Honda, and hightailed it to Poppy's condo in Saint-Eustache. For several months he worked odd jobs, followed coverage of the Villejoin investigation, and lay low.

As time passed and Johnny Law failed to come knocking, Adamski grew increasingly confident he'd gotten away with murder. As was his pattern, he also grew increasingly disenchanted with his living arrangement.

During this period, Adamski logged a lot of couch time with Poppy's TV. And bless her, she had cable. Along with hockey and reruns of *The Rockford Files* and *Miami Vice,* he followed news of a series of home invasions across the border in upstate New York. He learned that, over a two-year span, three senior citizens had been robbed and beaten to death.

Adamski began thinking about the old lady who'd disappeared from L'Auberge des Neiges. About the Villejoins. Though it had been years since he'd seen his former wife, he thought of her, too. He remembered Keiser's threats to pull her money from the bank, wondered if she'd followed through.

He'd married Keiser for financial gain. But the old lady was nuts, still wanted sex. Living with her was intolerable. As with everything in his life, the plan hadn't worked out. Like Poppy wasn't working out.

Adamski did some calculation. Marilyn Keiser would be seventy-two. He'd killed the Villejoins and skated. The women were feeble, provided little challenge.

Adamski established that Keiser still lived in the same building. For weeks he sat in Poppy's Honda on Édouard-Montpetit, watching his former wife's comings and goings. He followed her to a synagogue, a market, a community center, a yoga studio.

One Friday, Keiser emerged with an overnighter and drove to Memphrémagog. Adamski followed. To his surprise, she went to his old hunting shack.

Three times he observed this weekend routine. When Keiser wasn't there he checked security. Visibility. The proximity of neighbors.

Slowly, a plan took shape. He'd break into the cabin, hide Poppy's car in the shed, and wait. When Keiser arrived he'd demand her stash. If it was hidden at the cabin, perfect. If it was at the apartment, he'd drive her back to town and kill her there. Either way, he'd make it look like a home intrusion.

Except Keiser didn't surrender as easily as expected. When she finally broke, Adamski was so furious he doused her body with kerosene and tossed a match.

According to Adamski, the women were mostly to blame for their own deaths. His reasoning ran thus. He has problems with rage. They shouldn't have crossed him. Flawless.

After nearly ten hours of watching the sleazy bastard, I was ready to burst my skin. Or shed it in disgust. Partly the coffee? Maybe.

My brain was still ragged from staring first at the microfilm, then at the grainy image on the closed-circuit TV. Exhaustion had scrambled my emotions, and I had no desire to sort my psyche. I felt sadness, sure. Repugnance. Anger. Yeah, a boatload of anger.

Anyway, by four I'd had it.

With Ryan's promise to keep me looped in, I headed home.

That night I dreamed again of moths and skeletons and incinerated corpses. Ryan was there, Ayers, Chris Corcoran. Others, too murky to name.

I awoke at eight, again sensing a missed shoulder-tap from my subconscious.

What? The Jurmain, Villejoin, and Keiser cases were closed. The Lac Saint-Jean bones would soon be identified. Nothing remained but Edward Allen's accuser. Was that the cause of the *psst!* from my id?

While feeding the cat, I realized I'd failed to tell Ryan about my discovery of the Sainte-Monique boating accident. No biggie. He'd call shortly with an update on Adamski.

"Big day today, Bird."

Birdie kept crunching his little brown pellets.

"First, I'm going to resolve the Lac Saint-Jean case. Then I'm going to nail the rat bastard who smeared my name."

Bird shot me the cat equivalent of a reproachful glance. At my use of language? The rodent reference?

I left him to breakfast alone.

At Wilfrid-Derome, a small tan envelope lay on my lab desk. Finally, Joe had taken postmortem X-rays of all the teeth recovered with the Lac Saint-Jean remains.

Sliding the little black films onto a light box, I examined each tooth.

The spot of dullness on the second upper baby molar glowed white and radiopaque. A restoration. Interesting, but of little value without antemortem dental records.

Next, I reexamined each of the Lac Saint-Jean skeletons. Then I called Labrousse, the gynecologist-coroner in Chicoutimi.

After describing my library microfilm find, I asked Labrousse to see what he could dig up locally on the drowning victims. He agreed to look for surviving family members, medical, and dental records. He also offered to check the coroner archives, but doubted anything would remain from 1958.

Agreeing that retention of fifty-year-old files was unlikely, I asked Labrousse to query three things. Was Richard Blackwater First Nations? Was Claire Clemenceau given antibiotics as an infant? Did she have any fillings?

Labrousse said he'd get back to me.

Next, I called the chief coroner.

To describe Hubert's reaction as skeptical would be akin to calling Bull Run a minor skirmish. Or maybe he hated to admit that *my* skepticism was justified. Whatever.

His parting remarks: Valentin Gouvrard took tetracycline at age seven months. The kid from the lake had defective baby molars. *Quelle coincidence!*

Coincidence is right, I thought, hand lingering on the cradled receiver. A coincidence the size of Yankee Stadium.

Sometimes you just know. Call it intuition. Call it deductive reasoning based on experience and subconscious pattern recognition.

I was certain in my gut that the people from Lac Saint-Jean were the Sainte-Monique picnickers. I simply had to prove it.

I searched my brain. Was there *anything* to indicate the gender of the juvenile skeletons? Given the condition of the bone, measurement was impossible.

I came up blank.

I was gnawing on the problem when Ryan called. He sounded as tired as I felt. That didn't surprise me. His update did.

"Adamski's copping to Keiser and the Villejoins, coughing up detail like he's writing a novel. But he's adamant about having nothing to do with Jurmain."

"Do you believe him?"

"Why own three murders and lie about the fourth?"

"You did suggest a little American custom called capital punishment."

"Adamski lawyered up. He now knows extradition's not on the table."

"Is that little trick going to come back to haunt you?"

"No one told Adamski he'd go to the States. It's not our fault if the moron misinterpreted reference to Jurmain's citizenship. We were just placing her death in context."

I thought a moment. Rose Jurmain's bones had no signs of violence.

"Maybe being at the auberge was nothing more than bad luck for Adamski," I said.

"Meaning the initial finding was correct. Jurmain wandered off drunk and froze to death."

"There was no trauma to her skeleton."

"Except for the bears."

"Except for that. And her body wasn't buried or hidden in any way."

"Speaking of trauma, here's another kicker. Adamski swears he gut-punched Keiser to death."

"Why lie about shooting her?"

"Beats me. But the story skews right with his history."

"But I saw the bullet track. Ayers showed me photos."

"Maybe Adamski has self-image issues. You know, guns are for sissies, that sort of thing. Or maybe the gun belongs to someone he's trying to protect. We're still working him. It's harder now that he's hired a mouthpiece."

I told Ryan about the '58 boating accident on Lac Saint-Jean.

"Did you ask Jacquème about his brother-in-law's ancestry?"

"Yes, ma'am. Achille Gouvrard was *pure laine.*"

Pure laine. Pure wool. Translation: old-line white Québécois.

"And Jacquème remembered something else. Gouvrard fought at the battle of Scheldt in 'forty-four. Came home with shrapnel in his right thigh. Complained of bone pain when temperatures dropped."

After disconnecting, I got up and popped an X-ray onto the light box. There wasn't a trace of metal in the male's right femur.

I studied his broad cheekbones and shoveled incisor.

More than ever I was convinced the man was not Achille Gouvrard.

My eyes shifted to the younger child's discolored molars.

Again, shame burned my chest.

Briel spotted the tetracycline staining. I did not.

I looked away, out the window. At the scene I'd found calming for so many years. The river. The bridge. The drivers and pedestrians pursuing their everyday lives.

A moth lay on the sill, legs crimped, wings museum-mummy dry. Dead since this summer?

The little corpse triggered recall of my nighttime visitations. The moths. The skeletons. The burned corpses.

Something sat up deep in my brainpan.

I looked back at the bones.

Briel found the staining.

The something rippled the surface of my subconscious.

Briel found the bullet track.

The bullet track.

The something broke through into conscious thought.

GRABBING THE RECEIVER, I PUNCHED THE NUMBER FOR THE COOK County Medical Examiner. When my call was answered, I asked for Chris Corcoran.

Chris's extension rang three times, then rolled to voice mail.

I left a message. Call as soon as you can. It's important.

I looked at the wall clock. Nine thirty. He was probably carving out someone's liver.

The bullet track. Natalie Ayers, a veteran pathologist, missed it. Marie-Andréa Briel, a rookie, found it. That was the flag my subconscious was waving.

The case was a stunner for Chris Corcoran. He described it in detail when I was in Chicago. The woman dead on her living room floor. The autopsy revealing no sign of trauma. The grandson admitting to capping his grandma. The reautopsy. Chris found the injury so unique he wrote it up for publication.

OK.

I hurried to the library.

Where to start? Chris was working the case when Laszlo Tot's body turned up in the quarry. That was July of 2005.

It takes time to write a scientific article, to revise, to await your place in the publication queue. Pulling the November 2007 *Journal of Forensic Sciences,* I checked the author index.

Nothing. I checked 2006, 2005, 2008. Nothing.

So much for that.

Back to the lab.

While awaiting word from Chris about his bullet track case, and from Labrouse about the Sainte-Monique drowning vics, I decided to do some Internet research.

Googling the name *Marie-Andréa Briel* generated an astonishing number of links. In addition to numerous online papers and blogs, Briel had coauthored articles for the *Journal of Forensic Sciences,* the *American Journal of Forensic Medicine and Pathology,* and a number of Canadian and British journals. All with the first sacked student assistant. All in the past year.

Briel had given dozens of interviews in both French and English. She'd served on panels directed at student career networking. She was listed among the faculty of the Department of Pathology at Laval University, and on a dozen sites hawking biomedical experts. She'd joined every forensic society in the free world.

As I followed loops into loops, I was aware of Joe moving around in the lab, logging tissue samples, shooting photos, entering data into the system. Of Jean Leloup, Isabelle Boulay, Daniel Bélanger, and, of course, Céline crooning from the radio.

In all the cyber bytes tilled, I turned up nothing predating Briel's arrival in Quebec. No biography. No résumé. No mention of past employment or educational background.

When I finally peeled my eyes from the screen, I noticed a figure behind me. I turned.

Joe's arms were crossed on his torso.

"I'm sorry. Did you say something?" I was surprised to see him there.

"The dental X-rays. Lac Saint-Jean. They were OK?"

"Yes." Had I not thanked him? "Thanks. They were fine."

I hesitated, debating whether to share my revised take on the vics. Why not? It might appease him, make him feel part of the breakthrough.

Joe listened to my new theory, face utterly blank.

"What about the staining?" he asked.

"An excellent question," I said. "For which I *will* find an answer."

"Do you—"

The phone rang.

I swiveled, hoping it was Chris Corcoran. It was.

"Something breaking? You sounded revved."

"Thanks for calling back so fast. When I was in Chicago last December you described a homicide in which a single bullet shot straight down the victim's back, remember?"

"Damndest thing. The trajectory followed the alignment of the muscle fibers, completely masking the presence of the track. I did an informal survey. No one had seen anything similar. The case was so freaky, I wrote it up for the *JFS,* got a revise and resubmit. I still haven't gotten to the cuts the reviewers suggested. Want a copy?"

"Can you fax it to me now?"

"Sure."

I gave Chris the number, then hurried to reception. Minutes later his article came clicking in.

An Unusual Gunshot Death Involving Longitudinal Tracking Through a Single Erector Mass.

Twenty-four pages. I agreed with the reviewers. Overkill.

I did a speed-read while walking back to my lab.

A sixty-eight-year-old female was last seen alive at a family picnic on the Fourth of July. . . . Daughter discovered decedent in an advanced state of putrefaction. . . . Absence of organ perforation. . . . Absence of skeletal trauma. . . . Absence of metallic trace. . . . Cause of death undetermined. . . . Victim's grandson confessed to shooting. . . .

My eyes froze on a sentence in a section subtitled *Second Autopsy Findings.*

Cross-sectional dissection demonstrated a single bullet track running longitudinally down the right erector mass.

Throat constricting with anger, I skimmed the rest.

. . . wound orientation suggested the victim was moving at the moment of projectile impact. . . . Cause of death reevaluated as homicide. . . . Extremely rare. . . . Review of the literature revealed no reported cases. . . .

I tossed the fax onto my desk, thoughts firing like kernels in a popper.

The bullet track was extraordinarily uncommon and difficult to spot. Ayers missed it with Keiser. Chris missed it in his Chicago case. Both are experienced pathologists.

Briel found it.

Luck? Skill? Coincidence?

Not a chance.

Briel couldn't have read about Chris's case. The article wasn't yet in print.

My Internet search had turned up zip on Briel's past. She claimed to have done a number of postdocs. Might one have been with the CCME?

My id popped another flashbulb image. Friday night's dream. The tendrils floating from Rose Jurmain's skeleton, one inscribed with the initials *ML.*

But that was wrong. ML analyzed Lassie's bones. Not Rose's.

Suddenly the skin on my face felt tight.

Briel was keen on anthropology. She'd taken a short course. Done the reexcavation at Oka. Jumped on the Lac Saint-Jean vics in my absence.

Might Briel be ML?

My cortex scoffed at my lower centers. Waaay overreaching.

Yet.

I dialed Chris again. This time he answered.

"I read the article. Good job."

"You think it's too long?"

"A little. Do you remember having a pathologist at the CCME named Marie-Andréa Briel?"

"No. But they come and go."

"You did the bullet track autopsy around the time Laszlo Tot's body was dragged from the Thornton Quarry, right?"

"Yes."

"You said Walczak uses freebies for skeletal cases, pathologists, residents, anthropology grad students, right?"

"It's not my decision."

"Someone named ML did the anthropology on Laszlo's remains, right?"

"Sorry. I don't remember. I'd have to recheck the file."

"Can you do that for me? And if ML examined Lassie's bones, find out who that person was?"

"Does this have to do with the jerk who called Edward Allen Jurmain?"

God Almighty.

Suddenly, it all made terrible sense.

Briel found the bullet track.

Briel found the phalanges.

Briel found the staining.

My competence wasn't slipping. I was being sabotaged.

Was Briel the one who'd contacted Jurmain? She was here. She'd have known about my involvement in the case.

But why?

"Earth to Tempe."

"Sorry. I'm not sure, Chris. Maybe. But I know one thing for certain. The *merde*'s about to hit the *ventilateur.*"

The line beeped.

"Gotta go. Let me know what you learn. And thanks."

I clicked over.

Labrousse. I was on a roll.

"Good thing this area is so inbred." Labrousse wasn't using the expression metaphorically. Being an isolated population that had bottlenecked genetically and reproduced wildly, over the years the folks of Lac Saint-Jean had been mined extensively for medical research. "Families stay put around here. And have memories deeper than a hooker's cleavage. On Blackwater, everyone's in agreement. He was half Montagnais."

Yes!

"And Claire Clemenceau?" I asked. "Any history of tetracycline?"

"No one remembers anything like that. Brother says Claire was a healthy baby. Local GP's dead, but he had a young associate just coming on in the fifties. The guy's retired now, but remembers Claire. Says she was seen mainly for well-baby checkups. Guy's ninety, but seems sharp enough."

"But there are no written records to back him up."

"No."

"How about dental work?"

"The brother says none of the kids saw a dentist."

That tracked. Based on the adult female's teeth, it didn't appear dental hygiene was a big priority.

Yet the younger child had a filling. That didn't track.

"Did the brother remember staining on Claire's dentition?"

"Says she had perfect teeth."

Silence hummed down from the north. Then,

"Family version could be revisionist thinking."

"Meaning?" I asked.

"Tragic accident, years pass, the dead kid becomes the perfect little girl."

"Or the doc could be right. Claire was healthy."

"Could be," Labrousse said. "Let me know what you decide."

After hanging up, I crossed to my worktable and scooped up the younger child's two baby teeth.

I closed my eyes and digits and willed the tiny molars to speak to me. Claire Clemenceau, drowned while boating? Valentin Gouvrard, killed while flying?

I felt only a prickly hardness in my fist.

Uncurling my fingers, I studied the small crowns with their discolored enamel.

A phrase whispered through my brain.

Cusp of Carabelli.

No surprise I'd missed it. The tiny bump was barely visible, a wee bulge on the lingual surface of the mesiolingual cusp of the upper M2.

I picked up the permanent molar. No cusp.

Odd, but no big deal. The variation is most common on permanent first upper molars, but can be present on baby second molars as well.

Carabelli's cusp varies in frequency of expression between populations, occurring in a high percentage of Europeans. Its presence suggested the Lac Saint-Jean child was probably white. I already suspected that. The variant was little more than a curiosity.

Frustrated, I returned the teeth to their vial.

Then I paced, thoughts buzzing like yellowjackets in my brain.

Briel had done anthropology when her training was in pathology. Remains were now in danger of misidentification. Briel's motive didn't matter. I had to demonstrate her ineptness to Hubert. To stop her over-reaching her professional competence.

Gnawing a thumbnail, I reviewed the facts.

Achille Gouvrard was white. The male skeleton had features suggesting Mongoloid ancestry.

Richard Blackwater was half Montagnais.

Achille Gouvrard had shrapnel embedded in one thigh bone. The man on my table did not.

Claire Clemenceau was a healthy infant.

The younger child's baby teeth showed tetracycline staining. Obvious. Yet I'd missed it during my preliminary examination.

Claire Clemenceau probably never saw a dentist.

The child on my table had a restoration.

A Carabelli's cusp on one baby tooth.

Useless.

I'd missed that, too.

Or had I?

Briel found the bullet track.
Briel found the phalanges.
Briel found the staining.
The truth blasted through.
I knew what had happened.
And what I had to do to prove it.

LEAVING MY LAB, I CHECKED THE BOARD AT THE END OF THE HALL. The letters *AM* were written beside Briel's name. *Absence motivée.*

Briel had requested the day off.

Excellent.

I proceeded to admin. Claiming need of a file, I asked for a key to LaManche's door. No big deal. With the chief on sick leave, the pathologists and I occasionally required dossiers from his office.

My watch said eleven fifty. Back in my office, I forced myself to wait. Twenty minutes. Then my coworkers would be downing lunch meat and microwave pizza.

Overestimation. In ten minutes the medico-legal wing was deserted.

Moving quickly, I went to LaManche's desk and removed his master keys. Then I let myself into Briel's office, closed the door, and began searching.

The desk produced nothing.

I worked through the bookshelves, then the credenza. Still nothing.

My palms were damp. I felt like a thief.

With jerky movements, I began pulling drawers in the first filing cabinet. Nada.

Second. Nope.

My eyes flicked to the narrow window paralleling the door. Through the blinds I detected no movement in the hall.

Deep breath.

I started on the last cabinet.

And struck gold.

The ziplock lay in the bottom drawer, in a gap behind the last file separator. Inside were at least forty teeth.

High-fiving myself, I slipped from the room, locked up, and returned the chief's keys.

Back in my lab, I spread the collection on my blotter. And sagged in dismay.

There wasn't a baby tooth in the lot, stained or otherwise.

Had I erred? Misjudged Briel? Was I desperately seeking a way to let myself off the hook?

As before, my gaze drifted to the window over my desk. A frost blossom spread from a lower corner of the glass. I saw a peony. An owl. An old man's face.

I thought of Katy, our cloud games when she was a little girl. I wished myself home, on my back in the grass on a summer afternoon.

I remembered my conversation with Solange Duclos. Her "spider" molar from Bergeron's tub. *The itsy bitsy spider went up the waterspout.* I hadn't been amused. A sign I was growing old? Losing my ability to imagine? To laugh?

To function professionally?

Hell no. I hadn't really inspected the damn tooth.

The tooth.

The tub.

I pictured the "spider" itsy bitsying through the air.

My eyes closed.

Flew open.

Carabelli's cusp!

Grabbing my keys, I shot to the closet, unlocked a cabinet, and yanked out Bergeron's tub of teaching specimens.

Back to my desk for another triage.

The collection contained twelve baby teeth: eight incisors, three canines, and Duclos's "spider" molar, an upper first from the right side.

Sonovabitch. The molar had a Carabelli's cusp.

I carried it to a table-mounted magnifying lens. I was rotating the molar, studying every surface, when the door opened, clicked shut.

I glanced up.

Joe.

Too amped for small talk, I turned back to the lens, hoping, but not really expecting to find what I needed.

I was about to give up when a pinpoint of dullness caught my attention, not so much a stain as a subtle flattening of the enamel.

Barely breathing, I took the molar to the stereomicroscope and cranked up the power.

Yes! A wear facet.

After sealing the molar in a vial, I scrolled to a number on my mobile and dialed.

"Department of Anthropology."

"Miller Barnes, please."

A voice answered, broad and flat as a Kansas prairie.

I said hi. Miller said hi. We both agreed it had been a long time. Miller asked about Katy. I asked about his wife. Finally, I was able to make my request.

"Is there a scanning electron microscope on the McGill campus?"

"Engineering has one. What do you need?"

I explained.

"When do you need it?"

"Yesterday."

Miller laughed. "I play racquetball with one of the guys over there. Always get my ass whupped. Should work for us."

I paced, gnawed.

Joe cast curious glances my way. I ignored him. I'd buy cookies.

An eon later the phone rang.

"Ever watch *The Price Is Right*?" Miller asked.

"Back in the Pleistocene." Quiz shows?

"Come on down." He mimicked the coveted invitation.

Locking Briel's ziplock in my desk and Bergeron's tub in its cabinet, I pocketed the vial containing Duclos's "itsy bitsy spider" tooth, an upper-right M1, and the one containing the teeth from the Lac Saint-Jean child. Then I grabbed my jacket and purse and flew out the door.

McGill University lies in the heart of *centre-ville,* so parking a car is like dumping nuclear waste. Not here, sister.

After three loops up University and through a neighborhood dubbed the McGill ghetto, I spotted a possibility. Playing bumper cars for a good five minutes, I managed to wedge the Mazda into a gap probably vacated by a scooter.

I got out. The vehicles fore and aft had at least a foot each.

Attagirl!

The sky was tin, the temperature up a notch. Moist air pressed down on the city like a heavy wet quilt.

As I entered campus through the east gate, fat flakes began lazing down. Most melted on contact with the pavement. Others lingered, minimally enthused by thoughts of collective action.

Around the main quad, gaunt stone buildings climbed from Sherbrooke to Docteur Penfield, gray and solid as Mont Royal at their backs. Students scurried the pathways, shoulders rounded, heads and backpacks coated with wet snow doilies.

Above me, the spiffy new Wong Building looked square and stark, a poster child for modern efficiency. Its neighbor, Strathcona, was a sterner vision from a different time. Constructed in the late nineteenth century, Strathcona's architect had not striven to showcase his feminine side.

I trudged uphill and pushed through the door of Wong. Miller was waiting inside. I got a bear hug.

"My contact is in Materials and Mining."

"Lead on."

He did. To an office with the name *Brian Hanaoka* beside the door.

The man behind the desk wore clothes that looked older than he. Plaid shirt, faded jeans, ratty wool sweater. I put their owner at maybe thirty-five.

Miller made introductions. Hanaoka was short and pudgy, with a very round face and very black hair.

"Please. Make yourselves comfortable." More an exaggerated correctness than an accent.

We all sat, Miller and I facing the desk, Hanaoka behind it.

"My friend tells me we can be of help to your lab." Hanaoka's face went even rounder when he smiled.

I considered, decided against righting the record on exactly who was asking the favor. If my suspicions were upheld, the lab would benefit.

"While consulting to the United States central identification laboratory in Hawaii awhile back, I learned of research involving wear facets on isolated teeth. The study used scanning electron microscopy and energy dispersive X-ray spectroscopy."

"That is the facility that identifies your lost soldiers from southeast Asia, yes?" Miller asked.

"Yes. And Korea and World War Two," I said.

"A difficult task."

"Very. Remains are often fragmentary. Sometimes a few teeth are all that return, and dental records become very important. Occasionally an antemortem file documents a restoration in an *unrecovered* tooth. The record might say 'gold crown,' or 'amalgam,' for example. In such cases it can be useful to detect and identify specific elements on an adjacent though unrestored tooth that *has* been recovered."

"That's where these facets come in," Miller guessed.

"Yes. Wear facets are tiny abrasive patches that form between teeth. To the naked eye they appear to have little relief. When viewed microscopically, they're actually all corners and angles."

"Making them great repositories of particulate debris."

"Exactly." This guy was smart. "The CILHI researchers used SEM to visualize the facets and EDS to determine the elemental composition of restorative residue trapped inside them."

"Good." Hanaoka did a continuous, bobble-head nod. "Very good."

I unpocketed the Lac Saint-Jean vial and set it on his desk. Then, avoiding specifics, I shared my idea.

"Teeth A are associated with a recently recovered juvenile skeleton. The two baby molars exhibit features inconsistent with the rest of the remains. One is an upper-right second, the other a lower-right second."

"You refer to the brown, smaller ones?" Hanaoka was holding the vial inches from his face.

"Yes."

"One has a filling?"

"The upper."

I produced the vial with the "itsy bitsy spider" tooth from Bergeron's tub.

"Tooth B was obtained from another context. It is also a baby molar, an upper-right first. It has a wear facet on its distal side. It has no restoration."

Hanaoka got it right away. "You want to see if upper-first baby molar B, which has a wear facet, once sat beside upper-second baby molar A, which has a filling."

"Bingo."

"Why are child A's baby teeth brown?"

I explained the link to tetracycline, and the timing of crown formation.

More nodding. Then a pause. Then, "I like this."

"Can you do what I've proposed?"

"I can do it."

"When?"

"If you wait twenty minutes I will do it now."

While Hanaoka was gone, Miller described his recent fieldwork in Jordan. Distracted by thoughts of Briel's treachery, I took little in. But talk of archaeology reminded me of Sebastien Raines. When Miller had finished, I asked about Briel's husband.

"Know him? Yeah, I know the weasely goat turd. Wait. That's unfair to goats."

"What about weasels?"

"Friendly amendment accepted. Raines is mean as a snake and a disgrace to the profession."

"Don't hold back."

"The guy would dynamite Machu Picchu if someone offered cash. And write his report any way the buyer requested." Miller's face contorted in anger. "Raines had the cojones to apply for a position in our department. When we vetted his résumé, we found he'd fabricated almost everything."

"He has a master's degree, right?"

"Oh, yeah. Purchased online. Raines did enroll in a legitimate program in France, but got kicked out halfway through his first year of study. The project director caught him stealing artifacts."

"Raines is a Quebecker. Why study in France?"

"No graduate program here would accept him."

"I'm told he's a separatist."

"The guy's a fanatic. Refuses to speak English unless forced."

"Why apply for a job at McGill?"

"U of M and UQAM bonged him."

"Raines's specialty is urban archaeology."

"Yeah." Miller snorted in disgust. "The jerk can't score funding, so he digs anything that's close and not nailed down. You hear about his latest scheme?"

"Body Find?"

"*Corps découvert, madame, s'il vous plaît.* But, yeah. The concept is classic Raines." Miller shook his head. "Turn big bucks by skimming off the tragedy of others."

I remembered an incident that occurred shortly after Briel was hired. I was eating lunch on one of the cement benches outside Wilfrid-Derome. A man was waiting by the door, smoking and looking very uptight. Briel came out and the two argued. The man stormed off and she went back inside. Barely knowing Briel, I paid little attention.

"Is Raines a tall muscular guy? Dark eyes, long black hair tied back at his neck?"

"That's him. Thinks he's Grizzly Adams. Here's a story you'll love. One time Raines—"

Hanaoka reappeared. Miller and I rose.

Apologizing for the length of his absence, our host led us to the basement, down a long narrow corridor, and through a blue door into a secure area marked *Microscopy Center.*

Indicating a stereomicroscope, Hanaoka asked that I locate the facet on the tub tooth. I did. At low magnification the contact point looked like a small dark spot.

The SEM system wrapped one corner of the room. Cylinder tanks, CPUs, monitors, a couple of keyboards, a gaggle of gizmos whose function eluded me. I'll admit, I was clueless as to which part was actually the scope.

We moved to the setup. There being one chair and two men, Hanaoka insisted I sit. Or maybe he feared I'd mess with his dials.

"Do you require high-quality photos?"

"For now I'd just like to see if there's debris in the facet. If so, I want to know if that material is consistent with the material used in the other kid's filling."

"Very well. If you need high-quality images later we'll coat the surface with evaporated carbon or sputtered gold."

Hanaoka took what appeared to be clay, positioned the tub tooth on a little platform, and inserted it into a rectangular airlock.

"This is the vacuum chamber. The process should require but a minute."

Once vacuum was attained, Hanaoka flipped a switch to activate the electron beam. An image appeared on one screen.

The facet now looked like the Thornton Quarry. Piled in its corners and crevices were what looked like stones and pebbles.

"Wow," I said.

"Wow," Miller said.

Hanaoka beamed like a kid with a Kit-Kat.

After increasing magnification, Hanaoka used the screen image to focus the electron beam on a particularly impressive cluster of rocks. He continued speaking as he worked.

"I'm setting the spectrometer to collect characteristic X-rays emitting from the sample."

When satisfied, Hanaoka indicated that I should roll my chair to a monitor at the far end of the setup. Miller clicked along behind.

A landscape materialized, green underbrush with three narrow pines spiking skyward. A two-letter code identified each tree. *Yb. Al. Si.*

"Ytterbium. Aluminum. Silicon. Does the combination mean anything to you?"

I shook my head, confused. I wasn't a dentist, but I knew something about amalgams. I'd expected very different elements. *Hg. Sn. Cu. Ag.* Mercury. Tin. Copper. Silver. The stuff usually found in fillings.

"That's the spectrum for the material in the facet. I'll make a copy for you." Hanaoka hit a button and a printer whirred to life. "Now, on to the filling."

Hanaoka removed the tub tooth from the airlock, inserted the Lac Saint-Jean tooth, and repeated the process.

Moments later a second landscape filled the screen.

"Wow," Miller said.

"Holy shit," I said.

38

THE SECOND LANDSCAPE WAS IDENTICAL TO THE FIRST. *YB. AL. SI.*

The material in the filling was consistent with the debris in the facet. And unusual. That suggested that the tub tooth and the Lac Saint-Jean tooth erupted side by side in one child's mouth.

Sonovabitch!

Two scenarios fountained up in my mind.

Scenario A. Briel read about tetracycline in Valentin Gouvrard's antemorts, took the stained molars from the tub, and substituted them for the ones found with the Lac Saint-Jean bones.

Scenario B. The Lac Saint-Jean child's first baby molar somehow migrated to Bergeron's tub.

Migration was as likely as nooky in church.

My fingers tightened into fists.

Briel had sabotaged my case.

Would others be convinced?

"Consistent with" and "unusual" weren't enough to nail her. I had to have more.

The elemental spectrum describing the stuff in the filling. That was the key.

Hanaoka's voice broke through.

". . . you could ask around, see if some type of database exists. Do you have a thumb drive? I can save the spectrum to an EMSA format if you like."

"Yes," I said, digging a drive from my purse. "Yes I do."

* * *

It was dark when I left the Wong Building. The snow was still coming down, though not with much gusto.

Instead of returning to my car, I trudged uphill to Strathcona at the corner of University and Pine. Originally headquarters for the medical faculty, the old fortress is currently home to the anatomy department and the school of dentistry.

It was Tuesday, the Tooth Sleuth's teaching day at McGill. I didn't make that up. Bergeron actually wears a shirt embroidered with that moniker. And likes it.

I found Bergeron in an office on the second floor. The overheads were off, and a green-hooded bankers' lamp cast soft yellow light across the carved oak desk.

I outlined the problem, leaving out only the role played by his tub. Bergeron listened, long bony fingers intertwined in his lap. When he nodded understanding, I asked about the existence of a dental materials database.

Bergeron remembered talk of a project at the FBI's Quantico SEM lab.

He made a call. Explained. Jotted notes. Uttered endless "Uh-huh's" and "I see's." Finally hung up.

Such a database existed. Its developer was now retired, so the software was under the custody of an SEM lab at the State University of New York at Buffalo.

Bergeron made a second call. Again explained the problem.

Uh-huh.

I see.

I was almost wetting my shorts.

Finally the call ended.

The man's name was Barry Trainer. Bergeron handed me a scribbled e-mail address. If I transmitted the spectrum as an EMSA file, Trainer would run it through the database.

Thanking Bergeron, I practically skipped down the hill.

And hydroplaned.

As I landed, something popped at my wrist. Inside my mitten, I felt hardness between my palm and the sidewalk.

Rising gingerly, I collected my purse, brushed myself off, and continued to my car at a more dignified pace.

Sherbrooke was a clogged artery. Between drumming the wheel and cussing at traffic, I fastened my watch. The crystal looked like I'd smashed it with a hammer.

Thirty minutes later I arrived at my condo. The underground garage was dark and deserted.

I was whrp-whrping my car lock when I thought I heard movement.

A footstep?

I froze.

Another.

Another.

I spun. A figure was emerging from the shadows of one corner.

My brain took in the basics.

Male.

Moving fast.

Instinct short-circuited my adrenaline-pumped nerves.

Whipping my purse, I caught the guy square in the ear.

His hand flew up and he bent at the waist.

"Fucking sonovabitch!"

Shit. Sparky.

"You startled me."

"You broke my fucking eardrum."

"Not likely."

Sparky straightened, ear shielded theatrically. "You're certifiable, you know that?"

I'd lacked the patience to placate my wounded assistant. I definitely had none to soothe my headcase neighbor.

"You came at me out of nowhere. What are you doing down here?"

"None of your fucking business, but I was getting shit out of my trunk."

"You have a real way with words."

Sparky shook his head, then pounded his ear with the heel of one hand. "I'll probably need a doctor."

"Send me the bill."

Shouldering my purse strap, I strode toward the door.

"Wait." Sparky dogged me, whining to my back. "I've got something to say."

"Put it in writing. I'm busy."

"Your fucking cat's driving me nuts. You gotta do something about the meowing."

Sparky lives one floor up, in the wing across the courtyard. Birdie would have to be electrically amped for his vocals to project that far.

The anger switch tripped.

I pivoted.

Sparky slammed into me.

I pushed him back with a hand to the sternum.

"You're done with my cat, you sniveling weenie. No more complaints. No more dead birds. No more feces. Got it?"

In the dimness, the planes of Sparky's face hardened.

"Yeah? We'll see who's done."

Upstairs, I told Birdie what a magnificent feline he was. Then I booted my laptop, downloaded and e-mailed the spectrum to Trainer.

To kill time, I zapped some frozen spinach ravioli. As the microwave hummed, I checked my watch. The digits were obscured by a network of cracks.

"Crap."

Digging an old Swatch from my dresser, I returned to the kitchen.

I'd finished the pasta and moved to the study when the phone rang. I grabbed it.

"Say you love me." Chris Corcoran sounded excessively pleased with himself. Ebullient, almost. It was annoying as hell.

"I love you."

"A lot?"

"What did you find, Chris?"

"You used to be fun."

"I also used to be queen of the hop."

"No you weren't."

"I'll ask for a recount."

"Be that way." Mock hurt. "You remembered correctly. ML. A pathologist named Miranda Leaver did the anthropology on Laszlo Tot's bones. Leaver was in Chicago for a one-year postdoc at UIC. No one at the CCME remembers much about her. One tech recalls that while here she got screwed over by her husband, got divorced, and went back to using her maiden name."

"Briel!"

My yelp sent Birdie shooting down the hall.

"Yeah, that's it." Surprised. "After getting dumped, Briel went to

France to pick up the shattered pieces. Her therapy? A cram course in bones for nonanthropologists."

"Where in France?" I could feel my nerves humming.

"Montpellier."

I grabbed paper and pen. "Do you know the name of the institution—"

"Down, girl. I can dial a phone, too. The program was offered jointly through the University of Montpellier and the Department of Forensic Sciences at the Hôpital Lapeyronie.

"While in Montpellier, Miranda Leaver, now back to her maiden name, Miranda Briel, became more French than the French. Bought très chic shoes, a beret, started saying *je m'appelle* Marie-Andréa. Eventually, she met a *garçon* with similar leanings. Or maybe he was the cause of her Gallic reawakening. Who knows?"

Normally, I'd have smiled at Chris's French pronunciation. I was too torqued by his news.

"An archaeologist."

"*Voilà.*"

"His name?" I knew the answer. Just wanted to hear it.

"Sebastien Raines."

"Did you learn anything about him?"

"While a student, Raines was nailed for pilfering artifacts. Apparently, he beat the snot out of the prof who fingered him. He was kicked from the program and, for a while, moved around working archaeological digs for pay. Eventually he split *la République* for *La Belle Province.* He's reputed to have a temper, and to carry a chip on his shoulder the size of Marseille."

"Against?"

"PhDs in general, academics in particular."

My laptop trilled as an e-mail landed. I crossed to it.

BTrainer@buffalo.edu.

"Thanks, Chris. This is really great."

"Was it this Briel who jammed you up with Edward Allen Jurmain?"

"I think so. Or Raines. He's her husband now. The two have a scheme to get rich off forensics."

"Which hop?"

"What?"

"Over which did you reign? There were a lot in the old hood."

"All of them."

I clicked open Trainer's e-mail.

The message was succinct.

Its last line screamed from the page.

Molar B. The cavity was restored with Heliomolar, a resin whose elemental composition and atomic percentages, to my knowledge, are unique. Al 2.85. Si 87.4. Yb 9.75.

Molar A. The debris in the wear facet produced a spectrum identical in elemental composition and atomic percentages to that obtained from molar B. Al 2.85. Si 87.4. Yb 9.75. It is my opinion this facet also contains residue from Heliomolar resin.

Trainer had included a few comments.

Heliomolar HB Resin Composite is an esthetic, high-viscosity, packable, light-cured restorative material designed for use in posterior teeth (Classes I and II).

Heliomolar is more radiopaque than enamel and dentin, and shows up brighter on X-rays.

Heliomolar is produced by Ivoclar Vivadent Inc., in Amherst, New York.

I reread the last line, fingers tight on the mouse. *Heliomolar was introduced on the market in 1984.*

The Lac Saint-Jean child's tetracycline-stained molar was filled with a resin called Heliomolar. In life, that molar had butted cusps with the molar I'd found in Bergeron's tub. It had Heliomar residue in its wear facet. Both molars had Carabelli's cusps.

Heliomolar was introduced in 1984.

The Sainte-Monique picknickers drowned in 1958.

The Gouvrards crashed in 1967.

Again, I was faced with two scenarios.

One, both teeth belonged to the Lac Saint-Jean child. Ergo, the vics were neither the Gouvrards nor the Sainte-Monique drowning victims, or;

Two, neither tooth belonged to the Lac Saint-Jean child. Ergo, both had been taken from the tub to replace that child's real second molars.

By Briel.

A maelstrom of emotions surged through my mind.

I hadn't missed the staining. Or the restoration. They hadn't been there because I'd viewed the child's real teeth.

Before Briel swapped them out.

Briel found the phalanges.

My ass, she did. She palmed them from the lab and planted them at Oka.

Briel found the bullet track.

Had she created it during one of her midnight sorties to the morgue? I pictured Briel shooting a bullet into Marilyn Keiser's corpse. The image was appalling.

For the next half hour I considered and reconsidered my shocking epiphany.

Could this really be?

Nothing else fit.

The phone rang as the full scope of Briel's treachery was sinking in.

"How's it hanging, buttercup?"

I was too upset to nitpick Ryan's endearment. Without asking about his day, I relayed everything I'd learned. Chris Corcoran's bullet track case in Chicago. Miranda Leaver, alias Marie-Andréa Briel. Sebastien Raines's violent and unsavory past. Heliomolar. 1984. The tooth swap. The phalanges theft.

"The call to Edward Allen was the kickoff for Briel's plan to torpedo me."

"What's the motive?"

"To enhance her reputation. To lend dazzle to Body Find so it can generate contracts with the government, private companies, and lawyers."

"I can see gunning for Ayers, if you'll pardon the expression, but why go for you?"

"In France, pathologists do everything, anthropology, odontology, whatever. It's an archaic approach to forensic medicine, but there you have it. While taking her short course, Briel probably developed delusions of grandeur."

"She thinks she can do bones and you are competition."

"That's my theory."

"If you're right about all this, Briel is looking at a hard slap. Tampering with evidence, obstruction of justice, improper handling of human remains."

"Good for starters."

"What's your plan?"

"First I'll take it to Hubert. If he's nonreceptive, I'll go to LaManche. This is serious. Briel's actions could cause serious blowback on Keiser and Villejoin. On every case she's worked."

So far the conversation had been all about me.

"What's happening with the investigation?"

"Florian Grellier picked Adamski out of a lineup. Says he's definitely the bar buddy who talked about a grave at Oka. We've got a Canadian Tire clerk says he sold a garden spade to Adamski the day Anne-Isabelle Villejoin was murdered. We've got a gas station attendant says he sold kerosene to Adamski the week Keiser went missing. There's a waitress puts him in Memphrémagog about that time. The net's closing."

"How about Poppy?"

"A judge cut paper. A team's tossing her place in Saint-Eustache as we speak."

"Claudel is still working Adamski?"

"It's harder now that the hairbag's lawyered up. But the crown prosecutor feels the confessions on Keiser and Villejoin are solid. Adamski's still not budging on Jurmain. Also insists he never shot anyone."

"So my Briel theory fits."

"Like a pair of commandos. How's Birdcat?"

I told Ryan about my latest encounter with Sparky.

"You want Sparky to have an encounter with the long arm of the law?"

"Thanks," I said. "I'll handle it."

There followed one of those awkward pauses. Then, "Want company tonight?"

The offer dropped my stomach. I wanted nothing more than Ryan snoring at my side.

But no. It didn't yet feel right.

I deflected the hit with humor.

"Whose?" I asked.

"Why do I put up with you, Brennan?"

"My scintillating wit and awesome good looks. Neither of which will win a high star count tonight."

"I'll award you my unwavering five."

"Thanks. But I'm staying cloistered with Birdie. When I shared Sparky's comments on his vocal carrying power, the little guy decided to get the band back together with new amps. I need to talk him down."

After disconnecting, I returned to my computer and opened a file. I wanted my ducks in perfect formation for tomorrow's face-off with Hubert.

I'd been at it an hour when movement caught my eye. I glanced into the hall.

Birdie was doing crouching panther.

"Bird."

The cat didn't move.

"What is it, fur ball?"

Birdie flattened his ears.

Flashback. The shattered window.

A chill spread through my body. Small neck hairs upright, I crept down the hall and peered into the bedroom.

On the drawn shade, backlit by a street lamp, was a human silhouette. Close. Very close.

New adrenaline started making the rounds.

"Sparky! You sonovabitch!"

I grabbed a sneaker and blasted out the front door, thumbing the bolt so the lock wouldn't engage. Firing around the hall corner to an emergency entrance in back, I hip-slammed the release bar, pushed through the door, and jammed the shoe into the crack.

The temperature was still mild, but the dampness was biting. Goose bumps quickly puckered my arms.

Snow melted on the strip of lawn below my bedroom and study. I remembered searching that grass with the cops. Lamplight winked from a few missed shards, reminders of the assault on my home.

My psycho neighbor was nowhere to be seen.

Hugging my torso, I crept across the yard, already regretting my impetuousness in flying out coatless.

"Sparky!"

My voice sounded loud in the after-snow hush.

"Where the hell are you?"

I stopped.

Listened for movement.

A car whooshed by on the street, tires spinning up slush. Water dripped somewhere.

My eyes swept the yard.

In the peach glow of an alley light, the bushes looked like humped-up coral. The pine needles wore designer pink coats that were slowly dissolving.

"Show your face. I know you're out here."

No response.

Whatever Sparky's plan, it was meaningless now. Apparently, I'd scared the little skank off.

Shivering, I turned to retrace my steps.

I made it to the door.

Then reality fragmented.

And cut to black.

I *CROUCHED MOTIONLESS, PEERING INTO THE ENDLESS BLACK VOID.*

Clearly, I hadn't broken through to the aboveground world. But to what? A basement? A tunnel? Another catacomb, long ago sealed and forgotten?

Impressions churned in my head.

The outside air was dank, colder than that in the tomb.

My nose sorted new smells. Mud. Stagnant water. Mold. Piss?

"Hello? Help!"

My voice echoed, suggesting a cavernous space.

"Anyone out there?"

Nothing but the hollow rollback of my words.

I squinted into darkness so absolute it seemed to have life.

Based on the time it took the door to sail down to terra firma, I gauged distance to the ground as just a few feet.

Could my injured ankle take the hit?

It had to. Staying put wasn't an option.

Rolling to my bum, I scooched forward, eased my legs over the edge, then turned onto my stomach. I tried to stretch to my full length while keeping a grip on the door opening. The brick was too slick, my fingers too numb. I dropped off.

The landing sent a sharp slap of pain up my left leg. The knee buckled and I tumbled sideways. My shoulder hit hard, and rough ground claimed what skin remained on my right cheek.

I lay a long moment, waiting for the throbbing to subside. My hands and feet were almost dead from the cold. My head pounded. My mouth and tongue were parched.

I was gagging from the smell of sewage and sludge.

Sudden flashbulb images. A quarry. Boxed bones. Chris Corcoran. Vecamamma. Cukura Kundze.

Lassie Tot.

At last. Memory was trickling back.

I'd traveled to Chicago when? Vecamamma's Christmas decorations were up. December. How long ago? What had occurred since?

Recent history remained elusive, so I tried to focus on the present situation.

In the stillness, faint but close, I heard twittering and scratching.

Adrenaline shot from synapse to synapse.

Rats!

I lurched to my feet.

And cracked my skull.

My heart went into claustrophobic overdrive.

Easy!

I drew a steadying breath. Another.

Bent at the waist, I tested with one tentative step.

My injured ankle breathed fire.

I gulped several more mouthfuls of air. Then, crouching with arms outstretched, I painfully backtracked.

I'd landed not far from the mouth of the tomb. I explored the wall with my hands.

I was in a brick, tubelike structure with a sloping floor. The tomb entrance was near the tube's top on one side.

The scrabbling sounded closer now, robust. I shivered from cold and disgust.

The tube leads somewhere. Follow it.

Using the wall as both guide and crutch, I began hobbling through the dark.

The air was dank, the ground slick underfoot.

I imagined beady red eyes. Naked tails. Yellow teeth bared in long pointy snouts. I had to force my fingers to stay on the brick.

The smell was overpowering, a mixture of garbage, feces, and slime. Was I in a drainpipe? A sewer?

Yes. It had to be a sewer.

Active? Abandoned?

Sudden terrifying thought.

In older neighborhoods, Montreal relies on a combined drainage system, with sewage and rainwater running through the same pipes.

The air was frigid. What conditions prevailed up top? Snow? Sleet? Was it too cold for rain?

Might a surge of black water suddenly engulf the space I was in? Would it carry me downstream or drown me?

What was wrong with my mind? Why contemplate Montreal's public works and not recall what brought me to this hell?

Think! Think!

More firefly images.

The Oka skeleton. The Memphrémagog corpse.

I took five more tortuous steps. Seven.

Names.

Rose Jurmain. Christelle Villejoin. Anne-Isabelle. Marilyn Keiser.

Nine.

Ten.

Then, my hand met emptiness.

Heart hammering, I yanked it back.

Something rolled. Hit brick.

An anemic yellow beam arrowed the floor.

I blinked at the first illumination I'd seen in hours. Days?

Oh, sweet Jesus, yes! Yes!

I lunged and snatched up the flashlight.

The beam wavered.

Please!

I tightened the casing. The beam steadied. I swept it around my feet.

Filthy water puddled the brick, iridescent black in the pale yellow glow.

I slid the beam up the curve of the wall.

The little oval jitterbugged in my shivering grasp. Sniffed the flashlight niche. The small space was empty now, save for rat droppings.

I pointed the beam up.

Sludge-coated brick arched over my head. Not good. Whatever flowed through here must at times fill the whole space. The tunnel I was hunch-walking through was no more than four feet in diameter.

I aimed the beam in front of me. Behind. Six feet out the tiny shaft of light was devoured by darkness.

A tremor shook my body. My teeth chattered.

Keep moving. Must keep moving.

I resumed creeping, wall-leaning, flashlight arcing from side to side. The feeble beam was already starting to weaken.

With each yard, I felt more wetness, more drag on my feet. The puddles merged. The water rose up the sides of my soles. Sewers have to empty into something.

Please, God, don't let me be walking upstream.

Now and then I stopped to dip a finger. Was the water level rising? Should I turn back? Ahead, I sensed, more than heard, a low murmuring, like wings beating somewhere in the darkness.

One flashlight sweep illuminated an armada of tiny heads rippling the slick surface. I slogged on, refusing to consider what was swimming at my feet.

The filthy water. The rats. The anger and fear. Whatever the trigger, jigsaw memories now winged at me hard.

Adamski.

Claudel.

Ryan.

The confession.

I sloshed on.

The water covered my laces.

The missing phalanges.

The Lac Saint-Jean molars.

Marie-Andréa Briel. Miranda Leaver.

Sebastien Raines.

Had Raines put me here? Had he and Briel learned that I was onto them?

My abduction was still a void. Had I been drugged? Hit on the head? What did it matter? I was here and I had to get out.

Ten steps, then the beam sputtered.

Please, God. No!

I thumbed the switch to preserve the batteries, casting myself into absolute blackness.

The murmuring now had a backbeat of gurgling and slapping. Water covered my laces. My back and hamstrings screamed from the strain of doubling over.

Reverse?

Go forward?

I'd lost all feeling in my fingers and toes. I was shivering wildly. Fever? Hypothermia?

Find an out! Break free!

I continued onward, every cell in my body dedicated to escape.

My scalp tingled.

I ignored it.

Again the tingle, now on my forehead.

Feathery legs brushed my eyelid. The bridge of my nose.

A spider!

My hand flew up and my fingers raked at my face.

Trembling from revulsion, cold, and exhaustion, I leaned into the wall, despair threatening to overwhelm me.

Screw the batteries. I had to have light!

I flicked the switch.

The beam was almost useless except as an emotional crutch. I aimed it ahead, toward the source of the murmuring sound. Saw inky black.

My body was racked with ever more violent shivers.

As I wrapped my arms around my torso, amber light skimmed the brick at my shoulder.

Picked out something.

Breath suspended, I drew the flash close to the wall.

*T*HE FUZZY AMBER SPOT CRAWLED BLACK MARKS ON THE BRICK.

Stenciled letters, faded and chipped.

I inched the light along, forcing my addled brain to fill in the blanks, form words, derive meaning,

ALEX DRE DE S VE ET DU PAR L FONT INE

Street names.

Rue Alexandre-de-Sève Rue du parc Lafontaine.

An intersection.

Dear God, that corner was just blocks from the lab!

The brackish water. The stench.

The tunnel had to be a sewer. Did it underlie one of those streets?

But I'd awakened in a tomb.

It made no sense.

The bitter cold was jumbling my newly emerging cognition.

I struggled for a mental map of the terrain overhead.

Veterans Park. The entrance ramp toward the Jacques-Cartier Bridge. Rue Logan. Malo. Avenue Papineau. De Lorimier.

Another flash. Not recent. This synapse came from way, way back. From a written page.

Veterans Park was the site of the Old Military Burying Ground.

Had I been sealed in a tomb built for dead soldiers?

No way. Those graves were exhumed and moved in the forties.

Had some been missed? Raines was an urban archaeologist. He'd know about cemeteries. Tombs. Sewers.

My abductor had to be Raines.

I was starting to feel dizzy.

How much time had passed since I'd left the tomb? How long until I succumbed to hypothermia?

I tried to think clearly.

My brain screamed one word.

Move!

Jaw clamped against the tremors, I resumed hunchbacking forward, palm skimming the wall.

The downhill slope sharpened.

The murmuring-gurgling-slapping grew louder.

Water now lapped my ankles.

I slogged on, beam reduced to one strip of amber filament.

Another ten feet and I came to an opening, round, the lower half filled with broken brick and debris. From beyond came the unmistakable rush of moving water.

I pointed the beam through the gap.

The sewer I occupied was joining another. A main collector? Water ran through the larger shaft, a knee-deep river of swirling black sludge.

My eyes squinted for detail the light couldn't find. Saw only a collision of shadows.

My ears told me the current was swift, strong enough to sweep my feet from under me.

My only choice lay behind me.

The tomb. The silent dead.

Don't be stupid. You'll never get back into it. The opening is too high.

It was then that the beam died altogether.

Desperate, I shook the flashlight.

The bulb sputtered to life, wavered, went out for good.

Using the cadence of my hammering heart, I hypnotized myself calm.

You're OK! You're OK!

How long since I'd left the tomb? An hour? A minute? Time still meant nothing.

Plan your next move. Think. You have to keep moving.

Then, over the watery snarl, my ears picked out another sound. Grating, like metal scraping concrete.

Craning my head into the junction, I peered in both directions down the main line.

To the left, light seeped from a circular opening in the tunnel's arched dome.

Had it been there before? Had I missed it?

No.

Then how?

A manhole!

Someone was entering the sewer!

As I stared, two legs appeared. A torso. A human figure began descending a ladder now visible against the curved tunnel wall.

"I'm here." Pure instinct. Yet the cry was feeble.

The figure continued its downward climb.

"Je suis ici." *Still hoarse, hardly above a whisper.*

Two more rungs. The figure gleamed oddly, as though made of satin or plastic.

"Help me!" This time I shouted with all my strength. "Please!"

The figure froze.

"Over here." My shout echoed.

The figure scrabbled down the last few rungs, then scuttled into shadow.

I waited, blades of hope and fear windmilling in my chest.

Had I imagined it? Was I hallucinating?

No, the man was real.

Why didn't he answer?

My stomach curdled at a terrifying thought.

The man was not a city worker.

My abductor had returned to finish me off!

It had to be Raines.

But no.

Raines was a gorilla. The figure on the ladder had long spider legs.

Spider.

The spider on my face.

Duclos's "spider" tooth.

The itsy bitsy spider went up the waterspout . . .

My lids felt heavy.

I allowed them to drift down.

Briel took the spider tooth from Bergeron's tub and placed it with the Lac Saint-Jean child.

Down came the rain and washed the spider out . . .

Like I'd soon be washed out.

In a sewer.

What do you explore?

Underground stuff.

Drainsplorers.

Joe.

Joe had access to the tub.

Not Briel.

I had a key.

Joe had a key.

I was so tired. I wanted to drag myself back uphill to the tomb. To hide.

Spine to the wall, I slid downward into the fetid water. Hugged my knees in an attempt to preserve heat.

A million miles away I heard splashing. Shouting.

No. Not distant.

Here.

Now.

Dragging my lids apart, I muscled myself forward and peeked into the intersecting sewer.

A two-headed monster-marionette stumbled and splashed in the pale circle of gray cast by the open manhole. Four legs struggled in the swirling black water, two glistening, two dark. Four arms flailed.

As I watched, the marionette-monster exploded down the middle. Two puppets emerged. Both were tall and lanky. One wore a tassled hat. The other had hair that was spiked on top.

Spike lurched left.

Tassle lunged after and grapple-hooked Spike around the throat.

Both puppets toppled backward but were not swept away. Their thrashing sent waves cascading outward into the darkness.

Angry shouting bounced down the tube. I could not catch words.

My vision was swimming.

I blinked. Still the images seemed disjointed, like frames of film disconnected by edits.

Spike staggered to his feet.

Tassle clung to Spike's leg, was dragged.

Spike turned and kicked out with one foot.

Tassle's head snapped back. He pinwheeled, then fell. Filthy brown water covered his face.

Spike slogged toward the ladder.

Tassle struggled to his feet, pistoned, caught Spike from behind and drove him face-first into the wall.

Spike's hands flew up and his neck whiplashed.

Tassle body-slammed Spike a second time, harder.

Spike's head again smashed brick.

Tassle stepped back.

Spike slid downward into the watery scum.

"Here." Barely a whisper. "I'm here."

With that, I crawled to a hidden corner of my mind. To the reassuring cadence of blood pulsing in my inner ear.

The sewer evaporated. The water. The cold. The rats.

Moments, or hours, later I saw a flashlight bob toward me.

Time passed. Or didn't.

I became aware of a presence. Of my shoulders being raised. Deep rasping breaths. The smell of wet wool. Male sweat. Warmth.

I forced my eyes open.

A face floated inches from mine.

Slowly, the features shaped up.

"Hold on, buttercup."

STAGE TWO HYPOTHERMIA.

That was the diagnosis. When Ryan found me, my body temperature had dropped to 95 Fahrenheit.

For mammals, that's not good.

I have only dim memories of my last moments in the sewer. By then I was feeling warm and sleepy, ready for cocoa and cookies and bed.

I remember being jostled. Something padded under my back, probably a stretcher. Gray sky. Flashing red lights.

Then nothing.

I woke in a hospital room. It was dark. Then light. Then dark again. Nurses adjusted tubes, changed drip bags, checked my hands and feet, shined lights into my eyes.

I'd suffered frostnip, not frostbite. The doctor had chuckled on explaining that. I'd been far less amused. But relieved that I'd keep all my digits.

I was also relieved that my treatment involved only heated blankets and hot drinks. No sloshing warm liquids through my bladder, stomach, and other hidden places. Lavage. He'd described that, too.

Hallelujah.

During lucid periods, I learned that cold hadn't been my only aggressor. Joe Bonnet had also contributed his share of hurt. In the course of abducting, transporting, and dumping me, he'd concussed my brain, sprained one ankle, and converted one cheek to raw flank steak.

Yeah. Joe. The drainsplorer. I'd gotten that right.

I let my gaze travel the room. IV drip. Cardiac monitor. Water pitcher. Wall-mounted TV. Visitor chair, one of those convertible plastic types originally designed to crack secret agents. A paperback novel lay on the arm rest.

I checked the title. *Playback.* Raymond Chandler was Ryan's favorite author.

I smiled. It hurt like hell.

I recalled talking to Ryan during one waking phase. Grilling him would be more accurate. I'd been abducted at 10 Tuesday night. It was now 10 a.m. Thursday. I did some calculation. Thirty-six hours had passed since I'd charged from my condo. Twenty-eight since Ryan had sprung me from the sewer. More math. I'd spent eight hours underground.

The flukey warm spell had been a mixed blessing. Milder temperatures had aided my survival. They'd also spurred melting, sending gallons of runoff into the sewers.

As if cued by telepathy, Ryan appeared, bearing a bouquet of pointy orange things that looked like they fed on small lizards.

Seeing me awake, Ryan hurried to the bed.

"Are those things dangerous?" My voice sounded hoarse and croaky.

"Only if you threaten their young." Ryan set the flowers on the bed, took my hand.

"Holding only. No caressing or massaging." He stroked a thumb lightly across my knuckles.

I floated a brow. I think. My questioning brow is on the right. That side of my face was toast.

"Rubbing could dislodge ice crystals intent on bushwacking your heart."

"I hate when that happens," I said.

Ryan dragged a chair to the bed. Sat. Reclaimed my hand.

"OK, Galahad," I said. "Dish."

"Everything?"

"For now, just the highlights. My abductor was Joe Bonnet, right?"

Ryan nodded. "Long story short, your beloved assistant felt under-appreciated and overworked."

I rolled my eyes. That hurt, too.

"Sensing disaffection, Briel schmoozed Joe up. Said he was a superstar. Offered a golden future with Body Find."

"Joe stole Christelle Villejoin's phalanges for her."

"No, that was Briel's handiwork. She overheard your conversation with the Villejoins' doctor, figured the finger bones would be important because of the camptodactyly."

I thought back to that day. "Briel pinched them while I was upstairs getting a Diet Coke."

"She reasoned that since the phalanges would be 'discovered' during her follow-up dig, no harm no foul."

"How did she know Hubert would send her to Oka?"

"If not, she planned to find the phalanges in the lab. Either way, you'd look bad."

"Briel also swapped out the Lac Saint-Jean teeth?"

"Yep. Read Valentin Gouvrard's antemorts, remembered Duclos mentioning a dental collection with brown baby teeth. Joe let her into the cabinet containing Bergeron's tub, she found the stained deciduous molars, palmed and planted them with the remains. Who cares after all these years?"

"Decades-old bones, case going nowhere, what's the difference, right?"

"Exactly her thinking."

"That's what tipped me in the sewer that my attacker was Joe. I realized Briel had to have gotten access through him. Only Bergeron, Joe, and I had keys. That and the long spider legs."

"Long spider legs?"

"Never mind."

Ryan let it go. "Both with Oka and Lac Saint-Jean, Briel felt she could make herself dazzle while doing no harm."

"Except to me."

"Another plus."

"Did Briel call Edward Allen Jurmain?"

"She had Raines do that. Wanted it to be a male voice in case anyone asked Edward Allen. He used a pay phone at the gare Centrale to avoid blowback on either of them."

"Did she shoot the bullet into Marilyn Keiser's corpse?"

"Briel insists that was all Joe. Says she'd never do anything to compromise a police investigation. Claims she was horrified by Joe's action. I suspect it was a joint effort. Joe wouldn't have known anything about that kind of bullet track. Briel remembers Richie Cunningham's case in Chicago—"

"His name is Chris Corcoran."

"—sees another chance to shine. Three-month-old homicide, probably never be solved. If it is, so what if cause of death's a little off. I'm thinking she held the body while Joe fired the shot. She dissects out the bullet, announces the track, *voilà,* she's a hero."

A nurse entered the room, rubber sole squeaked to the bed. She took my pulse, then stuck a thermometer into my mouth, strapped my arm with a blood pressure collar, and pumped the little black ball.

"Those flowers must go into a vase." Without looking at either Ryan or me.

"Of course." Ryan offered his most engaging grin. "Would you possibly happen to have an old one lying around?"

We all waited out my thermal performance.

The nurse entered vitals into my chart, hurried off.

"Don't cross that woman," Ryan said.

"Not a chance," I said.

"Did Briel write the *Go home damn American* note?"

"That was Joe's little touch."

"Nice. I suppose she leaked the Keiser ID to the press."

"How better to score tube time."

"What happened Tuesday night? Where was I?"

Ryan's brows definitely rose. "You explained it to *me,* sweet pea. Don't you remember?"

Sweet pea? That was a new one. Or was that a medical reference? I did have a catheter and tinkle bag.

I shook my head.

"I found you in a sewer below Alexandre-de-Sève. You'd crawled along a semi-abandoned collector to its junction with a main line. You'd broken out of an old tomb below Veterans Park. Searchers learned about that today."

"Part of the Old Military Burying Ground," I said. "But that cemetery was relocated long ago."

"Right you are." Ryan assumed a professorial tone. "At one time, acreage around what is now Veterans Park served as a final resting place for both the British military garrison, and for a fairly large number of civilians." Ryan broke character. "Average joes and janes got planted there, too." Back to Herr Professor. "From 1797 until the mid-nineteenth century, more than one thousand soldiers and their families were interred in what became known as the Old Military Burying Ground. Over the years, neglect and vandalism took their toll, and the cemetery became an eyesore. In 1944, the British soldiers were disinterred and moved to the Field of Honour in Pointe-Claire."

"But here's the catch." Simple Ryan-speak. "There was never any systematic attempt to unearth Jane and Joe. The gravestones went away, but many ordinary citizens were left behind."

So were some soldiers, I thought, remembering my fellow tomb occupants.

"Every now and then a stiff surfaces, much to the dismay of public utility and construction crews."

Ryan smiled, exceedingly pleased with himself.

"How do you know all this?" I asked.

"We contacted an archaeologist at U of M and an historian at the McCord. The former agreed to go down with the SIJ team. The latter declined. The archaeologist thinks burials were probably unearthed when the sewer was constructed, sometime around the turn of the century. He hypothesizes that, unnerved, workers slapped up a quickie tomb, sealed the displaced corpses inside, and moved along. Being geographically apart, the makeshift crypt was missed when the cemetery was moved in the forties."

"At first I thought Raines was my attacker," I said. "He'd know about historic tombs and burial grounds. Then I zoned in on Joe. He stumbled on the tomb while drainsploring, right?"

"Right."

"Joe planned to have me simply disappear. No body. No explanation. Just gone."

"Yes." Ryan's grip tightened and his thumb moved more rapidly across my knuckles. Stopped. We both waited out an arterial ice crystal assault. Nothing.

"Was Joe acting for Briel?"

"Again, she says it was all Joe all the way. Denies knowledge of any plan to harm you."

"Where is he, anyway?"

"Enjoying a cage and a bright orange jumpsuit. While I searched for you, my backup team fished him out of the sewer."

"Did Joe give a reason for wanting to kill me?"

"He says Briel danced around the subject, but that her meaning was clear. Says she constantly mentioned things would go smoother without you. Hinted it would be nice if you went away and never came back."

"How did you find me?"

"Around eleven, I called your condo and your cell, got no answer. I found that odd, since you'd just told me you planned to stay home with the cat. After phoning repeatedly, I began to worry that you were sick again, so I decided to swing by your place. The emergency exit was jammed with a shoe. Your front door was unlocked. Your watch lay smashed on the floor. Your jacket was there but you were gone."

Watch on the floor? I guess I had Birdie to thank for that.

"You'd just told me your suspicions concerning Briel, and described Raines's temper and sketchy past. You'd also just had a nasty encounter with your neighbor."

I'd forgotten all about Sparky.

"I called Claudel and told him to net Briel and her hubby. I found your neighbor asleep in his recliner. Sparky's boss vouched that he'd been filling potholes on the Décarie Expressway until eleven. By the way, Sparky admitted to smashing your window."

"How?"

"Metal baseball bat. He'll pay damages. But that's a story for another day."

"That sonovabitch."

"Briel and Raines stonewalled at first, but Claudel came down hard and they cracked under threats of multicount indictments. Briel agreed to phone Joe.

"Needless to say, we were listening. Joe said he'd seen you rifling drawers in Briel's office, overheard you talking about the Lac Saint-Jean teeth and the SEM and EDS tests you intended to run. To protect Briel and his future at Body Find, he told her he'd taken you out."

Ryan's jaw muscles bunched and the pressure on my hand increased.

"Joe bragged that he'd buried you alive in a place you'd never be found. Briel asked where you were. Joe refused to disclose the location. She begged. He held firm. As per our prearranged plan, she demanded he meet her at the lab.

"When Joe arrived, Briel told him you had something she desperately needed. Otherwise her deceit would be uncovered, her reputation ruined, and Body Find destroyed. She asked again where you were. Joe still refused to tell her.

"Acting distraught—very convincingly, I might add—Briel begged that he retrieve a bag of teeth she knew you were carrying on your person. Threatened to have nothing further to do with him if he refused."

"The dolt really thought I was toting evidence around?" I couldn't believe anyone could be that stupid.

"Briel said you'd called and accused her of professional misconduct, said you'd claimed to have proof in your jeans pocket. She told Joe she'd checked her filing cabinet and found teeth missing. Incriminating teeth. It rang true. Joe had seen you take something from Briel's office."

"All this time you're waiting in the wings."

"Yes, ma'am. Joe led me to you. The rest is history."

"How the hell did he get me into that tomb?"

"There's a manhole just yards past the tomb opening. You went the wrong way, though you wouldn't have been able to see the manhole from inside in the dark."

"Figures. How did he seal the damn door so effectively, and why?"

"Quikrete Exterior Use Anchoring Cement."

Ryan beamed. I waited for the explanation.

"You can buy the stuff at any hardware store. Joe hid a ten-pound bucket in the sewer and brought hot water with him. After shoving you inside the tomb, he mixed the cement, jammed the plank into place, and filled the gap. The stuff sets up in thirty minutes, reaches a compression strength of two hundred psi in two hours, four hundred psi in twenty-four. You probably started banging away around two or three a.m. By that time the pull-out strength would have been pretty impressive. He probably sealed it because he didn't want another drainsplorer getting in there and finding a modern body."

I thought a moment.

"Why not use the same manhole when he returned?"

"When Joe arrived, shortly before dawn, a street crew was setting up over his original entrance point. Undaunted, he hied himself to the next manhole, donned his drainsploring waders, and headed down. With yours truly close on his tail, of course."

In the corridor, a bell bonged softly. A cart rolled by. A voice paged Dr. Someone. Behind me machines beeped softly.

"Thanks for being there, Ryan."

"My pleasure."

Pleasure?

"It was a sewer."

"You were in it."

The nurse entered, placed a vase on my bedside table, cranked her lips into something that looked like a smile. Ryan and I both thanked her.

"I remember one thing," I said when she'd gone.

"What?"

"You were wearing really bad headgear."

"My tassle tuque?" Feigned affront.

"The thing has a pom-pom."

"It's a man tassle. I love that hat."

43

SATURDAY MORNING, RYAN HELPED ME CHECK OUT OF THE HOSPITAL. Drove me home. Settled me on my couch. Lit a fire. Made lunch.

My ankle ached. My cheek was congealed tar. I had a lump on my occipital that could wrestle as a heavyweight. The Weeki Wachee Mermaids were still doing wheelies in my brain.

What the hell? I needed nurturing.

Over tomato soup and peanut butter on toast, we treaded safe conversational ground.

Ryan told me that on Wednesday results had come back on my Lac Saint-Jean vics. The adult female's femur had produced sufficient organic material to sequence mitochondrial DNA.

"Did the brother provide a sample?"

"Yes, ma'am."

"And?"

"Being congenial pays off. You have a reputation for being congenial. People like you."

"Ryan." I gave him the steely-eyed look. Squinting irritated the scab on my face.

"In deference to your recent excellent adventure, an SQ officer drove the sample from Sainte-Monique to Montreal personally. The DNA boys leapfrogged it to the front of the queue."

"And?"

A grin spread over Ryan's face.

"Tell me."

The grin widened.

Leaning forward, I punched Ryan's bicep.

"Give the lady a gold star."

"Yes." I arm-pumped the air. It hurt. "The Clemenceaus and Blackwater, not the Gouvrards."

Mostly, we discussed the growing evidence against Adamski.

A warrant had been served and an SIJ team had tossed Poppy's condo in Saint-Eustache. Much to her displeasure.

"A hollow beneath a waterbed produced a duffel containing two thousand dollars."

"From the Villejoins' pantry?"

"Could be. Someone's checking for prints, looking for trace DNA."

"Prints would be good. Trace DNA is a long shot."

"Better than—"

"No shot at all. Poppy didn't know about the money?"

"You think she'd have left it there after Adamski's arrest?"

"Did SIJ find anything else?"

"A shovel in the garage. A sedimentologist is comparing dirt from the blade to samples you collected from Christelle's grave at Oka."

"Any blood?"

"Biology is looking at a stain. Trace evidence has some hairs. The garage was also home to a lovely little chain saw. A botanist is comparing gunk from the teeth to pine logs stacked in the Villejoins' backyard."

"Wowzer."

"Wowzer. If Adamski's confession is kicked, the crown prosecutor wants beaucoup backup."

The buzzer sounded. Again. Ryan answered the door, returned bearing yet another gift. I'd already received a gazillion flowers, a pajama-gram from Ayers, and a fruit basket from Santangelo. This time it was a floral arrangement the size of Denver.

Ryan set the vase on the table and handed me the card.

"Claudel," I read.

"What's he say?"

"Claudel."

"See. He likes you."

Ryan took our dishes to the kitchen, then we rifled Santangelo's basket. A clementine for me, a banana for Ryan.

"Adamski admitted to forging Keiser's old-age pension checks. Discovered all three in her purse. After cashing them, he tossed the purse into a Dumpster on Saint-Laurent and found himself a bar."

"Open a tab. It's on my dead wife." My voice conveyed the disgust I felt.

"He's holding firm on Rose Jurmain. Denies killing her. Adamantly."

"So the original coroner's finding was probably correct. Rose overdrank, underdressed, wandered off, and died of exposure."

"Adamski's only admission concerning Jurmain is that her disappearance triggered the idea of going after his former wife. That and news coverage of elderly victims in upstate New York."

"And getting away with murdering the Villejoins."

"And that."

"What's happening on the Joe-Briel-Raines front?"

"They've turned on each other like hyenas on a carcass. Ballistics is checking out a Browning twenty-two semiautomatic pistol found in Briel's condo. They'll all go down."

"Was Raines involved?"

"Indirectly. Body Find was his baby. He brainwashed Briel into believing that if she gained celebrity status it would get the venture off the ground. Also, he called Edward Allen."

"Briel's a viper," I said.

"Let's not be overly harsh. Briel believed she was neither setting a criminal free nor convicting an innocent person. She was knifing some colleagues to promote herself, but that doesn't make her Adamski, unless you think she really did want Joe to kill you. Also, once the jig was up, she was instrumental in your rescue."

"Probably to avoid being an accessory to murder."

"Probably."

The fire had died to embers. Ryan got up to poke them.

"It's people like Briel who give forensic science a bad name," I said.

"Adamski's dirty and he's going away for a very long time, but Briel's actions make you wonder." Ryan spoke without turning to face me. "How many guilty have gone free, and how many innocent have been convicted because of bad police or forensic work?"

"You've heard of the Innocence Project?"

Ryan nodded.

"In the last twenty years there have been over two hundred exonerations in the U.S., some involving inmates on death row. More than a quarter, fifty-five cases with sixty-six defendants, involved forensic testing or testimony that was flawed. And those stats don't begin to tell the whole story."

Ryan added a log. Embers spiraled, Lilliputian fireworks in the dim hearth.

"Forensic science is popular right now, and people with minimal or no training are hot to be players. Briel is a perfect example. She learned a little about bones and hung out her shingle as an anthropologist."

"With predictable results," Ryan said.

"Whether it's bad methodology, sloppy performance, or intentional misconduct, jurors can't always spot junk science. If an expert wears the white lab coat, it's science."

Returning to the couch, Ryan sat closer.

"Cops and lawyers have the same problem," he said. "How are we average joes supposed to know who's legit?"

"That's the point of board certification. Every field has it now. The American Board of Forensic Anthropology, Engineering, Entomology, Odontology, Pathology, Toxicology, etc. Accreditation is a rigorous process.

"Board certification isn't a perfect answer, Ryan. Sure, some incompetents slip through, just as in law or medicine. But it's a start. Those letters behind a scientist's name aren't just for show. They're hard-earned. And they're a message that an expert has undergone peer scrutiny and meets a high set of ethical standards. And being certified in one field doesn't mean you're an expert in another."

"Briel's not certified in forensic anthropology."

"Of course she isn't. It takes a PhD and years of experience to qualify for ABFA candidacy. Being a pathologist doesn't make you an anthropologist, or vice versa."

For several moments we listened to the hiss and pop of the logs.

My eyes drifted to a bouquet on the dining room table. LaManche. His gift had been the first to arrive.

"This would never have happened on LaManche's watch," I said. "He'd never use a noncertified expert."

"The old man would have seen through Briel," Ryan agreed.

"I hope he's doing well," I said.

"So do I."

Ryan took my hand. Firelight danced in his eyes and bathed his face with a warm, honey glow.

"Are we, buttercup? Doing well?"

I hesitated.

"Yes, dandelion."

I smiled.

"Very well, indeed."

FROM THE FORENSIC FILES OF DR. KATHY REICHS

CAMELOT? OR SCAM A LOT?

In this special essay, Kathy Reichs discusses the imperfect relationship between science and the criminal justice system.

"How many guilty have gone free and how many innocent have been convicted?" Why does Tempe ask that of Ryan?

She's worried about bad forensic science.

A lot of us are.

Today, science is a routine and crucial tool of the criminal justice system. A latent fingerprint places a defendant at a crime scene. DNA from sperm links an accused to a rape victim. Chemical analysis determines that a drug is illegal. An autopsy establishes that a death is homicide.

The forensic science community includes a wide array of practitioners: anthropologists, biologists, chemists, entomologists, odontologists, pathologists. On television these scientists are portrayed as knights in shining lab coats.

No question. Science is powerful. But does it always smite with the unerring stroke of Excalibur? Is every expert a gallant champion for justice and right?

Recent findings suggest things aren't perfect in Camelot.

Thus Tempe's unease.

"Whether it's bad methodology, sloppy performance, or intentional misconduct, jurors can't always spot junk science," she says.

Tempe speaks of the Innocence Project, a national litigation and public policy organization dedicated to finding justice for those wrongfully imprisoned. Numbers have risen since her fireside chat with Ryan. As of this writing, 234 convicted persons in the United States have been exonerated through DNA testing.

How could our courts err in so many cases?

Each "forensic science" has its own methodologies, technologies, practices, and standards. There is significant variability with regard to reliability and potential for error. Some specialties are analytical and laboratory based: DNA analysis, toxicology, drug analysis. Terra firma. Others rely on pattern interpretation: fingerprints, hand writing, tool and bite mark analysis. Shakier ground.

"If an expert wears the white lab coat, it's science," Tempe says. She is worried about testimony based on faulty science, on imperfect testing and analysis, or on imprecise, exaggerated, or false claims.

Examples abound. An expert in Illinois relocated to Texas testified on lip print analysis, an anthropologist on identification through shoe prints. Neither methodology had been validated. Using goggles and a blue laser, a dentist in Mississippi identified bite marks, scratches, and other injuries that no one else saw. His results can't be photographed or reproduced.

A chemist in Tennessee, later Texas, routinely presented inconclusive findings as conclusive, altered laboratory records, and reported scientifically impossible or improbable results. A Toronto doctor performed over a thousand autopsies on children, though he never certified in forensic pathology.

Innocent people went to jail. Mothers lost custody of their kids. Perpetrators who could have been convicted were acquitted.

Tempe doesn't like it. And she's not alone.

Recently, the Science, State, Justice, Commerce, and Related Agencies Appropriations Act of 2006 became law. Under the terms of the statute, Congress tasked the National Academy of Sciences with evaluating the state of forensic science in the United States. On February 18, 2009, the NAS issued its long-awaited report.

It was a doozy.

The report described disparities in forensic science operations in federal, state, and local law enforcement jurisdictions and agencies. It found that medical examiner systems vary in the extent of services and the level of expertise provided. Given these factors, the committee concluded that the reliability and quality of information arising from the forensic examination of evidence available to the legal system varies substantially across the country.

Bottom line. In America justice isn't equally available to all. Why? Understaffing and underfunding.

The NAS report also highlighted a credentialing problem. Most jurisdictions do not require forensic practitioners to be certified by reliable legitimizing organizations. Most forensic disciplines have no mandatory certification programs internally.

Sound familiar? It's one of Tempe's favorite themes. Here's what she says:

"Board certification. Every field now has it. The American Board of Forensic Anthropology, Odontology, Entomology, Toxicology, Engineering, Psychiatry, Pathology, etc. Full accreditation requires attainment of a specified educational level, a lengthy application process, and rigorous examination. And it's not just a one-shot deal. For continued certification, diplomates must participate in ongoing professional activities and adhere to ethical standards."

Among its eleven recommendations, the NAS report called for mandatory certification of all forensic scientists and medical examiners. The same way that, for example, states require lawyers to be licensed.

But back up, you say. Weren't these issues addressed years ago by the Supreme Court?

In 1993, in *Daubert vs. Merrell Dow Pharmaceuticals, Inc.*, the Supreme Court ruled that a "trial judge must ensure that any and all scientific testimony or evidence admitted is not only relevant, but reliable."

Bravo! So what's the problem?

First, the Daubert standard applies only to federal courts and to state court systems that choose to adopt it. Second, Daubert appoints the judge as gatekeeper. But how does his or her honor distinguish legitimate forensic methodologies and their practitioners from junk science and charlatans?

Tempe's point precisely.

"Board certification isn't a perfect answer, Ryan, but it's a start. Those letters behind a scientist's name aren't just there for show. They're hard-earned. And they're a message to judges, prosecutors, law enforcement, whomever, that an expert is legit, that he or she has undergone peer scrutiny and meets a high set of standards."

Contrary to the television myth, laboratory workers differ from crime scene searchers. Scientists, most with advanced degrees, differ from the technicians who lend them support.

It is the scientists who wield the mighty swords. And, sadly, not all are equally competent. Not all view themselves as champions of scientific truth.

206 Bones is the story of a scientist who wished to become the Grail Knight. Though qualified in one field, the individual aspired to much more. The result was disastrous.

I have selected forensic science as my life work. Like the vast majority of my colleagues, I have sworn to a code of chivalry. The pledge: To protect the innocent from wrongful conviction; to help convict the guilty.

The fulfillment of this twofold promise requires assurance of professional competence across all disciplines, and enforcement of rigorous ethical standards.

How to ensure both?

Tempe and the NAS are right on the mark. Board certification must become mandatory in the hiring of scientists, and in their qualification as experts in court.

And existing boards must not relax their standards to accommodate all. Technicians are not scientists. The skill sets are different. Certification standards must remain rigorous to clarify this distinction.

Not perfect. But it's a start.

What do I propose?

Proclaimed to all knights of the realm. Going forth from this day. To sit at the round table ye must:

Suck it up, take your boards, pass the king's muster.